MW00941998

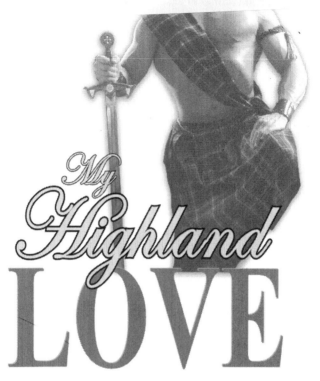

My *Highland* LOVE

Highland Lords Series

TARAH SCOTT

BROKEN
ARM
PUBLISHING

ISBN: 978-1482676235
ISBN 13: 978-1482676235

Author's Website: www.TarahScott.com
Facebook: Facebook.com/TarahScottsRomanceNovels
Twitter:@TarahScott
Blog: TarahScott.TarahScott.com

Interior Book Design and Cover Design by Melissa Alvarez at BookCovers.Us
Cover Art: Background © DepositPhotos.com/Oliver Taylor
Cover/Interior Art: Highlander © RomanceNovelCenter.com/ Jimmy Thomas

First Trade Paperback Printing by Broken Arm Publishing: March 2013

This is the second edition of My Highland Love. The first edition was previously published by Silver Publishing.

10 9 8 7 6 5 4 3 2

Reviews

The chemistry between these two characters will leave you breathless! This is one book I will defiantly read over and over! *Starry Night Book Reviews*

The story is not only well written, but flows at just the perfect pace. One of the most important things in this genre is chemistry between the characters. My Highland Love's Marcus and Elise will set fire to the pages, or your e-reader screen! It's romantic and sensual with a good dose of suspense and action added in. Set in the beautiful Scottish Highlands this tale of love and second chances truly shines among other Highland novels. If you're looking for the next greatest Highland tale, pick this one up! *Kristina Haeker's Reviews*

Dedication

This book is dedicated to my two very good friends and critique partners, Kimberly Comeau and Evan Trevane. You guys read this book above and beyond the call of duty. *Thank you!*

Chapter One

America
Winter 1825

"*T*he *Lord giveth and the Lord taketh away.*" Or so her eulogy would begin.

The heavy gold wedding band clinked loudly in the silence as he grasped the crystal tumbler sitting on the desk before him. He raised the glass in salutation and whispered into the darkness, "To the dead, may they rot in their watery graves." He finished the whiskey in one swallow.

And what of that which had been hers? He smiled. The law would see that her wealth remained where it should—with him. A finality settled about the room.

Soon, life would begin.

Solway Firth, Scottish-English border

Elise jumped at the sound of approaching footsteps and sloshed tea from the cup at her lips. The ship's stateroom door opened and her grip tightened around the delicate cup handle. Her husband ducked to miss the top of the doorway as he entered. He stopped, his gaze fixing on the medical journal that lay open on the secretary beside her. A corner of his mouth curved upward with a derisive twist and his eyes met hers.

With deliberate disinterest, Elise slipped the paper she'd been making notes on between the pages of the journal and took the forestalled sip of afternoon tea.

She grimaced. The tea had grown cold in the two hours it had sat untouched. She placed the cup on the saucer, then turned a page in the book. As Robert clicked the door shut behind him, the ship's stern lifted with another wave. She gripped the desk when the stern dropped into the swell's trough. Thunder, the first on the month-long voyage, rumbled. She released the desk. This storm had grown into more than a mere squall.

Robert stepped to her side. "What are you doing?"

"Nothi—" He snatched the paper from the book. "Robert!" She would have leapt to her feet, but her legs were shakier than her hands.

He scanned the paper, then looked at her. "You refuse to let the matter lie."

"You don't care that the doctors couldn't identify what killed your daughter?"

"She is dead. What difference can it possibly make?"

Her pulse jumped. *None for you. Because you murdered her.*

He tossed the paper aside. "This has gone far enough."

Elise lifted her gaze to his face. She once thought those blue eyes so sensual. "I couldn't agree more."

"Indeed?"

The ship heaved.

"I will give you a divorce," she said.

"Divorce?" A hard gleam entered his eyes. "I mean to be a widower."

She caught sight of the bulge in his waistband. Her pulse quickened. Why hadn't she noticed the pistol when he entered?

Elise shook her head. "You can't possibly hope to succeed. Steven will—"

"Your illustrious brother is in the bowels of the ship, overseeing the handling of the two crewmen accused of theft."

Her blood chilled. When her father was alive, he made sure the men employed by Landen Shipping were of good reputation. Much had changed since his death.

"One of the men is wanted for murder," Robert said.

"Murder?" she blurted. "Why would a stranger murder me?"

Robert lifted a lock of her dark hair. "Not a stranger. A spurned lover." He dropped the hair, then gripped the arms of her chair and leaned forward. "Once the board members of Landen Shipping identify your body as Elisabeth Kingston, the stipulation in your father's will shall be satisfied and your stock is mine."

The roar of blood pounded through her ears. If he killed her now, he would never pay for murdering their daughter. And she intended that he pay.

Elise lunged for the letter opener lying in one of the secretary compartments. The ship pitched as her fingers clamped onto the makeshift weapon. As Robert yanked her to her feet, she swung the letter opener. Bone-deep pain raced up her arm when the hard mass of his forearm blocked her blow. The letter opener clattered to the wooden floor.

She glimpsed his rage-contorted features before he whipped her around and crushed her to his chest, pinning her arms to her sides with one powerful arm. He dragged her two paces and snatched up the woolen scarf lying on the bed. In one swift movement, he wound it around her neck.

Robert released her waist, grabbed the scarf's dangling end, and yanked it tight around her neck. Elise clawed at the scarf. Her nails dug into the soft skin of her neck. Her legs buckled and he jerked her against him. His knees jabbed into her back and jolts of pain shot up both sides of her spine. She gulped for air.

His breath was thick in her ear as he whispered, "Did you really think we would let you control fifty-one percent of Landen Shipping?" He gave a vicious yank on the scarf.

No! her mind screamed in tandem with another thunder roll. Too late, she understood the lengths to which he would go to gain control of her inheritance.

The scarf tightened. Her sight dimmed. Cold. She was so cold.

Amelia, my daughter, I come to you—the scarf went slack. Elise dropped to her knees, wheezing in convulsive gasps of air. Despite the racking coughs which shook her, she forced her head up. A blurry form stood in the doorway. *Steven.*

The scarf dropped to her shoulders and she yanked it from her neck. Robert stepped in front of her and reached into his coat. *The pistol.* He had murdered her daughter—he would not take Steven from her. Elise lunged forward and bit into his calf with the ferocity of a lioness.

Robert roared. The ship bucked. Locked like beast and prey, they tumbled forward and slammed against the desk chair. The chair broke with the force of their weight. The secretary lamp crashed to the floor. Whale oil spilled across the wooden floor; a river of fire raced atop the thin layer toward the bed.

Steven yanked her up and shoved her toward the door. Robert scrambled to his feet as Steven whirled and rammed his fist into Robert's jaw. Her husband fell against the doorjamb, nearly colliding with her. Elise jumped back with a cry. Robert charged Steven and caught him around the shoulders, driving him back onto the bed.

The ship bucked. Elise staggered across the cabin, hit her hip against the secretary, and fell. The medical journal thudded to the floor between her and the thick ribbon of fire. Her heart skipped a beat when Robert slammed his fist into Steven's jaw.

She reached for the open book and glimpsed the picture of the belladonna, the deadly nightshade plant. Fury swept through her anew. She snatched up the book, searing the edge of her palm on the fire as she pushed to her feet. Elise leapt forward, book held high, and swung at Robert with all her strength. *May* this *belladonna kill you as your powdered belladonna killed our daughter.* The crack of book against skull penetrated the ringing in her ears. Robert fell limp atop Steven.

4

The discarded scarf suddenly blazed. Elise whirled. Smoke choked her as fire burned the bed coverings only inches from Robert's hand. Steven grabbed her wrist and dragged her toward the door. He scooped up the pistol as they crossed the threshold and they stumbled down the corridor to the ladder leading up to the deck.

"Go!" he yelled, and lifted her onto the first tread.

Elise frantically pulled herself up the steep ladder to the door and shoved it upward. Rain pelted her like tiny needles. She ducked her head down as she scrambled onto the deck. An instant later, Steven joined her. He whirled toward the poop deck where Captain Morrison and his first mate yelled at the crewmen who clung to the masts while furiously pulling up the remaining sails and lashing them to the spars.

Steven pulled her toward the poop deck's ladder. "Stay here!" he yelled above the howling wind, and forced her fingers around the side of the ladder.

The ship heaved to starboard as he hurried up the ladder and Elise hugged the riser. A wave broke over the railing and slammed her against the wood. She sputtered, tasting the tang of salt as she gasped for air.

A garbled shout from the captain brought her attention upward. He stared at two men scuttling down the mizzen mast. They landed, leapt over the railing onto the main deck and disappeared through the door leading to the deck below. They had gone to extinguish the fire. If they didn't succeed, the ship would go down.

Elise squinted through the rain at Steven. He leaned in close to the captain. The lamp, burning in the binnacle, illuminated the guarded glance the captain sent her way. A shock jolted her. Robert had lied to the captain about her—perhaps had even implicated Steven in her so-called insanity. The captain's expression darkened. He faced his first mate.

The ship's bow plunged headlong into a wave with a force that threw Elise to the deck and sent her sliding across the slippery surface. Steven shouted her name as she slammed into the ship's gunwale. Pain shot through her shoulder. He rushed down the ladder, the captain on his heels. Another wave hammered the ship. Steven staggered to her side and pulled her to her feet. The ship lurched. Elise clutched at her brother as they fell to the deck. Pain radiated through her arm and up her shoulder. The door to below deck swung open. Elise froze.

Robert.

He pointed a pistol at her. Her heart leapt into her throat. Steven sprang to his feet in front of her.

"No!" she screamed.

She spotted the pistol lying inches away and realized it had fallen from Steven's waistband. She snatched up the weapon, rolled to face Robert, and fired. The report of the pistol sounded in unison with another shot.

A wave cleared the railing. Steven disappeared in the wash of seawater. Elise grasped the cold wood railing and pulled herself to her feet. She blinked stinging saltwater from her eyes and took a startled step backwards at seeing her husband laying across the threshold. Steven lay several feet to her right. She drew a sharp breath. A dark patch stained his vest below his heart. *Dear God, where had the bullet lodged?*

She started toward Steven. The ship listed hard to port. She fought the backward momentum and managed two steps before another wave crested. The deck lurched and she was airborne. She braced for impact against the deck. Howling wind matched her scream as she flew past the railing and plummeted into darkness—then collided with rock-hard water.

Cold clamped onto her. Rain beat into the sea with quick, heavy blows of a thousand tiny hammers. She kicked. Thick, icy ribbons of water propelled her upward. She blinked. Murky shapes glided past. This was Amelia's grave. Elise surfaced, her first gasp taking in rainwater. She coughed and flailed. A heavy sheet of water towered, then slapped her against the ocean's surface. The wave leveled and she shook hair from her eyes. Thirty feet away, the *Amelia* bounced on the waves like a toy. Her brother had named the ship. But

Amelia was gone. Steven, only twenty-two, was also gone.

A figure appeared at the ship's railing. The lamp high atop the poop deck burned despite the pouring rain. Elise gasped. Could he be—"Steven!" she yelled, kicking hard in an effort to leap above another towering wave. Her skirts tangled her legs, but she kicked harder, waving both arms. The man only hacked at the bow rope of the longboat with a sword. "Steven!" she shouted.

The bow of the longboat dropped, swinging wildly as the man staggered the few steps to the rope holding the stern. A wave crashed over Elise and she surfaced to see the longboat adrift and the figure looking out over the railing. Her heart sank. The light silhouetted the man—and the captain's hat he wore. Tears choked her. It had been the captain and not Steven.

Elise pulled her skirts around her waist and knotted them, then began swimming toward the boat. Another wave grabbed the *Amelia*, tossing her farther away. The captain's hat lifted with the wind and sailed into the sea. She took a quick breath and dove headlong into the wave that threatened to throw her back the way she'd come. She came up, twisting frantically in the water until she located the ship. She swam toward the longboat, her gaze steady on the *Amelia*. Then the lamp dimmed... and winked out.

Chapter Two

Scottish Highlands
Spring 1826

Engength lay far behind him, though not far enough. Never far enough. Marcus breathed deep of the crisp spring air. The scents of pine and heather filled his nostrils. Highland air. None sweeter existed. His horse nickered as if in agreement, and Marcus brushed a hand along the chestnut's shoulder.

"It is good to be home," Erin spoke beside him.

Grunts of agreement went up from the six other men riding in the company, and Marcus answered, "Aye," despite the regret of leaving his son in the hands of the Sassenach.

He surveyed the wooded land before him—MacGregor land. Bought with Ashlund gold, held by MacGregor might, and rich with the blood of his ancestors.

"If King George has his way," Erin said, "your father will follow the Duchess of Sutherland's example and lease this land to the English."

Marcus jerked his attention onto the young man. Erin's broad grin reached from ear to ear, nearly touching the edges of his thick mane of dark hair. The lad read him too easily.

"These roads are riddled with enough thieves," Marcus said with a mock scowl. His horse shifted, muscles bunching with the effort of cresting the hill they ascended. "My father is no more likely to give an inch to the English than I am to give up the treasure I have tucked away in these hills."

"What?" Erin turned to his comrades. "I told you he hid Ashlund gold without telling us." Marcus bit back a laugh when the lad looked at him and added, "Lord Phillip still complains highwaymen stole his daughter's dowry while on the way to Edinburgh." He gave Marcus a comical look that said *you know nothing of that, do you?*

"Lord Allerton broke the engagement after highwaymen stole the dowry," put in another of the men. "Said Lord Phillip meant to cheat him."

"Lord Allerton is likely the thief," Marcus said. "The gold was the better part of the bargain."

"Lord Phillip's daughter is an attractive sort," Erin mused. "Much like bread pudding. Sturdy, with just the right jiggle."

A round of guffaws went up and one aging warrior cuffed Erin across the back of his neck. They gained the hill and Marcus's laughter died at sight of the figure hurrying across the open field below. He gave an abrupt signal for silence. The men obeyed and only the chirping of spring birds filled the air.

"Tavis," Elise snapped, finally within hearing range of the boy and his sister, "this time you've gone too far and have endangered your sister by leaving the castle."

His attention remained fixed on the thickening woods at the bottom of the hill and her frustration gave way to concern. They were only minutes from the village—a bare half an hour from the keep and safely on MacGregor land—but the boy had intended to go farther—much farther. He had just turned fourteen, old enough to carry out the resolve to find the men who had murdered his father, and too young to understand the danger.

Bonnie tugged on her cloak and Elise looked down at her. The little girl grinned and pointed to the wildflowers surrounding them. Elise smiled, then shoved back the hood of her cloak. Bonnie squatted to pick the flowers. Elise's heart wrenched. If only their father still lived. He would teach Tavis a lesson. Of course, if Shamus still lived, Tavis wouldn't be hunting for murderers.

Those men were guilty of killing an innocent, yet no effort had been made to bring them to justice. The disquiet that always hovered close to the surface caused a nervous tremor to ripple through her stomach. While Shamus's murderers would likely never go before a judge, if Price found her, his version of justice would be in the form of a noose around her neck for the crime of defending herself against a man who had tried to kill her—twice.

Any doubts about her stepfather's part in Amelia's death had been dispelled a month after arriving at Brahan Seer when she read a recent edition of the London *Sunday Times* brought by relatives for Michael MacGregor. She found no mention of the *Amelia's* sinking. Instead, a ten thousand pound reward for information leading to the whereabouts of her *body* was printed in the announcements section.

Reward? Bounty is what it was.

The advertisement gave the appearance that Price was living up to his obligations as President of Landen Shipping. But she knew he intended she reach Boston dead—and reach Boston she would, for without her body, he would have to wait five years before taking control of her fifty-one percent of Landen Shipping. She intended to slip the noose over his head first.

Elise caught sight of her trembling fingers, and her stomach heaved with the memory of Amelia's body sliding noiselessly from the ship into the ocean. She choked back despair. If she had suspected that Robert had been poisoning her daughter even a few months earlier—

"Flowers!"

Elise jerked at Bonnie's squeal. The girl stood with a handful of flowers extended toward her. Elise brushed her fingers across the white petals of the stitchwort and the lavender butterwort. She was a fool to involve herself with the people here, but when Shamus was murdered she been unable to remain withdrawn.

"Riders," Tavis said.

Elise tensed. "Where?"

"There." Tavis pointed into the trees.

She leaned forward and traced the line of his arm with her gaze. A horse's rump slipped out of sight into the denser forest. Goose bumps raced across her arms.

Elise straightened and yanked Bonnie into her arms "It will be dark soon—" Tavis faced her and she stopped short when his gaze focused on something behind her.

Elise looked over her shoulder. Half a dozen riders emerged from the forest across the meadow. She started. Good Lord, what had possessed her to leave Brahan Seer without a pistol? She was as big a fool as Tavis and without the excuse of youth. She slid Bonnie to the ground as the warriors approached. They halted fifteen feet away. Elise edged Bonnie behind her when one of the men urged his horse closer. Her pulse jumped. Was it possible to become accustomed to the size of these Highland men?

She flushed at the spectacle of his open shirt but couldn't stop her gaze from sliding along the velvety dark hair that trailed downward and tapered off behind a white lawn shirt negligently tucked into his kilt. The large sword strapped to his hip broke the fascination.

How many had perished at the point of that weapon?

The hard muscles of his chest and arms gave evidence—many.

The man directed a clipped sentence in Gaelic to Tavis. The boy started past her, but she caught his arm. The men wore the red and green *plaide* of her benefactors the MacGregors, but were strangers.

"What do you want?" She cursed the curt demand that had bypassed good sense in favor of a willing tongue.

Except for a flicker of surprise across the man's face, he sat unmoving.

Elise winced inwardly, remembering her American accent, but said in a clear voice, "I asked what you want."

Leather groaned when he leaned forward on his saddle. He shifted the reins to the hand resting in casual indolence on his leg and replied in English, "I asked the boy why he is unarmed outside the castle with two females."

Caught off guard by the deep vibrancy of his soft burr, her heart skipped a beat. "We don't need weapons on MacGregor land." She kept her tone unhurried.

"The MacGregor's reach extends as far as the solitude of this glen?" he asked.

"We are only fifteen minutes from the village," she said. "But his reach is well beyond this place."

"He is great, indeed," the warrior said.

"You know him?"

"I do."

She lifted Bonnie. "Then you know he would wreak vengeance on any who dared harm his own."

"Aye," the man answered. "The MacGregor would hunt them down like dogs. Only," he paused, "how would he know who to hunt?"

She gave him a disgusted look. "I tracked these children. You think he cannot track you?"

"A fine point," he agreed.

"Good." She took a step forward. "Now, we will be getting home."

"Aye, you should be getting home." He urged his horse to intercept. Elise set Bonnie down, shoving her in Tavis's direction. "And," the man went on, "we will take you." The warriors closed in around them. "The lad will ride with Erin. Give the little one to Kyle, and you," his eyes came back hard on Elise, "will ride with me."

The heat in his gaze sent a flush through her, but her ire piqued. "We do not accept favors from strangers."

His gaze unexpectedly deepened.

She stilled. *What the devil? Was that amusement on his face?*

"We are not strangers," he said. There was no mistaking the laughter in his eyes now. "Are we, Tavis?" His gaze shifted to the boy.

"Nay," he replied with a shy smile. "No' strangers at all, laird."

"You know this man?" Elise asked.

"He is the laird's son."

"Marcus!" Bonnie cried, peeking from behind Elise's skirts.

Elise looked at him. Marcus? *This* was the son Cameron had spoken of with such affection these past months? It suddenly seemed comical that she had doubted Cameron's stories of his son's exploits on the battlefield. She had believed the aging chief's stories were exaggerations, but the giant of a man before her was clearly capable of every feat with which his father had credited him.

Prodded by the revelation, she discerned the resemblance between father and son. Though grey sprinkled Cameron's hair, the two shared the same unruly, dark hair, the same build... and... "You have his eyes," she said.

He chuckled.

Heat flooded her cheeks. She pulled Bonnie into her arms. "You might have said who you were." She gave him an assessing look. "Only that wouldn't have been half as much fun. Who will take the child?"

His gaze fixed on the hand she had wrapped around Bonnie and the small burn scar that remained as a testament of her folly. His attention broke when a voice from behind her said in a thick brogue, "'Tis me ye be looking for, lass." She turned to a weathered warrior who urged his mount forward.

Elise handed Bonnie up to him. Stepping back, she bumped into the large body of a horse. Before she could move, an arm encircled her from behind, pulling her upward across hard thighs. A tremor shot through her. She hadn't been this close to a man's body since—since those first months of her seven-year marriage.

Panic seized her in a quick, hard rush. The trees blurred as her mind plunged backward in time to the touch of the man who had promised till death do them part. Her husband's gentle hand on their wedding night splintered into his violent grip the night he'd tried to murder her—the movement of thighs beneath her buttocks broke the trance as Marcus MacGregor spurred his horse into motion. His arms tightened around her and she held her breath, praying he couldn't hear her thudding heart.

The ambling movement of the bulky horse lifted her from Marcus's lap. She clutched at his shirt. Her knuckles brushed his bare chest and she jerked back as if singed by hot coals. Her body lifted again with the horse's next step and she instinctively threw her arms around Marcus's forearm. His hold tightened as rich laughter rumbled through his chest.

"Do not worry, lass. Upon pain of death, I swear, you will not slip from my arms until your feet touch down at Brahan Seer."

Elise grimaced, then straightened in an effort to shift from the sword hilt digging into her back.

"What's wrong?" He leaned her back in his arms and gazed down at her.

She stared. Robert had never looked so—she sat upright. "I've simply never ridden a horse in this manner."

"There are many ways to ride a horse, lass," he said softly.

Elise snapped her gaze to his face, then jerked back when her lips nearly brushed his. She felt herself slip and clutched at his free arm even as the arm around her crushed her closer. Her breasts pressed against his chest where his shirt lay open. Heat penetrated her bodice, hardening her nipples. A surprising warmth sparked between her legs. She caught sight of his smile an instant before she dropped her gaze.

Their ascent steepened. Marcus closed the circle of his arms around the woman's waist. She leaned into him. It was a shame she wore a cloak. Without it, her bare arms would lay against his chest. He hardened. *Bloody hell.* Shift even a hair's breadth and the challenge he'd seen in her gaze an hour ago would resurface, accompanied by a slap across his face.

She had betrayed no fear when he came upon her—other than her open assessment of his weapon. Odd his sword should be what frightened her. She must have known if he meant mischief, he needed no weapon save his body. An erotic picture arose of her straddling him, breasts arched so he could suckle each until she begged him to lift her onto his erection.

He forced back the vision and focused on her determination to defend the children with her life… or perhaps, her body. He smiled, then gritted his teeth when he further hardened at the memory of her leaning over Tavis's shoulders as she scanned the forest for the riders he'd sent. Hands braced on her knees, her posture revealed the curve of a firm derriere.

When she turned at their approach, the wind had blown her brown hair about her shoulders, bringing his attention to the sensual curve of modest breasts visible just above the edge of her bodice. He envisioned hips tapering into long legs and wondered what those legs would feel like wrapped tightly around his waist while he thrust deep inside her.

Her accent had caught him off guard. What was an American woman doing on MacGregor land, and how had she come to know Tavis and Bonnie well enough to track them through the woods? Hot fury shot through him. The little fool. Had the wrong man come upon her, she might well have ended up like Katie.

The majestic heights of Brahan Seer's west tower abruptly loomed in the distance. Marcus's steed unexpectedly faltered, then steadied. The woman tensed and Marcus's body pulsed. He closed his eyes, breathed deep of her hair, then looked again at the tower. For the first time in his life, he regretted the sight. His ride with her cradled in his arms would soon end.

Higher they climbed, until Brahan Seer's walls became visible. The gates were open. At their approach, his captain Daniel hailed from the battlements. Marcus nodded as they rode through the entry. Inside the courtyard, he halted and Daniel appeared at his side.

"Elise," he addressed the woman, surprise apparent on his features. He glanced at the children, his gaze lingering on Bonnie. His mouth tightened. "Mayhap Marcus can take a hand with you, Tavis. Get along, and take your sister. Your mother will be worried."

Marcus handed Elise down to him. Before Marcus's feet touched the ground, she had started toward the castle. He dismounted and clasped Daniel's hand while watching from the corner of his eye the sway of her cloak about her hips as she answered a welcoming smile from two of his men headed toward the stables.

"What were they doing out alone?" Marcus demanded of Daniel.

"I've ordered the boy not to go wandering the woods," he replied.

"And Bonnie?"

"This is the first. I imagine she chased after her brother."

Elise turned the corner around the castle and Marcus cut his gaze onto her the instant before she disappeared. Lust shot to the surface and tightened his shaft, but he turned back to Daniel. "Why is Shamus letting his children run wild—never mind. I'll speak to him. You look well."

Daniel hesitated, then said, "Chloe is with child."

Marcus smiled in genuine pleasure. "Congratulations, man."

Daniel smiled, then took the reins as Marcus

turned toward the castle.

Through the busy courtyard, he answered greetings, but his thoughts remained on the image of Elise as she vanished from sight. She had a forthright, strong quality. Yet—he bent his head to breathe her lingering scent from his clothes—the lavender bouquet in her hair was decidedly feminine. It would be some time before he forgot the feel of her buttocks across his thighs. But then, perhaps he wouldn't have to. Marcus entered the great hall to find his father sitting alone in his chair at the head of the table.

Cameron brightened. "So, ye decided to come home?"

Relaxing warmth rippled through Marcus.

"Tired of wandering the land?" Cameron made a wide sweeping gesture.

"You knew I was on my way, but, aye." He stopped at the chair to his father's right and lowered himself onto the seat. "I am pleased to be home."

"How is my grandson? I see you did not bring him with you."

Marcus sighed. "Nay, Father. You knew I wouldn't."

Cameron snorted. "We would not want to offend the mighty Sassenach."

"Father," Marcus said in a low tone.

Cameron shook his head. "The clan never asked you to concede to the English, you know. *I* never asked for it. Did you ever wonder if the sacrifice is worth your son?"

"Aye," Marcus murmured. He'd wondered. Politics had ruled the MacGregor clan for centuries and that wasn't easily changed. He paused. "Have I been gone too long, or is something different about the great hall?"

"You have the right of it, lad." Eyes that mirrored his own looked back at him. "More than you can imagine."

Marcus looked about the room. "I can't quite place it. What's happened?"

17

Cameron took a long, exaggerated draught of ale. "*Cameron.*"

"Enough of your looks, lad. They do not work with me." He chuckled. "I taught them to you. Remember? It is no mystery, really. Look around. When did you last see the tapestries so bright, the floors so clean?" He motioned toward the wall that ran the length of the room, framed by stairs on either end. "When have you seen the weapons so polished?"

Marcus scanned the nearly two hundred gleaming weapons mounted across the wall. He rose and walked the wall's length, perusing the weapons. Each one glistened, some nearly as bright as newly forged steel. He glanced at the floor. The stone looked as if it had just been laid.

He looked at his father. "What happened?"

"The women came one day—or rather, one month—and swept out the cobwebs, cleaned the floors, the tapestries, weapons."

Marcus rose and crossed the room to the kitchen door where the women worked. The housekeeper sat at the kitchen table. Ancient blue eyes, still shining with the bloom of youth, smiled back at him. Winnie had been present at his birth. Marcus knew she loved him like the son she'd never had. He, in turn, regarded her with as much affection as he had his own mother.

She turned her attention to the raw chicken she carved. "So, you've returned at last."

"Aye, milady."

A corner of her mouth twitched with amusement.

"I am looking forward to the company of some fine lasses tonight," he said. "'Tis a long and lonely trip I've had. Perhaps next time I shall take you with me." He gave her a roguish wink before striding back to his seat in the hall.

Marcus lowered himself into the chair he had occupied earlier. "Must have taken an army just to shine the weapons alone. Not to mention the walls and floors."

"It did. You will see the same throughout the

castle. Not a room went untouched."

"Whatever possessed them to do it?"

"It was the hand of a sweet lass," Cameron replied.

"Which one? Not Winnie—"

"Nay. The lass Shannon and Josh found washed ashore on the coast. They brought her when they returned from the south."

"Washed ashore?"

"An American woman. Her ship perished in a fire."

"American?"

Cameron scowled. "Are you deaf? Shannon is the one who discovered her at Solway Firth."

"What in God's name was she doing there?"

Cameron gave his chin a speculative scratch. "Damned if I know. They were headed for London."

"London? Sailing through Solway Firth requires sailing around the north of Ireland. That would add a week or more to the journey."

His father's mouth twisted into a wry grin. "You know the English, probably got lost."

"I thought you said she was American."

"English, American, 'tis all the same." Cameron's expression sobered. "But dinna' mistake me, she is a fine lass. She came to us just after you left for Ashlund four months ago. You should have seen her when they brought her here. Proud little thing."

"Proud, indeed," Marcus repeated.

"'Tis what I said." Cameron eyed him. "Are you sure something isn't ailing you?"

Marcus shook his head.

"At first, she didn't say much," Cameron went on. "But I could see a storm brewed in her head. Then one day, she informed me Brahan Seer was in dire need of something." He sighed deeply. "She was more right than she knew."

Marcus understood his father's meaning. His mother's death five years ago had affected Cameron dramatically. Only last year had his father finally sought female comfort. The gaping hole created by her absence left them both thirsting for a firm, feminine hand.

"It's a miracle she survived the fire," Cameron said. "'Course, if you knew her, you would not be surprised."

"I believe I do," Marcus remarked.

"What? You only just arrived."

"I picked up passengers on the way home—Tavis, little Bonnie, and an American woman." Marcus related the tale. "I recognized her accent," he ended. "Got accustomed to it while on campaign in America."

Cameron smiled. "Elise is forever chasing after those children."

"Why?"

His father's expression darkened. "Shamus was murdered."

Marcus straightened. "Murdered?"

"Aye."

"By God, how—Lauren, what of her?"

Sadness softened the hard lines around his father's mouth. "She is fine, in body, but… her mind has no' been the same since Shamus died. We tried consoling her, but she will have none of it."

A tingling sensation crept up Marcus's back. "What happened?"

"We found him just over the border in Montal Cove with his skull bashed in."

"Any idea who did it?"

"Aye," Cameron said. "Campbells."

Marcus surged to his feet. He strode to the wall, where hung the claymore belonging to his ancestor Ryan MacGregor, the man who saved their clan from annihilation. Marcus ran a finger along the blade, the cold, hard steel heating his blood as nothing else could. Except… *Campbells.*

Had two centuries of bloodshed not been enough?

Fifty years ago, King George finally proclaimed the MacGregors no longer outlaws and restored their Highland name. General John Murray, Marcus's great uncle, was named clan chief. Only recently, the MacGregors were given a place of honor in the escort, which carried the "Honors of Scotland" before the sovereign. Marcus had been there, marching alongside his clansmen.

Too many dark years had passed under this cloud. Would the hunted feeling Ryan MacGregor experienced ever fade from the clan? Perhaps it would have been better if Helena hadn't saved Ryan that fateful day so long ago. But Ryan had lived, and his clan thrived, not by the sword, but by the timeless power of gold. Aye, the Ashlund name Helena gave Ryan saved them. Yet, Ryan MacGregor's soul demanded recompense.

How could Ryan rest while his people still perished?

Marcus removed his hand from the sword and faced his father. "It's time the MacGregors brought down the Campbell dogs."

Feminine laughter spilled from the kitchen into the great hall during the evening meal. Marcus sighed with contentment. Light from sconces flickered like a great, filmy curtain across the room. Two serving girls carrying trays of food stepped from the kitchen, and the men, who blocked the doorway, parted. The sense of contentment came as an almost unconscious realization. He had missed sharing the evening meal with his clansmen. Marcus leaned forward, arms crossed in front of him on the table, and returned his attention to the conversation with Cameron and Daniel.

"We will be ready at first light, laird," Daniel said.

"The Campbells will not be expecting trouble," Cameron put in.

"If word has reached them that I've returned, they may be," Marcus said.

Cameron grunted. "Lot of good it will do."

The feminine voice Marcus had been waiting for filtered out from within the kitchen. "Easy now, Andrea," Elise said.

The conversation between his father and Daniel faded as Marcus watched for her amongst the men who crowded between the door and table. The thought of seeing her beautiful body heated his blood. Elise stepped from the kitchen, balancing a plate of salmon. She passed the table's end where he sat and carefully picked her way through the men until reaching the middle of the table. She set the oval platter between the chicken and mutton.

"Beth, place the carrots to the left. Andrea—" She took the plate of potatoes from the girl, then set it to the right and turned toward the kitchen.

"Elise," one of the young warriors called, "come, talk with us, lass."

Her mouth quirked. "If I play with you, who will finish dinner?"

The man's hearty chuckle gave evidence she hadn't fooled him, and he approached with friends in tow.

Cameron stood. "Elise," he called over the men's heads, "come here."

She turned. When her gaze met Cameron's, warmth filled her eyes. She dried her hands on her apron and headed in his direction.

"Go on, lads," Cameron said to the men who teased her. "You have better things to do than dally with the lassies."

When she came within arm's reach, he gripped her shoulders. "Meet my son. He's returned today." He turned her.

Her gaze met Marcus's. Her smile faltered but quickly transformed into polite civility. "We've met."

"Oh?" Cameron replied, all innocence.

"Yes. He came by when Tavis, Bonnie, and I were on our way home this afternoon."

"Ahh," Cameron said, then turned and gave the man beside him an energetic greeting.

Elise looked again at Marcus and motioned toward the kitchen. "I have work to do."

"Aye," he said. The memory of her breasts pressed against his chest caused him to harden.

She backed up a few steps, then turned and ran headlong into the man behind her. He reached to steady her. A flush colored her cheeks and Marcus bit back a laugh when she dodged the warrior. Marcus leaned forward, catching one last look at her backside before she disappeared through the kitchen door.

Chapter Three

At the sound of horses padding past the cottage she shared with Winnie, Elise looked up from the table where sat the teacup she had been refilling. She glanced from the curtained window to Winnie, who remained bent over her needlework. Elise took two steps to the fireplace, hooked the kettle over the fire, and went to the window. She pulled back the lace curtain to see a procession of warriors filing past the cottages.

Marcus MacGregor rode at the head of the company. He sat straight, his body shifting in easy motion with the horse's rhythmic movements. Her father had exuded the same careless confidence. Elise recalled her mother often watching from a window as he rode away. The warmth spreading through Elise now gave her an understanding of what her mother must have felt.

"Ridiculous," she muttered.

"What?" Winnie called, but she didn't answer, mesmerized as Marcus turned his profile to her and addressed the man to his left.

The edges of his dark hair curled along the line of his ear and down his neck. He smiled. The remembered feel of his solid chest against her breasts arose with surprising intensity. What would his chest feel like beneath her fingers? Her pulse quickened. Where had that thought come from? Marcus's horse disappeared around a sharp turn in the path. Elise surveyed the long

24

line of men following.

"Where are they going?" she murmured.

"To the Hastings Campbells," Winnie said.

"I thought the MacGregors and Campbells were feuding."

"They are."

The last of the men disappeared from view. "Why go then?"

"To deal with Shamus's murderer."

Elise swung her gaze back to Winnie. "Shamus has been dead two months. Why has Cameron waited so long to bring the guilty man before the law?"

"Cameron *is* the law," Winnie replied.

A tremor rippled through Elise. Price, too, had appointed himself law. "How can Cameron be impartial? It is his kin who was murdered."

The housekeeper grunted. "How impartial should he be?"

"Surely he wouldn't kill in cold blood?"

Winnie's head snapped up. "Cold blood? What the Campbells done—killing Shamus—*that* was cold blood."

Elise realized she had crushed the curtain and released it. She crossed to the table and grasped the back of the chair across from Winnie. "Has Cameron identified the killer?"

"Each kinsman is responsible for the other."

Elise stared. "Have you any idea what you are saying?"

"Every Highlander will tell you the same."

"Even the Highlands of Scotland can't be so uncivilized as to seek recompense of the guilty party's neighbors. The man who committed the crime, he alone is responsible."

"Mayhap," Winnie said as she squinted at the tiny stitching. "But his kinsmen would have to hand him over to his accusers, and the Campbells are not known for thinking themselves guilty for ridding the world of a MacGregor."

Elise kept her tight grip on the chair. Would

the MacGregors hand her over to Price? Would the ten thousand pound reward sway them? "So an entire clan will suffer for one man's wickedness?"

"'Tis a funny thing you'll find in the clans," Winnie said, her attention intent on the sewing. "Some do nothing but fight. Others are peaceful, while some are just plain scoundrels. Whatever they are, 'tis generally agreed amongst themselves. Like begets like. If a man differs, he can take refuge elsewhere."

Warmth rippled through Elise. Just as she had taken refuge here. She watched Winnie stitch the intricate needlework on the linen blanket meant for Chloe's new baby. How much like her were these people? Sadness wound through her. What did it matter? When Price finally believed she had perished at sea and stopped advertising the notice, she would then board a ship without fear a bounty hunter was looking for her. Her wedding band, hidden behind a loose stone in the ladies' drawing room, would buy passage to America. There she would testify that she shot Robert in defense of her brother and herself.

Would her word be enough? She wasn't the only person who had survived the sinking of the *Amelia*. Someone had reported to Price that she shot Robert. Was that person friend or foe? Would that person try to stop her from bringing Price Ardsley to his knees? Elise startled at the realization that she intended to dispense her own brand of justice.

"Justice isn't always what it should be," she murmured.

Winnie snorted. "It is the law of the land—every land—and the Campbells know it. They're a bloodthirsty lot." Her countenance softened and she nodded toward her teacup. "Fill my cup."

The normalcy of the request loosened the tightening in Elise's stomach. She retrieved the kettle from the fire and poured hot water into Winnie's cup, then dropped in a tea ball.

"You canna' know," Winnie began, still working her stitching, "what it is to have everyone against ye, even your own king."

Elise returned the kettle to its place and seated herself at the table. Her soul grew heavy at hearing how more than two hundred years ago the government gave the Campbells all MacGregor land, heedless of the fact the property was occupied.

"Even the MacGregor name was outlawed," Winnie said. "Our line would have died if not for Ryan MacGregor."

Winnie went on to tell how the foresight of a single man saved an entire people. Ryan MacGregor, traitor to the Scottish crown, married a woman wealthy enough to shun the insidious alliance of the merchants and government, then bought land and furnished his people with weapons to keep it.

"How he angered the Campbells," she said with satisfaction. "We still lived and died by the sword, mind you, for a Campbell cannot bear to see a MacGregor at peace. But we had a sword to fight with."

But the horror had only begun, Elise realized as Winnie went on. The political tide then turned against all Highlanders.

"Clearances, they call it. *Evictions.*" Winnie jabbed her needle into the cloth. "*Murder.* Our chiefs evicted us. *Their own kin.* All in the name of *progress.* But the Duchess of Sutherland, she is the devil incarnate. Ninety families, she started with, but the numbers got as high as two thousand families in a single day."

Elise gasped. "Dear God, how is that possible?"

"It happened."

"Who is this duchess?"

"The most powerful woman in all Scotland— mayhap, the world. She owns tens of thousands of acres of land. When she realized ranching held better profit than farming, she began evictions. Thousands thrown out of their homes no matter their age or infirmity. Many were left by the wayside to die like animals. Not a family lives who hasn't been touched by the clearances. My great uncle Duncan McKay," Winnie's voice grew shaky, "he and his family, caught in the dead of night. Four bairns burned in their beds."

Elise's throat constricted at the picture of burning beds and children screaming for their parents.

Soundless tears rolled down Winnie's cheeks. "Duncan lived, poor devil, despite being nearly burned to death. They brought him here."

"Here?" Elise asked in a choked voice.

"Aye. My mother was Cameron's father's healer, then his for many years. But she couldna' do a thing for Duncan. He could have lived, or so she said, but the spirit died with his wife and children. There are others, but Duncan I remember best." She looked up "Have you ever seen a man burned?"

Unreasonable panic rose with the memory of the fire that had so quickly spread across the *Amelia's* cabin floor. Elise shook her head.

"Pray you never do." Winnie returned to her embroidering. "The Campbells stood alongside the duchess. They had government *and* church sanction. We were to be broken, you see. It did not matter that our men fought for the crown while their families died at home. We never bowed to their authority and that pricked them."

"And the Campbells," Elise said, "they took part in the… the…"

"Aye." Winnie nodded. "They made it their business to see to the MacGregors."

Elise's heart swelled when she learned of those few leaders who stood by their own. Of how the MacLeod chiefs improved the lives of their clansmen by ensuring their monies were shared amongst the people. The MacDonalds, too, had not partaken in the atrocities.

"Then," Winnie said, her voice softening, "we have the MacGregor."

Warmth emanated from her as she related how Cameron MacGregor, along with his young son, Marcus, defended their people. Only a few scant years ago Marcus picked up the gauntlet passed from father to son and returned to Brahan Seer with over a hundred ragged and defeated Highlanders. They were all he could save from the Sutherlund riots at Gruids.

"The Campbells were there," Winnie went on. "They gained noble rank—at the expense of the MacGregors. It's our wealth they stole. But we didn't lay down for it—and how they hate us for it." Her fingers convulsed on the embroidery needle. "They hate Cameron even more because he offered asylum to *any* Highlander. Two years ago, Marcus met them with a fist of iron when he attacked the Bannatyne Campbells."

"Dear God, why?"

"Katie MacGregor. If you had seen what they did to the lass—" Winnie forced the needle through the soft linen as if it was leather and gave a sudden cry.

A small pearl of blood splotched the beige cloth from beneath.

"Winnie!" Elise jumped to her feet.

Winnie snatched up the cloth and began sucking the blood from the linen. Elise grabbed the rag hanging over the hearth and wrapped it around Winnie's finger. Elise gripped it tightly, stanching the flow of blood. Winnie examined the cloth, then began sucking again.

"Shall I fetch some water?" Elise asked.

"Nay," Winnie replied, still sucking. "The saliva of the blood's owner is what takes blood from cloth." She looked at the cloth. The blood had disappeared. "This isn't the first MacGregor blood spilled because of Campbells, and it will not be the last."

A chill snaked through Elise. Would the next dead MacGregor be amongst those who just set out for Campbell land?

Elise bolted upright in bed, the echo of a scream giving way to the pounding in her ears. She looked wildly about the room but, instead of flames surrounding her as they had an instant before, only the hearth burned with soft, red embers. A faint light radiated from the coals. She gulped a deep breath upon recognizing the shadowed contours of the cottage she shared with Winnie. Which dream had awoken her this time? The one where she *hadn't* escaped her stateroom before it went up in flames, or the one where the flames of hell surrounded her?

Dear God, forgive me.

She choked back tears. He might forgive her, but Amelia and Steven wouldn't.

"Elise."

Elise jerked her attention to the far side of the room where Winnie slept.

"What is amiss?" the housekeeper asked in a sleep-laden voice. "You cried out—" Her gaze swung in the direction of the door. "What in God's name?"

The insistent knocking at the door penetrated Elise's brain and she realized the noise had yanked her from the dream.

Winnie threw back the covers and jumped out of bed. She draped a wrap about her shoulders and hurried to the door. "Who is it?" She yanked open the door. "Mary, girl," Winnie growled at the maid, "you had better—"

"The men have returned," the maid interrupted. "They're demanding supper."

"Mother of God," Winnie whispered. "Go along, child. I will follow in a minute." She shoved the door shut and scampered on tiptoe across the drafty floor to her bed.

"I'll come," Elise said as Winnie pulled off her shift and reached for the grey dress draped over her bed's foot board.

"No need." Winnie slipped the dress over her head.

Elise got to her feet. "No sense lying here while you work."

She quickly dressed, then grabbed the *plaide* from the foot of her bed and draped it over her shoulders as she followed Winnie out the door.

Minutes later, Elise slowed two paces into the kitchen, startled by the grim silence that pressed in about the room. Winnie hastened to the counter where

Mary and another girl were placing mutton and chicken on platters. Elise shook off the morose feeling and tossed the *plaide* she wore onto the counter, then hurried forward to join in the preparations.

"Nay, Wilma," Winnie admonished. "Leave the plate of mutton. You and Mary fetch wine from the cellar. The men will sleep better with a little help."

The girls hurried off. Cold chicken, bread, and peas were quickly placed on platters. Elise took the platter Winnie placed in her hands and headed for the great hall.

The camaraderie which generally characterized gatherings in the eating hall was absent. When Elise set the peas on the table, her heart stirred at sight of the men's exhausted faces. She cast a furtive glance at Marcus. The hard set of his mouth and hollow eyes startled her. What had happened to the carefree devil who held her in his arms only a few days ago? She returned to the kitchen.

"Take those." Winnie pointed to the bottles of wine sitting on the table, then turned back to the bread she had unwrapped from its cloth cover.

Elise hesitated. Four uneventful months at Brahan Seer had dulled her senses. Why hadn't she realized Cameron's son would be with his men tonight? A tremor rocked her belly. Neither had she considered that he could have read the wanted notice for Elisabeth Kingston while in London. He was far more sophisticated than Michael and, surely, far less trusting. Given time, would Marcus MacGregor recognize Elise as the nickname for Elisabeth?

"Elise."

She snapped from her thoughts and saw Winnie staring expectantly at her. Elise grabbed the bottles of wine on the table and reentered the hall. Marcus's plate was untouched. She set the wine on the table. His gaze met and held hers for an instant before he shoved back his chair and rose.

She remained rooted to the spot as he strode to the stairwell. At the stairs, he   paused and looked back at her, eyes dark with need. He turned suddenly and headed up the stairs. Her breath caught at sight of his shirt, taut across his shoulders, and her gaze dropped to his calves in the instant before he disappeared from view. Elise broke the stare and realized her pulse had jumped to a gallop. Good Lord, was the greater danger Marcus connecting her to the Elisabeth Kingston wanted for murder, or her reaction to him? Until now, she hadn't worried how long Price persisted in searching for her. She had been sure she could wait him out. Now, could she afford to wait—could she afford to remain even another night near Marcus MacGregor?

Marcus awoke, his body hard with arousal. He shifted his thoughts from Elise to the Campbells, but the memory of her face the night before persisted. Her eyes changed with her mood. Would those eyes darken with passion when she lay beneath him? He stirred restlessly. How might she cry out as he brought her to her pleasure? He would find out—and soon.

Ten minutes later, Marcus entered the kitchen to find the women busy with preparations for the meals. "Good morning, Winnie." He seated himself across the table from her.

She reached for a sprig of herbs from one of the piles before her and began grinding it in a mortar bowl. "Morning."

He glanced at the rear door.

"No sense watching the door. She isna' here."

He leaned forward. "You are a witch, Winnie, my love. Where is she?"

"Michael's. She set out early this morning."

"Why?"

"He broke his leg. She makes sure he is tended to."

"Indeed?"

"Indeed." Winnie reached for another sprig of herbs.

Marcus rose and kissed her cheek. "Making trouble while I've been gone, I wager?"

She looked up. "No more than usual."

"So I thought," he said, and left the kitchen.

Marcus looked from his father to the warrior entering the great hall. The man strode past the men gathered for the evening meal and stopped at the table opposite him.

"Lady Ross to see you, laird," he said.

"And you back but a day from fighting with Campbells," Cameron said.

Marcus sighed. "I suppose she knows I'm here."

The guard looked uncomfortable.

"You can escape out the back," his father suggested, but the door opened again and Lady Margaret Ross entered dressed in a tightly fitting riding habit that said she'd been in the saddle the better part of the day. "I told ye not to dally with noblewomen," Cameron added under his breath, and stood as she approached. "Margaret, lass, how are you?" He clasped her hands in his.

"Your Grace." She dipped into a deep curtsy.

He shot Marcus a dry look while her head was bowed. "Enough, lassie." He pulled the petite woman to her feet. "We are not in Edinburgh." He released her hands. "You will forgive me, if I dinna' stay. I have a mare that bears attending." He winked. "You won't miss me, I feel sure."

"It is always good to see you, Your Grace."

"It is good to see you, as well."

"You haven't had your supper, Cameron," Marcus remarked.

"Aye, well, I cannot leave Coreen alone too long. She is due to foal any time."

"Craig can watch after her."

Cameron snorted. "The boy doesna' know a gelding from a stallion."

"The next time you geld a stallion, have him watch. He'll remember after that."

His father cast a sheepish look at Margaret. "Well,

I do not think—"

"Never mind," Marcus cut in. "As you say, you have a mare to attend to."

"I do," he agreed, and made a hasty exit.

Lady Ross looked to Marcus. "Lord Ashlund." She started to curtsy again.

"None of that, Margaret," he said.

She paused and studied him from beneath her lashes then, with an incline of her head, straightened. She gave him an inquiring look and he stood.

"Gille," he addressed the man seated to his right, "give your seat up to the lady."

The man stood and bowed.

Lady Ross angled her head in thanks, then sat. "You are looking well," she said. "Did you enjoy London?"

Once again, the postern door opened and Marcus paused in sitting to look see who entered. Recognizing the newcomer as another of his men, he seated himself.

"Lord Ashlund," came Margaret's insistent voice.

"My visit went well." He forced his attention to her.

"I'm sorry I could not accompany you as you wanted."

"It was you who requested an escort, Margaret, not I who requested your presence."

"A shame my plans changed," she went on. "Unfortunately, I now must go to London." She smiled. "I would be glad of your company."

He gave a mirthless laugh. "London twice a year is quite enough. I have no wish to make it three."

She laid a hand on his arm. "Not long ago you would have done this for me."

"Made a special trip to London? You're confusing me with another of your admirers."

The women began serving the food and he glanced at the clock over the mantle. The evening grew late. "Did you come alone?" he demanded.

"I did."

Marcus frowned. "Very foolish."

The postern door creaked open again. Daniel stepped in. He looked in Marcus's direction. Amusement flicked across his face before he turned and exited.

"Are you expecting someone?" Margaret asked.

A maid placed a platter of mutton on his side of the table and he reached for it. "I will have one of my men escort you home." He dished a helping of meat onto his plate.

"It is so late, I thought perhaps…"

Marcus paused and looked at her. "You knew you would arrive after dark. Why do it?"

She stiffened. "Sheathe your conceit, Marcus. You were not the only person I visited today." She pursed her lips. "If my staying is too much of an inconvenience…"

He glanced again at the clock. Elise wouldn't journey home in the dark. He sat the platter of meat on the table. If she did, he would clip her lovely wings.

When Elise didn't return the following afternoon, Marcus went in search of his father and found him in the stables keeping watch on Coreen.

"It isn't unusual for her to be gone a day or two when she goes to Michael's," Cameron said. "She likes to make sure he is well-cared-for."

"What the blazes does that mean?" Marcus demanded.

His father stopped mid-stroke as he ran his hand across the mare's distended belly. "Hell, lad, the man is my age. What would he want with a lass Elise's age?"

"Age has not stopped you of late."

Cameron flushed. "A man cannot resist the charms of a woman forever, you know."

"That's exactly what I am afraid of," Marcus muttered.

"Although," Cameron said, his tone thoughtful, "I didna' see young Erin return with you. Did he go directly to Michael's? He has not seen his father in months."

"Yes, by God. How long did you say she usually stays with Michael?"

The mare nickered and Cameron began stroking her again. "She does, *on occasion*, stay a couple days, but, certainly, never longer."

"And it has been two days."

"It has," Cameron said with such emphasis that Marcus looked at him.

"I'll ride out and make sure she is safe."

"A fine idea. We would not want anything to happen, would we?"

Marcus gave his father a recriminating look, then snapped out an order for his stallion to be saddled.

Marcus stopped in front of Michael's cottage, dismounted, and tossed the reins over the post to the right of the porch. He entered the cottage without knocking.

"Back for more, lass?" came Michael's voice from behind the curtain that enclosed the corner bed.

"More of what?" Marcus demanded.

Michael drew back the curtain with a flourish. He met Marcus's gaze and grinned. "Marcus, this is a surprise."

"I imagine so," he said as Michael rose and hobbled toward him.

The old man halted. "Is something wrong?"

"Nay. Where is Elise? She's been gone some time and Cameron is concerned."

"Concerned?" Michael looked puzzled. "I cannot imagine why—" He stopped, his eyes narrowing shrewdly. "Are you sure 'tis not you who is worried?"

Marcus relaxed. "Where is she?"

"Marcus, you've come all this way, and I haven't seen you in age. Surely, you can spare a civil word? Sit down." He motioned toward the table sitting before the hearth. "Have a drink. Dinna' fash over Elise. She'll return soon."

"Return?" Marcus started. "Where is she?"

Michael sighed and gave him a disgusted look. "Out in the barn with Erin."

Marcus left the cottage, the words *with Erin* ringing in his head as he strode across the meadow to the barn.

"I want to thank you for all you've done for my father." Erin's voice filtered from the barn as Marcus neared.

"It's nothing," Elise replied.

Marcus paused at the open door. The sound of milk squirting into a pail was followed by a low moo from the heifer.

"Nay," Erin went on, "you lifted his spirits. It's difficult, him out here alone."

"Why hasn't he moved into the village?"

"This land has been worked by our family for generations. He refuses to give it up."

"I can understand—" She cried out in unison with the clang of a hoof against metal.

Marcus shot forward but halted inside the door at seeing Elise on her backside in a puddle of spilt milk, the pail on its side beside her. Erin leaned with his arms over the cow's back, staring down at her.

"Oh, dear." She looked up at Erin. "I haven't quite got the hang of it."

The young warrior came around the cow and squatted beside Elise. "Are you all right?" His voice betrayed the mirth he clearly felt.

"Fine," she replied wryly and extended a hand. "If you please?"

He stood, pulling her to her feet. She twisted in an effort to examine the back of her skirt.

"You have milk in your hair. How did you manage that?"

Elise gave him a dry look and shook out her skirt. "Perhaps I need a dip in the loch."

"Rather cold."

"True, but it would be better than this milk. It's getting late and I doubt I'll return to Brahan Seer

37

tonight."

"Aye," Marcus said. "You will return to Brahan Seer tonight."

Her head snapped in his direction as Erin whirled. "Marcus, what is amiss?"

Marcus looked at Elise. "I am here to take Elise home."

"Take her home?" Erin echoed.

"Aye. It's late, and Cameron was growing concerned." Marcus wondered at his rapidly increasing ability to lie with such ease.

"Of course." Erin faced Elise and bowed. "Thank you for coming. I know my father was pleased to see you."

He stepped back, and Elise turned a calculating eye on Marcus. His body tensed under her scrutiny.

"I am not going anywhere."

"Nay?" he asked, quelling the tightening of his groin at the cool note of confidence.

"My visit here is not finished."

"Nay?" he repeated.

She glanced at the pail laying near her feet and Marcus prepared for a quick retreat.

"No," she answered, and he relaxed upon seeing her turn her attention, albeit reluctantly, from the pail. "It's late and I have no horse," she said. "The trip home on foot after dark is dangerous."

"Aye," Marcus agreed.

Her brow knit in confusion, then her eyes widened. "I will not make another trip with you on your mount."

The statement was made with such force that Marcus nearly laughed.

"I will lend you a mare," Erin offered.

Marcus regarded her and lifted a brow in question.

"I promised Michael dinner."

"Elise," Erin put in, "my father will understand."

She kept her gaze on Marcus. "You may leave. I will find my way home."

His heart beat wildly at the open defiance expressed with such aplomb. He stepped forward and

Erin moved to intervene.

"Laird." The young man's voice hit like ice water and Marcus looked at him. "She doesn't know our ways," Erin said.

Marcus relaxed and shifted his gaze to her. "If it pleases her to stay, we shall. But only for dinner."

She gave a snort, then strode past them and out the door.

As the evening wore on, Marcus watched Elise entice them into becoming willing participants in the preparation of the meal.

"You three will not sit idle while I do all the work," she said.

"Lass," Michael protested, "what would poor men such as ourselves know of preparing food?"

"Enough, I'm sure." She thrust the handle of a knife into his hand.

An instant later, she'd replaced the copy of the *Sunday Times* sitting on the table beside him with an onion. Michael looked at her as if she were mad but, in the end, peeled and sliced the onion, his lip twitching with barely suppressed amusement.

"Erin." Elise placed a bowl of flour, sugar, and cream of tartar in his hands. "You stir the biscuits. Marcus," she said, surprising him, "see to the grouse on the fire."

Marcus obeyed, but turned a moment later when she cried, "Erin!" and saw Erin had spilled flour from the bowl onto the table.

Erin looked to his father.

"Do not look at me, lad. 'Tis not my fault you can't stir flour without dumping it all over yourself."

Elise grasped Erin's hand, trying to show him how to gentle his touch. Marcus jolted at seeing her slender fingers covering the young man's large hand. *Damn it, surely the boy posed no threat?* Marcus knew he'd lost his mind. Bloody hell, he was jealous.

"Ohh," she said in frustration as more flour went

over the side of the bowl.

Marcus laughed at the sheepish look on Erin's face. She snatched up the bowl and Michael joined in when she muttered incoherently and strode to the stove to finish the biscuits.

"So, tell me, Marcus," Michael said through his laughter. "How was London?"

"The same as always."

"And Kiernan?"

At the mention of his son's name, Marcus recalled his surprise at how much the boy had grown in the last year. At only eighteen, he towered over most Englishmen. Referred to as the dark giant, he deserved the nickname. Still, Marcus never ceased to marvel at the fact that one noticed his mother's raven hair and blue eyes when he entered a room. Unbidden, his father's words echoed in Marcus's mind, *"Do you not wonder if the sacrifice is worth your son?"*

"Is it worth it?" he said under his breath.

"What's that you say?" Michael asked.

Marcus focused on him. "The lad is doing as well as can be expected, considering."

"Considering?" Elise asked.

"Aye," he said, glad his father wasn't present to hear his response. "Considering he lives among the Sassenach."

At meal's end, Marcus insisted they go. Elise's expression darkened and she looked as if she might protest, but he caught her glance in the direction of father and son and relaxed when he saw she had chosen discretion over pride. Anticipation surged through him, despite the knowledge she considered him the lesser of the evils.

They stood at the door. Elise rose on tiptoes and planted a kiss on Michael's cheek. "Stay off your wounded leg."

"Thank you. You're a good lass." He gave her a bear hug.

"No toying with me."

The impish wink she gave Michael made Marcus regret ending the evening. She would be more reserved with her charms once they were alone. She went outside where Erin waited with their horses.

Marcus clasped Michael's hands.

"Do not wait so long to come back," Michael said.

Marcus started to release his hand, but Michael's grip tightened. "Be careful." He glanced in Elise's direction. "The dark has been known to bite."

Chapter Four

*T*o be bitten in the dark.

Marcus glanced at Elise. Moonlight filtered in dim rays through the trees, making it impossible to distinguish her features atop the mare. He slid his gaze over her figure. It was a shame Erin had a mare she could ride.

"Marcus," she broke into his thoughts.

He checked the surge of eagerness that leapt to life. "Aye?"

"Why does your son live in England?"

"Politics, love."

"Ah," she replied. "I see."

He was sure she didn't but was pleased nonetheless.

"Having your son living amongst a people so different from your own can't be easy."

"Nay?" They moved out of the trees into pale moonlight and he discerned an indulgent smile on her face.

"I'm not ignorant of the differences between the Highland life and that of London."

"You have been to London?" he asked.

"No, but where I'm from can't be much different."

"Where might that be, lass?"

"Boston."

"Do you miss it?" he asked.

"No."

He wondered at the quick answer, then his gaze caught on her mouth. What would it be like to kiss those lips? Moonlight glistened on the dark hair that cascaded down her cloaked shoulders. She straightened in the saddle, sharpening the curve of her breasts. He imagined his hand sliding over them and downward to the soft curls nestled below. Marcus shifted in the saddle to accommodate his growing arousal. Elise shook her head and ran a hand through her hair. What would she do if he took her now? Just when he'd convinced himself she wouldn't resist, his mind snapped to attention at hearing an unexpected noise.

"Do you—" she began.

"Hush," Marcus commanded in a whisper.

He reined in alongside her. Grabbing her mare's bridle, he pulled both horses to a stop. He dismounted, then hauled her down from the saddle and drew her close to whisper in her ear, "There is a hill just ahead. I'm going for a look. Do not move." He shoved the reins into her hand and slinked into the darkness.

Near the top of the hill, Marcus crouched, then finally went to his knees, crawling the last few feet to the crest. Between the hill where he crouched and the opposite hill, three men on horses picked their way across the rocky ground. Their colors were indistinguishable, but he knew they were Campbells.

When he had demanded Shamus's killer be turned over to him, John Campbell had complied *after* Marcus and his men threatened to take John in his kinsmen's place. The fact the man was turned over to Peter McKinlay of the Glasgow police for a proper trial made no difference. John Campbell had been furious.

The men disappeared into the trees, and Marcus hesitated. The keep was another ten minutes' ride. Could he send Elise on alone? He remembered Katie MacGregor and cursed. He couldn't gamble with Elise's safety.

Marcus quietly made his way back down the hill and, minutes later, distinguished her form in the darkness. "Elise," he called in a whisper.

Her head jerked in his direction, but she didn't cry out. After another instant, he reached her side. He grasped her shoulders and pulled her close, whispering, "We must ride—and fast." She started. "All will be well." He squeezed her shoulders. "You ride with me. Can you stay in the saddle?"

She nodded.

"Good lass." He reached for the reins

She grabbed his arm. "What's happened?"

He hesitated. "Campbells."

She glanced at the hill. "So close to Brahan Seer?"

"Aye."

Marcus vaulted into his stallion's saddle, then extended a hand toward her. Elise yanked her skirts thigh high, grabbed his hand, and jumped nimbly up behind him as he pulled. She wrapped her arms around his midsection. The soft contours of her breasts pressed into his back. He gritted his teeth and nudged the stallion into a quiet walk, keeping the mare close until they were well out of earshot of the small camp. Then he urged the stallion into a gallop.

The men on the castle walls sprang to life at their approach half an hour later. Marcus brought their horses to a skidding halt before the gate. "Open!" he shouted. "'Tis me, Marcus."

The gate creaked open and he drove the horses through before the doors had swung wide. He halted amongst the gathering warriors and brought his leg over the horse's head, sliding from the saddle.

"Marshall," he called to the nearest man as he pulled Elise from the saddle, "find Daniel and have him gather twenty men. We ride in ten minutes. Where is my father?"

"I dinna' know," Marshall answered. "Mayhap the great hall?"

Marcus started off, then stopped and whirled to see Elise standing where he left her. "Go to your cottage," he ordered then, cursing the powers that be, set out after his father.

*   *   *

Elise glanced at Michael, who rode alongside her. His gaze remained directly ahead. The rigid set of his mouth indicated he was still angry with her for coming alone to his cottage. Guilt unsettled her. His anger was born out of concern, and he was more right than she cared to admit. To make matters worse, the trip had been a waste. He hadn't received a recent copy of the *Sunday Times.*

Birds abruptly took flight in the trees up ahead. She gave a small cry. Michael shot her a look that said, *Not so sure there aren't any Campbells on MacGregor land, are you?*

Heat warmed her cheeks and she looked straight ahead. The Campbells had eluded Marcus that night three weeks ago. No further trace of them or their kinsmen had been found since, but Marcus was on a mission to discover who had trespassed onto his land. As a result, she wouldn't be able to ride more than an hour without encountering one of his men.

Damn him. If not for his watchful eye, she would be on a ship to America. The night he fetched her from Michael's, she had decided not to return to Brahan Seer but to continue to Glasgow and chance the first ship away from Scotland. The wanted notice had been in the *Sunday Times* dated three weeks prior, but Price could have given up since then.

She took a shaky breath and closed her eyes. Price stared back at her from behind her father's mahogany desk at Landen Shipping. MacGregor men wouldn't crawl the land like mice much longer. Soon she would return for the man who had put her mother in an early grave, then quietly took part in her daughter's murder. Her heart constricted. Steven was a casualty of *her* making—a casualty she knew Price Ardsley relished. Elise forced back tears.

Beware, stepfather. I will return.

"Will you come to the great hall?" Elise asked Michael when they passed through the castle gates.

"Aye," he replied shortly.

"Michael," she began, but he pulled his horse to a halt beside her and dismounted.

He came around to her and helped her from the saddle. "Go on." She hesitated, and his eyes softened. "I'll be along after I have seen to the animals."

She pressed a kiss to his cheek. "You're a good man, Michael MacGregor."

He shook his head, but she could see that he was pleased. He limped off leading the horses, and Elise headed for the great hall. At the postern door, she entered and saw Marcus standing near the hearth. He broke off his conversation with the two men who stood with him and glanced over his shoulder. The drawn look on his face snapped into a dark scowl. He started forward. Elise faltered when she saw he meant to intercept her. His companions disappeared up the nearest staircase and a hum of apprehension began deep in her stomach.

Marcus rounded the table and reached the midway point when she blurted, "Good afternoon, Marcus. How are you?"

"Where have you been?" he demanded.

"I—" She fell back an unsteady step when it seemed he would ram into her. He halted three feet from her. "I have just returned from visiting Michael."

"So I was told," he replied curtly. "Winnie's warning did nothing to deter you?"

"Winnie's warnin—" Elise recalled her encounter with Winnie that morning. Good Lord, Winnie had told him she saw her leave.

Marcus's eyes narrowed. "Aye, you remember. Fortunately for you, I only just discovered your absence. Unmanageable wench," he added in a dark voice.

"You have your answers," she shot back. "Why bother asking?"

"Because I couldn't believe you were traipsing

about the countryside."

"I was not *traipsing* about the country. Not that it's your business."

"It is my business—and I will see to it you no' do it again."

She ignored the warning bell the definite hardening of his brogue set off inside her head. and said, "You're insane if you think I'll be ordered about."

"Ye will do as you're told," he said in a quiet voice that was perversely more unsettling than a shout.

"I come and go as I please, just as everyone else at Brahan Seer."

A keen light shone in his eyes. "If you will note, the women are staying close to home." His expression hardened. "At the express command of their men."

Elise gasped, then glanced past him, gauging the distance between him and the freedom the kitchen offered. He stepped closer and her temper flared. She raised her hands to shield herself from his advance and her palms met the unexpected warmth of his chest. She gaped at her fingers splayed across tanned skin where his shirt lay open, and her senses reeled at the raw power in the heavy rise and fall of his chest.

"Lord," she whispered, and yanked her hands away.

The vague realization that strong fingers had gripped her wrists was overshadowed by the jolt she felt when Marcus forced her hands back to his chest. Her mind screamed to break free, but the sight of her palms gliding over his dark skin—the need to touch every contour, to know intimately his powerful body—held her rooted to the spot. She tore her gaze from his chest and looked into his eyes. The fire blazing there drew her—commanded her—and she leaned into him.

"There ye are, lad. I was just look—"

Elise twisted as Cameron reached the bottom of the nearest staircase. He lifted a bushy brow. She looked back at Marcus. His hold loosened and she snatched her hands away. She retreated, stumbling over her own feet. Marcus reached for her, but she

47

dodged his hand with another unsure step backward.

"I-I must go," she stammered, and fled the room.

"*Elise*—bloody hell!"

Marcus's voice echoed off the stone walls as she shoved through the postern door.

Elise avoided Marcus that night. Yet his memory persisted. Alone in bed, her cheeks burned with the recollection of how he had forced her hands against him in a rough caress. Though only a moment passed between them, her senses had taken in every contour as her fingers glided along the unyielding muscle. The hint of brandy on his breath, the hammering of his beating heart, his hard body—with a flourish, she threw back the covers. Cold air crept over her. Yet it wasn't the cold that made her shiver, but the vision of Marcus's hands touching her as she had touched him. Oh, treacherous body! To be undone by desire.

A desire beyond that which drew you to the man you shot, her mind whispered.

Elise examined her hands in the moonlight that spilled across the bed from the window above her head. It hadn't occurred to her she would touch another man as she had Robert. A porcelain doll, Robert had called her, to be admired but not touched. The fact he had suffered her in his bed only long enough to get her with child had proven even her beauty had been lacking. Yet the memory of Robert's scorn didn't stop the leap of her heart at the thought of Marcus.

Time grew short—shorter than she had realized. Dare she wait another week or even a day before leaving Scotland?

Marcus stood on the battlement speaking with Daniel when he spied Elise emerging from the stables astride a horse.

"By God," he cursed.

"What is it?" Daniel looked in the direction Marcus stared.

"Stop her!" Marcus shouted down to the guards, then hurried down the stairs.

Her gaze met his as he leapt from the battlement steps into the courtyard. "Out of my way," she ordered.

"Woman, only yesterday you fled from me as if I were an ogre. Now you dispense imperious orders as though you are a queen. Where are you going?"

"To find Tavis and box his ears. Then I'll drag him and his sister back."

Marcus raised a brow. "Tired of chasing the little fools all over God's green earth? A pity they won't listen to good advice. Come down from there." He reached to pull her from the mare's back.

She slapped his hand. "They purposely sneaked out."

"Disobedient brats," he said.

Her eyes narrowed.

"Never mind," he said.

"Never mind?" she choked. "If I hadn't heard it myself, I wouldn't have believed it." She jerked on the reins. "Out of my wa—" Elise shrieked when he yanked her from the saddle.

Marcus brought her face level with his. "Yesterday, you left against my command. Will you attempt to disobey me again today?"

Her eyes narrowed. "I planned to enlist Brady's help in finding the children."

"And if he's not available?"

"He's the stable master. He is always in the stables."

"Aye," Marcus said. "But if he isn't, you will use good sense and return to the keep?" He added before she could argue, "I'll fetch the children."

Her eyes lit. "I'll wait while you get a horse."

He released her, then pried the reins from her fingers and mounted. "I will go."

"But—"

"Elise," he growled, "are you saying I cannot deal with two errant children?"

"No-no, of course not. It's just that Bonnie is

49

so little, and Tavis—" Her eyes blazed. "The boy is going to get them both killed."

"Why does he take his sister with him?" Marcus asked.

"He doesn't. She's a clever child. She watches, then follows."

"Bloody hell," he said under his breath. "She is but seven."

Elise laid a hand atop Marcus's hand, which rested on his thigh. "Why does Tavis persist in going out like this? I thought you dealt with his father's murderer."

"Revenge is never satisfied," Marcus replied.

Her fingers moved against his and he looked at her hand. His gaze caught on the long, thin scar on the outside edge of her palm. He had noticed it before, had meant to ask her—She snatched her hand back.

Marcus looked down at her and smiled softly. "It is all right, love. I will bring them safely home." He brushed a finger across her cheek.

She looked startled and a blush crept up her cheeks.

Marcus urged his horse forward, satisfied.

Two hours later, Elise looked up from her seat in the kitchen to see Marcus enter with Bonnie on his shoulders. A general round of praise went up from the women. He gave a gallant bow, very obviously pretending to forget Bonnie, then grabbed her at the last moment and shoved her back into place on his shoulders.

Warmth rippled through Elise at sight of him pausing to pluck slices of apples from a bowl on the counter. She silently cursed her schoolgirl giddiness. Marcus popped a slice into his mouth, then passed one to Bonnie. Elise's thudding heart kicked up a notch when he looked in her direction. He started toward her and she hastily returned her attention to the potatoes she was peeling. He pulled Bonnie from his shoulders and lowered himself into the chair beside Elise. Bonnie settled on his lap and leaned back in the crook of his arm. Absorbed in her apple, she munched contentedly.

"I think we need not worry any longer about Bonnie running after Tavis," Marcus said.

Elise looked to find a lock of hair had fallen across his forehead, making him look very much like a large child himself. She resisted the urge to smooth the lock back into place.

Focusing instead on her potatoes, she said, "Why is that?"

"Because he won't be taking any more trips."

"How can you be sure?"

"I told him not to."

Elise sighed. The boy would probably obey without even a whimper. She hazarded a glance at Marcus. He was grinning.

Her heart unexpectedly constricted. How would she live without seeing that smile every day?

When Elise entered the kitchen the following afternoon, she frowned at finding the room empty. Winnie napped in the early afternoon and several of the younger women tended to their families' needs, but Jinny was usually present, starting preparations for the evening meal.

Jinny's voice abruptly sounded from the eating hall. "Please, milaird, let me go."

"Come now," a male voice boomed, "'tis only a friendly gesture."

A round of riotous laughter followed this statement.

"Nay, laird," Jinny pleaded, "I dinna' want you to be friendly."

"You haven't given me a chance," the male voice began as Elise retrieved a large cast-iron pan from the ten plate stove located against the wall near the hearth. She crept toward the door leading to the great hall and heard, "I can be verra friendly, given the proper incentive."

From the kitchen door, she saw Jinny, held on a man's lap, twist in an effort to avoid his kiss.

Elise stepped through the doorway. "Enough!"

The command rang through the stone chamber, quieting the group.

The brute blinked. "Who might you be?"

"Let her go," she ordered.

He shared an amused look with his comrades, then lifted Jinny from his lap and rose.

"Go along, Jinny," Elise said.

The girl whirled and fled out the postern door. The brute strode to where Elise stood.

He clasped his arms over his large chest and cocked his head to the side. "Now what?"

"You released her. Satisfy yourself you've escaped intact."

"I need a replacement." He reached for her.

In one long movement, Elise swung the pan, bringing the cast iron pot across his shoulder. Metal met muscle with a loud crack, and the blow sent the sizeable man tumbling to the floor. He lay sprawled on the floor, blinking up at her.

Elise stared down at him. "Try such nonsense again, and the next one will be across that thick Scots head of yours."

Howls of laughter filled the room from the brute's comrades. He pushed to his feet. "Seems you need a lesson, lassie."

"Nay, Declan," came Marcus's voice behind her.

Elise whirled. Marcus caught the hand holding the pan. She glimpsed Jinny near the kitchen door.

"You won't be needing this anymore." Marcus gently worked the pan free of her grasp.

She looked down at the pan and released it.

Declan grabbed for her, but Marcus pulled her to his side. "No touching the lass."

"But you saw what she did. I willna' hurt her." He gave her an appraising look. "Not really."

Elise shot him a recriminating look.

"You brought this on yourself," Marcus said.

"You aren't taking her side?"

"I am."

"Nay," he said in clear disbelief.

"Aye."

He gave Marcus a dubious look, then grumbled as he retreated to his seat, "Probably not worth the trouble, anyway."

Marcus placed the pan on the counter, then started for the great hall.

"Marcus," Elise said as he brushed past her.

He stopped and turned.

"Keep him away from Jinny."

Marcus reached for the pitcher of ale sitting on the table before him and Declan and refilled their glasses. "How many cattle were stolen?" Marcus set the pitcher back on the table. The man to his right snatched up the pitcher and passed it down the table to the men gathered for dinner.

"Thirty or forty head," Declan replied.

"Within two months?" Marcus gave a low whistle. "My guess is Campbells."

"Aye," Declan agreed. "But I havena' been able to catch the bastards in the act."

"We've had Campbells on our land of late."

"The bastards," Declan said with feeling. He picked up a piece of bread from one of the platters sitting before him and stuffed a piece into his mouth. "They get around, eh?" His eyes gleamed. "If it's a fight they're wanting, I'll oblige."

"That would be nothing to scoff at," Marcus said.

Declan's own men, plus extended relatives, rallied a force of six hundred men. Add the MacGregor forces, which numbered nearly twelve hundred, and they commanded a small army.

"I can't blame you for wanting to put an end to the foolishness," Marcus said, "but a little rustling isn't worth a war." Declan started to reply, but Marcus cut him off. "War it would be, Declan. There isn't a clan in the district who would pass up the chance to even the score against the Campbells."

"And the Campbells hold their own grudges," Declan put in. "They haven't forgiven you for your assault on Assipattle two years ago."

Marcus's jaw tightened. They had better not forget. He hadn't forgotten Katie MacGregor. "The next time they attack a MacGregor woman, I will raze every Campbell keep from the border to Assipattle."

Chapter Five

A branch snapped with a loud crack. Elise jerked her gaze onto her companion Allister, then twisted in the saddle and peered over her shoulder. A blur of green and blue *plaide* shot from the trees at the top of the hill. She gasped.

Campbells.

Elise faced Allister. The young man stared back at the Campbells, eyes narrow with fury. Dear God, she hadn't believed them to be a genuine threat, but in an effort to buy time when she didn't return to Brahan Seer, she had asked Allister to accompany her to Michael's. If anything happened to him—

He yanked the dirk from the leather scabbard strapped to his horse and snapped his eyes onto her. "Ride."

She kicked violently into the mare's belly. The mare lunged forward alongside Allister's gelding. The sound of pursuing hoof beats bore down upon them. She hugged the horse's neck, urging the mare into a harder gallop down the mountainside.

The heaving horses closed in from behind. Elise's heart thudded in unison with the pounding of her mount's hooves. Tears stung her eyes as she clung to the horse, the jerky rise and fall of the animal's neck jolting her body with each swift stride. Allister's horse nosed ahead and Elise knew the young man was restraining him in order to keep pace with her.

From the corner of her right eye, she glimpsed the nose of a horse gaining—then a flash of metal and a man's cry as Allister's dirk found its mark. The other men shouted and her heart leapt into her throat. She cracked the reins over the rump of the horse, then suddenly pitched forward. She tumbled over the horse's head as the mare hit the ground nose first. Allister shouted her name.

The mare somersaulted over herself, and Elise saw the hooves bearing down on her as she and the mare plummeted downhill. The wind gushed from her lungs, then a splitting pain shot through her head when she thudded to the ground, grinding her cheek into the hard, rocky soil. The blurry figure of the horse landed a few feet away, rolled, then jumped up, and disappeared.

A shot sounded.

"Bloody animal got away," a man muttered as horses drew up alongside her.

Booted feet appeared at her side.

"She's broken her neck," another said.

"What of the boy?" another asked.

Fingers gingerly probed her forehead, then temples.

"Dead."

"She's hit the front of her head," said a deeper voice—not Marcus's voice, but who—Sudden pain registered through the fog as she was rolled to her side. She groaned.

"She's not dead," the deep voice said.

Fingers ran along her spine.

"She hasna' broken her back. She'll live."

Arms slid beneath her, then lifted her from the ground and pressed her against a warm body. She opened her eyes, but her blurry vision made out only the wall of flesh her face was shoved against.

"Leave her," said the other. "If we bring her back damaged, it'll be our heads."

"Toss the saddle over the mountain." The speaker shifted her in his arms. Pain splintered through her back "Round up the gelding," the man said, "and throw

Greig's body over his back. Damn the MacGregor dog who killed him. If he wasn't already dead, I would kill him myself."

Shock reverberated through Elise. Young Allister was dead?

As Marcus approached the village stables, he glimpsed movement through the open door. He yanked aside his steward Harris as a rider burst from the stables. The youth riding the horse seemed not to notice he had forced them from his path and galloped toward the village.

"Youth," Marcus muttered, and entered the stables. "I want Gaelan's, Logan's, Sloan's, and Neal's places finished by summer's end." He strode along the line of stalls.

Harris made notations in his notebook. "We can have them patched by month's end."

"Patch Sloan's," Marcus said. "The others, replace."

"That'll take 'til Fall, and we will need materials."

"Order what you need from Edinburgh. In the meantime, get started on the minor repairs for the other cottages. I want you back in Ashlund by month's end. I don't plan on returning for"—he thought of Elise in his bed, her hands on him—"for some time." Marcus halted at the stall that housed the horse he wanted to examine. "Gerald," he murmured to the gelding, who stood, head hanging over the stall door. Marcus rubbed Gerald's nose while he unlatched the door and stepped inside. "Getting along in years, are you, lad? Harris," Marcus called.

Harris entered the stall.

"What do you think?" Marcus ran a hand down the horse's leg. "He stumbled last week."

Harris squatted and looked closely at Gerald's knee. "A might knobby." Harris stood and walked around the horse, feeling belly and rump as he went. "His coat is dull and"—the steward came around to the horse's head again—"his head is hanging low."

"Aye," Marcus agreed. "We'll need two more plow horses then. Alen could last another season, but we will use him for delivery. Don't order from MacFie. I have another seller in mind. Belgian draft horses."

"Aye," Harris replied.

Marcus went around the rump of the horse. "Go yourself. There's a Russian Trotter I want you to look at. You can order the supplies while in Edinburgh."

"What are ye saying?" A shout from outside the stall intruded upon their conversation.

Marcus recognized the stable master's voice.

"Where did they go?" Brady demanded.

"Mary didna' g-go with Elise," Craig, the stable boy, stammered.

Marcus stilled.

"Bloody fool," Brady shot back. "You didn't wonder why she wanted the mare?"

Marcus cursed and started for the door.

"W-why should I wonder?" the boy stuttered. "You let Mary use your horse before. How could I know you changed your mind?"

"Christ," Brady's voice was hoarse. "MacGregor will whip us both."

Marcus lunged from the stall and Craig went pale. Brady glanced over his shoulder and his eyes widened.

Marcus strode toward them. "Hold," he commanded when it looked as if they would bolt.

"I had no notion—" Brady began, but Marcus raised a hand.

He grabbed Craig by the collar, nearly lifting him from the ground. "What happened?"

"Th-they came a-a-and g-go—"

"Pull yourself together," Marcus snapped.

Craig swallowed. "M-Mary and Elise came and s-saddled Brady's mare. I didn't know they were not supposed t-to take her."

"Nay?" He gave the boy a hard shake. "How long ago did she leave?"

Craig hesitated, and Marcus said, "It is nearly

58

three now. How long?"

"This morning. Mayhap eight."

"You helped them saddle the mare?" Marcus snapped.

"No! I heard them saddle the horse." He hesitated.

Marcus's lips tightened. "Sleeping?"

Craig dropped his gaze.

"What did they say?" Marcus demanded.

"Elise was g-going to Michael's."

Marcus shoved Craig from him. "Saddle Alexis."

"That devil?" Harris blurted.

"Alexis," Marcus repeated. "I will take even the devil's help."

Ten minutes later, Marcus galloped out of the stables. He left the path as soon as he found a reasonable place to drive the stallion down the steep hills, cutting off more than half the time Elise would have taken to reach Michael's. The resolve he had made to whip her to within an inch of her life died when he reached the cottage to discover she hadn't been there.

"I'll come with ye to find her," Michael said. He turned and started toward the corner containing his bed.

Marcus glanced at Michael's leg. The splint was gone. "There's no time to saddle your horse."

"There is," the older man said, his voice firm. "It will take but three minutes."

Marcus started to argue, but Michael strode the last two paces to his bed, saying, "We can waste time arguing if you like, but I'm going." He snatched up the coat lying on the chest at the foot of the bed and turned to Marcus. "Go on ahead. I can follow. Dalton will give Alexis a run for his money." He gave Marcus a hard look. "If there is trouble, you'll be needing all the help you can get." He strode past Marcus and out the door.

Cursing, Marcus followed. Three minutes later, they rode.

Marcus yanked Alexis up short and leapt to the ground when he at last sighted Elise's tracks.

"They went down here." He squatted, examining where the mare had lost her footing on the mountainside.

"Aye." Michael dismounted.

"The mare threw Elise." Marcus motioned at the wide swath of crushed ground dented from the mare's landing.

He rose, moving slowly forward, ignoring the tracks he knew had to be Campbells as his gaze scanned the ground. He squatted again and carefully ran a finger over a smattering of dried blood on a rock. Marcus looked onto the turf churned up where riders had pulled up hard and fast alongside the place Elise had fallen. He traced the tracks with his fingers, noting the change in weight when they had dismounted.

"If she were dead, they would have left her," Michael said.

"Or they could have kept the body as a bargaining tool. Where is the saddle? It fell off." Marcus scanned the surroundings but found no sign of the saddle.

"They probably threw it down the mountainside or took it," Michael said.

Marcus stood. Had he not taken the shortcut, he would have noticed the tracks forty minutes ago. "Fetch Johnson from Brahan Seer. He's our finest tracker. I'll follow the tracks."

Marcus grasped his horse's pommel, then froze at the sound of a low moan. "Did you hear," he began, but Michael was already starting down the hill at a near run.

"Michael," Marcus shouted. The fool would break his leg again, or worse.

Marcus raced after the old man and reached him just as a body came into sight beyond the nearest fir tree. Marcus's heart thudded in the instant before his mind registered that it wasn't Elise but a man. Allister, he realized. The young man's father had recently died and Allister had taken over the land his father had tilled.

Marcus dropped to one knee beside him. Allister stared up, eyes dark with pain.

"What happened, lad?" Marcus asked.

He licked his lips, then rasped, "Campbells."

Fear knifed through Marcus. "Elise?" he asked.

"Fell from her horse," Allister managed.

"There was no body, MacGregor," Michael reminded him. "Allister is alive, so is she."

Marcus nodded and forced calm as he made a quick assessment of Allister's injuries. His arm had been gashed and a bruise had begun to form on his forehead, but no blood gushed from any part of his body.

"Can you move?" Marcus asked.

"My leg… broken," he said.

Marcus nodded. "Hurts like the devil, I wager."

Allister winced with what looked like laughter at the obvious understatement.

"Can you manage until help arrives?" he asked.

A steely glint lit the young man's eyes. "Leave me a pistol and any Campbell that comes near will die."

"That's the spirit," Marcus said.

"I got one."

"What?"

"My dirk," the boy said.

"You did well." Marcus rose. "Michael will leave you his weapon. If I overtake the bastards, I plan to use my pistol."

Marcus hurried back up the hill with Michael close behind.

Marcus mounted his horse. "You'll reach Brahan Seer in ten minutes. I doubt any Campbells stayed behind, but leave the boy your knife as well." Michael nodded. Marcus gave the stallion a kick, and the beast lunged forward.

"MacGregor!" Michael shouted.

Marcus brought Alexis around in a sharp turn.

"Dinna' do anything foolish. We'll be no more than an hour behind. If—when—you find the lass, wait for us."

"Make it forty minutes," Marcus said, and dug his heels into the belly of his horse.

*   *   *

Elise blinked. The darkness around her gave way to formless shadows that shifted before her eyes. She jostled and groaned at the pain that spiked in all directions through her body.

"Awake, eh?" The male voice crashed through her head like a wave against a cliff.

She lay in the arms of the speaker, her back against a muscular chest. A distant memory hovered. "Mar—" her voice cracked. Then in a half whisper, "Marcus?"

He grunted. She went rigid. This wasn't Marcus.

Elise closed her eyes, forced back the queasy upheaval of her stomach, then opened her eyes again. All before her looked as if she were looking through a fog. She squinted at the blurring shadows. Slowly, images formed, and she realized she was staring down at the moving ground. They were riding—her mind registered the horse's rhythm beneath them. *The horse's rhythm.* She had been riding—hard. The crystal-clear memory of the mare bearing down on her when she'd been thrown caused her to shudder.

Then she remembered Allister.

Tears sprang to her eyes. The young man had died because of her. His mother—Elise choked back a sob and a wave of dizziness wrenched her stomach. She forced her breathing to slow. At last, the nausea subsided and she shifted. Pain lanced through her head, but she squinted at the blur that had come into view on her right until the figure of a man riding came into focus. He stared unabashedly.

Elise ignored the tremor his stare elicited and looked past him, skyward, where dim points of light showed through thin, grey clouds. She shifted again and found herself staring up at the jut of a square jaw. Above that, the bluish hue of moonbeams filtered through clouds. The pain relaxed to a dull throb and her stomach settled. The clouds parted and the moon blazed in her vision. She squeezed her eyes shut, but registered its position and estimated the time as just past midnight.

"There's been no sign of MacGregor," her captor said.

Marcus would have expected her to be at supper tonight. He might not notice her absence, but Allister's mother would notice his.

"The horses need rest," the other man said. "They're spent."

"We stop up ahead," the man who held her said. "Leave them saddled and tether them."

A few minutes later, they halted. Elise's captor handed her down to the man who had stared at her. He pressed her close to his chest. The hand wrapped around her legs slipped beneath her skirt. She thrashed. Hot spikes of pain fingered out through her body. His hand rubbed her outer thigh. She gave a weak scream. He laughed, lowering his head toward her mouth.

"Rory!" her original keeper shouted, and took her into his arms.

Elise fought tears as he turned and her heart lurched when she caught sight of several more riders dismounting. She kicked and slammed a fist down onto her captor's chest.

"Cease," he growled. "Fighting will do ye no good."

She yielded, too spent to do anything else. He strode to a cluster of medium-sized rocks, then set her down against the rocks and returned to his horse. Rory approached, horse's reins in hand. Elise tensed. Their gazes remained locked until he disappeared from view behind her. Another man followed, then the next and the next, and she realized the horses were being tethered near where she lay.

Her keeper approached carrying a tartan and a small pouch. He stopped beside her, shook out the tartan, and squatted, settling the blanket over her. He regarded her. "We left MacGregor land long ago. You are in Campbell territory and wouldn't have a chance in hell in these hills. You cannot see, but 'tis barren country. Nothing for miles."

"Why—" she stopped, seeing the implacable set of his jaw.

He reached into the pouch and produced a biscuit. He handed it to her. Elise took the food and watched him stride to where his comrades sat huddled on smaller rocks. She looked at the biscuit, then sniffed it. To her surprise, she detected no mold. A small nibble and her stomach rumbled. She pulled her knees up and reached for her foot. She unlaced one boot, took it off, then did the same with the other. She arranged the boots beside her and took another bite of the biscuit, while edging herself into a more prone position. She took another, larger bite.

"We should bind her hands." Rory's voice abruptly broke the silence.

"Touch her and I'll kill you," her captor said through a mouthful of food.

A pause followed, and Elise shivered as much from the threat as the cold. She pulled the tartan up over her shoulders, closing her eyes.

"You wouldn't be wanting her for yourself, would you, William?" Rory demanded.

"She isn't yours, Rory."

"What if she escapes?"

"She was knocked half senseless," William replied. "She couldn't manage it."

"I know women who could," Rory retorted.

"She wouldn't know which way was home." William paused. "She's asleep."

"Easy pickings," Rory commented.

Grunts of approval from the men sitting in the group sounded.

"Mayhap not so easy." William shifted, the sword strapped to his hip scraping against rock.

Elise shrank beneath the tartan and ate the last bit of biscuit. Finally, the men's voices quieted. A moment later, she heard a nearby rustling. She peered past a corner of her tartan and discerned the forms of men lowering themselves to the ground. She recognized William, still sitting with his back to her.

A close snigger told her Rory was among the men bedding down nearby. Her stomach wrenched. She glanced heavenward. Dawn was no more than four hours away. MacGregor territory lay southeast of Campbell land. They had ridden approximately fifteen hours. She could reach Brahan Seer by tomorrow afternoon. Marcus might not welcome her back, but she had to make sure he knew who was responsible for Allister's death. She thought of the wedding band sewed to the lining of her shift. She had planned to go from Michael's to Glasgow and catch the first ship away from Scotland. But Allister deserved recompense just as much as Amelia and Steven.

When snores at last told Elise the men had fallen asleep, she crawled from beneath her blanket. The biscuit had settled her stomach, but the trembling deep within persisted.

"Where are ye going?"

She stopped at the sound of William's voice and twisted to look over her shoulder. He still sat on the rock, back to her.

"I-I need a moment of privacy."

"There are guards," he said.

"What?"

"Out there." He motioned with his head to the blackness beyond their camp.

Her blood chilled, but she forced her body into motion and crawled around the rock.

Marcus tensed at sight of a figure moving in the shadows where the Campbell horses were tethered. "Did you notice any of the guards returning to camp?" he demanded of Michael, who squatted beside him on the hill from which they watched.

"Nay," Michael whispered.

Marcus strained to make out the figure's form in the moonlight, but the hill cast too dark a shadow on the valley. "God damn it," he muttered. "If anyone has given away our presence—" The loud neigh of a horse broke the quiet. "What the bloody hell?"

"The horses," Michael hissed as the Campbell horses bolted.

Shouts rose, and the Campbells sprang up and after their mounts.

"What are they up to?" Marcus yanked his gaze back onto the figure in the shadows near the horses. He leaned forward in the saddle and was riding to the left of the camp.

"Take two men and bring back that rider," Marcus said. "Be careful not to alert the others to our presence."

Marcus turned his attention onto the Campbell men running through the trees in an effort to retrieve their scattered horses. Then waited.

The light sound of a boot treading close came from the darkness and Marcus jerked his head around.

"Laird," one of his men said, "come quick. We have the rider."

He pulled his cloak close and backed away from the crest of the hill, jumped to his feet, then hurried downhill at a near run. At the bottom, he broke through the circle of his men, hand on the hilt of his sword.

"Nay! Laird, stop!" came a chorus of low voices.

Marcus felt his sword arm jerked back, but he saw the prisoner even as someone grabbed his other arm. He went stock still. "Elise?"

"Yes," she replied.

Even in the shallow light of the cloudy darkness, he could discern her drawn expression. "Are you unharmed?"

She smiled, her mouth quavering a little. "I have a blazing headache, but I'll live."

Marcus started forward, but two of his men seized his arm. "Release me." He yanked free, then took two steps and halted before her. "You are the rider?"

"Yes."

She swayed. Marcus caught her to him.

Elise clutched at his shirt, burying her head in his chest. She didn't move for a long moment, then took a shuddering breath and mumbled against him, "If I could sit down."

He whipped off his cloak and wrapped it around her. Marcus slipped an arm beneath her and she threw her arms around his neck when he lifted her into his arms. He knelt and gently settled her in a seated position on the ground. Her arms remained tight about him for a moment, then finally relaxed.

Marcus straightened, his gaze falling on her bare feet. "Where are your shoes?"

She glanced from her feet back at him. "I took them off. What woman attempting an escape would go barefoot?" She gave him a hopeful look. "Sensible, don't you agree?"

"Sensible?" he repeated.

Elise abruptly grasped her stomach. Marcus held her head to the side as she wretched violently. The convulsion ceased and he wiped her mouth with the tartan.

She sat up. "Had to happen eventually," she croaked.

"Will you be all right?"

She nodded but averted her face. "I'm much better."

Marcus stood. "Michael, you, Brian, and Finn remain here. Get the horses," he said to the remaining men, then looked at Elise. "I assume you freed their horses?"

She nodded.

"Marcus," Michael said. "We stumbled upon two Campbells. They were the guards west of the camp. Seems we were wrong. They had moved. Probably the only ones who had horses."

"Dead?"

The older man nodded.

Marcus's men returned with the horses.

He took Alexis's reins and mounted, then

said to Michael, "It may take some time, but I won't leave before catching every last one of the bastards. If so much as a shadow flickers, get out."

Michael nodded, and Marcus reined his horse around, his men following.

Marcus stood, legs apart, staring down at Elise. She sat on the couch, head bowed, her gaze on the carpeted floor of his library. He took a deep breath and seated himself beside her.

"A day on the trip home and I held my tongue," he said. "Then a day here at Brahan Seer. You're well enough now to answer to me. What in God's name were you doing?"

"I promised Michael I would come."

"Michael would not hold you to any such promise."

She lifted her chin and met his gaze. "I didn't go alone, as you know."

"You took a boy, Elise."

Pain flickered across her face. "I will not make that mistake again."

"Nay, you will not, but that doesn't explain why you insist upon going. Bloody hell, Elise, no one but you is a risk-taker."

She stiffened. "I am sorry you had to come for me—"

"*Sorry I had to come for you?* You little idiot. It wasn't the coming for you that you need be sorry for, but the fact you nearly got yourself killed. It's a miracle you survived the fall from your horse."

Marcus shifted his gaze to her right cheek where the light yellow of a severe bruise peeked out from beneath her thick hair. He was well aware of the gash that lay hidden beneath her hair. She had taken great pains to hide the wound. *What else did she hide?*

"What of the Campbells, Elise?"

She frowned. "I don't understand why they took me."

"Nay?"

She started. "I'm not a complete fool. I understand their intentions. But why make off with me? Why not attack me there?"

A mental picture of them *attacking* her there rose on a tide of a fury that forced Marcus to his feet. He strode to the sideboard, poured a whiskey, drank it in one gulp, then set the glass down and faced her. He leaned against the sideboard and folded his arms across his chest.

"They like to savor their victims."

Her lips parted in a soft gasp.

"Did you think otherwise?" he asked.

"The beady-eyed one, Rory, would have taken me there, but their leader, William—"

"William?" Marcus interjected savagely. He started toward her. Her eyes widened when he closed the gap between them. He yanked her from her seat. "What did *William* want, Elise?"

"He stopped Rory from…"

"Did he now?" Marcus shoved her onto the couch, pivoted, and returned to the sideboard. He poured another drink and emptied the glass as he had the last, then faced her again. "It didn't occur to you he didn't want a woman who was used up?"

Her cheeks reddened, then her expression hardened. "There had been no sign of Campbells for weeks. How long am I supposed to let your fears rule me?"

"Until I say otherwise. Just be glad I don't tie you to your bed."

Her eyes narrowed. "What sort of threat is that?"

"The kind I will enforce with relish."

Elise jumped to her feet. She swayed slightly. Marcus started forward, then stopped when she fisted her hands at her sides.

"Ooooh." She drew the word out in a long frustrated breath. "You are an arrogant knave, Marcus MacGregor, not to mention foul natured. Does it give you pleasure to threaten me?"

"Threaten you?" He gave an exasperated laugh. "I haven't given you even a small sample of my power."

"I advise you to keep such threats to yourself," she said through clenched teeth.

"God help me, I should turn you over my knee—which is what I planned in the beginning."

Elise took a step back and he advanced. "In fact, if you have any defense, say your piece now, for you shall receive the only recompense your sex allows."

"I have nothing to tell you." She retreated another pace.

Marcus halted. Bloody hell, were his suspicions right? "What are you hiding, Elise?"

Her eyes flashed but not before widening enough to tell him he'd caught her off guard. "What could I possibly—"

"You're a fool if you expect me to believe you simply want to visit Michael. We both know he is well. Who do you meet when you leave Brahan Seer?"

Her eyes lit with indignation.

Feminine fury. Had he hit the mark? Had she taken a lover?

The blood pounded in his ears. "You would risk death—or worse—for a common liaison?"

Her expression flashed to hauteur. "Any assignations I have are none of your concern."

Relief rammed through him. Womanly pride drove her, not fear of discovery. Why, then, the insistence on going to Michael's?

She turned, but he caught her wrist and whirled her around. "What are you hiding?"

Elise clenched the hand he grasped. "Is it so hard to believe someone might care enough about another human being to take a risk?"

"You expect me to believe you are so foolish?"

She gave a harsh laugh. "Believe what you will."

"I believe you are lying."

"Why bother coming for me, then?"

For the thousandth time, Marcus saw Elise as Katie MacGregor had been when she was found raped and beaten. He yanked Elise to him, his mouth crashing down on hers. She shoved at his chest, but he only tightened his arms around her and roughened the kiss. He thrust his tongue inside her mouth and felt her body stiffen in surprise then slacken against him. Her breath quickened. Marcus remembered the couch only a few feet away, but she abruptly wrenched her mouth free. He hugged her close, burying his head in her hair.

"Elise," he whispered hoarsely. "When I think—" his voice caught. "They had their hands on you." He hugged her even closer. "Never again."

He kissed her neck, placed gentle kisses behind her ear and down to where neck met shoulder. She gasped, and he lifted his head to look down into her wide eyes. He lowered his mouth to hers, tenderly this time, moving slowly until her lips softened beneath his. She gave a sudden small gasp, then pushed away, her hand going to her lips. He focused on the action.

"Ohhh," she drew out the word on a soft breath.

Marcus stepped toward her. She backed up until the chair before his desk barred her retreat. He halted, his body inches from her. She gripped the top of the chair, then stepped aside, shoving the chair toward him. Marcus reached for her. The chair hit his shin. Pain shot through his leg, but he stumbled forward, grabbing for her. His fingers closed around thin air as she dashed for the door and disappeared down the corridor.

Chapter Six

Movement to his left caused Marcus to jerk his head in the direction of the woman emerging from the kitchen into the hall. She was not Elise. The woman's brown hair had fooled him for an instant. He shoved his chair back, rose from his seat, and strode to the kitchen. He stepped aside for another serving maid as she hurried past into the hall with a plate of food in hand. He scanned the kitchen. Elise wasn't among the women serving the evening meal.

By God, she was avoiding him.

Why she was avoiding him, he knew; how she had managed to do so for a day and a half, he suspected could be answered by Winnie, who, oddly enough, was also absent. He turned and headed for the postern door, wincing at the ache in his knee. Once in the quiet of the brightly lit courtyard, he veered north toward the cottages.

"Marcus."

Marcus glanced over his shoulder at the sound of his father's call and stopped at sight of the MacLaren warrior walking alongside Cameron. They halted in front of Marcus.

"Brian here has brought a message from Declan." Cameron looked at the man. "Go ahead, lad."

"Declan wanted ye to know there's been Campbells on MacLaren land."

"When?" Marcus demanded.

"Three days in a row now."

"You haven't caught any of them?"

Brian snorted. "The bastards are getting better at running."

"They are," Marcus agreed, then asked, "You will stay the night?"

"Aye."

"Good. Be ready at first light. I'll travel back with you. Have some supper." He motioned toward the great hall, then looked back at his father. "Cameron, I wish to speak with you." Marcus waited until Brian was out of earshot, then said, "Have Elise moved into the castle while I am gone."

Cameron showed no surprise at the request. "What reason should I give?"

"Ask if she plans on living with Winnie the rest of her life."

His father gave an approving look. "I will put her in the west wing's private suite."

"Nay," Marcus said. "The east wing, the room nearest mine.

Cameron frowned. "'Tis hard on you, her sharing a cottage with Winnie, but to put her in the lady's quarters next to yours is going a bit far the other direction."

"The guest room, Cameron," Marcus said. "Not in the adjoining room—at least, not yet."

"*At least, not yet?*" Cameron exclaimed.

Two men passing turned their heads at his raised voice.

He glanced at them, then leaned in closer to Marcus. "That's a bit obvious, don't you think, lad? A man doesna' flaunt his mistress."

Marcus raised a brow. "Aye."

His father blinked. "What? Are you saying what I think you're saying?"

"I am."

Cameron rubbed his chin. "I have never known you to take advantage of a woman under your protection."

"I have no intention of doing so now," Marcus replied, though he couldn't help the mental image of how much he would relish *taking advantage.*

Cameron regarded him. "I thought you would not marry again. 'Tis ten years since Jenna died."

"I hadn't planned on remarrying."

"You have a son and, at your age, you need not marry."

Marcus gave a short laugh. "I needn't do much of anything, Father."

Cameron gave a single nod. "Your marriage to Jenna wasn't one of love." His mouth turned down wryly. "You always were the politician. You should have told King George to go to the devil when he insisted you marry the wench."

"I have no regrets," Marcus replied. "And I shall have none now."

"Tiring of the demimonde?"

He gave a slight smile. "'Tis not the same."

Cameron grinned. "I thought you would want the lass, but I hadn't realized how badly."

Marcus exhaled. "No one is more surprised than I."

Marcus and his men dismounted in the outer bailey of the MacLaren holding. He tossed his horse's reins to a MacLaren guard and waited. A few moments later, Declan entered the bailey.

Marcus stepped forward and caught Declan's hand in a firm grip. "Good of you to allow us entrance."

Declan's eyes twinkled. "Aye, considering your treatment of me when last I visited Brahan Seer."

"I recall your night ended well."

Declan grinned. "Aye, a fine night it was. What brings you here? Have I ruined the MacGregor lasses for you? Josephine cried when I left."

"I heard she got rather feisty," Marcus remarked.

Declan laughed. "Aye, she's a sassy one, but nothing like your *Ceasg.*"

Marcus gave a rueful grimace. "Elise's temper is much like the Highland mermaid's."

"A resemblance? If the lass were a Highlander, she could grant the mythical three wishes." He gave Marcus a shrewd look. "Perhaps she has already granted yours, eh?'

Marcus snorted. "I suspect granting any wish I have is the furthest thing from her mind."

"Ahh," Declan intoned. "You haven't exactly endeared yourself to her?"

"Not quite."

"Mayhap, you should have let me teach her a lesson after all." His brows lifted. "Break her in, so to speak."

"I would have had no sympathy for you when she broke you."

Declan grimaced. "Aye, well, 'tis best, then, that I leave you with the taming."

"God help me," Marcus said under his breath, then gave him a serious look. "I hear you have had Campbells on your land."

"Aye." Declan led Marcus toward the great hall.

"Elise was kidnapped by the Campbells six days ago," Marcus said.

"Kidnapped?" Declan gave Marcus an appraising look. "You don't look broken up like you were with Katie. Is the lass…?"

"She is well, though only by the grace of God. We need to talk."

Marcus shook his head at the serving girl who offered to refill his dinner plate, and she moved to the man sitting to his right.

"They never touched her?" Declan asked.

"Nay."

"Can you be sure?"

"Bruised a bit, but nothing like Katie."

"Aye, well," Declan said, "I suppose if she wasn't in the same shape as Katie…"

"She wasn't," Marcus replied. "Which is damned lucky for the entire Campbell clan."

Declan leaned back in his chair. "Too close for comfort."

"They were within half a mile of Brahan Seer."

"Jesus, they've grown bollocks of late. I am surprised they didn't do the deed right there." His mouth twitched. "You don't suppose they suddenly got religion?" He laughed, giving the table such a slap it rattled the plates.

"Nay," Marcus replied, his mouth twisting into a grim frown. "But they did meet their maker."

"Good. You have been too soft with them in the past. Aye," he went on when Marcus started to interrupt, "ye made them pay for Katie, but there have been other times."

Declan reached for his mug and took a long draught. He set the mug on the table while watching the serving woman who approached from the far end of the table. She looked up and Declan winked. His gaze remained on her as she passed. He took another drink of ale, then turned back to Marcus.

"They've been spending an unusual amount of time on MacGregor land of late."

"So I have noticed." A pause followed, and Marcus said. "You have something on your mind?"

"'Tis interesting they made off with her. One would expect them to take care of business and be done with it."

"I'm not one to question good fortune," Marcus said.

"But you are." Declan's expression sobered. "What do you know of the lass?"

"She's American, as you know. The ship she and her husband sailed on went down in a fire. Shannon and Joshua found her washed ashore at Solway Firth."

"She is no serving wench," Declan commented.

"Nay."

"Have you any idea why she is acting the part?"

Marcus gave a single shake of his head. "Nay, but I will find out."

Hooves pounded on moist ground, the roll of their thunder cutting in heavier strikes as they neared the castle. Swirls of thick fog whipped upwards and into the night as the gates of Brahan Seer swung open by an unseen hand. One after another, men forced their way in until the keep overflowed with the blue and green of Campbell plaide.

Fear lodged in Marcus's throat at sight of his enemies' raised swords.

"Buadhaich!" came the battle cry.

A shudder shook Marcus.

The devils' weapons stabbed through the grey of the murky fog. Pleas for mercy resounded. Still, Marcus remained rooted to the spot, watching until the last MacGregor fell.

A Campbell glanced at him, the first to acknowledge his presence. The man smiled, stepping on the head of a vanquished enemy and grinding the skull with his foot. As if magically freed from unseen bonds, Marcus lunged at him. They crashed to the ground, Marcus's grasp closing around nothing. He leapt to his feet, seizing another Campbell. He, too, vanished. One by one, they disappeared each time he grabbed their necks. His mind sought for purchase within the ghostly battle, his senses reeling with the echo of laughter that rose from the curling mist.

Finally, every Campbell gone, Marcus stood, his breath coming in labored gulps. Torn and twisted bodies lay scattered about him—the ruin of his clan. A cry broke the silence. He whirled. Elise lay on the ground, a trembling hand raised to him.

Marcus rushed to her side. He fell to his knees, lifted her head, and cradled it in his lap. Tears streamed down his cheeks, splashing onto her lips. With gentle fingers, she wiped a tear from his cheek.

"Shh," she murmured. "It's not your fault." Her hand fell away and her eyes closed.

He tightened his grip but she vanished, causing him to tumble forward. Her garments twisted in his hands. He shoved and kicked, trying to dislodge himself from the fabric.

Leaping up, his fingers closed around a post—

Marcus stood in darkness, gasping in heaving gulps of air. His grip on the bedpost tightened as he looked about wildly in the darkness. No moon shone overhead. No bodies lay around him—a soft chime sounded—*a clock.* A shudder reverberated through him and he fell to his knees on the stone floor of the bedchamber. The cold of the floor against his knees contrasted the sweat that beaded his forehead. A drop trickled along his hairline. *A dream.* But Elise's kidnapping had been no dream. Had she not escaped... Marcus bowed his head, the cold barely noticeable to his naked body, and he touched the tear trailing down his cheek.

The clock chimed again. Four gongs this time.

His heartbeat had slowed and his body chilled. Fingers still wrapped around the bedpost, Marcus pulled himself onto shaky legs. He gathered his kilt from the floor near the foot of the bed and wrapped the *plaide* around his waist. Brahan Seer lay but half a day's ride away. Marcus paused.

A dream.

To return home before visiting the young MacFarlene chief would be foolish.

A dream.

His heart rate increased. A dream where everyone he loved had perished. Where Elise had perished. He grabbed his belt from the chair, then halted. He had left the keep well-guarded. He would wake his man Kyle. One day for Kyle to ride to Brahan Seer and make sure all was well, then meet them tomorrow at the MacFarlene holding.

Marcus studied the men gathered in the MacFarlene great hall, then returned his attention to Langley, the young MacFarlene chief, who stood beside him at the massive hearth. Marcus set his glass of scotch on the mantel. "No sign of Campbells on your land?"

Langley nodded to one of his men. "Nay." He finished his scotch, then placed the glass next to

Marcus's. "If I had, they would be buried—and King George would never find them."

Marcus well remembered Langley's uncle, Cory MacDonald. The MacDonalds had not forgiven the Campbells for the Glencoe massacre over a hundred years ago. MacDonald blood flowed as hotly in Langley's veins as did MacFarlene blood.

"Ye have a spy, MacGregor."

Marcus's attention snapped back to the young man. "What?"

"How else do you explain their success in creeping about your land? You say Shamus was killed in Montal Cove. That isna' MacGregor land. I remember hearing about Katie MacGregor. She was in MacLaren territory when they attacked her." Langley regarded him. "Before this last incident, how long since they were seen on MacGregor land?"

"Two months." Marcus stilled. "The night I escorted Elise back from Michael's."

"The same lass they made off with?" Langley grunted. A young woman carrying several bottles of whiskey wound her way through the crowd. "Brenda," he called. "Bring me one of those bottles, lass."

She turned and hurried forward. He took a bottle from her tray. She glanced at Marcus.

"Off with you," Langley said.

With a flash of a smile for Marcus, she sauntered away.

Langley opened the bottle, filled their glasses, then set the bottle on the mantel. He took a large drink before wiping his mouth with the back of his hand. "Two months ago, you say?"

"Aye," Marcus replied.

"What came of it?"

"Nothing. They were gone when I returned."

"A shame, and a little strange, wouldn't you say?" Langley finished the drink, reached for the bottle, and refilled his glass.

"They may have heard me passing by and ran, or luck might have been with them."

"Aye," Langley agreed. "They're a cowardly lot. But considering they returned, that makes the situation more strange than lucky." He shrugged again. "Think what you like, but you have a spy." He lifted a brow. "Mayhap it's you they want?"

"They had their chance when they abducted Elise. They knew I would pursue them yet didn't lay in wait for me."

Langley grunted. "The pleasures of the flesh are a powerful distraction."

Marcus's jaw tightened.

"Dinna' lose your temper," the young chief said. "'Tis an observation, nothing more."

"An astute observation," Marcus muttered, then added, "Someone who is reporting the comings and goings."

"What they are reporting, I can't say. But 'tis clear they are hunting. I wager it's big game. 'Course, we will fight alongside you."

Marcus smiled to himself. The clans feuded far less in these modern times, giving a restless Highland heart such as Langley's no outlet for its brand of justice.

"You will stay until tomorrow morning and train?" Langley motioned toward the men who tonight sported with whiskey and lasses, but tomorrow would train hard.

"Aye," Marcus replied, the memory of Kyle's report that all was well at Brahan Seer fresh in his mind.

Langley gave an acknowledging nod, then grabbed the bottle and strode toward several men who vied for the attention of two kitchen maids.

Marcus watched him go. A lot of Langley's father Glen lived in the boy. Glen had refused to give up the old ways and he had fought English injustice the only way he knew how: midnight raids. Marcus smiled, remembering the chief's delight in slaughtering the sheep of an offending lord, then leaving the animals on the lord's doorstep. As a young man, Marcus had ridden with him three days from MacFarlene territory on just such a raid. Unfortunately, Glen went on one too many clandestine rendezvous and was felled by a young baron on the English coast. Marcus understood the battle cry that had driven the old chief. However, in their modern age, it was bad business to consider teaching the Sassenach the error of their ways.

Suddenly, Marcus wearied of politics and war. Even wealth and power hadn't exempted the MacGregors from the English disdain for Highlanders. Still, Ryan MacGregor had done well in choosing a woman of courage. Thank God for a good woman. His loins stirred at the thought of another good woman. Desire swept through him, bringing his body to the now-familiar ache.

Marcus left the revelry. He fell into bed, his body hard with the memory of Elise's touch. In his mind's eye, he saw her wrap slim fingers around his shaft. He reached down, his hand closing over hers. She called to him, her song as sweet as that of any *Ceasg*. He groaned. Slowly, and with great precision, she pulled him into murky depths where willowy shapes tortured his body and held him hostage long into the night.

Elise sighed when Winnie shoved the book across the kitchen table toward her.

"Nay," Winnie shook her head, "I canna' do it. I have no brain for it."

"Ridiculous," Elise snorted. "Now, calm yourself. We aren't finished."

"Aye, we're finished." Winnie jumped from her chair and began pacing. "We're finished for good." She rubbed her temples as if to drive the frustration from her mind.

"But you were doing so beautifully. Come," Elise entreated, "sit and rest."

The housekeeper paused, eyes narrowed, but flung herself into the chair, nonetheless.

Elise repressed a smile when Winnie picked up the offending book and glanced in the direction of the fire.

"Winnie—"

"Dinna' try to talk me into any more reading." She dropped the book on the table as if horns had sprouted from the cover. "'Tis no use. I haven't the brain for it."

Elise raised a brow. "Surely you're not afraid of a little effort?"

The housekeeper shot her a shrewd look. "Isna' that and you know it."

Elise shrugged. "It's not for me to judge. You will be the one to explain to your friends why you cannot read to them as promised."

"You think you're mighty smart, eh, lass?" She snatched up the book.

Elise leaned back in her chair and closed her eyes. "The next two lines, please."

"O, woo-would, or I," she began slowly, "had seen the d-ay that tre-tra—" She snorted in frustration.

"Treason," Elise prodded softly.

"—treason thu-s cud—"

"Could," Elise corrected.

"Could sell us, my au-ld grey heed—" Winnie grunted, then repeated with vehemence, "head," then again slowly, "had lien in c-l-ay wi' Bruce and loyal Wallace," she ended with a flourish.

"Excellent. Read half an hour tomorrow and the next day. Then we'll review those pages."

Winnie hesitated.

"Don't worry." Elise smiled. "In no time at all you will have everyone in the village begging you to read for them."

"Well, I don't know about that," Winnie replied, but her nonchalant attitude didn't hide the small smile at the corner of her mouth.

"I do," Elise said with conviction.

"So do I," added a deep voice from the kitchen doorway.

Elise twisted in her chair to stare at Marcus

He lounged against the doorframe. "I believe, milady," he addressed Winnie, but never took his eyes off Elise, "if your teacher has her way, you will never have a moment's peace."

"Nothing will have changed then." Winnie sniffed, then rose.

"No need to go," Elise said too quickly.

"Aye, there is." Winnie gave her a knowing look as she brushed past. "Good night to ye, Marcus," she said on the way out the door.

"You're back," was all Elise could say.

"Aye, love. 'Tis my home, remember?" He pushed off from the doorframe, his gaze holding hers as he walked forward. He stopped by her side.

The embers in the fire crackled, causing her to jump. "The fire needs more wood."

He gave no indication he'd heard, then turned and went to the hearth. Marcus grasped the poker and stoked the fire. "How have things been during my absence?"

"The same." She prayed he didn't read into her answer the fact that every day he had been away she had recalled the look on his face when he'd burst through his men and saw her after she escaped the Campbells, and the whispered words *"Never again"* when he pressed her close… and the kiss that had followed.

Marcus reached for a log from the pile beside the hearth. He bent to one knee, his kilt falling across the calf of the bent leg. She tried tearing her gaze away. Instead, her attention fixed on the play of muscle in his shoulder as he tossed the log onto the fire. Here was the reason behind his command to move her into the castle. If she were nearer him, how long could she resist his advances? Damn him. He had further hampered her movements. In the three days he'd been gone, she had yet to leave the castle without someone marking her movements. Had he enlisted all MacGregors as spies?

Marcus unexpectedly glanced back over the shoulder she was staring at. Her heart pounded wildly in the moment he studied her. How transparent were her thoughts? He rose. She tensed when he leaned the poker against the wall and turned.

"Elise," he began as he approached, "I handled things badly." He halted before her.

"Well, you were a bit…" She gave him a rueful look. "I haven't been a saint." Her heart lurched at the understatement, then fluttered at the thought of confessing the truth. What would he do if she threw herself into his arms and told all?

Marcus smiled. "No matter." He extended a hand. "Come, love, walk with me."

She stared at his outstretched hand, held steady for her. The gentleness there belied the strength.

"'Tis all right," he coaxed. "I promise not to bite."

Elise looked up at him. "Are you in the habit of making promises you cannot keep?"

He reached for her and she resisted the urge to slap his hand back.

Marcus stood behind Elise on a hill overlooking the village. Lights dotted the valley, shining in haloed rings from the cottages. A balmy breeze blew, yet Marcus saw her shiver.

Marcus resisted the urge to wrap an arm around her and stepped up beside her, fingers laced behind his back. He turned his attention to the flickering lights below. "What do you think of the Highlands, lass?"

She said nothing for a moment, then, in a quiet voice, "The Highlands are… unusual. Despite all odds, life thrives here." She laughed softly. "At least, the Highland notion of life." She slanted a smile in his direction. Marcus stilled, afraid the spell would dissolve. "Highland life is full and lush." She returned her attention to the valley. "Yet, some would say, like a woman, it changes at a moment's notice, suddenly wild and furious."

Did he detect a sensual note in her voice? Marcus tightened the grip on his emotions. Now wasn't the time to test her. Yet a voice from within asked, *If not now, when?*

"The rugged wilderness here is frightening," she

went on. "Yet, at the same time, it is compelling to the extreme." Elise motioned with her head at the broad expanse before them. "Those hills lure with a beauty uniquely their own. They call to the soul, drawing it into their mystery like..."

Marcus leaned toward her before catching himself. Inhaling a deep breath, he said in a hushed voice, "Like a lover."

She looked at him, her expression open. "Yes, you've captured the heart of it."

Not yet, love, he thought, but soon, very soon. "How did you come to be in Scotland?"

Surprise flickered on her face, but instantly relaxed into the even reply, "Surely you know I was washed ashore when our ship went down in a fire."

"Aye. I mean, why were you in Solway Firth?" Elise frowned, and he added, "Sailing from America to London, you would pass the south of Ireland. To reach Solway Firth you must pass north of Ireland, then head south between Ireland and Scotland. The route would add a week or more to your journey."

Surprise flashed across her face. "A week?"

"Aye."

Her expression clouded and she murmured, "Amelia."

"What?"

She started. "What?"

"Who is Amelia?"

Elise looked out over the valley. "Amelia was my daughter."

"Was—*Elise*."

She shook her head. "Odd, isn't it? I sail from America for London, am shipwrecked—barely on Scottish soil—and here I am, miles away, in the Highlands."

"Strange, indeed," Marcus murmured, sending up silent thanks for the huge difference in that short distance. "And why come here to Brahan Seer?"

She gave a small laugh. "I had nowhere better to be."

"Are you happy?"

Can you be happy without husband and child?

"Your father has been kind. I liked him the moment I met him."

"What did you think upon first meeting me?" At the startled look on her face, he cursed his foolish curiosity.

"Why, milord," the title fell in teasing accents from her lips and her eyes widened with mock gravity, "I thought you were the fiercest warrior I'd ever had the misfortune to meet."

Marcus blinked, then threw his head back and laughed, for he remembered her assessment of his sword—not to mention his open shirt.

"Sit with me." He took her hand, settled her on the ground, and lowered himself down beside her. Marcus turned his gaze onto her and gave a soft smile. "Tell me about Amelia."

Pain flickered across her features and she lowered her gaze. When, at last, she spoke, her words were flat. "Amelia was six years old and very ill. We were traveling to England to see a specialist. I should have known she wasn't strong enough for the journey—I did know—but I couldn't bear the thought of never again looking upon her sweet face.

"Selfish," she muttered. "When Amelia smiled…" Elise's breath quickened and Marcus tensed, recognizing the anxiety in the sudden rise and fall of her breasts. "The corners of her eyes crinkled and her eyes sparkled as only a child's can." The moon illuminated Elise's face, revealing the part of memory that couldn't be conquered, and a pain that would never wholly die. "She died three days before the fire."

"*Three days?*" Marcus exclaimed. "Had you not gone by way of Solway Firth—"

"Yes," Elise agreed in a voice far removed from Scotland—from him. "Yes."

"Why take that route?"

She shrugged. "We encountered bad weather and must have been blown off course. I didn't concern myself with the route." The bitterness in her voice said she now counted that a mistake.

Marcus kept to himself the knowledge that a storm couldn't have taken them to Solway Firth had they not been north of Ireland to begin with.

"You can't know what it is to watch your child die." She looked down into her lap where her hands lay clasped. "We could do nothing. When Steven heard of a specialist in England, we set sail immediately. I thank God she died in peace. Facing what came afterwards would have been far worse."

"And the others on the ship?" Marcus asked.

"We traveled on a barque, three-masted. Not a large ship, with only a crew of eleven. Then there was Steven, R-iley and I."

"Riley?" Marcus repeated.

"My husband."

"Who is Steven?"

"My brother." Elise stared out over the valley. "The commotion woke me in the middle of the night. By the time Steven came for me—"

"Steven, not your husband?"

"No. By the time Steven got to my cabin, smoke filled the corridors. He dragged me up on deck. I was sure we wouldn't make it; the corridor was so thick with smoke."

"No chance the ship could be saved?"

"They tried. Flames lapped up from the galley and the sails were ablaze. The wind blew hard. A storm had kicked up and the sails flapped furiously. Oh, how the wind can howl."

"Storms are common in the sound," Marcus said. "What started the fire?"

She grunted, a low but distinctly disgusted sound. "Likely an unattended lamp." She gave a mirthless laugh. "I knew what Steven meant to do. But, damn him, he knew me just as well. He gave me no chance." She looked at Marcus, her gaze burning into him. "Threw me overboard without so much as a by-your-leave."

"Indeed?"

"Damn you, one and all," she said under her breath.

Marcus cleared his throat. "He managed a boat, I take it?"

"What?" she answered on a distracted note. "Oh, yes." All bitterness had vanished from her voice. "I should have warned him, but I never dreamed—" her voice broke and Marcus realized she was weeping.

"Elise, love."

She shook her head, turning away. He sat up and reached for her. She tried to stand but couldn't manage her skirts quickly enough. He hauled her onto his lap and hugged her close.

"I would like to go home," she said into his shirt between quiet tears.

"Love," he whispered, "you are home."

"Amelia was gone," she said as if not having heard him. "But Steven—"

Some minutes passed. At last, her soft cries subsided and Marcus felt her chest expand with a deep breath. "A piece of him died each day with Amelia. When she—" Elise fumbled in her pocket. Marcus calmed the nervous search by placing his hand over hers. She stilled.

Marcus brushed the tears away with a thumb.

"I should have allowed Amelia to die in her own home," Elise said when he'd finished. "Steven would still be here."

"Steven suggested the doctor? He must have been as anxious as you to see her recover."

"Of course," she answered crossly.

"Could you have stopped him?"

"He couldn't have gone without us. Yes. I could have stopped him."

"Somehow, I doubt that."

"He was a determined fool," she cut in, "but had I told him it was best—"

"He would have carried you onto the ship."

"Damnable men," she muttered.

"What of Amelia's father?"

"He did not survive."

That Marcus knew, but he found it strange that Elise's story didn't include her husband. Too painful, he realized, and said, "I'm sorry, lass."

"Fate is strange," she murmured.

"You can't blame yourself for their deaths," Marcus said.

"You would be amazed at what I can do."

Marcus felt a tremor pass through her. He hugged her closer. "Dinna' say more."

"Seems a bit late for that," she remarked in a dry tone.

He sighed. "Lass, you could remain here quiet all night and I wouldna' complain."

She looked up at him. "It is not… common—for a brother and sister, that is—but Steven was my friend. I shall never find that kind of trust again."

His gaze fell on her left hand and the spot where he knew the scar was on her palm's edge. She hadn't escaped the fire completely unharmed. He took the hand, lifted it to his lips and kissed the scar. He placed the hand around his waist, then slid a hand into her hair and tilted her head upward.

"Are ye sure?" he asked.

Her mouth parted with quiet surprise. He had promised himself he wouldn't touch her. Yet his head lowered and his mouth covered hers of its own volition. Elise offered no resistance when he parted her lips with his tongue. He tightened his hold, the fire in him hot. Still, he kept the kiss soft, his tongue thrusting gently in her mouth. She relaxed. His groin tightened and he ended the kiss. He sighed. His only choice now was to take her home or *take* her there.

Chapter Seven

"*Are you sure?*"

The memory of Marcus's warm breath brushing her skin as he whispered the question made Elise shiver. She squinted up at thick morning sunlight streaming down between heavy storm clouds. Daylight brought no more clarity than had the sleepless night. She paused at the rock, which marked the halfway point on the hill between Brahan Seer and the village, and sat down. She worked the boot from her left foot.

"Infernal pebbles." She turned the boot upside down and shook the irksome item free.

The pebble hit the stony ground with a click. Elise strained to see it, then, shaking her head, stuck her foot in the boot and tugged. Her heel caught on the heel grip. She tugged harder but to no avail.

"Good Lord." She jumped to her feet.

She stomped her foot on the ground. The heel jammed even harder on the heel grip and her foot turned, tumbling her to the ground. She sat for a moment, surveying the skirts thrown up around her thighs, and sighed. Drawing her knees to her, Elise tugged the skirts down over her legs. She propped an elbow on one knee and placed her chin on the heel of a palm.

Foolish endeavor. All the peevishness in the world wouldn't change the fact she wanted him—more than that—hungered for him. Last night had passed in snatches of erotic dreams with Marcus suckling her breasts, then sliding down along her belly and finally between her legs.

Even in better days, Robert hadn't moved her as Marcus had by simply holding her close as he had last night. Her pulse quickened. She had nearly blurted Robert's name. How many more days—and nights—could she hazard with Marcus MacGregor?

Marcus glanced at the hearth as he entered his library. The fire burned low but cast enough light so he could make his way through the shadowy darkness to his desk. He lit the candle sitting there and seated himself before an open ledger. Despite the hour, sleep eluded him.

He laughed. "It wouldn't be the taste of Elise's lips that has your mind churning?" he mused, but knew good and well his cock and not his mind was doing the *churning*. He forced his attention to the numbers.

Sometime later, Marcus glanced at the hearth, abruptly aware of a chill in the room. The fire had all but expired. He rose and went to the fireplace. He threw a log on the dying embers and stoked them. After hooking the poker in the holder, he lowered himself into the armchair beside the hearth. Stretching his legs out before him, he crossed ankle over ankle and relaxed against the cushion. Heat slowly worked its way up his body. He closed his eyes and dozed.

Marcus jerked awake, aware someone had entered the room. He glanced at the mantel clock. Just after two. Who would invade his library at this hour? The shadow cast by the intruder's taper glided across the wall then came to a halt. He heard the clink of the brass holder being placed on his desk and twisted to peer around the edge of his chair. His body tightened when he saw the prowler was none other than the *Caesg* responsible for his sleepless night.

Elise stood, wrapped in a *plaide* blanket, perusing the books on the shelf behind his desk. His gaze dropped to the shoulder laid bare where blanket and chemise had slipped to her arm.

She shivered and drew the blanket closer about her shoulders as she glanced in the direction of the hearth. Their eyes met and he grinned. She started.

Her eyes flashed. "It's extremely impolite to spy on people. Or didn't your mother teach you manners?"

"Aye, love." He grinned even wider. "But you made such a pretty picture standing there, I couldna' help myself. 'Tis verra' unfortunate you spied me so soon."

Her eyes narrowed in the instant before she whirled and headed for the door. Marcus jumped up and, in four long strides, stepped in front of her.

"Now, lass," he drawled in an even thicker brogue, "you wake a man in the middle of the night, then run away so quickly? 'Tis no' verra' bonnie of you, and you are a verra' bonnie lass."

Elise gave him a dry look. "I warn you, Marcus MacGregor, step aside."

He grinned. She was in a fit all right and he felt the desire to see her at full sail.

"Come, love," he said, "what will ye do?"

She didn't answer and his curiosity piqued at the realization that the wheels in her head were turning at a furious rate.

"Do you plan to stand there all night?" she finally said.

He raised a brow and her expression darkened. Marcus gave a hearty laugh. "Do you expect me to capitulate to so easily?" He laughed even harder. "Lass," he shook his head, "you are—" Marcus halted when she started forward.

He reached to grab her shoulders, thinking she meant to escape after all, then realized her intention even as her foot snaked around his boot and yanked. He fell to his backside with a heavy thud. Stunned, he blinked up at her. He suddenly realized how Declan must have felt. Perhaps she did need a lesson. Her gaze darted to the door.

"Should have thought of that before you laid me on my arse," he said. "You have no chance of getting past me without my bringing you to the carpet with me." Marcus looked down the length of her. "A prospect which has its appeal."

She leapt back, but he caught the edge of her blanket and yanked it free.

He took in the bare arms, the hint of rosy nipples beneath the thin night rail, and the shadow cast by the curls between her thighs. Elise glanced down at her scantily clad body. She flushed and an answering flash of heat coursed through him.

"This is unkind of you," she said.

"Unkind?" Marcus cocked a brow. "You dare send me to my backside then lecture me on the etiquette of kindness?"

"A gentleman does not strip a lady of her clothes."

Marcus stood and tossed the blanket well out of her reach. "I have not stripped a lady of her clothes—yet."

Her brow knit and he read genuine indecision in her expression. She took a step back.

Lesson learned, he thought, and started for the blanket, but the sight of a slow smile on her lips halted him.

"Why, Marcus, you fraud. Trying to teach me a lesson."

His heart rate kicked up. Had she no idea what her soft tone did to him? "Love," he scooped her to him, "'tis not the lesson I would teach ye, given the chance."

To his surprise, she didn't pull away but wrapped her arms around his neck. "What lesson would that be, milord?"

He slid a hand up her back and wrapped his fingers in her soft, brown hair. He brought his mouth slowly down on hers. She sighed. He deepened the kiss. She pressed closer. He cupped her buttocks and backed her against the door. He tugged at the strap of her nightgown, pulling it down over her arm. Elise moved her fingers in light movements along his arm.

Marcus groaned. "You keep me on the precipice between heaven and hell."

He bent and took a taut nipple in his mouth, drawing on the pink bud through the fabric of her nightgown. She gripped his shoulders and arched toward him. Marcus ran a flattened palm up her thigh and across the roundness of her buttocks. He continued down to the underside of her knee, then lifted her leg over his hip. The nightgown rucked up and he rubbed the hard length of him between her legs. She gasped. He trailed moist kisses from neck to ear. She softened against the motion and contours of his body. He became aware of her breasts pressed to his chest, the nipples brushing in tantalizing strokes as he rocked gently against her.

"Elise—" Marcus froze at hearing footsteps in the hallway.

She opened her eyes, confusion mingled with the clouded look of desire. He yanked her away from the door and stepped in front of her as it swung open and a warrior entered.

"Forgive the interruption, laird." The man kept his gaze on Marcus's face. "A rider from Drummond territory is demanding to see you. Says it's important."

Fear displaced passion. *Drummond. At this hour? Had the old chief finally died?*

Marcus gave the man a curt nod. "See him to the hall."

The door closed and Marcus faced Elise. Her cheeks were flooded with color. She had pulled the nightgown straps back over her shoulders and her arms were crossed over her breasts. He reached for her, but she stiffened.

"You have a guest waiting," she said.

He clasped her arm and directed her the few steps to where the discarded *plaide* lay on the carpet. Marcus released her and bent to pick it up. He settled the blanket around her shoulders, drawing her close once again.

"One more stolen moment, aye?" he asked.

94

Marcus wrapped his arms around her, pinning her arms between them, and kissed her. She breathed through parted lips, and he answered the invitation with a slow thrust of his tongue. He gently drew out her passion until she trembled with the final tracing of his tongue along her lips. He forced himself from her. Her head fell to his shoulder, and relief mixed with the lust still churning in him. He waited, unwilling to part even for his old friend.

She raised her head. "I should go."

Marcus walked with her to the stairwell that led to her chambers. He gave her a final kiss on the cheek. "Go, love." He urged her up the first step.

He watched the sway of the blanket until she disappeared around the bend, then turned on his heel and headed for the great hall.

Distant footsteps sounded in the hallway outside the drawing room where Elise sat. She looked up from the book she was reading. Surely Marcus hadn't returned from the fields so early? She hadn't seen him since last night. If he were to catch her here alone… would they finish what they'd started? The footsteps stopped in front of the door. Her heart thudded. The door swung open and a petite woman, smartly dressed in a burgundy velvet riding habit trimmed in gold, stood in the doorway.

"Have tea served here," the woman ordered Mary, who stood behind her. The woman concentrated on the gloves she peeled from small, elegant hands. "I am hungry, as well. The ride this morning—" She looked up, her gaze on Elise, and she halted the tug on her glove.

No warmth shone in the woman's blue eyes and Elise wondered that such porcelain-like beauty should be marred with a statue's coldness. The woman's expression turned appraising.

"Do Brahan Seer's servants habitually lounge in the drawing room during the day?"

"Just myself," Elise replied.

The woman's gaze sharpened. She stared for a moment, then waved a dismissive hand at Mary.

"Thank ye, Lady Margaret." Mary bobbed a curtsy and backed out of the room, leaving Elise alone with the stranger and an increasing sense of apprehension.

Elise rose, hugging the book to her breast.

"You are American." Lady Margaret yanked off the remaining glove.

Elise halted. "I am."

"How long do you think you can hold his interest?"

Elise frowned. "What—" She froze.

"Let us get to the point," Lady Margaret said in crisp tones. "He is a man, and there are certain things we must accept in men."

Anger heated Elise's belly, but she replied in a cool tone, "Perhaps we have different standards."

Surprise flickered across Margaret's face, then disdain settled on her features. "I have seen it before and with women possessing far more charms than you." She raised a brow. "You are… twenty-six, twenty-seven, perhaps?"

Despite the fact Elise knew it made no difference—tomorrow she would be gone—the barb hit its mark. Marcus never asked her age. He, too, probably thought her younger than her thirty years.

Margaret raked her eyes over Elise in an unladylike fashion. "Men are intrigued by the new and unusual." She waved her hand in the same dismissive manner she had with Mary. "That will change once we are wed."

Elise couldn't prevent a gasp.

Margaret lifted a brow. "He did not tell you? Pity. You can't be surprised he kept the news from you, of all people."

Elise narrowed her eyes. "Marcus is no liar."

"He hasn't lied. The news has not yet been announced. We are awaiting permission from King George." Margaret regarded her with a curious intensity. "You don't believe me." She laughed, the sound filled with disdain and, to Elise's surprise, pleasure. "Tell me," Margaret said, "do you like the way he slides his tongue over your lips?"

A chill pooled in Elise's belly.

"Or perhaps you find the way he runs his hands along your body more memorable. He is a man who enjoys touching a woman—and let us not forget the way he moves in a deliciously languid motion—"

"What do you want?" Elise demanded.

Margaret slapped her gloves against her hand. "You have nothing I want. His fancy will pass soon enough—as it always does." Then, under her breath, "Though it doesn't please me he has so openly taken his pleasure while I have been away."

While I have been away. A clear explanation for why Marcus had avoided the issue of his wife-to-be.

"He has not taken his pleasure, madam," Elise shot back, remembering all too well how he had nearly done that very thing just last night. How she was just hoping it was he who came looking for her to *take his pleasure.*

Surprise shone on Margaret's face. "Why, there must have been many opportunities..." Her eyes widened. "You mean to marry him."

Elise jerked. "What?"

"You think if you make him wait, he will marry you. My girl, Marcus does not marry out of lust. The Marq—"

"It is quite evident love is not the driving factor in your marriage," Elise snapped.

Margaret's eyes blazed.

"My congratulations, madam. I wish you, Marcus, and all his paramours a happy union." Elise hurried past her toward the door.

"How dare you, you little—"

Elise yanked the door open and slammed it behind her as she stepped into the hallway, leaving Margaret's final words behind. She stumbled forward. Tears clouded her vision. She reached out a hand to the wall, steadying her progress, and discovered she still held the book. She gripped it tighter and took one wobbly step after another until she reached the stairs. She started down, but the sound of voices echoing up the stairwell stopped her. *Cameron.* She turned, scanning the hall for some form of escape, then remembered the small alcove around the bend she had just passed. She dashed up the stairs and down the corridor.

Elise reached the alcove and yanked back the tapestry, nearly falling headlong inside. She straightened, then turned and backed up, stopping only when her shoulders touched cold stone. Sliding to the floor, she dropped the book and hugged her knees to her chest.

"Nay." Even from the distance of the stairwell, Cameron's voice boomed within the narrow confines of the corridor. "'Tis likely he won't be back for several days."

"I hadna' realized he meant to stay so long in the fields," came Daniel's voice.

"He believes the Campbells mean to do mischief during the harvest."

"The guards around the wall remain on double watch," Daniel said.

Elise held her breath as they passed the alcove.

Cameron sighed. "His thirst for revenge is likely never to be quenched. He cannot forgive them for taking Elise."

She stifled a gasp. Winnie's words unexpectedly rang in her mind. "*…it was Marcus who made it clear threats against his own would be met with an iron fist.*"

The male voices faded down the hallway and Elise rose to her feet. She tiptoed to the tapestry and drew the fabric back a fraction. She glanced left then right in the empty corridor, then stepped from the alcove and hurried to the stairs.

Memory of the previous night rose in even more vivid detail than when she'd faced Margaret. If not for the arrival of Marcus's guest, she would have given herself to him. Heat flared in her cheeks. He had held her intimately. So intimately that in her dreams he had caressed her, taken each nipple in his mouth as he slipped a finger between the wet folds of her womanhood. She had never experienced a dream so real... so erotic. Her vision blurred on the stairs and she slowed.

In her dream, it hadn't been him who took her, but she who had willingly parted her thighs, then pulled him between them. She had wrapped her hand around his swollen rod and teased him—teased herself—by rubbing the tip against her throbbing sex, then between the folds before finally guiding him inside her. Elise halted and collapsed back against the wall, her breath heavy and the throb between her legs as real now as it had been in the dream.

The cool of the stone penetrated the thin fabric of her servant's dress. She forced her breathing into a more natural rhythm, then started down the stairs again and didn't stop until she reached her room. Elise closed the door with a soft click. Her knees shook and she suddenly doubted her ability to cross the few paces to the bed.

"Fool," she hissed. She had almost spread her legs for him. A stab of longing startled her. Dear God, the deed would have meant nothing to him.

The unexpected sound of footsteps racing down the hallway jerked her attention to the door. The light tread belonged to a woman and she approached at a run. Elise darted from the door, headed for the screen in hopes of ducking behind the barrier. The footsteps halted outside her bedchamber and the door burst open before she reached the screen.

"Thank God!" Mary cried.

Elise whirled.

"You must come quickly!" Mary dashed across the room and grabbed her arm, then tugged her toward the door.

"What in God's name is wrong?" Elise wrenched free.

"'Tis Lady Margaret," Mary wailed. "She's in an awful fit and is sure to beat Jinny."

Elise pushed past Mary and rushed from the room, along the corridor, then down the steps into the great hall. She raced across the great hall, coming to a skidding halt in the kitchen.

Jinny cowered in a corner with Margaret standing over her.

"What is the meaning of this?" Elise demanded.

Margaret turned.

"Cease this nonsense," Elise ordered.

Margaret stared, slack-jawed.

"Close your mouth," Elise snapped. "In polite circles, it is considered rude to stare."

Margaret's mouth twisted into a gruesome frown. "How dare you?"

"What right have you to terrorize this household?"

Margaret's eyes gleamed with malicious satisfaction. "I have every right—as you know."

"Don't count your chickens before they are hatched. I venture Marcus will not take kindly to your actions."

"Marcus again, is it?"

Elise recognized the jealousy in the woman's eyes and gave her a calculated look. "Jinny," she addressed the young cook who still cowered, "fetch Cameron."

"Cameron?" Margaret's brows rose in a mocking manner.

"Yes. Jinny, I saw him upstairs only a few minutes ago. He was probably on his way to the library."

"Stay where you are," Margaret threatened.

Jinny's wary glance darted from Margaret to Elise.

"It's all right," Elise urged.

Jinny shot a sidelong look at Margaret, then eased a foot to the side. Lady Margaret took a step toward the girl. Elise slid between them.

"Don't take your petty jealousy out on her." Elise stepped so close Margaret was forced to look up in order to maintain eye contact. "Are you such a coward you will only fight those who don't have the power to fight back?"

Margaret raised her hand and swung, palm open, for a hard slap. Her gaze flicked past Elise and her eyes widened as a much larger hand intercepted her palm before it hit its intended mark.

"Enough, lass," Cameron commanded softly.

"I—" she began.

"Never mind," he said. "Marcus isna' here. 'Tis best if you go."

Margaret looked as if she would say more but lifted her skirts and headed for the door.

Cameron looked at Elise. "Are you all right, lass?"

She kept her gaze on Margaret's retreating form then, as Margaret stepped from the kitchen to the great hall, Elise started forward. Cameron stayed her with a firm grip on her arm.

"Whoa, lass. Where are you going?"

She shook his hand from her arm. "Why did you interrupt?"

"I heard you tell Jinny to fetch me. I would think you were glad for my timely arrival."

"A timely arrival would have been three seconds later."

"But she would have struck you by then."

Elise saw Margaret open the postern door. "Correct."

"You wanted her to hit you?"

"Yes."

"Why?"

Elise looked at him. "Because then I could have hit her back."

Elise stopped before Winnie's cottage. Her sharp rap on the door quieted the evening crickets and she entered without waiting for an invitation.

Winnie looked up from where she sat at the table. "What's wrong?"

"Something must be wrong?" Elise asked.

Winnie rose and bustled to the door. "Supper is finished and you are visiting me. If you had good news, you would have told me then." Winnie prodded her into a chair at the table, then turned to the hearth and grabbed the kettle from the fire. "Have some tea."

She set a cup in front of Elise, picked up a tea strainer from the basket sitting on the table, and plopped it into the cup. Winnie filled the cup with hot water, then did the same for herself. She replaced the kettle over the fire, seated herself across from Elise, and stared, an expectant look on her face.

Elise dipped a finger inside her cup and fiddled with the tea strainer so that it bobbed in the water. "I haven't spoken about my life before Brahan Seer."

"Nay."

"Perhaps that was unfair."

A silence drew out between them before Elise said, "The details no longer matter, only that I lost everything. I began again here," a tremor rippled through her at the lie, "but now I see myself entangled in a mess no better than the one I came from."

"A mess?" Winnie repeated.

Elise smiled gently. "By now, all of Brahan Seer knows what happened today between me and Lady Margaret."

"Aye, though no one was surprised by such mischief from Lady Margaret."

Elise lifted a brow. "Indeed?"

"Aye," Winnie said. "She's a bitch."

Elise blinked, then couldn't help laughing.

Winnie frowned. "Well, she is."

Elise released a breath. "That doesn't change the truth… or the fact I must leave."

"Leave?" Winnie snorted. "Surely not because of Lady Margaret?"

Elise leaned forward on the table. "Winnie, he is to marry her."

The older woman's shocked expression said she knew nothing of the betrothal. Elise experienced a sense of relief she hadn't hoped for. Winnie hadn't been a part of the deception.

"I don't believe it," Winnie said.

"No?" Elise asked. "Because you don't like her?"

"Nay." But this time, the denial held less conviction.

"I am going. Tomorrow."

Winnie's brows snapped together. "So soon? Mayhap you should wait just a little while, give Marcus a chance—"

"A chance for what?" *To win me over?* The very thing she couldn't allow. For she would submit, then the leaving would only break her heart all the more. And she would leave. For Amelia. For Steven. And because he had lied to her.

"Marcus is away," she said. "It's better I go now."

"You plan on returning to America?"

Elise nodded.

"I suppose you can manage there as well as here."

"I need your help."

Winnie gave her a wary look. "I dinna' like the look in your eye."

"I must leave early if I am to reach Glasgow before nightfall. Leaving so early is sure to raise suspicion. If you and I go together to the village—"

"Lord save us." Winnie rolled her eyes heavenward.

"You know it will take trickery."

"Oh, it will take trickery."

"If you know another way?"

"There is a secret passage leading outside the gates."

"A secret passage? Where does it emerge?"

"Near the gate."

"That might work," Elise murmured.

Winnie unexpectedly shook her head. "Nay. 'Tis a bad idea."

"Why?"

"If you are caught, the jig is up. We will do as you said and go early. Only you cannot go all the way to Glasgow alone. Peter will   go with you."

"Peter?" Elise's heart thumped. "I won't risk another person's life."

Winnie's face softened. "Peter is no green boy. He's my niece's cousin, a seasoned fighter and a crack shot. And," Winnie paused for emphasis, "he knows nothing of Marcus's, er, desire for you to stay." Elise hesitated, and Winnie added, "He would have returned home anyway. Glasgow is not far out of his way. Trust me, he can get you there safely."

Elise nodded, despite the knot in her throat. God help her if she miscalculated again.

Chapter Eight

Marcus stared at the warrior standing before him in the great hall. The anticipation he had felt only an hour ago had given way to a throbbing in his head that threatened to incite him to violence. "You found her buying a ticket for an Australian-bound packet?" he managed in an even voice.

"Nay, laird," the warrior replied.

"Ah," Marcus said, "I forget, you intercepted her at the pawnbroker's shop."

"Not in the shop, exactly," he hedged.

Marcus glanced at his father, who sat in his chair sipping ale as though they were discussing nothing more important than the weather. Marcus looked back at the warrior. "Where, then?"

"She, er, had left the pawnbroker—you see, Daniel reasoned we couldna' just go inside and take her. She would bring all of Glasgow down upon us."

"Indeed," Marcus murmured.

"She near did—or would have, had we not dragged her into the alley."

"Dragged her into an alley, you say? This alley was deserted then, a place you could have done with her as you wished?"

The man swallowed. "Aye."

"Angry, was she?" Marcus realized he had clenched his hand into a fist.

The man looked sheepish. "You can't blame the

lass, she thought—"

"Aye," Marcus interrupted savagely, "I know what she thought. The little fool is damned lucky that isn't what happened. You are certain no Campbell accosted her?"

"Not so much as a scrap of Campbell *plaide* was found between here and Glasgow."

"How far behind were Elise and Daniel when you left them?"

"They were riding fast—not so fast she couldn't keep up," the man added quickly, "but I rode harder. I left them at early light."

"By all rights, they should be arriving anytime," Marcus calculated.

"Aye," the warrior agreed.

Marcus jerked his head toward the postern door in an indication the man should leave, and he hurried from the great hall. Marcus faced his father. "What the bloody hell was she selling—and Australia? I thought Winnie said she was bound for America."

"'Tis strange," Cameron agreed.

"If anything has happened to her…"

Cameron's gaze remained steady. "Ye heard what John said. She is well." He motioned to the seat beside him. "Sit, have an ale, and wait."

"By God, she had three days head start." Marcus slammed a fist down on the table. "*Anything* could have happened."

"Not three, less than two. 'Tis been three days since she left. I can see how you would confuse the time, but our lads took after her night before last. Elise and Peter's tracks indicated they rode slow, and our men rode fast. Did you not comprehend John's report?" Marcus opened his mouth to retort, but Cameron added, "Our men lagged but two hours behind them yesterday afternoon. I sent more men to meet them. They are on their way home and willna' dare dally."

"How could you have let her go?"

"I didn't let her go." Cameron regarded him. "You plan on making her a prisoner?"

106

"Would you have her alone on that ship?" Marcus demanded.

His father's mouth thinned. "We should beat them both." He glanced in the direction of the kitchen where Winnie worked.

"Aye," Marcus said, agreeing with his father for the first time since he'd returned home an hour ago. "Beat her, I will. If I don't get the chance, I will take it out of your hide, *Father.*"

Cameron took a large swig of the ale sitting before him, then set the mug on the table. He wiped his mouth with the back of his hand. "The lads will return with her soon."

Marcus shot his father another unforgiving look. "So you have said a dozen times the past hour."

His father's expression hardened. "I realize you are upset, lad, but you aren't giving me enough credit. Do you believe I would sit here drinking ale if I thought she was in danger?"

Marcus hesitated.

"She will arrive safe."

Tramping feet approached the postern door. Marcus whirled as the door opened and Daniel entered, followed by half a dozen men.

"Where is she?" Marcus demanded.

The men parted to reveal Elise, head downcast, hair damp. Marcus frowned, his first thought was *Why had she not been given a tartan?* But she raised her head and the fire in her eyes ignited an answering fury in him. He strode to her, grabbed her by the shoulders, and began shaking her.

"What do you think you were doing?" He shook her harder with every word.

"Marcus!" Cameron's sharp voice cut through the haze. "You'll shake her to death."

"Or mayhap shake some sense into her." He shoved her away from him and raked his hand through his hair.

"Laird," Daniel said.

107

Marcus looked at Daniel, who tossed a small pouch to him. He caught it and the clink of coin rattled inside the leather.

"'Tis Elise's—"

Marcus jerked his gaze onto his captain.

"The money she received from the pawnbroker," Daniel finished.

Marcus loosed the tie and emptied the coins into his palm. He counted five sovereign. A small fortune. He looked at Elise. "What were you selling?"

She remained mute. He turned to Daniel.

Daniel cleared his throat. "A wedding ring, according to the bill of sale."

Marcus watched dumbfounded as Daniel produced a piece of paper from within his sporran. He strode to the table and laid the bill of sale on it.

Marcus looked at Elise. "A hefty sum, even for a gold band."

She lifted her chin a fraction. "How did you find me?"

He slipped the coins back into the pouch, then tossed it on the table. "The MacGregor can track you, remember?"

Her cheeks colored and he knew she remembered that day in the meadow when she had threatened him with the MacGregor fury should he harm her and the children. *'I tracked these children. You think he cannot track you?'* she had said.

He broke eye contact. "Go change into dry clothes." Silence followed and he looked to see she hadn't so much as twitched a muscle. Marcus narrowed his eyes. "I warn you, Elise, do no' try my temper any further. Go upstairs. *Now.*"

She remained motionless. He lunged forward and scooped her onto his shoulder. Whoops and cheers rang throughout the room.

"Marcus MacGregor!" She thrashed.

He answered with a hard squeeze to her legs. The men responded with more raucous laughter. Applause followed as he strode across the room and bounded up the stairs. She twisted in his grasp, but Marcus ignored the futile effort until he reached her bedchamber, where he kicked the door open and, in three paces, tossed her onto the bed. She landed on the mattress and immediately made to scramble to her knees. Marcus leapt forward, one knee on the bed, and planted his hands on each side of her.

"Get away!" she shouted as she scooted backwards.

She fell back against the bed when he brought his face to within an inch of hers.

"If you do not change into dry clothes, I will do it for you."

Elise remained motionless, but he caught the flicker of uncertainty in her eyes. He pushed away from her and stood. She crawled off the bed, her gaze on him, as she fetched the dress hanging in the closet. She faced him. Marcus waved toward the screen in the corner.

"Kind of you," she retorted.

"Do not try me," he growled.

"Try *you?*" Elise snorted, then stepped behind the screen.

"All I want to know is why?" he demanded.

The rustling of clothing paused. A long moment of silence passed, then she said, "Exactly my question."

Marcus started to reply but threw himself, instead, onto the couch opposite the bed. A moment later, she appeared from behind the screen.

"Why did you leave?" he demanded.

"Why did you bring me back?"

He frowned. "I didn't. Cameron did. I wasn't aware you had left until an hour ago."

"Cameron?" Her eyes darkened. "So I have him to thank for scaring me half out of my wits."

Marcus leapt from the couch. Elise retreated several steps.

"You truly have taken leave of your senses." He stopped two paces from her. "Had I known—had I come for you—I would have given you a scare you wouldn't have forgotten. Being kidnapped by the Campbells clearly left no impression on you."

109

"I was well out of MacGregor territory when Daniel found me. *I was safe.*"

Marcus seized her hand and yanked her close. "So safe you were accosted in an alleyway. And a woman on a ship alone—bound for America—no, Australia. No money, no escort—although, money you had in abundance. Why did you leave?"

Her lips pursed. "That is none of your business."

"None of my business? Bloody hell, Elise, I will have my answers." He yanked her so close he could feel her breath on his face. "Why?"

He twisted her wrist slightly and she winced.

"Elise," he repeated.

Silence followed, then she said, "I decided it was time to go."

Marcus tightened the tenuous hold on his temper. "Well, you can't go." He shoved her away from him. He closed his eyes, massaging the bridge of his nose with thumb and forefinger.

"I can't go?" she repeated softly.

He whirled on her. "I have just spent one of the most hellish hours of my life and you think I'll be swayed by your indignation?" Marcus moved an inch closer. "Think again, my sweet." He inched even closer and she backed away from him. "I am the master here, and I will let you push me only so far." He slid closer.

Elise sidled to her left, but he grasped her shoulders. He forced her back against the wall and pressed himself against her. Their eyes locked. He broke the standoff, his gaze dropping to her lips. The beat of his heart pounded against the swell of her breasts. He breathed deep, then pulled her to the couch and shoved her onto the cushion.

"Now, what is this foolishness?"

"I can't stay here forever. It's time I go."

"It is not," he growled.

Elise jumped.

"Do not move. I won't strike you. Though, God knows, I would love nothing more than to turn you over my knee."

"Comforting," she said with a snort.

"Listen, you little fool, when I think it's time for you to go, *if* I ever think it's time for you to go, I will tell you."

"You can't stop me."

Marcus stared. "You think I can't stop you? I can do anything I damn well please." Though this was the first time he'd used his power to take advantage of a woman. *"Do you plan on making her a prisoner?"* his father had asked.

"Cameron is master here, not you," Elise said. "He can let me go."

"There's no real difference between my father's authority and mine."

"There is enough difference. If he says I can go, then I can."

"It doesn't matter. He will not."

"You are so sure?"

Marcus exhaled loudly.

"You don't mind, then, if I ask." She stood.

He couldn't believe it. "You would ask him?"

Elise raised a brow. "Afraid?"

Marcus paused. "You will let this rest if he agrees with me?"

"He won't."

Marcus followed two paces behind as Elise stepped from the staircase into the great hall moments later. It was mid-afternoon, and only the men who had fetched her home lingered in the hall with Cameron. She smiled and approached him while Marcus sauntered to the hearth and propped an elbow on the large mantle. Elise stopped before Cameron, who glanced from her to Marcus, then back again.

"I would like to speak with you, Cameron," she said.

He motioned the men to leave. She seated herself in the chair beside his. Once the men were gone, he looked expectantly at her.

"Marcus tells me I can't leave."

"'Tis his decision."

111

"You can countermand this edict."

Cameron laughed. "I can, but will not."

"Aren't I free?" she asked. "Don't I fall under the same law as every Highlander?"

Cameron's mouth twitched and he looked at Marcus. Marcus raised a brow and his father turned back to her. "Why do you want to leave, lass? Have we not been good to you? Have no' we cared for you as one of our own?" His expression softened. "You're a sweet lass. We would miss you."

Her eyes narrowed. "I feel certain you would survive quite well without me." Her voice quieted. "I don't belong here."

He frowned. "Who has been filling your head with such silliness?"

She hesitated. "No one. It's simply obvious, is all."

"Nonsense."

Elise leaned on the table and said in lowered tones, "I must go."

"Why?"

She dropped her gaze to her hands clasped atop the table. "There are certain… rumors about me."

His brow furrowed. "Such as?"

Elise leaned closer. "It is said that I am Marcus's mistress."

"What?" Cameron burst out.

Marcus dropped his elbow from the mantel.

"Nay, lad." His father held up a hand. "Stand where you are." Marcus halted and Cameron focused again on Elise. "Who said this?"

She shook her head. "That isn't important."

"But it is."

"No—"

"If I am to consider any petition," he interrupted, "I must know all the facts."

After a moment's silence, she mumbled an answer.

"What? Speak up, lass."

Marcus strained, but missed the single word she repeated.

"Margaret?" Cameron repeated loudly.

112

Marcus started forward.

His father's attention jerked to him. "Hold, Marcus." Their gazes locked, Cameron's mouth twitching, then he looked back at Elise. "Is this what the two of you were fashin' over?"

"Margaret?" Marcus echoed.

Elise released an audible groan.

Cameron looked at him. "You should have seen 'em. Had I not arrived when I did—"

"It isn't funny," Elise snapped.

"Aye, lass"—his shoulders began to shake with laughter—"it is."

"All this over a silly conversation with Margaret?" Marcus demanded.

"It would seem so," Cameron said between fits of laughter.

"I will put an end to Margaret's troublemaking." Marcus muttered. His father had been right; he should have dallied with the demimonde and left the noblewomen to their own devices.

Elise grabbed Cameron's arm. "But, Cameron," she shook his arm, "it's not true."

"Wha—"

"She's lying," Elise insisted

Marcus's mind snapped to attention.

Cameron gave a final grunt, then sobered. He focused on Marcus. "Is this true? I had thought—" he broke off with a slight cough and a sideways glance at Elise.

Marcus swung his gaze onto Elise. "What are you doing?"

"Marcus," Cameron cut him off.

Marcus looked at his father.

"Is it true?" Cameron repeated.

"Damn close," Marcus replied with force.

"Marcus!" Elise cried.

"Do not act as if it isn't true," he replied irritably.

She shot to her feet. "You are no gentleman, sir."

"Elise," his father said, "sit."

She cast a dark glance at Marcus. He

113

raised a brow, but she did as ordered and reseated herself.

Cameron addressed Marcus. "Is it true, lad?"

"Aye, she speaks the truth."

"Margaret ought not to have lied." Cameron gave Marcus a quick glance. "'Course, she had no way of knowing it was a lie." He rubbed his chin. "If ye don't belong to Marcus—"

"Cameron!" Marcus strode across the room to his father's side.

Elise leapt from her chair. "Be quiet, Marcus MacGregor, and let your father speak."

"She may have a point," Cameron said.

Marcus kept his gaze on Cameron. "Father," he growled, "you know my feelings on this."

"Aye, lad, but if you haven't done anything about it yet—"

"Cameron—"

"I warn you, Marcus." Elise stalked toward him. "Remain silent and let your father finish, or I'll…" she stopped, looking wildly about the room. Her gaze stopped on the weapons mounted on the wall, and she ran to them.

Marcus cast his father a look and they both burst out laughing. Elise made a frustrated sound as she began tugging on a scabbard containing a large sword. The weapon remained fixed and she moved to another. That one didn't budge, nor the next or the next.

"Elise, lass," Cameron said between howls of laughter, "you're tugging on the scabbards." He laughed even harder. "If you wish to draw a weapon"— he slapped the table with his hand, "grab the"—he gasped with laughter—"hilt." He doubled over with laughter. "By God," he wheezed, "are ye sure you're not Irish, lass?"

"Irish?" She laid a hand on the hilt of a lady's *sgian dubh* mounted above the swords she had already tried. "You've never seen an Irish temper like my father's. Except, perhaps"—she turned back to the wall— "mine."

Elise pulled the dagger free of its scabbard. She stepped a pace from the wall, drew back, and threw the knife. The *sgian dubh* whizzed between Marcus and his father, entering the wooden table with a loud *thwang*.

Aside from a "Sweet mother of God" from the kitchen doorway, silence reigned. Both men stared at the knife.

Marcus pulled the dagger free of the wood and held it up, looking at her. "You missed."

She raised a brow. "I did not."

"Sweet mother of God," Cameron repeated. "Where did you learn to throw a knife like that?"

She gave him a disgusted look.

"Are you sure you want her, Marcus?"

"Aye," he replied, not taking his eyes off her.

Cameron slapped the table again. "A Celtish woman who can throw a knife. I knew I liked you." He patted the chair. "Come, sit."

Marcus tensed for the moment she studied them before crossing to the chair and reseating herself.

Cameron leaned back in his chair. "Why didn't you tell us you are Celt?"

"I didn't know it mattered."

He gave Marcus a satisfied look.

"What?" she demanded. "What has happened?"

"'Tis as you said," Cameron said, "you fall under Highland law. You're an Irishwoman. We are family."

"I am free to go, then?"

"Well," he answered slowly, "'tis not so easy."

"But Winnie said any clansman who didn't agree with their clan could leave."

Cameron's lips thinned. "I wouldn't speak of Winnie. That isn't working in your favor."

"But—"

He shook his head. "She would be the first to admit that she wasn't talking about women traipsing off alone."

"What?"

Cameron gave her a considering look. "Did she not send Peter with you?"

"Yes, bu—"

"And did she not tell you it was a bad idea?"

"I wouldn't say—"

Cameron raised a brow.

"I have a right to come and go as I please."

"You're a woman," he insisted. "You must submit to your lord."

She stiffened. "I have no lord. I am unmarried."

"All women have a lord," he explained gently.

Elise shook her head. "I am free."

"Aye, you are a free woman—not a slave—but I am your lord."

"You? Ridiculous."

"You are under my roof. You are a part of us."

"Cameron—"

"It would be wrong of me to let you go," he interrupted gruffly. "You should never have run off in the first place."

"But you were going to let me go," she insisted.

He shrugged. "I was considering it, but I hadn't made up my mind either."

Elise jumped up and whirled on Marcus. "This is your fault."

"My fault? This was your idea."

"Now, lass," Cameron interjected, "tomorrow Marcus will deal with Margaret and she'll never interfere again."

Elise turned on Cameron. "Cameron, please—"

He brought his palm down on the table. "Enough." He looked to Marcus. "Marcus, take her upstairs and put her to bed—once and for all."

Marcus took hold of her arm. She started to resist, but Cameron gave a single shake of his head. Marcus prodded her toward the stairs and her shoulders slumped.

"This is wrong," she said, taking the stairs with deliberate slowness.

"It's finished," Marcus replied.

"You have nothing to say about it."

"I have been patient," he said, as they reached the

116

top of the stairs.

"I never asked for your patience."

He placed a hand on her back and urged her down the hallway at a quicker pace. "Count yourself fortunate that's what you've gotten. Now go to bed."

They came to a halt before her bedchamber door.

"I'll go to bed when I am good and ready," she retorted.

Marcus leaned in close behind her. "Go to bed before it's too late."

She shook her head.

"You play a dangerous game." He opened the bedchamber door and shoved her inside.

"What the devil are you talking about?"

He stepped into the room, shutting the door behind him. "By God, did your husband teach you nothing of respect? What of trust"—desire flared to life inside him—"or...desire?"

Elise paled.

Marcus started at her sudden expression of pain. "Bloody hell." He reached her side in an instant. "Forgive me, love."

She turned away, but he grasped her shoulders.

"Please go," she said, her head averted.

"Did you love him deeply?" Marcus asked. She grasped his wrist and tried to disengage them from her hands, but he tightened his grip. "Elise?"

She lifted her head and met his gaze. "*No.*"

Marcus blinked. Her eyes widened and he was unsure if he read fear or remorse. "What happened?" he asked.

Her expression hardened. "That is none of your concern."

"Mayhap, but I want the answer."

At first it seemed she wouldn't comply, then in a tired voice, "Riley shouldn't have married. He didn't want the ties of a wife, and certainly not the responsibilities of a child."

"How can a man not love a beautiful wife who gives him children in his   own image?"

She dropped her gaze, but he didn't miss the scarlet that crept up her cheeks.

"Elise."

"You have your answers. Now go."

With a finger, he forced her chin upwards. "The man was a fool. How he could not want you—"

She twisted from his grasp. "I never said he didn't want me. We had a daughter."

"A child need not come of passion."

She shot him a defiant look. "You tread on dangerous ground."

He slid an arm around her back. "Tell me, love, did he kiss you like this?"

Marcus pressed his mouth to hers, gently caressing her lips with his. She squirmed, but he tightened his hold. Slowly deepening the kiss, he parted her lips with his tongue, tasting the hot moistness of her mouth and encouraging her to enjoy him. Her breath quickened, and he slid wet kisses across the smooth skin of her neck. He grazed a breast with his hand and felt her sharp intake of breath. He kissed her mouth, harder this time. At last, he released her.

Elise looked into his eyes, her expression flat. "That is lust. Any man can feel lust."

"True," Marcus agreed. "And I can find a woman to satisfy lust. But this is need. A need," he cupped her bottom, pressing her to him, "born of strong desire, fueled by something much deeper. This leads to true passion."

Keeping her close, he lifted her from the floor and carried her to the bed. He settled her upon the bed, then lay down beside her.

"This is a need so great it drives a man wild." He stroked her neck. "That's what I felt our first meeting in the meadow. You have no idea what you do to me." He nuzzled her neck. "Even the ride home with you in my lap was painful." He kissed her neck. She shook her head, but he went on. "Just the thought of you incites me like a raging fire."

Marcus rolled onto her. He stroked her shoulder,

118

then slid his hand down to cover a breast. He kissed the base of her neck. She gripped his shoulders and it seemed she would resist. He slipped a finger inside her bodice and brushed a nipple. Her hold tightened on his shoulders.

"Sweet," he whispered, "ye are beautiful. I want you." He tugged her bodice down and grasped the nipple between thumb and forefinger, rolling it gently. She arched a breath's movement toward him. "Aye," he coaxed. "You want me." He moved against her. "Tell me you want me. Come, sweet, surely you can give me those simple words." He kissed her, moving against her more ardently.

She abruptly shoved at him. He rocked against her again. She shoved harder.

"No," she said in a voice hoarse with effort.

"Wha—?" He tried to focus his eyes.

She arched.

"*Elise.*" He buried his head in her hair.

"Get off me." Her fingernails pressed through his shirt, biting into his shoulder.

Marcus lifted his head. "What has happened? What's wrong?"

Elise pushed harder, grunting with the useless effort. "I will not be your mistress."

He frowned. "I'm not asking you to be my mistress."

She stopped pushing at him. "Then what is this all about?"

"What does it look like?"

"Why don't you ask the woman you are going to marry?"

"I would be glad to, if she would allow it."

Elise stared. "What kind of man involves his future wife with his mistress?" She began struggling again. "Let me go!"

"Not until you explain what this is about."

"I have told you."

"Nay. You've only spoken in riddles."

"I'm sure Margaret   would not think it was

much of a riddle," she retorted.

"Margaret? You're still fretting about her silly comments? I told you, tomorrow I will—" The horrified look on Elise's face halted him.

"Marcus," she said in a trembling voice, "if you have any feeling for me, you will not do this. Margaret made it perfectly clear how she felt about you flaunting your mistress—"

"Flaunting my mistress?" Anger flooded him. "This is none of her bloody affair."

"None of her affair? For God's sake, you are to marry her. I certainly wouldn't—"

"I what?"

Elise blanched.

"Margaret," he said through gritted teeth, "I will wring your meddling little neck."

Elise bristled. "You have no right to be angry just because she spoiled your plans."

"Aye, but I do."

"You think you can use women as pawns."

"Love—"

"Do not address me in that familiar fashion. I tell you, I will not be your mistress." She struggled beneath him. "I won't change my mind, no matter what you say."

Marcus caught her face between his hands. "No matter what I say?"

She tried shaking her head, but he held her firm.

"I am happy to hear that," he said. "For 'tis not Margaret I intend to marry, but you."

Chapter Nine

A hard knock sounded on the door of Winnie's cottage. Elise started from her concentration on the teacup Winnie stood filling with hot water. They exchanged a questioning look before Winnie called "Come in" as she turned and replaced the kettle over the fire.

The door opened and Mary entered. She brushed back the shawl thrown over her head as cover against the light rain and addressed Elise. "Ye must come to the castle."

"Why?"

"'Tis the MacGregor's command."

Elise bristled. His imperious commands—her stomach did a somersault—were those of a husband-to-be. She summoned a believable amount of female condescension. "What does he want?"

"He and Lady Ross are in his library. Says you must come without delay."

"Margaret?" Elise shot a glance at Winnie.

"The man keeps his promises," Winnie remarked.

"The *man* is an idiot." Elise turned back to Mary. "Tell him I'm busy."

The girl gasped. "I canna' do that. He'll have my hide."

Elise's stomach gave another turn. It was her hide he wanted.

Tell him the truth, her mind insisted, but she

ignored the urging now as she had last night when Marcus said it was her he wanted to marry and not Margaret. He wasn't the sort of man who would let his wife set off to America with the intention of avenging herself against a killer. And Amelia and Steven deserved more than to be forgotten at sea.

"Tell him I'm busy," Elise said.

Mary shot Winnie a beseeching look, but Winnie shrugged. "Lady Margaret can go to the devil."

Mary looked at Elise again. "You can't refuse."

Elise gave a single shake of her head. Mary looked from one to the other, then whirled and left the cottage.

Elise still sat across the table from Winnie, deep in conversation, when another rap sounded on the cottage door, this one sharper than the last.

"Who in the world?" Winnie complained. She hurried to the door and threw it open. "Marcus." The housekeeper stepped back.

Elise flicked her gaze from Marcus to Margaret, who stood beside him, then narrowed her eyes on him. He lifted a brow as if to ask where she would now hide and, despite her efforts, her heartbeat accelerated.

"May we?" Marcus indicated the interior of the cottage with a nod.

"Aye, of course." Winnie stepped clear of the doorway.

Margaret glided into the room ahead of him and sat in the chair Winnie had occupied. Marcus leaned against the doorframe.

A moment of silence passed before Margaret addressed Elise. "I understand there has been a misunderstanding between us."

For the hundredth time, Elise thanked God for the *misunderstanding*. Otherwise, Marcus would have looked deeper for the reason behind her running away.

"I wish to apologize for any distress I caused," Margaret said.

Elise quirked a brow. A tinge of red heightened the color in the woman's cheeks. Satisfaction shot through Elise. What would the woman think of

Marcus's marriage proposal to a lowly servant? The thought vanished with the realization that Marcus might have told her. Who else might he have told? The possibility of spending the rest of her life with this man—

"I regret you misinterpreted my words," Lady Ross went on.

"I understood you perfectly," Elise replied.

Another long silence drew out before Margaret looked at Marcus. "Now that this is all settled, your—" She stopped, and Elise caught sight of the now hard set of his jaw. Margaret turned her attention back to Elise. "We understand one another, then?"

"We do."

Lady Ross angled her head. "I shall be going." She glanced at Marcus. "If I may?"

With a brusque nod, he straightened from the doorframe. "Winnie, escort Lady Ross to the stables, if you please."

Margaret rose and walked to the door. She paused beside Marcus as though to say something but, with a curtsy, left with Winnie closing the door behind them.

When they'd gone, he closed the door and faced Elise. "I sent for you."

"Yes."

"Yet you forced me to bring Margaret to you."

"Yes."

"And when we arrived, you were less than gracious."

"*Milord*," Elise said in exaggerated tones, "you can force me to sit quietly while you issue commands, but you cannot force me to agree."

Marcus blinked, then started toward her. She tensed as he threw himself into the chair beside hers, folded his arms across his chest, and regarded her.

"Is it so difficult to do as I ask?"

"In this case, yes," she replied.

"This request, then, went against your... moral fiber?"

"That is one way of   putting it."

A gleam appeared in his eye and a prickle of dread crept up her neck.

"This means," he went on, "you will honor future *requests* so long as they do not go against your moral convictions?"

"Perhaps," she answered tentatively.

"Mayhap a distraction would help." His gaze held hers. "Would you like to know what sort of distraction I have in mind?"

"No," she replied, and mentally cursed the all-too-quick response.

"Too late."

Marcus stood. In one quick motion, he grasped her waist and lifted her onto the table. With a single finger, he tilted her chin upward so she was forced to look directly into his eyes.

"I have found my threats are meaningless. Probably because you know I am incapable of carrying them out against your beautiful body."

He shifted his gaze to her neck and moved his finger lightly on the hollow of her throat. Elise tried to quell the quiver in her stomach, but the almost imperceptible, yet arrogant twitch at the corner of his mouth said she hadn't been completely successful.

"I am, however, more than willing to do this every time you disobey me." He cupped the nape of her neck as he bent and covered her mouth with his.

Elise twisted in an effort to distance their bodies. Marcus gave a satisfied grunt and shoved her thighs apart with his knee. He pulled her close, pressing her stomach against his erection. A gust of desire startled Elise. He slipped a hand beneath her skirt.

She wriggled in an attempt to break the kiss. Her belly rubbed across his hard shaft. She jerked back, but he hugged her closer as he traced circles up her inner thigh. She seized his shoulders and tried to shake his immoveable body. His tongue slipped past her lips and thrust gently against her tongue.

In her mind's eye, she saw him ease her back onto the table and pull up her dress until she lay bared before him. How easily he could spread her legs, then lift his kilt and—Elise jolted. His hand had moved farther up her thigh. She swayed with dizziness. Body and mind seemed connected only through the roiling in her stomach. His fingers brushed the sensitive skin on the uppermost part of her thigh.

Elise tore her mouth from his and buried her head in his shoulder. "Enough," she said between heavy breaths.

His hand stilled. "Have I selected an effective distraction?"

"You know perfectly well what you've done."

Marcus removed his hand from her thigh, then grasped her shoulders, holding her at arm's length. "Beware," he said, and something suspiciously close to a smile played on his mouth, "for, if I find you disobeying me too often, I will conclude you crave the *distraction*."

Realization washed over her. "You odious man!" She pushed him from her.

Clutching his breast, Marcus took a step back. "You wound me, my sweet."

"I'm in no mood for games." She stood and began smoothing her rumpled skirts, slowing the action upon seeing her hands tremble.

"I assure you," he said with a seriousness that yanked her attention onto him, "this is no game." The glitter in his eyes reflected the edge in his voice.

Elise stared. "You can't be serious. You wouldn't…"

"Do what I have just done? That and more. Passion is a powerful distraction."

His gaze held hers and she knew he was remembering his final words before leaving her room last night, *"I will wed you."*

He abruptly turned and strode to the door.

Elise tried tearing her gaze from his muscled calves but found herself unable to blink until the door closed softly behind him. How was she going to get out of this mess? If she told him she didn't love him, he wouldn't believe her.

Elise sat on the bed beside Chloe, gripping the girl's hands and keeping them pressed against the mattress as Winnie placed a hand on Chloe's stomach. Her deft fingers inched along the skin until she located the unborn child's buttocks. Winnie pressed hard, trying once again to coax the buttocks away from the birthing canal. Elise rubbed her forehead against her shoulder in an effort to brush back sweat-matted hair from her eyes.

Winnie suddenly pushed hard on the baby's rear. Chloe flinched, crying out. Elise twisted and met the older woman's gaze. Winnie straightened and gave a small but significant shake of her head. Elise gently massaged Chloe's wrists before reaching for the rag floating in a water basin beside the bed. Elise wrung out the rag and wiped the girl's forehead. Chloe writhed.

"Shhh," Elise soothed. "It'll soon be over."

"Nay!" Chloe shoved at her hand. "I've killed my own bairn."

Elise wiped Chloe's neck. The girl's body clenched. "Winnie!" Elise called, but Winnie was already pressing down on the baby.

Chloe jerked and would have bolted upright, but Elise grabbed her shoulders and shoved her deep into the mattress.

"I've killed him," Chloe whimpered.

She relaxed, the contraction receding, but her weeping continued. Elise looked at Winnie, who again placed a hand over the baby's buttocks and tried forcing the head into position. Elise watched the skillful hands at work. Winnie had an uncanny knack for understanding the core of a problem. She always had some potion ready for any ailment. But no potion could be concocted for Chloe. The girl no longer wept. She lay, eyes closed, her tear-stained face resigned.

With a short nod to Elise, Winnie pressed down

on Chloe's stomach again. Elise held Chloe's arms. The girl did little more than grunt when Winnie bore down on her stomach. Another contraction struck. Chloe's hips arched off the bed. Elise bit her lip to keep the tears in check. How much more could the girl endure? She'd labored for twenty-two hours. Soon, she would grow too weak to birth the child.

Winnie pressed down on the baby for an agonizing hour and a half, then abruptly took a quick step back and reached beneath the sheet covering Chloe's legs. Elise felt a sudden jerk on Chloe's body, and the girl nearly wrenched free of her hold.

"Hold her!" Winnie shouted.

Elise closed her eyes. Chloe screamed. Elise heard a loud swooshing noise and her eyes shot open as Chloe went limp.

No loud wail followed.

Chloe bolted upright. "Give him to me!"

"Now, Chloe," Winnie cooed, her back to them. "Let me take the babe and—"

"Nay!" Chloe screamed. "*Give me my bairn.*"

Winnie looked over her shoulder. "Chloe, 'tis best if ye don't see him." Her eyes softened. "Trust me, lass, I know."

Chloe looked at Winnie, her face suddenly far older than her nineteen years. "He's mine. I have the right to hold him." Her pained expression deepened.

A pain of the soul, not the body. One Elise knew all too well.

"The bairn is a part of me," Chloe ended simply.

Winnie sighed, then faced them. Elise told herself to avert her gaze, but maternal instinct, the memory of her own lost child, brought her gaze to bear on the beautifully formed babe. Winnie placed him in his mother's arms. Chloe cradled him as tenderly as if he had lived. She wiped the blood from his face, then traced his mouth with a gentle finger. She looked up at Winnie.

"He has Daniel's mouth."

"Aye," Winnie replied.

Chloe began to rock as she sang in a low voice. The Gaelic words were as Greek to Elise but the meaning was clear. Unshed tears stung her eyes. The picture of mother and child blurred with the memory of holding her own dear Amelia, the feel of her daughter's skin, baby soft against her breast. Elise's gaze focused on the blood-smeared body of Chloe's child. Were things so different for her? Did Chloe love the nameless child any less than she had loved Amelia?

Love had deepened for Amelia as time passed. Yet she and Chloe shared the same pain that came with lost possibilities. The young woman had glimpsed her husband in their child. Elise had seen much of Robert in Amelia. Who would the children have grown up to be? Who would they have fallen in love with? What children might they have brought into the world?

Winnie snatched the child from Chloe's arms. Chloe's tear-filled gaze locked on the babe as Winnie whirled and disappeared through the door. Elise froze. She was alone with the grief stricken mother. Her own loss, instead of creating a bridge between them, had widened the chasm, bringing her to the precipice where roiled unrealized emotions, more bittersweet memories—and another, deeper, more concrete conviction that she, too, had failed as a mother.

"I killed him," Chloe whispered.

Elise stared. When had it happened? What had been the defining moment in history when womankind became convinced that if anything went awry in the lives of those they loved, they were somehow responsible? Had it begun with Eve? Had the beguiling serpent planted the seed that all mankind would suffer as a result of her misdeed? Elise fell to her knees beside Chloe's bed.

"No." She took the shaking girl into her arms. "It isn't your fault. It's no one's fault."

Chloe clung to her, her tears bathing Elise's neck.

It seemed hours later when Elise heard the creak of the door and looked up to see Winnie standing in the doorway. Winnie's gaze went to Chloe, who slept, then came back to Elise. Elise rose from the bed and tiptoed across the floor. Winnie stepped from the doorway and Elise followed, quietly closing the door behind her. The porch, not long ago filled with friends and neighbors joyously awaiting the arrival of the newest MacGregor, now held only silence.

"You told Daniel?" Elise asked.

"Aye."

"Where is he?"

She nodded to the left of the cottage where the path led into the cover of the moonless night. Elise started down the steps.

"Perhaps ye had best leave him to his grief," Winnie offered.

Elise paused, then disappeared into the darkness.

Daniel hadn't gone far. She saw him, arm outstretched on a tree, shoulders shaking with silent tears. She halted a few feet from him. "Daniel." She heard his quick intake of breath and stepped closer in order to put a hand on his shoulder. "Daniel."

His shoulder stiffened beneath her fingers. She turned him toward her. Without hesitation he fell into her arms and wept.

"A son," he said between sobs.

"I know," she replied, and his tears fell even more freely.

At last, he released her and stepped back. He straightened, again the proud warrior. Elise breathed a silent sigh of relief. He would recover. Now for Chloe. "Daniel, the loss of the child is terrible, but you have something else which must be dealt with now."

"What?"

"Chloe."

"Is something amiss? Winnie said she would live." He looked as if he would race back to the cottage.

"No," Elise quickly put in, "you misunderstand. She will live. However..." Elise hesitated. These Highland men weren't known for having a deep understanding of their women, and she, a stranger, stood before one of them, presuming to tell him how to better deal with one of his own.

"Out with it," he growled. "If she is in danger—" His voice lowered. "Did Winnie lie?" He seized her shoulders.

Elise laid a hand on his arm. "The danger doesn't lie with her body, but her heart."

"Her heart?"

"She blames herself. What's worse, she believes you blame her."

His hands dropped away. "Of course I don't blame her."

"She thinks otherwise."

He gave a dismissive wave of his hand. "She'll think differently tomorrow."

Anger shot through Elise. "You, sir, have no idea what a woman thinks."

A silence drew out between them before he said, "What did she say?"

"She didn't tell me outright, but I… I understand how she feels."

Daniel studied her. "You lost a child?"

"Yes."

He breathed deep. "What's to be done?"

"Go to her. Be with her. Let her know you still love her. It's you she needs."

He stared for a moment then, without a word, strode toward the cottage.

Elise watched until he disappeared into the darkness. A moment later, she heard the shuffle of boots on the porch. With the click of the cottage door, exhaustion washed over her. She took three steps to the closest tree and leaned against the trunk, resting her head. What a fool she was to have become too entangled with these people. They were no longer faceless strangers, but named friends whose lives had touched her. Friends she had deceived—Marcus most of all. She pushed from the tree and started down the path.

No guard remained to escort her home. The moon peeked from behind clouds. She welcomed the solitary walk. The moment the thought formed, tears rolled down her cheeks. Elise gave her head a hard shake but only succeeded in further blurring her vision. The moon dipped behind the clouds again and she was plunged into shadows. Her toe slammed against a rock. She lurched forward. She thrust her hands out in defense of the fall, but large hands seized her waist and yanked her against a hard body. Elise opened her mouth to scream but the arm tightened around her and the scream emerged a squeak.

"Re-release me you brute!" she wheezed, giving her assailant a hard kick to the leg.

He cursed softly. Her stomach did a somersault. *Marcus.*

"Brute, is it?" he murmured. A strained note in his voice said the kick had been successful. "You dare call me brute when I saved you from a nasty fall?"

Elise sagged against him. "You gave me a scare." She took a deep breath.

He ran a hand over her shoulder, following the caress with a kiss to her neck. "'Tis not nice for a lady to call her lover a brute." Another kiss followed on her shoulder.

"*Good Lord.*" She broke free and faced him, trying to discern his features in the darkness. When unsuccessful, she muttered, "You truly are a man."

He chuckled. "That doesn't please you?" Marcus took her hand and started down the path. "Never mind. It will soon enough."

They walked for a few moments, then he slipped an arm around her waist. A shock rippled through Elise, settling between her legs. This feeling she had to guard against. When she left—her heart wrenched and she became painfully aware of his arm around her. His warmth had seeped through her dress, comforting, offering the promise—Elise clamped down on the burgeoning desire. She wouldn't hurt him by giving herself to him then leaving. She had to keep him at a distance for just a little longer.

"You must be exhausted," he said.

She thought of Chloe. "I'm worried about Chloe."

"She'll be fine. Daniel loves her."

"Yes. Their love is their salvation."

"'Tis always the case," Marcus stated matter-of-factly.

Her heart leapt. "Oh?"

"Aye. The love between a man and a woman is salvation itself."

"Perhaps. However, they will be needing an extra dose now."

"You don't think Daniel loves her?"

"I believe he will do his best to comfort her," she replied.

"And who will comfort Daniel?"

"Chloe, of course. Who else?"

"Who else, indeed?" Marcus repeated softly, and this time she couldn't stop the flutter of her heart.

When they entered the castle's kitchen, Marcus ordered Mary to prepare a hot bath for Elise. She protested, but he shook his head.

"I planned on going straight to bed," she complained, as he escorted her through the kitchen.

"Trust me." He forced her to keep pace with him as they crossed the great hall. "You will thank me in the morning." They neared the stairs and he prodded her up.

She remained silent until they reached her door. "Really—" she began.

"Go," he interrupted. "I'll return in a moment."

Elise sighed but acquiesced.

Marcus strode down the hallway to his room. He pushed past his bedchamber door and crossed to the sideboard in the far corner. He poured a brandy and drank it in one swallow. He grimaced, then poured another and went back to Elise's room. Pausing at her door, he knocked once then entered. She looked up sharply, one hand on the remaining boot she was in the process of removing.

"You might have waited until I gave you permission to enter," she said, giving him a reproachful look.

"Drink this." He handed her the brandy.

Elise set the boot on the floor, then took the glass. She sniffed and peered at him over the rim of the snifter. "Napoleon brandy." She drank it in nearly as quick a flourish as he had.

Marcus raised his brows. "Careful, lass. One should acquire a tolerance for spirits before gulping them."

"I wish you'd brought two. Mmm." She stood. "Makes me feel warm all over."

A knock sounded at the door.

"Come in," he called.

Elise frowned. "This is my bedchamber," she said, as the door opened and two men entered carrying the bathtub. "If you don't mind, I will be the one to allow visitors entrance." Her gaze shifted to the tub. She thrust the glass forward, bumping Marcus's chest. He grasped the snifter as she released it and stepped past him. "Over there," she instructed, "by the fire."

Two more men followed with pails of steaming water. "Mary said the rest of the water will take a little time to heat," one man said, as he dumped his pail into the tub.

Elise walked to the tub and peered into it. "Two pails of cool water will do."

The men nodded and were gone. She faced Marcus. He gave her a questioning look, knitting his brows as though not comprehending.

"*Marcus.*"

"Ah, yes." He set the glass on the nightstand, then came to stand beside her. He grasped her shoulders and spun her facing away from him.

"Wha—?"

He began unbuttoning the buttons down the back of her dress.

"Marcus!" She tried to twist free.

"Hold still," he commanded, holding fast

to the dress, "or you'll rip the fabric."

Elise reached back, slapping at him, and hit the hard muscle of his hip. She instantly snatched her hand back. He regretted his lack of foresight in not standing closer. An inch or two more, and she might have managed a nice swat to his groin.

"Release me," she growled.

"Not unless you intend to bathe in your clothes." He tugged on the final button, leaving the dress open to her waist.

She grasped the back of her dress, whirling just in time to hide her back from the man who entered with the two pails of cold water she'd requested. She stepped out of his way as he hurried past her and Marcus to pour the water into the tub. He turned and left. The door clicked closed behind him. Elise faced Marcus. He grinned and leaned against the bedpost.

Her eyes narrowed. "Marcus MacGregor."

"I could wash your back—"

"Out!" She pointed to the door.

He sighed, straightening from the bedpost. He started for the door then halted, and faced her. "Mayhap another brandy? It would take me only—"

"Ohhh!" She lunged forward and shoved at his chest.

He took a faltering step back. "It would relax you, lass. Trust—"

Elise released her hold on the back of her dress and used both hands to push even harder. He stepped back several paces until he came up against the door.

"Surely you don't mean to keep all the warm water to yourself," he said.

She leaned into him. "You want to share the water?"

His body tensed. "I would gladly share your bathwater, love."

Elise shoved away from him. "Fine. I will have it sent to your room when I'm done."

Marcus entered the kitchen an hour later to find

Mary sitting by the fire. "How is Elise?"

"I haven't heard a peep. Should I see to her?"

He shook his head. "I will go."

A few minutes later, Marcus opened Elise's door. He froze at the sight of her fast asleep in the tub. Mesmerized, he tried to throttle the dizzying current that raced through him. He had held her intimately. Yet those encounters had not prepared him for the sight of her naked. Earlier, he had teased her mercilessly, knowing full well she wouldn't give in. Now, she lay before him in all her womanly splendor, his for the taking.

In his mind's eye, he saw himself lift her from the water. Her eyes would flutter open to register first surprise, then desire. Desire streaked through him. A blush crept up her neck as he slid is gaze to her breasts. When he pressed her close, the moisture that clung to her skin dampened his shirt. Water dripped from her body and across the floor as he carried her to the bed. He laid her on the bed, coming down on top of her— Marcus jarred from the vision. The throb in his groin deepened and he couldn't halt his gaze from moving down Elise's body, past her breasts, along her stomach to the curls below. He closed his eyes. If he took her now, she might acquiesce but would later blame him, feeling he had taken advantage in a moment of weakness.

God help him, she would be right.

If he took a single step toward her, nothing could call him back.

Marcus whirled. Behind him, sweet victory whispered. Then laughed.

Chapter Ten

Elise awoke the following morning, the lingering warmth of Marcus's body from her dream state so real that she jolted awake upon reaching out and touching only cool sheets beside her. Sadness settled over her. There would be no mornings where they awoke together, no mornings where Marcus pulled her close and kissed her body before slipping inside her.

Tears stung her eyes. This time when she left, there would be no clues, no one to confess that she had gone with Peter McFie. She didn't blame Winnie. When confronted by her master, Winnie had told the truth. Elise expected nothing less. She had gambled and lost. She wouldn't lose a second time. Now, if she could only locate the secret passageway leading from the castle to the outside.

The mantel clock chimed softly. She looked at the clock. Nearly seven. Elise bolted upright. Marcus had likely already gone to the fields. She swung her legs over the side of the bed then paused before rising. He would be preoccupied with final preparations for the celebration starting that night. If she chose the moment with care, he might not overanalyze her request to go to Michael's.

A pang of guilt surfaced. Was the need to check for the notice in the *Sunday Times* worth manipulating him one last time? The question went beyond morality.

When she reached Glasgow, if no ship left immediately for America, she might have to go to another port. London was the best choice. But if the notice was still in the paper could she risk it?

When Elise stepped from the postern door ten minutes later, she spotted Marcus at the front gate. He stood among a group of men, his horse's reins in hand. She hurried across the courtyard toward him. He turned as she neared. A smile spread across his face. When she came within arm's length, he surprised her by dropping the reins and sweeping her into his embrace, then twirling her about.

"Marcus," she breathed, "put me down."

He twirled again. The ground spun around her and she squealed, burying her face in his neck. Her cheek instantly warmed with the contact of his skin. Her breath quickened. Good Lord, she'd forgotten about his open shirt! He stopped and she looked up into his grinning face.

"What brings you here this fine morning?" he asked, still holding her off the ground.

"Put me down," she said. His grin widened, and Elise felt her cheeks flush even warmer. "People are watching."

"Lass," he said, imitating her secretive whisper, "we have no secrets."

Elise glanced at the men who spoke amongst themselves as though she and Marcus weren't there.

"Have you come to wish me a good day?" he asked.

She looked back at him. "Of course."

"Then ye mean to leave me with one of your sweet kisses." He lowered her to the ground.

Her heart sped up.

Marcus's eyes darkened.

There was something warm and enchanting in his humor and, against her better sense, Elise wound an arm around his neck and pulled him to her. Their lips met. Marcus gave a gentle but firm thrust of his tongue against her mouth. She jerked, sure every man present knew of the intimacy, but   Marcus held her another

137

moment before breaking the embrace.

He nuzzled her neck. "You make me feel as though I err going into the fields today."

Elise pulled back and gazed up at him.

He smiled. "Surely my time would be better spent with ye in your bedchamber?"

She drew a sharp breath.

"Nay, sweet." She tried to break away, but he held her fast. "You don't kiss a man thusly and expect him no' to want more."

Elise dropped her gaze to his chest. Warmth flooded her midsection at sight of the tan chest visible through his open shirt. She had sped past embarrassment into idiocy. Michael MacGregor and the *Sunday Times* be damned, she should have stayed in bed.

"It was just a simple kiss," she said.

His masculine laugh rippled through the air. "I would say then that gives me much to look forward to."

She jerked her head up.

Marcus released her. "I had better go." He gave her a roguish wink. "Or I won't be going at all."

"Wait," she said. "I have a request."

"A request?" He turned to test the cinch on his mount's saddle.

"Michael hasn't arrived at Brahan Seer as Erin said he would. Lammas begins tonight, and he promised to be here yesterday. I would like to make a quick visit to see if he is well."

Marcus turned his gaze on her.

"I know there is a lot to do," she added hurriedly. "But I would only go there and back."

"Lass—"

"You can send someone with me. I don't mind."

"'Tis best—"

"You cannot deny me. It isn't right—"

Marcus grabbed her and she yelped as he clamped a hand over her mouth.

"Hush," he said. Eyeing her suspiciously, he loosened his hold, then removed his hand from her mouth altogether. "I will send Erin to fetch his father."

"And if Michael isn't feeling well?"

"I will send someone along with Erin. If Michael is unwell, the man can fetch someone to tend him. Erin will accompany me this morning. I'll send him to his father's this afternoon. They will be back in time for the festivities."

Her heart sank. "I wanted to see for myself that he is well."

"If he feels too poorly to make the trip, he'll need a more experienced doctor."

She scowled. "You think yourself clever, Marcus MacGregor." His mouth twitched and she gave him a dry look. "All right." Before realizing her own intent, she gave him a quick kiss on the jaw.

Surprise flashed in his eyes.

Elise backed away. "I have work to do." She whirled and hurried toward the castle.

A hard day's work hadn't dampened Marcus's anticipation. He spotted Elise standing on the far side of the courtyard, winding her way through the throng gathered in honor of Lammas. Her hair, piled atop her head, left the soft contours of her shoulders bare. With his gaze, he traced the low-cut bodice of the olive green gown that hinted at the tender, creamy flesh of her breasts. She had adorned herself with MacGregor colors—his colors. A red and green sash of *plaide* crossed one shoulder and fastened at her waist. She paused in the crowd to speak to one person, then another.

Musicians struck up, fiddle and bagpipe leading the music, and the crowd cleared the center of the courtyard for those who joined in dance. Brian MacGregor swept Elise into the barn dance being played. She threw her head back, her delight in her companion obvious. Marcus waited a few turns, then caught them as they neared.

"You can't keep the lady to yourself, Brian," he

said.

"Laird," Brian replied, and released his hold on Elise.

Marcus pulled her close. The music ended. He remained motionless, his gaze holding hers until the band began *The Scottish*. He realized the quickening of her breath in the rise and fall of her breasts as he swung her to the right in unison with other dancers.

Her gaze broke from his, her lashes dropping demurely. A tremor passed through him. Was she toying with him? Her fingers tightened on his shoulder as he executed a quick turn. Elise leaned into him, her hair brushing his jaw. She tipped her head up slightly. He felt her breath against his neck. A tiny smile lifted one corner of her mouth, then her brow puckered.

"Is something wrong?" she asked.

"Nay, love."

"You seem deep in thought."

Marcus dodged another couple who strayed perilously close, then looked down at her. "I was thinking how I would like to take you from here and ravish your sweet body until you cry 'enough!'" Her mouth parted in a tiny gasp and he went on. "Then I would slowly and methodically make love to every inch of your body until you lie exhausted beneath me."

She stumbled. If not for his tight grasp, she would have fallen. Delighted, he pulled her closer. "I see the idea appeals to you."

Her gaze dropped. When she brought her eyes back to bear on him, she looked at him through her lashes, a shy expression on her face. "I can only wonder, sir, if you have the strength to fulfill such outlandish claims."

Deviltry played in her eyes, and Marcus felt his body harden at seeing more than a little curiosity mixed in the bargain. "Aye." He pressed her more intimately against him. "I have the strength."

Her intake of breath told him she felt his arousal.

"Do you not agree?" he asked.

She remained silent for a moment. The noise of the

crowd filled the air, the music winding between the spaces as if for them alone.

Her eyes darkened, and she said, "It occurs to me, milord, that if you fulfilled such a promise, logic dictates it would be *you* who lay exhausted on top of me."

"Indeed?" he said with the raise of an amused brow.

He whirled her into the final spin of the dance before the music ended. The dance crowd dispersed and new couples assembled as the music began again. They stood, still in each other's arms. She moved to step away, but he held her fast. She gave him a quizzical look.

"Come, take a walk with me, love," he said.

The dancers began dancing around them.

Elise shook her head. "You can't abandon your guests, and I promised Winnie I would help with the food." She pushed his arms from her and backed away.

A couple danced between them. He saw the bemused look the woman gave Elise and realized she had seen it too. She was clear of the dancers now.

"I had better go see if any help is needed in the kitchen," she shouted above the music.

Marcus watched her turn and hurry away. So, the little minx had ventured a dip in the waters only to yank her foot back when it had been nibbled. Perhaps next time he would simply yank her in.

Marcus hadn't considered the possibility that Elise would wish to accompany the women the following day on the yearly tradition of swimming in the cool waters of Loch Katrine. Now, the procession had started and, per his order, his guards had stopped her from passing beyond the gates. He grimaced at seeing her agitated pacing as he approached. She stopped and glared at him.

"Do you mean to keep me here while the other women go to the loch?" Her narrowed eyes dared him answer *yes*.

"John," he called to the nearest guard, "fetch another man and the two of you accompany the women to the loch."

John's eyes widened. He cast a quick glance at Elise, then jerked his attention back to Marcus.

Marcus gave him a dry look. "You are to watch for trouble, John, not the lasses."

Marcus looked back at Elise and stifled a laugh at the tight-lipped look on her face. Apparently she didn't care for being singled out with an escort. Imagine how she would feel when he came for her in a short while. The most important part of the tradition was allowing the women enough time to discard their dresses and frolic in the water. The men later followed to engage them in a sporting game of chase.

Elise abruptly whirled and strode through the gates down the path.

"Hurry, lad," Marcus urged. "She's getting away."

John called to a man on the wall, then hurried through the gates after her.

Marcus turned his attention to Elise's retreating back. "Any antics, lass, and I'll turn you over my knee."

She didn't acknowledge the threat, but he knew she'd heard him. His first wife, Jenna, hadn't been predisposed to clan traditions and never participated in the game. This year, he had reason to participate. Elise disappeared from view down the path. She didn't understand the game. She soon would.

Twenty minutes later, unable to resist the idea of Elise's scantily clad body gliding through the water, Marcus emerged from the trees at the bottom of the mountainside. He hurried across the twenty-foot clearing where he ducked behind one of the larger patches of juniper bushes lining the jagged shoreline.

Peering through the foliage and across the rocky shore, he witnessed the exact scene he had imagined. Elise, stripped to her chemise, dove into the blue waters of Loch Katrine along with the other giggling women. The thin cotton chemise she wore the night he accosted her in his library revealed far more than the heavy flannel the women wore in the interest of modesty during this adventure, but he envisioned the revealing shadows he knew would be visible through the wet material. A giddy anticipation settled in his stomach. She would, at first, be furious. With gentle persuasion, however…

Marcus emerged from his hiding place and strode to the shore's edge. The women splashed one another, the recipients shrieking when their companions' aim found a mark. A woman squealed. He had been spotted. Elise looked his way. Just as he thought, the surprise on her face said she hadn't been informed of this part of the game. He suspected that, if she knew the real reason behind the yearly ritual, she would have declined participation. She insisted on being a part of Brahan Seer; logic dictated that she receive full measure.

Eyes steady on her, Marcus stripped off his boots. He stepped into the loch, his shins, then thighs, slicing through the water as he ventured deeper. The women blazed a path for him, shrieking with delight while Elise remained frozen.

"You had better move, lass," one woman called. "He's coming for ye, and if he catches you…" Peals of laughter followed.

Elise's eyes abruptly shifted and she scanned her surroundings before returning to him. Marcus smiled. Her eyes narrowed, then she dove into the water. He halted, waiting for her to resurface. Seconds ticked by and she didn't reappear. He scanned the water. A sudden round of triumphant shouts went up from the women and he whirled to see Elise rising from the water some thirty feet behind him. She started for the shore, her progress labored through the hip-deep water. By God, he would have to put his back into it to catch her before she reached her clothes! She glanced back, throwing him a satisfied smirk.

Oh ho! She may not have known the game, but she caught on fast. Marcus dove into the water, his strong strokes speeding him through the deeper water until he reached knee deep. He rose, the water no longer a hindrance to his fast pumping legs. His feet pounded onto the shore and, with a burst of energy, he closed the gap between them. In a final sprint, he dove for her, his arms encircling her waist as he brought her to the ground.

Elise sputtered and he realized she had gotten a mouthful of sandy dirt.

"Oh!" she spat. "Let me go!"

Marcus allowed her to thrash in his grasp until she had twisted into a prone position facing him. He settled his weight on her. She beat at his chest. He chuckled and hugged her closer, trapping her arms between them.

"Let me go!" she howled, kicking her heels on the ground like a spoiled child.

Marcus tried looking innocent but knew he failed miserably. "Nay."

"What in God's name are you doing? Why have you attacked me? This is an outrage!" Her voice rose as she twisted in a serious effort to dislodge him.

"Now, why do you say that, love? I am only playing with you."

She looked at him as if he had lost his mind. Her eyes narrowed to slits. "One does not attack a defenseless woman."

"Lass, I think you are anything but defenseless. Although, I am enjoying myself at your expense." Marcus bent his head to whisper in her ear, "The women didn't explain the game."

He went on to explain how, each year, the women came to the loch, and their men later followed. Those with wives sought them out, some in sport, some with the intentions of a child arriving nine months later. Those wanting to make a woman their wife came with the hope that the love play would lead to the consummation of a betrothal. When Marcus finished, a blush had made its way from Elise's cheek to the delicate ear he'd been whispering into.

"*No*," she said, her eyes wide.

144

Marcus grinned. "Aye."

She looked past him and he glanced over his shoulder to find several women regarding them with interest.

"I would like to get up now," Elise said.

He looked back at her. "Aye." He came to his knees. Before she could rise, he slid his arms beneath her, cupping her to his chest.

She gave him an impatient shove as he rose. "Set me down."

Marcus assumed a thoughtful expression. "Nay. I have won and deserve my reward."

Elise lifted a brow. "Just what reward would that be, sir?"

He grinned. Aye, she had learned the game. He stepped behind the cover of the bushes he had occupied earlier and paused, uncertain what he wanted to do with her. Marcus laughed inwardly. He knew exactly what he wanted to do with her. He simply hadn't decided how to go about it. One thing he did know, however, he was enjoying the feel of her wet chemise against him far too much to release her just yet.

He kissed her. She pushed against his chest and Marcus realized she wasn't about to let him make love to her in plain sight of the other women. He laid her on the ground and came down upon her, gently this time. He tugged her chemise high enough to free her legs and settle between them. Her grip on his shoulders tightened. He kissed her again. Hard. She tensed.

"Shh," he soothed. "Let me please you."

He slid a moist kiss down her cheek, then along her neck. "Just a little love play," he whispered.

He didn't intend on taking her there, tumbling her like a serving wench, but please her, he would. Slowly, he smoothed a hand along her outer thigh. Grasping her chemise, he bunched it until his fingers touched the soft flesh beneath. Elise turned her head, her cheek against his, and placed a kiss on his jaw. Marcus breathed deep.

He slipped his hand   beneath her and cupped

her buttocks. "I swear to only please you this time."

"We aren't—" She gasped as he lifted her buttocks, meeting her flesh with a gentle rotation of his shaft against her sex.

Her breath came quicker. He caressed her buttocks, her hip. A distant pounding of hooves stabbed through the cloud of desire. He paused, his hand on her pelvis. Again, a distant sound—a roll of thunder? He lifted his head. In a flash, the memory of the dream he'd had while at Declan's washed over him.

Elise's grip on his shoulder tightened. "What is it?"

Shrieks sounded.

The women.

Marcus shoved to his knees. He peered through the bushes. Riding like hell hounds toward them were seven Campbell warriors.

Seven, his mind repeated calmly, *not an army like that in his dream. Only seven.*

He leapt to his feet.

"Who are they?" Elise called.

His hand shot to his side. Bloody hell, he'd left his sword at the keep. *Foolish mistake.* Marcus swung his gaze to the two warriors sent to guard the women. He made out the red of their *plaide* behind bushes thirty feet down shore. He glanced up the mountainside at Brahan Seer. Why were no warriors charging down the hill? They must have seen the riders.

Elise scrambled to her feet and Marcus whirled. He shoved her to the ground. "Do not move!" He turned back to watch the Campbells approach.

The women shrieked. Those on the shore raced for the water, joining their comrades who had taken to deeper waters.

"Marcus!" Elise cried.

He looked to see her standing, then glanced at the oncoming men. His heart thumped wildly. *Had they seen her?* Marcus grabbed her wrist, yanking her back to the ground.

"Nell," she said, struggling to rise and pointing to
146

the right of their hiding place.

Marcus looked. There, sleeping soundly on the shore, lay Nell, a young maid who had only last week begun working in the castle. Despite the ruckus, she didn't stir. Marcus recalled that she was deaf in one ear. His heart leapt into his throat.

"Do not move," he ground out, and turned back to peer through the bush.

The other women had swum safely to deeper waters. Someone cried out Nell's name, but the girl didn't wake. Marcus looked at the Campbells. Two of the seven comrades reached the women's clothes and halted. More shrieks came from the women as they swam farther from shore. The two Campbells scanned the frantic women but made no move to pursue them.

One of the Campbells said something indistinguishable. Marcus strained to make out the other's response but without success. They continued to scrutinize the women, their attention moving farther to the right where Nell lay. They would see her in an instant. Marcus stood and stepped around the bush into full sight. He took two paces in the direction of his warriors' hiding place.

"Look!" one of the Campbells shouted, and the other turned in Marcus's direction.

Marcus spied a large piece of driftwood. He hurried the few paces to the wood and snatched it up. He kept his gaze on the Campbell who had called out as he snapped off two small branches and dropped them. Four of the five remaining Campbells joined their companions.

"Ha!" one of the newcomers exclaimed. "The MacGregor thinks to bring us down with a stick of wood."

The man unsheathed his sword and kicked his horse's belly. The beast lunged forward. The man bore down upon Marcus and swung his sword. Marcus deflected the blow with the driftwood as the horse shot past, and pivoted full circle, hitting the man across the back with the wood. A loud crack sounded and the man fell to the ground limp. Two more Campbells spurred their horses toward him.

He sprang forward, headed for the fallen Campbell's sword. He reached the weapon with a dive, barely missing the sweep of an oncoming rider's sword. The Campbell barreled past while his companion wheeled his horse hard right to intercept. The Campbells nearest the shore shouted and two more of them shot toward Marcus.

Marcus sprang to his feet, his steel meeting that of the man who had cut him off. Marcus faltered a step under the power of his opponent's swing. The man parried left, smiling as though already tasting victory. Marcus saw the man's fingers tighten around his mount's reins and, just as the horse turned, Marcus thrust his sword into his midsection. He twisted the weapon, then yanked it free.

The man cried out. He clutched his belly and slumped forward in the saddle. Blood gushed despite the arm he wrapped around himself. Marcus leapt forward and grabbed his shoulder. The Campbell swatted at him, his blood-soaked arm leaving a streak of blood down his arm, but Marcus's fingers found purchase, and he yanked him from the saddle.

Marcus grabbed the pummel and pulled himself into the saddle in time to see his two men close in on the Campbell warrior who had shot past him. The man gave a violent slap of reins against his steed's rump in an effort to elude them. John lunged forward, swinging the blunt side of his sword across the horse's knee. The horse stumbled, then fell to his knees, throwing its rider. Marcus wheeled his mount around to face the two Campbells who were nearly upon him when the thunder of hooves rolled down the mountainside. He cut his gaze to the left and saw a dozen MacGregor warriors speeding downhill.

A woman cried out, then Elise shouted, "Marcus! They have Nell!"

He jerked his attention to the girl. His gut wrenched when one Campbell rounded his attention on

Elise and stared. Marcus yanked his horse's reins to the right. The animal whirled and Marcus dug his heels into its flanks. In four great strides, he met his opponent's sword with his own. The Campbell pulled his mount hard left. Marcus gave his horse a fierce kick. The horse charged and he thrust his sword into the Campbell's side even as the man's gaze met his.

The man's eyes bulged. He reached out as if to grab Marcus. Marcus yanked his sword from the man's body. The man's mouth worked. Marcus whirled his horse toward the warrior who had captured Nell. The guards from Brahan Seer flew across the shore in his path, Erin in the lead.

"Erin!" Marcus shouted, then to one of the other men, "You!" Both men broke from their party and spun toward him. "Take her back to the keep." He jabbed his sword in Elise's direction. "Erin, you're with me."

In an instant, the warrior reached Elise. She shook her head.

"Take her!" Marcus ordered, and slapped the reins across his horse's rump.

He drove his mount, staying a nose ahead of Erin. Nell's heels unexpectedly kicked the belly of the Campbell's horse.

Fight, lass, fight! Marcus urged.

The Campbell's fisted hand rose and he tensed. The fist fell hard and Nell went limp. Marcus's blood froze.

The ground softened as the shores of Loch Katrine changed from rocky sand to marsh. Marcus smiled coldly. One had to know the land well to ride this section of the shore, which the Campbell warrior did not. The man's horse faltered. He glanced over his shoulder, then flung Nell to the ground. Erin cried out. An even darker rage shot through Marcus.

They reached Nell.

"Take her home!" Marcus shouted without stopping.

The Campbell's horse stumbled again, then crashed to the ground, pinning his rider's leg

149

beneath him. The animal struggled to rise, gave a shrill whinny, then heaved his full weight onto the man's leg. The Campbell arched in pain. After an instant's heavy breathing, he craned his head in Marcus's direction. Marcus lifted his sword. In ten seconds, the warrior would be his. The man shoved frantically at the horse's back, his gaze glued on Marcus.

Marcus tightened his grip on the sword. The man's gaze shifted to the raised weapon. He leveraged a foot on the horse's back, pushing with all his might. Marcus discerned strain in his arm muscles as, with one great heave, the man slid his leg from beneath the horse.

The warrior scrambled to his knees, lunging for his sword as Marcus raised his weapon and cried, *"Buadhaich!"* With one mighty swing of the claymore, Marcus sliced across the man's neck.

Marcus wheeled his horse around and, his gaze straight ahead, tread over the body as he raced toward home.

Chapter Eleven

Marcus closed the door of his library with a deceptively soft click and raked his gaze across the men standing in tense silence. "We have a traitor. When I discover who that man is—" His glare halted on his father, who sat in the chair nearest the hearth. Marcus caught the glitter of Cameron's eyes in the firelight before swinging his attention to Daniel. "You have made the changes in security?"

"Aye, laird," Daniel said, his mouth grim.

"Marcus," his father began.

"Aye?" Marcus took two paces and halted abruptly beside his desk.

Cameron sighed.

"The attack took place during the mid-afternoon change of guard." Marcus's words shook with the rage of self-reproach. "I should have realized—bloody hell, my thoughts were on what awaited me at the loch, just like those men who were hurrying from their duty at the wall. 'Tis true," he said, the reproach turned to bitterness, "logic bows to a man's cock."

He had always been prepared. The men who guarded the walls monitored the village to the east, the loch to the west, and the valley that stretched for miles to the south. The weight of guilt bore down in greater measure. His people depended upon him. Yet the enemy found a crack in his defenses. A shudder ran through him. Nell had very nearly been a casualty of his carelessness. Had Katie's life been forfeit because of such negligence? Aye, she still lived, her heart beat, she breathed, but her mind had ceased to work. Her spirit lay hidden in some dark corner of her being. He had failed her, as he had nearly failed—

Marcus slammed his fist down on the desk. "Who informed the Campbells of the routine? They attacked our women before our very eyes. Why such a bold move?"

Cameron answered in a low voice, "It doesn't seem strange to ye, lad, that we've had Campbells on our land three times in as many months?"

Marcus's mouth hardened. "Aye. But why?"

"Mayhap the why and who are the same?"

Marcus stilled. "What do you mean?"

They stared at one another for a moment before Cameron said to the men, "Lads, leave me with my son."

The men filed out, the last closing the door behind him.

Cameron looked at Marcus. "You mean to say you don't know?" Marcus only looked at him and his father went on, "You know well enough the trouble began with Elise."

"Aye, they are using her—"

"You are sure it's them using her?"

Marcus started. A surge of anger rammed through him, the first genuine hostility he'd ever felt for his father. "Bloody hell, Cameron, you're saying Elise is in league with the Campbells. They nearly killed her."

"Nay," Cameron replied. "In fact, the lass returned in remarkably good shape."

"The tracks I saw say otherwise."

"You are a fine tracker, but you are no master. You should have had Johnson—"

"I did take Johnson, if you recall," Marcus interrupted.

"But he did not see the tracks you interpreted as her capture."

"I made no mistake in my interpretation. What has

happened? You were in favor of my having her."

"Aye," Cameron said. "And I like her. But that does not change the fact she is the most likely suspect."

Elise's expression when he sent John with her to the loch came to mind. She had been angry. Any woman would be angry. He had nearly imprisoned her—and why?

"She lived here four months before I arrived with no such trouble," Marcus insisted.

"Mayhap the Campbells intended you to want her so they could use her against you."

Marcus laughed harshly. "The woman who escaped the Campbells was no collaborator. Nay, Cameron, you have no grounds for suspicion."

"How long have they hated us?" his father demanded with more vehemence than he'd heard in his voice since before his mother's death.

Blood lust shot through Marcus. "I will kill every last one of them."

"Aye. And condemn more men to die. What of their wives—their children?"

"We have dealt with them for years—centuries," Marcus snapped.

Cameron grunted. "King George is likely to tire completely of the fight and finance the MacGregor's annihilation."

Though King George had remained quiet, Marcus knew the king forbade any Campbell reprisal after Marcus attacked Assipatle in retaliation for Katie MacGregor's rape. His intervention had saved many lives. But the sovereign's mood swung between reality and fantasy, his mind controlled by liquor and the laudanum he kept ready at his bedside. Where his loyalties would lie tomorrow was anyone's guess.

"If he takes that course of action, he'll regret it as long as I draw breath," Marcus bit back.

Cameron slumped against the chair cushion. "I dinna' want to bury my only son." He looked directly into Marcus's eyes. "You have a son. What will be his legacy?"

153

"By God, Cameron, you would have me believe Elise is a spy and, in the same breath, demand I change the course of the raging river that is the Campbells." He strode to the door. "I will keep you apprised of my progress in discovering our traitor's identity." He yanked open the door. "Rest assured, when I find the guilty party—no matter who they are—there will be no place for them on this earth, save the grave."

Minutes later, Marcus entered the kitchen and scanned the busy room. "Winnie, where's Elise?"

Winnie turned from the counter, tray in hand, and handed it to a girl waiting nearby. "With Nell."

"Nell?" he demanded in a voice which quieted the bustle in the kitchen.

"Aye."

"Elise dared leave the keep after today—and especially at night?"

"So far as I know, she did not step foot outside the walls. I settled Nell in my cottage. With her mother dead and her aunt run off to wed, Elise offered to sit with her." He winced when Winnie added, "I feared leaving her alone." Winnie grasped a pitcher of water sitting on the cabinet. "Back to work," she ordered the women, shoving the pitcher toward a girl who took it and scurried toward the great hall. Winnie focused again on him.

"Elise will not be here for the evening meal then?" he asked.

"I sent their meals to my cottage."

Marcus gave a curt nod, then strode past the women and out the back door.

When he arrived at the cottage, he knocked lightly. Hearing no answer, he pushed the door open to find food sitting on the table untouched and both women missing. Marcus hurried back to the castle. He looked in Elise's room. His heart rate kicked up at finding it empty. He went next to the ladies' drawing room, but even as he opened the door he sensed the silence.

Dread coiled tight in his gut at sight of the empty

room. If she wasn't inside the keep and she hadn't attempted to pass through the gates, only one answer remained: she had left through the passageway leading from the dungeons. Why go to such lengths to leave unseen? His father's words earlier returned, *"...she is the most likely suspect."* He remembered her agitation when he sent John with her. She couldn't be the traitor, it simply wasn't possible. *Why,* his mind asked? *Because you love her?*

"Yes," he snarled, and slammed the door.

She could be in his library. But even the warmth that wafted out to meet him as he opened the library door didn't dispel the deadly silence. He looked at the chair his father had occupied earlier—the chair he had discovered Elise curled up in on many occasions. *"Mayhap the why and the who are the same,"* his father had said.

Marcus shook himself from the vise which gripped him, then closed the door on the vacant room. He considered employing more men in the search. Nay. If he found evidence of her culpability, he would deal with her before he could change his mind. He strode down the corridor, continuing through the castle until reaching the last sconce burning in that wing of the castle. He disengaged the light from the wall, then took the final steps to the staircase leading into the bowels of Brahan Seer.

Narrow step after narrow step, Marcus wound his way down to what, during his grandfather's rule, had been dungeons where he incarcerated criminals such as the one who betrayed them that afternoon. He paused in the long corridor before one of the cells and gave the door a shove. With a grinding creak, the heavy iron swung open. The sconce's flame jumped as if gasping for breath.

Marcus settled his gaze on the iron shackles hanging on the far wall in open defiance of time's passage. How would a woman survive chained in those irons? If Elise braved these dungeons, had even a tremor passed through her when she hurried by these rooms of torture? What sort of woman entered such a place?

A woman with something to hide.

He hurried past the cell to the next right turn, stopping at the sudden dead end. Squatting, Marcus lowered the sconce and slowly edged the light forward in order to examine the stone floor and discerned a single set of boot prints beneath the thin layer of dust. His heart pounded against his chest. He jerked the sconce up, searching the wall for the hairline crack recognizable only to one who knew it existed. He found the seam and depressed the spot. The panel sprang open with a squeal.

Marcus rose and stepped inside the passageway. Sconce low, he proceeded slowly, inspecting the packed dirt floor until he reached the end of the passageway. He faced left where lay the concealed door which opened to the outside and pushed against the door. The stone slid noiselessly open and he stepped into the night.

Ten minutes later, Marcus entered the kitchen again. "Elise is not to be found." He stopped before Winnie.

"Surely ye aren't worried," she said, but Marcus had caught the flicker of surprise in her expression.

"Who took the meal to them?"

"Bartholomew."

He started for the door.

"By now he's on duty at the wall," she called as he disappeared into the darkness.

Moments later, Marcus mounted the battlement stairs and found Bartholomew standing guard on the west corner of the wall. The guard straightened at his approach.

"You delivered the food to the women in Winnie's cottage?" Marcus demanded.

"Aye, laird."

"Were the women in the cottage when you arrived?"

Bartholomew shook his head.

Marcus narrowed his eyes. "And you thought nothing of it?"

He swallowed. "I didn't know I should."

Marcus hesitated, then turned and hurried along the battlements and down the stairs. He returned to Winnie's cottage but found nothing changed.

This time, when he entered the kitchen, Winnie halted the task of pulling scones from their baking pan and watched his approach.

He stopped beside the table. "They weren't in the cottage when Bartholomew delivered the meal."

Her gaze moved past him.

"What's wrong?" came Elise's voice at his back.

He pivoted to face her. Nell stood alongside her. "Where the blazes have you been?"

Elise's brow snapped into a frown.

"Well?"

"We were on the hill, near the storehouse," she replied.

Marcus looked at Nell.

"Aye, laird, we—" she looked at Elise.

"What is it?" he demanded.

"We were star gazing," Elise said in a reprimand.

He glanced at her, then looked back at Nell. "You two have been together all evening?"

"Aye," she said, obviously confused.

"By God," he muttered, and advanced toward them. Elise blinked and Nell retreated a pace, but he continued forward. When within reach of them, he grabbed Elise's wrist and started toward the great hall. Several men stared from the doorway.

"Be about your business," he ordered.

The men scattered in a hurried scuffle as he pulled Elise through the doorway and into the noisy hall. The din quieted slightly, men parting as he strode to the stairway.

"Marcus, what—"

"Hush," he commanded without looking back at her.

She didn't balk until they reached the door to her bedchamber. There, she yanked her hand free of his grasp.

He whirled on her. "Where were you?"

"I told you."

"I searched all of Brahan Seer."

"Clearly not all, or you would have found us. Ridiculous," she added in a mutter. "You act as if we need worry while inside the keep."

"Worry?" he repeated. "The Campbells meant harm, Elise. Did you think I would let them touch you?"

Her brow furrowed. He discerned the quick lift and fall of her breasts, the surprise—uncertainty perhaps? His body tightened. He realized the desire to take her with quick and hard actions.

"No," she replied.

He jarred from the erotic picture of her against the wall, him pressed between her legs. "Seeing you"—she faltered—"seeing them…" She shook her head, ending with a quiet, "It was strange."

"The Highlands are far more violent than Boston," he shot back.

She hesitated and his blood chilled when he realized it wasn't the violence of the Highlands that had startled her, but the violence in him. He felt anew the cut of his sword through Campbell flesh. He tensed, this time in fury.

"God damn bastards," he whispered, "they knew exactly what they were doing."

"What do you mean?"

He watched her carefully. "They knew when to attack—were aware of our weakness."

"Weakness?"

"Their attack coincided with the change of guard."

A tiny pause, then she said, "But that would mean—" She gasped. "That's not possible."

"Aye, 'tis not only possible, but true."

She shook her head vehemently. "I don't believe it."

The swirl of her hair, the tight-lipped determination, cut Marcus to the quick and he suddenly wished for nothing more than to hold her, to feel her heart beat against his chest as she slept in his arms. She fastened her gaze on him and he registered the lines of strain around her eyes.

"To bed," he said, and opened her bedchamber door. "And don't leave your room again this night."

She started to protest, but he shoved her inside and closed the door behind her. Marcus still gripped the handle. God damn it, he'd allowed his father's suspicions to poison his thoughts. Elise had been with Nell all evening. She wasn't the traitor... unless she had made those boot prints in the dungeon some time before tonight.

The following afternoon, Marcus entered his library to find Elise sitting in the chair before a low burning fire, looking just as he prayed he'd find her the night before. She jumped, the book she was clearly not reading sliding from her lap to the carpet.

He closed the door behind him. "You are the most unpredictable creature."

She bent to retrieve the book. "What have I done now?" She placed the book beside her on the chair.

Marcus walked to her and squatted beside the chair. He ran a finger down her arm. "Nothing, love. I'm preparing to leave for London and my mind is elsewhere." He smiled slightly. "It is my own shortcomings that plague me today. Not you."

Elise frowned. "Your shortcomings?"

He rose and strode to the sideboard "Never mind." He poured a drink. "It doesn't concern you."

A pause followed, then she said, "I think it does."

At her clipped tone, he looked over his shoulder. Her lips were pursed. Despite his mood, he smiled ruefully.

"I am no fool, Marcus MacGregor," she said.

He raised a brow.

"What shortcomings?" she demanded.

Marcus remained silent.

She shrugged. "I can easily find out."

He turned, leaving his drink untouched, and leaned against the sideboard. "How do you propose to do that?"

Elise slid him a sidelong glance. "Milord, do you think you are the only one with powers of persuasion?"

The sensual lift of her mouth startled him. He couldn't believe it. Was the little minx threatening to use her charms against him? A thrill reverberated deep within him. Lounging against the chair, she tipped her head back. His excitement grew as, closing her eyes, she reached back to tousle her hair. The locks cascaded in silken layers about her shoulders. Her fingers slid from her hair and along her throat. His body tightened when her fingertips skimmed the valley between her breasts. Her palms flattened across her belly, smoothing her dress, and finally came to rest in her lap. She toyed with him—but he wanted her. He commanded his gaze to break from the sultry picture, but his mind refused to comply.

Elise patted the tiny space on the seat beside her. "Come sit with me, milord."

Her use of "milord" tantalized him, despite the knowledge she used the title only when angry or mocking him. "Nay, lass. I think not."

"Afraid?" She gave a low laugh.

Confound the woman! She hadn't even bothered to open her eyes when addressing him.

"Not afraid, love," he replied. "Cautious."

"Ah, I see."

Aye, he was sure she did.

She stretched her legs in one fluid motion. She opened her eyes and, leaning forward, shook out her skirt, a flash of white chemise showing before the fabric settled about her. She rose and glided over to him.

"If you're not in the mood," she tugged the collar on his shirt, "we can discuss this later."

She smoothed his shirt with the same maddening

slowness she had used when straightening her dress. When her fingers tucked his shirt into the waistband of his kilt, he yanked her to him.

"You're playing with fire," he said.

She gazed up at him. "Am I?"

He bent to kiss her, but she dodged his mouth. He lifted a questioning brow and she met his gaze.

"You won't sit with me yet have no qualms about accosting me? Are you not tired?' she asked abruptly.

"Nay."

"Good. Then we shall talk."

Extricating herself from his hold, she wrapped a hand around his forearm and led him to the couch. Elise directed him down onto a cushion, then knelt on the cushion beside him.

"You are much too tense." She turned his back toward her.

With great care, she massaged the hard muscle of his shoulder. Marcus felt himself relax. He closed his eyes, contemplating ways to entice her hands lower. He became aware of her breath on his neck. He throbbed, anticipating her quick intake of breath when her gaze fell upon the noticeable lift of his kilt. She shifted and her breath came hot in his ear. Marcus shuddered as her lips brushed his ear.

"It wasn't your fault, you know."

His eyes flashed open and he twisted to face her. "I will not discuss this with you."

She shrugged, then nearly bounced into a sitting position beside him. "That doesn't change the fact I'm right."

"You know nothing of it," he snapped.

"I know enough."

Marcus faced her. Words poured from his mouth even as he blushed at defending his actions to a woman—especially this woman. "It is my responsibility to see that no harm comes to any here. I nearly failed."

"But you didn't."

The flat response brought him up short.

She shook her head   as if speaking to a child.

161

"You found a flaw in your defenses. Do you think it's the only one?"

Fear rushed through him. He hadn't considered there could be a single flaw, much less two, three or…

Elise took his hand in hers. "You aren't God. Close, perhaps," she gave a faint smile, "but still human. I understand how difficult this is, but you must accept the fact that, like most mortals, you are flawed." She paused. "Those attackers will never harm another person, and you learned a valuable lesson. Most would count themselves fortunate. Don't look so sullen. I am sure you will find a way to assuage your anger."

Marcus blinked, then grasped her shoulders and tugged her across his thighs. He pressed his lips to her ear and murmured, "What am I to do with you?"

Elise lifted a brow, saying, "Certainly not what you think," and gingerly shifted in his lap.

Marcus looked past his father and the other people crowding the courtyard until his gaze fixed upon Elise. She stood with a group of women, rifling through a basket of provisions they were distributing to the men who were to accompany him to London.

Cameron clasped his shoulder. "All will be well." He glanced meaningfully at Elise, his hand dropping back to his side.

Marcus focused on his father. "She isn't to leave Brahan Seer while I am away."

"Aye."

"If Loudoun doesn't agree to intervene with his clansmen, I will seek an audience with King George."

Cameron nodded. "The earl willna' relish the possibility of losing his property to one of our attacks. Castle Kalchurn is his pride and joy."

"I plan on using that fact," Marcus replied. He nodded toward Elise. "I had better say my good-byes."

Marcus strode to Elise. The warrior she handed a small cloth package to grasped it and murmured thanks before joining his nearby comrades. She turned, taking a surprised step back when she nearly collided with Marcus.

"You will honor your promise?" he asked.

"I won't leave Brahan Seer."

She couldn't leave. He had seen to that. The passageway had been boarded shut and the guards had orders not to let her pass. Marcus drew her to him. His heart pounded with every halting step closer she allowed until he could wrap his arm around her. Marcus cupped her neck in his free hand. Her gaze flitted to the side, but he cared nothing for the crowd. He kissed her. The familiar hunger lashed out. Had she any understanding of his need for her? She had called it lust. By God, he did lust after her.

Marcus took a long draught of her. When he returned, he would have set in motion what he should have done a month ago: discover her identity. He released her and motioned to the man who stood near the gate holding his horse's reins. The man pushed through the crowd and stopped beside him, reins extended. Marcus mounted, then paused, locking gazes with Elise.

"Elise."

She waited.

"I will return."

It seemed she didn't breathe.

"Be ready when I do."

Three days away from Brahan Seer—from Elise— had taken a toll. Marcus looked up from the letter he was reading to the grandfather clock in the far corner of the study in his London home. He curbed a growing irritation. He'd been forced to follow the Earl of Loudoun to London, and now that Marcus awaited his arrival, the fool had the temerity to be late. Marcus finished the drink sitting before him, then returned his attention to the note sent to him by Margaret's father, Lord Ross.

Marcus, the note began, *I was unexpectedly called to*

London and have just learned of your arrival two days ago.
He gave a low laugh. "You hate London nearly as much
as I do. What story did Margaret concoct to coerce you
into accompanying her?" Marcus continued reading the
note. *Lady Ross is giving a ball tomorrow evening. I trust
you will have time to attend.* Marcus tossed the invitation
aside. "You trust wrong, Ferris. I have no interest in
seeing your daughter."

Marcus looked up from reading the *Sunday Times*
when a knock sounded on the door nearly an hour later.
The door opened and his butler entered.

"The Earl of Loudoun to see you, Lord Ashlund."

Marcus glanced at the clock. An hour and a half
late. "Show him in, Bower." Marcus refolded the paper
and laid it on the desk as Loudoun entered.

He bowed. "Lord Ashlund, it has been some time."

Marcus indicated the chair in front of his desk. "It
has," he said, noting Loudoun hadn't had the good
grace to acknowledge his tardiness. It was impossible
to civilize a cur.

The earl seated himself. "I understand you wish to
see me on a matter of some importance." Bored
amusement shone in his green eyes.

"Have you seen your Hastings clansmen lately?"
Marcus asked without preamble.

Surprise flitted across Loudoun's features, but he
replied, the boredom reaching his voice, "Haven't been
to Scotland in an age. Why?"

"They attacked a group of women at Brahan Seer."

Surprise resurfaced. Then... satisfaction in the
guise of disbelief. "Come now," he drawled. "Surely,
you are mistaken."

"I was there."

"I suppose one cannot question the word of the
Marquess of Ashlund. Was your father, the duke, there
as well?"

"Nay. You know anything of the attack?"

"Me?" The earl laughed. "I never involve myself in

the petty squabbles on that side of the family." He studied Marcus. "Attacked your women, did they?"

Marcus nodded.

Loudoun shrugged. "Probably just wanted a bit of sport. Why bother yourself? If someone had been hurt or if it had been cattle—"

"Do not try my temper," Marcus cut in. "You know nothing of it?"

"As I said, I have little to do with those barbarians."

"In that you may be wise. I assume you still exercise some authority over them?"

"I suppose so. Can't say I've ever cared to try. Their actions are their own, so long as they don't interfere with my life."

"Spoken like a true Campbell," Marcus muttered.

Loudoun's eyes flickered, and there was a biting edge in his cultured voice when he said, "Unlike you, Ashlund, I am far removed from those people. I don't live in the wilds of Scotland, yearning for the days of old."

"It isn't the days of old I yearn for, but, like any civilized man, simple peace. Yet, it is *your* clansmen who make that impossible."

"Mayhap you should appeal to our king. He is in a better position than I to help."

"Mayhap," Marcus agreed. "Unfortunately, he's not in England. I should warn you, if trouble arises before he returns, you may find your clansmen intruding upon your life. Castle Kalchurn is between Brahan Seer and Assipattle, if I recall."

The earl's face tightened. "You have no cause to threaten me, MacGregor. I've done nothing. I am not involved in this matter, I tell you."

"Ah, but you are. Despite your complacent attitude, you would not be saddened to hear of my demise or the demise of any MacGregor, for that matter—man or woman—which makes you as guilty as your kinsmen. Now," Marcus leaned forward, elbows on his desk, "if there's a   possibility you can get to the bottom of this before it turns into something we will all regret, you would find me most appreciative."

"Just what the devil does that mean?" Loudoun demanded.

"It means, my dear Earl, that I might refrain from running a sword through your black heart."

Marcus found Kiernan at his favorite club. Pausing to observe his son as he lounged in one of the plush chairs, pride filled his heart at the man the boy was becoming. Kiernan's brow furrowed in response to something he read in the paper spread across the arm of his chair, and a tenderness stirred in Marcus at recalling where Kiernan had learned that look. It amazed him how much the boy resembled Jenna.

The old sadness revived in Marcus. There had been no great love between him and Jenna. The marriage could have been better. She hadn't been happy. Despite his noble blood, he was a Highlander—a clan leader—and Jenna couldn't comprehend the archaic way of life. Marcus hadn't been able to find it in his heart to blame her. She was of Scottish blood, not Highland. *Never the twain shall meet,* she had once said.

Still, he grieved when she died. Kiernan, a boy of ten, had been inconsolable. Marcus worried his son had never quite forgiven the world for taking her from him. Even now, he glimpsed flashes of resentment. They were rare, but the emotion ran deep. Kiernan always seemed to ask—to demand—why Marcus had been unable to save her when she'd been thrown from her horse. She hadn't died immediately. It would have been better if she had. Instead, she'd lingered a day, an afternoon, really.

Kiernan had stolen into his mother's room while she lay dying. Jenna hadn't wakened. Whether that was better or not, Marcus had never been sure. But Kiernan had said his good-byes. Marcus recalled seeing the lad on his knees beside his mother's bed. When he entered the room, Kiernan remained motionless. Neither moved for some time. At last, the boy rose and left.

Marcus shook off the morose memories. He crossed the room. Kiernan looked up from the paper. His face brightened and he stood, flashing a smile that dispelled the fear in Marcus's earlier memory. He grasped his son's hand and pulled him close. They separated.

"What brings you to London again so soon?" Kiernan pointed to a chair next to his, then sat. "I hadn't thought you'd be here until spring."

"Not glad to see me?" Marcus chided.

A corner of Kiernan's mouth lifted a little higher. "Never say you braved London for me. Why, Father, I don't know what to say." He motioned to a steward. "Two brandies," he said when the man reached hearing distance, then turned his attention back to Marcus. "Or are you missing city life?"

Marcus grimaced. "Nay. I had business with Loudoun."

Kiernan's smile vanished. "Damnation, Father, what sort of business?"

"Unsavory business."

Kiernan grunted. "That's about the only sort you could have with him."

Marcus gave an account of recent events. When he'd finished, he took the final swallow of his brandy.

An all-too-familiar gleam entered his son's eyes. "Perhaps I should return to Brahan Seer. You can use all the help you can get. I'm handy with a sword, if you recall." He flashed a cocky grin.

Aye, Marcus recalled all too well. His son had nearly bested him with his own sword just last year. Damn, the lad was truly grown.

"I do have some good news," Marcus said. He paused. "I am to marry."

Kiernan looked as if he had been hit in the belly. Marcus gave a quick explanation.

A moment later, Kiernan shook his head, his expression disbelieving. "You say she hasn't actually consented?"

"Aye."

"Isn't an announcement a bit premature?"

"No announcements. I am telling only you."

Marcus watched his son. He hoped to glean some insight into Kiernan's thoughts but, aside from obvious shock, he displayed no other emotion. The boy had grown too skilled at hiding the workings of his mind.

"Nothing to say on the matter?" Marcus finally asked outright.

"I assume you care for her."

"I do."

"Then congratulations are in order."

"Aye," Marcus replied, while wondering exactly how he would get Elise to agree. His gaze fell to the *Sunday Times* still open on the arm of Kiernan's chair. "Let me see that." He nodded toward the paper.

Chapter Twelve

The afternoon sun hung low in the overcast sky when Elise came to an abrupt halt outside the storehouse located in the southeast corner of Brahan Seer's compound. Marcus strode past the children playing at the bottom of the hill, headed up in her direction. Her grip on the small sack of flour she held tightened. He'd been gone less than a week. He hadn't delayed in returning to Brahan Seer—neither had he delayed in seeking her out. She had left the kitchen a few minutes ago and he hadn't been there. He could have only just arrived. Only one thing would cause him to come for her before even his horse could be unsaddled: he had found the notice and made the connection between Elise Merriwether and Elisabeth Kingston.

Her heart pounded against her ribs and she had to force herself not to run. *Where would you go?* she asked herself. He made escape impossible. *You think he couldn't find you within the confines of Brahan Seer?* He crested the hill and their gazes met. Her breath caught at the haggard look in his eyes.

He knows.

The children's shouts melted into the background as he halted so close, the warmth of his breath displaced the cool, early summer air against her face. She dropped her gaze and bit back tears. Why did he torture her so?

"Hello, love," he murmured.

169

Elise jerked her gaze up to his. No anger shone in his eyes. He tugged the sack of flour from her grasp and let it drop to the ground, then wrapped an arm around her waist and drew her close. Passion shot between them in a blazing kiss. She gasped when he showered lush kisses along her chin and down the base of her throat. She inhaled his scent and nearly cried when the familiar fragrance engulfed her senses.

Marcus wrapped his free arm around her and gave her a fierce hug. "I missed ye." He leaned back and looked into her eyes.

Her heart leapt with joy and sorrow in unison. Would it have been better for him to have found the wanted notice and confront her? He brushed aside locks of hair the breeze had blown across her cheek. He crooked a finger under her chin and tilted her face up toward his. Her cheeks warmed and she flicked a glance at the children who seemed oblivious of them. He stroked her lips with his thumb. A dangerous grin flashed across his face.

"Wha—"

Marcus dragged her behind the thick brush around back of the storehouse. He glanced at the massive oak tree behind them.

"Marcus—"

He backed her against the tree and pinned her with his body.

"You can't be seri—" The protest was cut off as much by the sudden awareness of the hard length of him pressing into her thigh as by his kiss.

Marcus broke the embrace just as abruptly as he'd begun, ending the kiss with a loud smacking sound. Elise stared. He grinned. She shoved at his chest. He bent over her once more and she heard his quiet laugh before his mouth covered hers. He parted her lips with his tongue, not asking, but taking. He shifted and the vague awareness of his fingers closing around her wrists penetrated her consciousness. He lifted her hands above her head, pressing them against the tree as he leaned his weight against her. A tremor ripped through her and her body coiled in readiness for the hard press of him against her thigh again. But Marcus released her mouth and, dipping his head, nipped at her flesh from cheek to ear.

"I haven't forgotten how mercilessly you teased me before I left." He rocked against her. The press of him against her weakened her knees. "Feel what you do to me, sweet," he said.

Elise inhaled sharply.

"Aye," he whispered.

Marcus rocked again, then again. She arched as he kissed his way down her neck. He released her hands and tugged down her bodice.

"Marcus!" She forgot the remonstration as his weight lifted from her and he bent, his wet mouth closing over a nipple.

Desire spiked through her. His tongue circled the nipple, then released it. She closed her eyes, shivering as the wind slid across her breast, puckering the bud to a hard peak. Marcus abruptly pulled her away from the tree. She snapped open her eyes. He eased her to the ground. The scent of crushed ivy ground cover enveloped her as he came down beside her.

"They're expecting me to return with the flour," she said. "When I don't—"

"They know I came in search of you." He slipped a knee between her legs. "They won't come."

He covered a breast with his palm and slowly teased the nipple with his thumb, while kissing the other breast. His mouth captured the nipple and a rush of pleasure shot from both breasts to the juncture between her legs. He lifted his head and she forced her eyes into focus. His gaze remained fastened on hers as he ran a hand along her ribs. His palm glided past her waist, then along her thigh. He grabbed a fistful of her skirt and pulled it up. She gasped at the feel of his warm hand flattening against her skin, then caressing her inner thigh.

"Marcus," she whispered.

He said nothing, only continued caressing

upward until his fingers tickled the hair between her legs. She tensed. He kissed the swell of her breast, her neck, her ear, then her mouth, lengthening the kiss as he slipped a finger between her folds. His thumb brushed the nub swollen with desire. She clutched his shoulders. His muscles tensed beneath her fingers. She ached to feel those arms around her. He stroked her deliberately while slipping another finger inside. He released her mouth and leaned his forehead against hers. His breathing grew ragged as he thrust gently with his fingers. His thumb stroked in quicker movements. Pleasure swirled in a restless coil deep insider her, spiking up in wide ribbons of intensity that took her breath away.

Marcus nuzzled her neck. "Come to me."

She started at the whispered words.

"Come to me," he repeated.

And she did.

Elise took one of the scones Jinny had baked that evening from the pan on the kitchen counter. They were still warm to the touch. She pulled the tartan covering her shoulders closer as she stuffed half the scone into her mouth and leaned against the counter. Despite a large supper and wine, she had been unable to sleep. Two glasses of wine hadn't been enough. She should have made it three. At least she would have slept, even if fitfully.

Why had she let Marcus touch her? When he left for London, she had counted on him being away longer than seven days and intended on being gone before he returned. Given enough time, Cameron would have seen her confinement for the prison sentence it was. She had planned on approaching him with care. When he thought she had been wronged by Margaret, he understood her desire to leave. An out-and-out demand for release, however, would be viewed with suspicion. After all, why would a woman with only fifty pounds to her name and no place to go want to leave?

She finished the second half of the scone. If she had listened to her head and not her heart and had shunned Marcus... Elise gave a mirthless laugh. She hadn't— and now she had to deal with him while searching for the secret passage Winnie had spoken of.

She reached for another scone, then decided to take some to her room. She found a cloth napkin in the cabinet and wrapped two scones. Male voices sounded in the direction of the great hall as she had folded the napkin's last flap.

Elise cocked an ear. They approached from the hall leading from the main entrance. Scooping up the scones, she froze at sound of a familiar laugh. *Marcus.* She tightened her hold on the tartan and darted through the kitchen door toward the stairs but was still half a dozen steps from the concealment offered by the staircase when the men burst into the room. Their laughter ceased.

Marcus's "Good evening, lass. What mischief brings you to the great hall tonight?" stopped Elise. She gripped the tartan more tightly about her throat and turned, lifting her hand to display the wrapped scones.

The men looked at the proffered scones and burst into laughter. She began to relax, then caught sight of Marcus's intense gaze.

The colors of the throw Elise wore dissolved in Marcus's mind in a blur of red and blue to the memory of her lying alongside him in the ivy. He felt again her body as she trembled beneath his hand, the moist heat of her—

"Good night, gentlemen," she said.

Marcus jerked his attention back to her as she turned to the staircase and started up. He brushed past his comrades and hurried after her. She paused midway up the staircase and looked over her shoulder. He continued forward and she hurried up the stairs and down the corridor to her bedchamber door where she whirled to face him.

"Marcus, perhaps—"

He leaned forward, his shoulder brushing hers as he reached around her and pushed open the door. The door swung wide and he cupped her bottom, lifting her from the floor. She squeaked and threw her arms around his neck, dropping the *plaide* and the scones. He stepped inside, kicked the door shut, and took the final steps to the bed. He fell atop her on the soft mattress.

"I need you," he whispered.

The spicy scent of clean bed linen met his nostrils as he kissed her. The fire crackled and it seemed the heat in his blood ignited in unison. Elise gripped his shoulders. The power in her hold belied the soft compliance of her lips. Marcus ended the kiss.

He rose to his knees and pulled her up and off the bed with him. He tugged the straps of her night rail down over her shoulders, forcing her arms down so that the garment skimmed along her body and pooled at her feet. His heart hammered. At last, she willingly stood before him, soft curves his to touch, her charms his to take. He forced back the need to crush her beneath him and pound into her heat with all the force in his body and drew her into his arms. She rested her head on his shoulder. He held her quietly until the pounding in his ears dulled to a low roar, then bent and brushed his lips across hers.

When Marcus lifted his head, he held her gaze as he rotated his hips against her. Uncertainty played across her face. She dropped her lashes at the second, more ardent grinding of his arousal against her mound. He stepped back and she looked up in surprise. He raked his gaze over her, then brought his attention back to her face. A furious blush crept up her cheeks.

He unbuttoned his shirt and dropped the garment on the floor. His left boot followed, then the right, leaving him standing in nothing but his kilt. Marcus studied her as he removed his belt and let it, along with the kilt, fall to the floor. The belt buckle clinked on the stone, but Elise's eyes remained fixed on his face. He took the few steps to her and, grasping her wrist, gently brought her hand to his shaft. Her gaze jerked down to where he firmly held her. He wrapped her fingers around him and nearly came to his knees at the cool feel of her fingers against his pounding heat.

"Do I frighten you, lass?" he asked.

Her head snapped up. "No."

Marcus gave a hoarse laugh. Bloody hell, mayhap she wasn't afraid, but he was. He picked her up and carried her to the bed. Placing her on the mattress, he lay down beside her. He ignored the hammering in his head and ran a shaky finger along her arm.

"I'll be gentle," he said.

She frowned. "I won't break."

"Nay, love," he agreed. "But compared to me, you are naught but a feather."

Elise sat upright. "I am no porcelain doll to be kept on a shelf."

Marcus opened his mouth to deny the implication but stopped. "Is that how your husband treated you?"

A long silence drew out.

"You cannot compare me to him," Marcus finally said. "I'm no fool."

She blinked, then rolled to her side and started toward the edge of the bed.

"Nay." Marcus grabbed her.

"You can leave now." She twisted as he yanked her back.

"Nay." He rolled on top of her. "Hush," he commanded when she opened her mouth.

He kissed her. She pressed herself into the mattress, but he lengthened the kiss. She wriggled as though to sidle out from beneath him, rocking their bodies together. Pleasure shot through him. Marcus ended the kiss, breathing hard.

"Elise," he whispered hoarsely, "you are not discouraging me."

She ceased.

Marcus slipped a knee between her legs. "I am a fool," he said. "I wanted you the moment I laid eyes on you. You know that."

He reached between them and drew apart the folds that protected her sex. He feared, at first, she would resist in earnest and he would be forced to spend yet another night without her, but an instant later, she wrapped her arms about his neck. Marcus touched her in heated strokes. He breathed deep of her scent filling his nostrils, stroking, petting until, at last, she cried out and buried her head in his shoulder. He trailed a long, moist kiss from her ear to a breast, taking the hardened nipple in his mouth.

"Marcus," she groaned.

He continued to tease her while settling himself between her legs. He probed for entrance into her body, aware of the sudden rise and fall of her breast, the subtle tension in her. His body tensed in response, hungry for the resistance. The tip of his shaft slipped into the moist opening.

"You're ready for me," he rasped, and in one swift motion, thrust.

Her nails pierced the flesh of his shoulders. She stiffened. Marcus stilled, waves of pleasure radiating from his groin. He took a shaky breath and focused on her face. His mind instantly cleared at sight of the drawn brow and hard lines around her mouth.

"Bloody hell," he cursed. "I hurt you."

"No," she denied so quickly he wouldn't have believed the pope had he said she spoke the truth.

"You may be no porcelain doll," he muttered, "but you aren't to be misused."

"You don't understand—"

"I understand well enough." He began to lift himself off her.

Elise held fast to his shoulders. "You do not, but it doesn't matter. If you will just continue, it will pass."

He frowned. "If you think I could misuse you—"

"Good Lord." She rolled her eyes.

"What in God's name has possessed you this evening?" he demanded, feeling frustration grow and himself soften.

"You, I thought."

Marcus blinked. He stared at her face for a moment, then dropped his gaze to her breasts. The nipples no longer stood erect. He lowered himself so that his chest brushed the soft peaks. They instantly stiffened. He hardened. He shifted slightly, gasping as the tight passage closed in around him in a hold he hadn't recalled since—Marcus froze, jerking his attention back to Elise's taut face—since he'd bedded Jenna on their wedding night. She'd been the only virgin he'd ever had, but the memory remained vivid. However, there had been no maidenhead with Elise. She had been married, had a child. She was no virgin.

"Elise," he said in a low voice, "how long since your husband bedded you?"

Her stricken look and the sudden moisture in her eyes told him all he needed to know.

"Love," he said, lowering his mouth to kiss her.

She turned her head aside. "Please."

Marcus kissed her neck instead. Not the kiss of passion he would have given her a moment ago, but a gentle, reassuring kiss.

"The man was a fool," he muttered, and moved inside her, slowly this time.

Her hold remained firm, but she shook her head slightly, refusing to look at him. Marcus lifted his weight from her, withdrawing slowly, then entering again with a quick but shallow thrust. He didn't mistake her tiny intake of breath, then the rise of her body to meet his next thrust. He pulled away, while running his tongue along the edge of her ear. When he thrust again, Elise wrapped her arms around his neck. He kissed her cheek, the corner of her mouth, then coaxed her to him, kissing her full on the mouth. She wound a leg around his calf and he thrust hard and deep before realizing the action.

He stilled. She opened her eyes. He saw no fear, only the question, *Why have you stopped?* He was a fool. Marcus moved again and again and again, until her arms tightened around his back and her walls closed around his shaft as she cried out in her pleasure. When the blinding light of climax shot through his body, he poured himself into her and knew he would never let her go.

Elise sat at Marcus's desk in the library and stared at the wanted notice in the *Sunday Times* dated the weekend he had been in London.

American-born Elisabeth Kingston wanted for murder is believed to have perished at sea off the coast of Scotland. A ten-thousand-pound reward is offered for information leading to the whereabouts of her body. Anyone with information contact Drew Cummins, Attorney at Law...

She closed her eyes, willing her pounding heart to slow. If this paper had been meant for Michael, why had it sat folded on Marcus's desk the last four days? The man who had demanded the Campbells deliver Shamus's killer to him wouldn't overlook a wife murdering her husband.

Marcus's anger at discovering that the woman he wanted to marry was a wanted criminal like Shamus's murderer would be even greater. She had eluded Price these past months. After what happened between her and Marcus last night, could she hide from *him?*

Marcus strode across the courtyard toward the gate. The drizzling rain, which had fallen since dawn, now turned into the large drops promised by the dark, low clouds. He would be surprised if Elise had ventured into the village on such a dreary summer day. In fact, he had expected her to be shut up in his library. He felt again the acute disappointment at not being able to make love to her before a low fire as he'd planned.

A moment later, he stood on the battlements, scanning the path leading into the village but saw no one approaching. He shifted his gaze to the dark shadows concealing the secret passage, then turned and surveyed the courtyard. The rain hadn't interfered with the daily goings on. People traveled to and from the castle and among the cottages beyond the bailey.

He scanned the grounds, his gaze centering on Winnie's cottage in the distance. He started to turn from the deserted-looking building when the door opened and a woman stepped out. Marcus studied the figure as she hurried down the single step onto the ground and started in the direction of the castle. He followed her progress until he discerned Mary's features, then turned from the wall. Perhaps she knew something of Elise's whereabouts. A moment later, he pushed through the postern door and strode through the eating hall to the kitchen. Mary appeared in the kitchen's back door as he entered.

"Have you seen Elise?" he demanded without preamble.

The girl paused in the doorway. "N-nay, laird."

Marcus surveyed the women in the room, all of whom had stopped their work and were looking at him. "No one here knows where Winnie is?"

A general "nay" went up and he turned from the kitchen. Where the bloody hell was Elise? And as for Winnie…

A cursory investigation of the castle turned up no sign of Elise. Only three weeks earlier he had been searching for her in much the same manner.

Her absence then was innocent enough. Yet the number of times she had gone to Michael's against his express command, combined with last month's disappearance, unsettled him.

Two hours later, after a more thorough search, including the dungeons, Marcus stalked toward Winnie's cottage. The secret passageway had become his nemesis. At every turn, he feared Elise had somehow managed to escape through it, despite the fact he'd had it sealed from the outside.

He found Winnie's cottage empty. Marcus worked his way through the keep, his temper rising with every step. At last, he reached   Lauren's home. Aye, she'd seen Elise, only that had been over an hour ago. He strode from her cottage, across the compound, and into the kitchen. Winnie, this time, sat at the table, plucking a chicken, just as she should have been.

"So, milady," he said, bringing her attention to him, along with that of the other women in the room, "you have returned to the roost."

Winnie looked up from yanking tail feathers from her victim's rump.

"Have you seen Elise?"

Comprehension shone on her face.

"Don't play games with me, Winnie," he warned. "You have seen Elise. I can see it in your eyes."

"No need to get testy." She turned to her chicken. "Try the women's drawing room."

Another five minutes and Marcus shoved open the drawing room door. The women jumped as the door hit the wall with a bang. He swept his gaze across the room before settling dangerously on Elise, who sat on the large couch against the left wall. No one moved as he strode toward her.

"Good Lord, what in the world is wrong?" she blurted when he halted in front of her.

With a jerk of his head, Marcus cleared the room. The door closed with a soft click and he demanded, "Where have you been?"

She blinked. "I-I have just come from Lauren's—"

"Not *just come*. You left there over an hour ago."

"What have I done now?" she retorted in the same dark tone he'd used.

"It never occurred to you to inform someone— *anyone*—where you were going?" Marcus grabbed her shoulders. "Don't do this again." He hadn't realized until seeing her, just how far his fear had run. He hugged her.

She wriggled within his grasp. *"Marcus."*

He leaned back and looked into her face. "The next time you leave the castle, tell someone."

Her brow furrowed, then her lips pursed. She wrested herself from his arms and tumbled back onto the couch. "Go away," she snapped, and reached to smooth her skirts, which had bunched beneath her.

Marcus sat beside her. "Listen to me. There is mischief afoot, and I won't live in fear for your safety, even within the walls of my own home. Do you understand?"

Her eyes narrowed. "What do you want from me? I am a veritable prisoner as it is. Now, like some child, I must ask permission before stepping outside my room?"

"Bloody hell, do you think the Campbells came here out of boredom?"

"What do you mean?"

"They wanted you."

She snorted. "That's ridiculous."

He raised a brow. "Is it?"

"What are you saying?"

He thought, *Who are you? Do the Campbells want you simply to hurt me?* But said, "They wish to hurt me. Remember, they tried once before."

"True," she agreed. "But why put themselves in danger in order to kidnap me again?"

"I beg you to trust me," he said. "Allow me some peace. Your confinement is for a short time, I swear."

Elise studied him. "Your father concurs with this *theory*?"

"He does."

"All right."

"There is something else that would ease my mind."

She sighed. "What is that?"

"I'm planning another trip to London. I wish to take you."

Surprise flickered across her face, then her brows rose. "This, after nearly chaining me to the castle walls?"

"Beware, my sweet. You may yet find yourself in chains."

"Sounds very nice, indeed," she muttered.

Despite the feminine nonchalance, Marcus detected caution. Did she suspect what he had in store for her? "I said your incarceration would last only a short time. I will feel more secure if you're with me."

"London?" she repeated.

Ah, there it was, a note of interest. "Aye."

She looked thoughtful, then said, "Perhaps the Campbells would forget about me in the meantime."

"Perhaps," he said, though a niggling doubt said otherwise.

"I will go," she said.

Marcus braced himself. "Good. Then I'll send for Father Whyte."

Chapter Thirteen

"**W**hat?" Elise asked softly—too softly.

"I'll send for Father Whyte," Marcus repeated.

"Why?"

"Last I heard, a priest was needed for a wedding."

Her eyes widened. "Married?"

"I said we would marry."

"I never agreed." She looked away.

"You swore not to become my mistress under any circumstances."

Elise looked sharply at him. "Yes, but—"

"Unless we marry, that is exactly what has happened."

She jumped to her feet, backing away several paces. "Not so."

Marcus raised a brow.

Her eyes darkened. "You know perfectly well what I meant when I said that."

"Aye, just as I have said."

"No," she retorted. "I would not be your mistress when you were to marry."

He lounged back against the cushions. "Interesting interpretation."

"It is not an interpretation!"

"Surely, you can understand my confusion."

"You are trying to trick me," she snapped.

"Nay, love. I only point out the facts. When you thought I was to marry, you left. You now know the truth yet are still here. Do you plan on running away again?"

Elise jerked her chin up with such a defiant gesture he had to stifle a laugh, despite knowing fear was the driving factor in her reaction. She blew out a loud, frustrated breath.

He stretched out a hand. "Come."

Elise responded with a quick shake of her head.

Marcus repressed a smile. He remembered the last time he'd offered her his hand. Though reluctant, she had accepted it then. Would she do the same now?

"Come," he repeated.

She again shook her head, but he noted the tiny puckering of her brows. *She doubted.*

"You fear me?" he asked.

Her brow puckered tighter. "You think you are clever, don't you?"

"Not so clever," he replied. "Come."

"I have no intention of being tricked."

"Aye," he replied.

"I-I have to go." She turned.

Marcus dropped his hand to his side. "Where will you go?"

She halted. Relief flooded through him. She wanted him. He stood and crossed to her.

"Come." He grasped her hand and drew her to the couch.

He sat, then gave a gentle but firm yank to her hand, and she tumbled onto his lap.

"I cannot—" she began, but he cut in.

"Let us be honest."

"I have been—"

"You say," he continued, "you *will* be my mistress now that you know I never planned to marry Margaret."

"I never—"

"But wouldn't it be more honest to admit you love me?"

Her eyes widened.

"You can trust me." Marcus discerned a

quickening of her breath. He'd hit the mark. "For you know," he added, "I love you."

Elise gasped. He felt the muscles in her body tense in readiness to push from his lap and tightened his hold. She thrashed, though without real violence, and he gripped her chin, turning her face toward his.

"Admit you love me." He kissed her.

She tried pulling away, but he held fast, his mouth gentle until he felt a slight tug when she grasped his shirt. He released her mouth and buried his face in her hair.

"Can you deny what you feel for me?"

"You don't know—can't possibly know—"

"I know all I need."

She grasped his shoulder and pushed him back until their gazes met. "Today doesn't matter. Tomorrow your fancy may change."

Marcus stared at her. "I am no young buck. I know what I want."

She gave a mirthless laugh. "Age has little to do with a man's desire."

He started to speak, to explain that her younger age might not allow for the understanding of his more experienced wisdom, but he stopped, remembering the empty marriage she'd endured.

"Hmm," he began slowly. "One day your feelings for me shall fade?"

"You are cruel," she cried. "You know that is not my meaning."

Marcus's chest tightened. She hadn't denied loving him. He gently squeezed her hand. "I am not Riley."

Elise twisted in his arms in an earnest attempt at escape. "You overstep your bounds, *milord*."

He barely repressed a sudden laugh when she thumped his arm with a small fist. She shoved at his chest and Marcus hugged her so close their lips almost met.

"Surely, I have proven I am not faithless," he demanded.

"Faithless? Good Lord, you're lucky I don't

sacrifice you for my own selfish needs."

"Needs? Aye, lass, you need me. Nay," he added when she opened her mouth to interject. "Don't think I am ignorant of your needs." He slid a hand into her hair. "They are not unlike my own."

Marcus kissed her. She breathed deep and he felt his body throb with a need that he now realized had only begun to surface. What would he have done that first day he saw her in the meadow had he known just how badly he would one day need her? Send his men away and take her there—leave her no choice, nowhere to go but to him? Turning and fleeing straight back to Ashlund would have been the wisest course of action. But he would not have—could not have—even then. He had loved—or thought he loved—other women. He had been hurt in the past, but Elise held the power to destroy him. He slid his mouth down her chin and along her neck to the swell of her breast. Her head fell back onto his arm without resistance.

"You would marry a stranger?" she murmured.

Marcus froze.

"Take a lowly servant girl to wife."

He jerked his head up. "I wouldn't relegate anyone to that status, least of all, you."

Her eyes unexpectedly softened. "I know, but that doesn't change the differences in our classes."

"I care nothing for so-called classes. I care about living life."

Her expression turned appraising. "Even you did not flout that responsibility. Didn't you marry out of a sense of duty?"

"Aye. Which is precisely why I will not do so again."

Marcus crushed her lips to his. She didn't protest this time, and he slid her from his lap and onto the couch. Grasping her hand, he slipped it beneath his kilt and forced her fingers around his erection.

Elise started.

"Nay," he breathed in her ear. "Do not run from me. God, you haunt me at every turn." Releasing her fingers, he yanked her dress up and reached between her legs. "Your body responds to me without reservation. Let your heart follow. I promise, I will love you."

He slipped a finger inside her slick heat. Her grip on his shaft tightened convulsively. Marcus drew in a sharp breath, gritting his teeth to keep from spending himself. He removed his hand and slid on top of her, pressing his lips against her ear.

"Guide me into you, sweet," he whispered. "Let me show you how much I want you. Let me show you what love is."

She did as he urged, and he caressed her with his movements, his body meeting hers, arching away, then gently thrusting again.

"Is marrying me so terrible?" he asked against her neck.

She breathed deep. "No, but after the fact you"— she gasped when he thrust with a quick motion—"you will regret being chained to me."

Marcus laughed. "It will be the sweetest of tortures." He drove deep again.

She cried out as her muscles clenched around him.

"It's not as if you *need* to marry me." She blurted in a strained voice. "I have not withheld myself from you."

Marcus halted. Bracing a hand on either side of her, he looked down at her. "I love you. I want you— *need* you." He held her gaze as he moved slowly, nearly filling her, then thrust quickly and pulled back.

"I haven't left you," she insisted.

"You withhold a part of yourself. If not, you would be dragging *me* to the altar."

Elise reddened.

"You don't trust me." He kissed her ear.

She shook her head. "I cannot believe we are having this discussion in the middle of… that is, I can't believe we are-are doing *this* in the middle of a disagreement."

Marcus chuckled. "'Tis a new experience for me, as

well. But, if we must disagree, this is a most pleasant way to do so." He slid his hands beneath her thighs, coaxing her legs around his waist. "Aye." He buried his face in her hair at the nape of her neck and drove into her. "I will protect you." He cupped a breast—she was breathing hard now, she wanted him—needed him.

He thrust quicker. Her breathless response told him she neared her pleasure. "You will be my wife, my marchi—"

"Your servant girl made mistress of the manor," she said.

Marcus jerked, his thrust going hard and deep. Elise gasped. He remained inside her, full to the hilt. "Why did you allow me to touch you?" he demanded. "Don't say it is because I am lord and you are servant. We both know better. I have the power to care for you, protect you."

At last, uncertainty shown in her expression.

"As my wife, your security is assured. No Campbells, or anyone else, can harm you."

"Nothing is that certain," Elise replied.

"I haven't failed you yet."

Her mouth parted in surprise.

He kissed her mouth and moved in her again. Kissed her forehead, cheek, then ear. "Admit you want me." He quickened his thrusts.

Her muscles tightened around him in readiness for her release.

"Admit it," he pressed. "You want me now and every day and night hereafter."

Elise hugged him tight. "Yes," she cried as her climax rolled over her.

"You are mine," Marcus rasped. "You will not regret the choice."

Elise found herself being pulled down the hall of Brahan Seer. Marcus intended to take her directly to his father to announce their *betrothal*. Her head whirled as much from his lovemaking as his proposal. He picked up speed, nearly dragging her down the hallway.

She needed more time. "Marcus, wouldn't it be wise to give this more thought before telling anyone?"

"Nay."

"Slow down. I can barely keep up with you." She tugged on the hand he grasped.

"I can carry you, if you like," he responded, still striding in long paces.

"Good Lord, no. *Marcus.*" Elise yanked hard on his hand.

He came to an abrupt halt and she tumbled into his arms.

"Aye, sweet," he drawled. "You wanted something."

"Slow down. I'm not a sack of potatoes to be dragged along behind you."

His gaze dropped to her breasts. "True, and I could easily forget myself even here in the common walkway."

Surely, he wouldn't have asked her to marry him if he'd seen the notice in the paper? Could she live with herself for deceiving him? "You needn't marry me," she said, then silently added, *This is your chance, Marcus MacGregor. Save yourself.* "I can't refuse you," she said, "even here."

His eyes jerked up to meet hers, the amorous light gone. "I believe we were on our way to see my father." Taking her hand once again, he continued at an even more relentless pace.

Five minutes later, they entered the stables where Cameron stood with the young foal born that summer.

"Father," Marcus called.

Cameron looked over his shoulder at Marcus, then her.

"We have an announcement," Marcus said as they drew up beside Cameron.

Cameron's expression turned bemused, but Elise knew better.

"Elise and I are to be married." Marcus's hold on

her hand tightened. "And soon."

Her heart jumped into a gallop. "No one said anything—"

"Hush," he commanded, and looked at his father. "Have you anything to say?"

Cameron shrugged. "You are old enough to make your own decisions."

Marcus grinned, and she muttered, "Bloody idiotic men."

Both men regarded her.

She looked back at them. How could she explain that the woman he wished to marry was wanted for murdering her husband? *You see, my husband poisoned my daughter with tiny doses of the deadly nightshade. The symptoms were subtle, which explains why the doctors couldn't pinpoint the disease. I never caught Robert in the act, but he knew I knew and tried to kill me. I shot him in self-defense. Ignore the wanted notice in the London* Sunday Times. *It will eventually go away.'*

Elise regarded Marcus. "As your wife, I am no longer prisoner?"

"You are not prisoner now," he replied. "You are in the castle for your safety."

"Safety," she murmured, then added, "If I wish to go to the village, you will allow it?"

He nodded. "If it pleases you. I have work I can take care of while we are there."

She narrowed her eyes. "I am no prisoner then?"

"Nay," he answered innocently, and she knew she would get no more.

He would ensure she was watched every second they were at the village. If she played the future wife, he would soon relax his hold. Pain stabbed at her heart.

She had to be gone before his priest arrived.

Elise paced her bedchamber. Marcus's son would arrive any hour. Only two days had passed since she'd agreed to marry Marcus. Was he hurrying to Brahan Seer to meet the woman who would marry his father, or to expose her as murderess? How in God's name was she to escape not two, but three MacGregor men?

The fire blazing in the hearth cracked and she jumped. She pressed a hand over her racing heart. Something must be done. She recalled the various decanters of liquor sitting on the sideboard in Marcus's library and hurried to the library.

She opened the door and met Marcus's gaze as he looked up from the work on his desk. "To what do I owe the pleasure of your company, love?" he asked.

She closed the door and headed for the sideboard. "I need a drink."

Elise ignored the quizzical lift of his brow as she stopped before the sideboard and surveyed the decanters. She spied the small square decanter filled with cognac. She removed the lid from the decanter, poured a healthy portion into a glass, then emptied it in two unladylike gulps.

She heaved a sigh, then poured another, and finished it just as quickly. She glanced at Marcus and saw he regarded her. "Oh," she said, "how thoughtless. Would you like one?"

He shook his head.

"Well, I do."

The glass reached her lips when Marcus's hand covered hers. "Slow down, lass. You're liable to regret this in the morning."

"Unlikely." She brushed his hand aside, then strolled to the hearth while sipping the cognac.

"Is something wrong?" Marcus inquired.

"Wrong?" She whirled. A delicious warmth radiated through her body. "A few months ago, I was shipwrecked, left penniless and alone, then, naïve little lamb that I am"—she narrowed her eyes at the mirth that leapt to his eyes—"I was pursued relentlessly by you."

"Perhaps what you need is a little comforting," he suggested.

Elise rolled her eyes. "What I need is another cognac."

TARAH SCOTT

"Nay."

She gave her head one single slow shake. "Do not think you can stop me from doing as I please. Now or after we're married."

Marcus caught her arm as she approached the sideboard. "Have you not had enough?"

She disengaged herself from his grasp. "I'm capable of handling my liquor. Be so kind as to move aside." She placed a hand on his chest and shoved.

He stepped back as she passed. "You're in a fine mood tonight. I have never seen you this way before."

Elise paused in filling her glass and looked at him. "Regretting your proposal?"

His mouth twitched.

Damn him, she mentally cursed.

"I think I will still wed you," he replied. "I'm looking forward to ravishing your sweet body every chance I get."

"I believe I pointed out you need not marry me to do that." She lifted the glass to her lips.

"Perhaps," Marcus said. "But it will be my obligation, and I will always know where to find you when my sense of duty calls me into service."

Elise halted mid-sip and narrowed her eyes. "What is that supposed to mean?"

He shrugged. "A wife is always in her husband's bed, aye?" His gaze made a possessive sweep over her body.

She lowered the glass from her lips. "Are you saying you're marrying me to ensure my... my availability?"

His wince and quick "Nay" confirmed the assessment. "I am marrying you because I love you and want you at my side."

A tremor passed through her at the declaration of love given so naturally, but she gave a feminine snort and retorted, "A masculine play on words."

"Nay," he denied even more vehemently.

Elise regarding him more closely. "You're jealous."

"Jealous?" His expression snapped to a stormy

192

darkness. "Of whom?"

She waved her glass, dodging the liquid that sloshed over the rim and onto the carpet. "The funny part is"—the funny part is, she should have created a fictional lover long ago—"you were afraid I would want someone else."

He looked startled and she couldn't help a laugh. Elise placed her glass on the sideboard and came to stand in front of him. A fuzzy sensation in her belly made her feel reckless. Wrapping one arm around his neck, she caressed his jaw with her free hand. She ran her gaze in a purposeful, slow motion from his mouth to his eyes. "Perhaps I should have considered another application or two for my hand."

His arm shot around her. She squealed with the hard yank of her body against his.

"I am marrying you because I cannot live without you," he growled.

But you will, she thought, and pulled away so he wouldn't see the pain that rose too easily to the surface. Elise started for the sideboard and her drink. She reached the tumbler and once again downed the glass.

"Elise," he growled. "Enough."

Despite the sudden fogginess of her vision, she reached for the decanter again. This time, strong fingers pried her hand from the stopper.

"You seem to forget," Marcus said, "my warning about disobeying me."

Elise frowned, the fogginess creeping into her brain. "Ahh, you mean the threat to *distract me with your body.*" She laughed. "I think that threat is a little old, don't you?"

Without warning, he swung her into his arms and, an instant later, she found herself on the couch, pinned tightly beneath him.

"I always keep my promises, love, even if it means finding a new twist to an old game."

"I'm not in the mood for your *games* tonight, *milord.* Let me go."

"Nay."

"Marcus." She groaned with the effort of attempting to shove him off her.

He shifted and, grasping her hands, wedged them behind her back. His weight lay fully on her and she wriggled, the increasing cloud across her mind impairing the ability to think. Even as she realized he'd lowered his head and his hair was tickling her chin, the sudden flicker of his tongue dangerously close to her nipple sent a jolt through her. She gave a tiny squeal and he responded with a noise deep in his throat. Gripping her wrists with one hand, he freed his other hand to reached down and yank up her skirt.

"Marcus," she breathed, unexpectedly clear headed, "we're in the library. You cannot!"

But he continued, his tongue—his tongue, she forgot in favor of the finger that slid across her pleasure point. Marcus wound a foot around her ankle and tugged her close until she felt the thick bulge pressed to her thigh. His grip on her hands loosened as a slow thrust slid along her thigh.

"I think ye will find your father in here," came Cameron's voice just outside the library.

Elise stiffened. Marcus yanked her skirt down as the door opened. She squeezed her eyes shut just before Marcus's gaze settled on his father.

"You chose a fine time to visit the library," Marcus said evenly.

"Aye," Cameron replied. "So it would seem. You look well this evening, lass," he added.

She buried her head in Marcus's shoulder, not quite stifling an oath.

"I think you had better do something about your lady's speech," Cameron said. "She's beginning to sound like a sailor."

"Was there something you wanted?" Marcus asked. "Kiernan," he exclaimed.

His muscles tightened and Elise realized he was rising. She grasped his shoulders.

He relaxed and said, "I'll be out directly. Give me a

194

moment." The door closed with a soft click, then he said, "You can open your eyes now, love. They have gone."

Elise opened her eyes while shoving at him. "Get up for God's sake."

He obliged. "Only a moment ago, you didn't want me to rise."

She sat up. "Your son—he saw me."

"Elise—"

She shot to her feet. "Good Lord, you shouldn't have—"

"Now, love, 'tis not all that bad. You were fully clothed after all"—she groaned and plopped back down onto the couch—"and, truly," he went on, "this has been a household of men for many years. We aren't shocked by a little love-play."

Elise shook her head harder this time.

Marcus gave her a gentle look. "You can't avoid him our entire marriage."

Her stomach did a flip.

"I'll take full blame for the situation."

She paused. "That is the truth."

"Aye," he agreed.

She kept her gaze fixed on him, but she was imagining his son's face as he stared down at them, Marcus on top of her while she arched toward him. If she could only leave the castle tonight. But even an hour's absence would be noticed. Not nearly long enough. She remembered how they had tracked her clear to Glasgow and the damned pawnbroker.

"Leave Kiernan to me." Marcus's voice jerked her back to the present.

She eyed him doubtfully.

He smiled. "Don't concern yourself over it, love. 'Tis nothing."

Elise rose. "I'm going upstairs to change."

"But you look beautiful."

"I can imagine just how I look," she grumbled.

His gaze traveled the length of her, his expression taking on a masculine pride, which started a

195

quiver in her stomach—and reminded her that his son had caught them when that same look was on Marcus's face.

Chapter Fourteen

When Elise finally stepped from the stairwell, Marcus had to remember to breathe. Pleasure rippled through him at seeing she had worn her hair loose. Her creamy skin, luminous against the soft brown of the modest gown borrowed for this occasion, radiated a sensuality, which revived the memory of their earlier lovemaking. Low bodice met high waist, emphasizing the curve of her breasts. The dress hung loosely around her slim body, transforming her into an ethereal creature drifting toward him. She stopped beside him and smiled at his son. Marcus watched Kiernan's acute scrutiny of her as introductions were made. She extended a hand as graciously as any duchess.

"Madam." Kiernan took her hand and brought it to his lips.

Her face lit with enchantment and Marcus breathed a sigh of relief that her misgivings seemed to have evaporated.

"Why, sir," she said, "I believe you are a heartbreaker."

Kiernan blinked in surprise.

"You didn't tell me he was such a rogue, Marcus. I wager the apple doesn't fall far from the tree."

Marcus smiled. "Kiernan is very much his own man."

Her expression softened. "Perhaps, but that raven's hair and those eyes…"

Memory of similar words spoken to him by her upon their first meeting stole over Marcus.

"They must be your mother's eyes." She smiled at Kiernan.

Marcus snapped back to the present.

Cameron joined them, his raised brow testament that he had overheard the comment. Marcus looked from his son to Elise. It hadn't occurred to him she might speak of Jenna. He had never spoken to her of his wife, and she had no idea of Kiernan's sensitivity concerning his mother.

Kiernan angled his head. "You are correct, madam. I did, indeed, inherit those traits from my mother."

"I see," Elise nodded. "But there's more." A corner of her mouth twitched upwards. "She imparted something of herself to you. A piece of her soul, perhaps." Kiernan looked genuinely shaken and Elise's smile turned gentle. "It is heartening that you carry her with you."

He looked hopelessly at his father but was doomed to find no solace there, for Marcus was as surprised as he.

"Well, now, Kiernan," Cameron's deep voice broke in, "what do you think of your father's future bride?" He gave Kiernan a crack on the back and winked at Elise.

Marcus noted the blush that crept up her cheek and wondered at a woman who could be so bold one moment, then so reticent the next.

The following day, Father Whyte arrived. Winnie announced the priest's arrival. Had it been Marcus, Elise would have taken the *sgian dubh* from the wall in the great hall and put it through his heart. That would be a more merciful end than the one he would suffer if his foolishness got them married.

Father Whyte asked if all were well with the wedding arrangements. "A week is a short time to prepare a wedding feast."

"A week?" Elise replied, then remembered Marcus saying the wedding would take place *soon*. He hadn't said how soon.

What if you did go through with the marriage, a quiet voice asked?

Then Price would go free, and Amelia and Steven wouldn't have recompense. But how many more would suffer as a result of Price? She had lost the two most important people in her life. Now she would lose Marcus. All because of her stepfather. But it wasn't so simple. If Marcus—or worse, someone else—discovered the truth, he would pay dearly.

In the end, Elise had seen to Father Whyte's comfort in the small abbey located on the southeast edge of Brahan Seer. Guilt piled higher at the realization that he was enthusiastic about the marriage. Why couldn't he have been one of those pinched-nose priests who believe rank shouldn't mix?

That night when Elise appeared in the great hall and started toward the kitchen, Marcus intercepted her and seated her beside him at the table.

"Winnie is expecting me." She tried to rise.

Marcus laid a firm hand on her shoulder. "Nay. She is not."

Elise glanced at the kitchen door.

"'Tis the way of things," he said. "You will have duties enough after we wed."

After we wed. Her stomach did a flip. Time running out and she had found no answer as to how she would safely and successfully slip away unnoticed. There remained only one answer; she had to tell Marcus she wouldn't marry him. When all was said and done, he was a good man. Once she demanded to be allowed to return home, he wouldn't keep her prisoner.

Kiernan seated himself beside her. She was surrounded. Elise listened as he talked of school, friends, and the upcoming season in London. Everything, she thought, except the one thing that must be in the forefront of his mind. How would she respond? What would she say to this keen young man if he questioned her about her past? Kiernan's gaze turned intense. Her heart rate accelerated. Had she missed something in the conversation?

"I do believe," he said, "the *ton* will be set on its ear by my father's new marchioness."

"Marchioness?" Elise repeated.

Kiernan nodded.

Marchioness… Marchioness—the wife of a marquess. Nobility, Marcus was nobility? Elise's mind raced. What rank was a marquess? Baron, viscount, earl, marquis—marquess—she abruptly felt as though a thick fog had enveloped her brain. If Marcus was a marquess, then Cameron—she nearly choked. Marcus was a high nobleman, and she was an accused murderess—a wanted criminal with a bounty on her head.

"Have I said something?" Kiernan demanded in a low whisper.

Elise's attention jerked back to the young man.

"I meant no offense," he went on. "Your forthright manner will be a breath of fresh air for London's tainted society."

"Of course," she responded in a whisper.

His brow furrowed in concern.

Elise shook her head. "Forgive me. The excitement of the wedding—and London…" she let her voice trail off.

Kiernan hesitated, then smiled in polite acceptance.

Supper ended. Elise waited until Marcus had joined his father and son near the hearth before slipping from the hall.

"Where are ye off to?" Winnie inquired as she hurried through the kitchen.

"I am in need of fresh air."

Winnie gave a grunt of understanding as Elise passed out into the night. She hurried across the compound and down the lane to the abbey. Father Whyte hadn't appeared for the evening meal and she prayed he wasn't already abed.

Elise entered the chapel to find him kneeling before the candlelit altar. She stopped, intending to make a quiet retreat, but he twisted and looked at her over his shoulder. The smile on his face died when their gazes met.

"What's wrong, child?" He rose and started down the aisle toward her.

Elise hurried forward, meeting him halfway. "Father," she said without preamble, "if I ask a question, you are obligated to tell the truth, aren't you?"

"Aye."

"What is Marcus's rank?"

"Rank?"

"Title—rank," she answered impatiently.

"He is the Marquess of Ashlund."

Her heart beat faster. "What is a marquess?"

"In this case, he is the son of a duke."

"A—" Her head reeled. "So Cameron really is a…"

"A duke," Father Whyte confirmed.

Elise collapsed onto a pew.

"Madam!" He caught her hand and fell to his knees before her. "Are you ill?"

"My God," she whispered. "My God." She looked at him. "This is… no mistake?"

He looked confused.

"There's no possibility Marcus will not follow his father's footsteps?"

"Marcus is the only son. He will one day be the Duke of Ashlund."

"My God," she repeated. Then, abruptly looking at the priest, she said, "If I cry off, Marcus couldn't force the wedding?" Would he—could he—actually force her to stay?

"Nay," the priest answered slowly. "He could not force you."

"Father, can you tell me why he hid his

identity from me?"

"Hid his identity? I dinna' see, exactly—" He frowned. "You knew nothing of his rank?"

She shook her head.

"But everyone knows. Perhaps he assumed you knew."

"He cannot stop me from changing my mind about the marriage—can he? I left once before and he brought me back."

Father Whyte looked surprised. "He is a powerful man. I hadn't considered such possibilities, but I suppose he could do almost anything." The priest hesitated. "My child…"

Elise's heart pounded. "Good Lord, what?"

"In society's eyes, you and Marcus are married. The wedding vows are a mere formality. You have been through a proper courtship." He didn't acknowledge her unladylike snort. "Everyone assumes—" He stopped. She frowned and he added, "That you already live as husband and wife."

A jolt of embarrassment warmed her cheeks. She'd been a virgin when Robert married her. The possibility of intimacy outside the marriage bed hadn't occurred to her. But then, she hadn't considered the possibility of intimacy at all after Robert.

"Of course," Father Whyte added, "if they are wrong…"

Elise laughed again, this time with bitterness. "You won't find redemption for me there, Father."

"You needn't worry. You are to be wed. As I said, 'tis a formality."

"A formality which carries the weight of the law."

"True."

"And I am free to go?" she insisted.

"Your reputation would be ruined."

"Bah! I don't care a fig for my reputation."

"It would be a terrible scandal for Marcus, as well."

"Would it?" she said with asperity, but guilt surfaced amongst the anger.

A mental picture flashed of the next big headlines in the London *Sunday Times,* "The Duke Who Married a Murderess." The fact it was a lie wouldn't matter.

"The announcements have already reached the papers," Father Whyte said.

"Announcements?" Elise echoed, then said, "But of course."

"Come," Father Whyte's expression softened, "there has been some mistake. Marcus is a good man. Surely, you will listen to his explanation."

"What explanation?" asked Marcus from the rear of the church.

Elise surged to her feet. "Lord Ashlund. Good of you to join us."

So she had discovered the truth. Marcus had no one to blame but himself for not telling her. He strode to them and halted beside Elise. He gave an acknowledging nod to Father Whyte, then said to her, "Aye, love. Lord Ashlund, Marquess of Ashlund."

"You lied to me."

He recognized the fear behind the curt statement and gently answered, "Nay."

Her lips thinned. "You deny it?"

"If I led you to believe I was of noble class but wasn't, you would have reason to be angry. The fact I *am* of the noble caste is of no consequence. Have you ever heard anyone here address me by my title?"

Her mouth tightened further. "You kept it from me."

"You are saying I instructed all of Brahan Seer to deceive you? How could I possibly accomplish such a thing? The fact that you learned about this before we signed the marriage certificate proves my point."

"The marriage certificate?" Elise repeated, then, as though to herself, said, "Of course, we would sign a marriage certificate."

"It doesn't matter," he insisted. "Especially here."

She canted her head. "And when we leave Brahan

Seer? Isn't that the reason we are doing this because you insisted we cannot leave Brahan Seer without being married?"

"Aye," he replied. "We cannot travel the country and live as we do here. Expectations are different outside Brahan Seer."

"Yes, they are," she retorted. "To the extent you are to be a duke!"

"You aren't being honest," he continued, forcing back frustration. "Admit it. Had you known in the beginning, you wouldn't have agreed to marry me *because* of my station."

"So you did lie."

"I did not."

"Father," she said, keeping her gaze on Marcus, "isn't the sin of omission the same as a direct lie?"

The priest took a deep breath. "It is."

"Are you saying you won't marry me because I will one day be a duke?" Marcus demanded.

"I am saying, I will not marry a man I cannot trust."

"Bloody hell," he cursed. "After all the years the MacGregors have fought for their good fortune, to have it turned against us—"

Her eyes flashed. "Make no mistake, Lord Ashlund, it isn't the MacGregors's good fortune I hold against you."

"It is," he cut in sharply. "If I were Michael's son instead of Cameron's, you would view my suit as proper."

"That is not the point—"

"It is exactly the point. With anyone else I would not have had to say, *You do realize I am a marquess?* Yet, you say that is exactly what I should have done."

"You knew *not* telling me was a manipulation."

"How am I to answer?" he snapped. "Had I made a point of telling you, you would have balked. Yet, *not* telling you is a grievous sin."

Elise eyed him critically. "When did you plan to tell me? Once we arrived in civilization and someone bowed before you?"

"Nay, as I just said, when you signed the wedding certificate you would have known."

"And when would that have been, the moment before we took the wedding vows?"

Marcus looked at Father Whyte. "When, Father?"

"Tomorrow."

Marcus looked back at her. "A far cry from the wedding day."

"But far too long considering the length of our *courtship*."

"You're being foolish." He grasped her arm.

She shook him off. "How did you expect me to react?"

He wished mightily Father Whyte weren't present. "I had hoped some feeling had developed that would negate these foolish concerns."

"I need to be alone with my *foolish concerns*." She brushed past him.

Marcus glanced at Father Whyte, who gave him a troubled look, then Marcus shifted his gaze onto Elise as she disappeared out the chapel doors.

Elise closed her bedchamber door, then walked to the couch and sat down. Placing a hand on her belly, she pressed it in an attempt to quiet the twisting, which had begun as a flutter and was now a wrenching unlike anything she had experienced since the last night on the *Amelia*.

Elise Merriwether would be the name of the woman to marry the Marquess of Ashlund. It was foolish for her to have given her great-aunt's surname, but when she'd come out of her delirium in Josh and Shannon's home, she'd given the first name that came to mind. Would Price connect that Elise Merriwether to her? Her mind raced. Would he see the notice? The announcement would go into the London *Sunday Times*, probably *The Scotsman* in Edinburgh, as well. But would the news reach America? She thought of the

Boston papers and recalled the news when King George III died and his son took his place. Occasionally, large business ventures were reported, but she couldn't recall any marriage announcements for the nobility.

Elise released a shaky breath. It was unlikely the announcement would make the American papers. She leaned back against the cushions and closed her eyes. Looking back, it now seemed ridiculous she hadn't realized there was more to the MacGregor men than mere wealth. She had missed all of the warning signs. How had she been so blind?

"Oh, Marcus," she whispered. "What have you done?"

A duke can protect even a murderess, her mind contended. Her insides gave a vicious twist. He could, she agreed. But could his reputation survive the scandal? And could she live with herself for hurting him?

First thing tomorrow morning, she would go to Cameron and demand to leave.

At the sound of voices in the great hall, Elise paused on the stairs. Who would be roused at this early hour? It wasn't yet dawn.

"I know what ye told me," a young male voice said. *Tavis.*

"Aye," came another, deeper voice. *Marcus.*

"I'm willing to take my punishment, laird," Tavis said.

Elise didn't breathe.

"I told you not to leave Brahan Seer again," Marcus said. "You are a man—the only man in your household. You're old enough to understand that responsibility."

Elise crept down the remaining four stairs and peeked around the corner. They stood on the far side of the table nearest the postern door, Marcus's hand on

Tavis's shoulder, Tavis's gaze downcast. The worry on Marcus's face stirred something deep within her. The day the Campbells attacked, he had been ruthless. But this was a gentleness as kind as his ruthlessness had been cruel.

"The thirst for revenge will eat a man alive," he said. "I swore to deal with your father's murderers, and did. Leave it be." He sighed, the action revealing a great weariness. "If those dogs came for you, even with a warrant from King George, I wouldn't give you up." A tiny smile played at his mouth. "Lad, we aren't as different from the Campbells as we believe. They were as unwilling to hand over their kinsmen as I would be."

Elise couldn't check a surge of hope. He would not give up one of his own—even in the name of justice?

Marcus crossed his arms over his chest. "I have no intention of facing your mother with the news that you have followed your father to the grave. Therefore, you go to London."

Tavis gasped.

"Nay," Marcus said. "You will have no more opportunities to go wandering off by yourself." He raised a brow. "You know your sister follows."

"I made sure she did not," the boy protested.

Marcus laughed. "Never underestimate a female, no matter her age."

"Laird," Tavis begged, "I promise—"

"Nay," Marcus said shortly.

"Not London then, but Edinburgh."

Another laugh from Marcus, this one tinged with fondness. "London it will be, lad. Edinburgh is too close for comfort."

"Laird," Tavis said, desperation in his voice.

The mirth in Marcus's eyes faded. "Erin will accompany you to England."

Elise felt her breath quicken. A decree she would have made had she the power. Realization washed over her in a tidal wave. If she confessed the truth, Marcus would sail across the ocean and kill Price with his bare hands. If she disappeared, he would leave no stone unturned until he found her. If she told him she would not marry a duke, he would follow her to the ends of the earth in order to change her mind.

God help him, he loved her.

And God help her, she wouldn't sacrifice him... not even for Amelia and Steven.

Marcus entered the great hall the following afternoon to discover the room filled with people and humming with unexpected excitement. He scanned the familiar entourage until his gaze settled on his cousin Sophie and, to his surprise, Elise, who looked as though she hadn't a care in the world. The two women stood, profiles to him, and neither had noticed his entrance. He hung back near the door, watching.

He hadn't spoken with Elise since she left him standing in the abbey the night before. He had gone to her room early this morning and found her bed empty. She had slept there, however, a fact he had verified in the dead of night. His search that morning didn't turn her up in the kitchen or the ladies' drawing room. Even his library, a favorite haunt, had been empty. The kitchen maids informed him she and Winnie had gone to visit Chloe.

Marcus studied Elise. What had transpired after she'd sequestered herself in her room? What other ridiculous considerations surfaced during those waking hours? She hadn't sought him out to inform him there would be no wedding. Neither had she confirmed there *would* be a wedding. No note, no message, nothing.

He shifted his attention to his cousin. Sophie, Lady Whycham, was one of the few Ashlund relatives he liked. Though petite, her flaming red hair and voluptuous body had made her all the rage before she wed Justin Ellington, the Earl of Whycham.

She caught sight of him, ceased speaking, and raised a meticulously plucked brow. Elise turned, and he started toward them.

"Sophie," he said as he neared. "What brings you

here, lass?"

"Don't play the innocent with me, Marcus MacGregor. You know full well I would not let my favorite cousin wed without me." The keen curiosity in her gaze vanished and her eyes narrowed in a fashion that Marcus knew well. "I am wondering, Cousin," she said, "why it is I read of your engagement in the newspapers instead of hearing it from you."

Marcus looked at Elise, whose impassive expression didn't quite hide the sense that she, too, wondered the same thing.

He slid an arm around Elise. She stiffened. The small hope inside him sagged, but he kept his gaze on her. "When last I visited Ashlund, I had no notion I would marry."

"No?" Sophie said, bringing both their attentions onto her. "Still, you could have sent a personal missive."

He again felt Elise's thoughts echo the question, and he looked down at her. "Forgive me, Sophie," he said, and smiled gently at Elise. "Since Elise agreed to be my wife, I have thought of little else."

"Not so, Cousin," Sophie replied. "You didn't forget the formal announcements."

Marcus shot his cousin a sharp look.

Sophie groaned. "Elise, are you sure you will be able to put up with him for the rest of your life?"

Marcus started. He cursed silently at Sophie, then his future wife when her expression remained unreadable save a hint of curiosity.

"Everyone is speculating about the woman who has captured Marcus's heart," Sophie went on.

"Good Lord," Elise blurted

Sophie laughed. "Didn't you know, my dear? Marcus is a confirmed bachelor."

Marcus stilled as Elise looked directly at him for the first time. "Really? I wouldn't have believed it."

"Why is that?" Sophie asked, the eagerness in her voice so transparent that Marcus wanted to thrash her.

"Because your cousin   pursued me with such a

vengeance that I would have thought he was desperate for a wife."

Sophie burst into howls of laughter, and his desire to laugh with her forced him to cough loudly several times.

"Does this," he began, but halted abruptly to clear his throat before saying, "Does this mean—"

"This means, sir," Elise cut in, "you should attend to your guests."

He opened his mouth to reply, then closed it again.

Elise opened the door to the library and stepped aside. "Forgive me, Lady Whycham. I hadn't expected company, so the ladies' drawing room isn't ready to receive guests."

"Call me Sophie." She brushed past Elise. "We shall soon be related. No need to stand on formality. Now," Sophie seated herself on the divan and waited until Elise had taken a seat beside her, "tell me what my cousin has done to annoy you."

Elise startled but managed a hasty, "I'm not sure what you mean."

Sophie's eyes twinkled. "I know my cousin." She laughed, a small snort escaping in the process. "Still, he did surprise me with the decision to wed again." She leaned close. "Marcus had formed no lasting attachments since Jenna's death. Though he is no womanizer—he is a remarkably discriminating man— he isn't one to refrain from female company."

"I didn't have the impression he denied himself the company of women," Elise said dryly.

Sophie's eyes widened with mirth and she clapped a hand over her mouth. Elise blinked, then gave into the infectious laughter.

Sophie lowered her hand. "All right, *Cousin*, what has he done?"

Elise hesitated. How did she explain that Marcus hiding the fact he was a rich and powerful man could prove to be his *and* her undoing?

When Elise had finished relating the tale of how she had come to Scotland and of Marcus's deception, Sophie took a deep breath. "I suppose learning the man you're to marry will one day be a duke could be a shock. But the fact he cares for you—" Sophie halted, and Elise knew her shock showed.

"You doubt his feelings?" Sophie asked.

She didn't, but she hadn't grown used to the idea, and the fact Sophie had so easily seen it made her want to cry. So, she countered with, "How can any woman know what a man thinks?"

"Come now, you must comprehend that Marcus isn't a man to make a commitment lightly."

"What I comprehend is that Marcus is a man accustomed to having his way."

"That is true of any man with half a wit."

Elise couldn't help laughing. "I suppose you're right."

Sophie's expression softened. "You aren't betraying your husband by loving again."

Elise nearly choked. "N-no, of course not."

"There is no one for you to return home to?"

She recalled the blood darkening Steven's coat. "No."

"Your husband's family, what of them?"

"There is no one."

Sophie sighed. "A shame."

"Yes," Elise replied, and couldn't prevent a picture of the two who waited for her at the bottom of the sea. Her chest tightened and she rose. "Would you care for a drink?" She crossed to the sideboard. "Marcus keeps an excellent Napoleon brandy."

"Brandy?"

Elise paused, her hand on the decanter lid, and twisted to look at Sophie. "Don't tell me you're going to lecture me. Are all MacGregors so puritanical?"

Sophie's eyes lit with amusement. "I've heard the MacGregors called many things—bloodthirsty, uncouth, barbaric, ignorant—but never have they been compared to anything so noble. Puritanical, indeed."

Elise couldn't resist. "There is port, if brandy is too strong for you."

"Brandy it is," she said without hesitation.

Elise poured two glasses of the brandy and returned to the divan. She handed a snifter to Sophie, then sat down.

"Did I mention that I tried escaping to Australia?"

"I do not recall the story," Sophie replied with such gravity that Elise couldn't help wondering if someone had indeed repeated the tale in the short time the countess had been there.

"Marcus's men retrieved me," Elise said.

"Retrieved you?"

"It seems strange now that I left," she said more to herself than Sophie.

"What happened when my cousin's men came for you?" Sophie asked.

"Cameron sent them. Marcus wasn't aware I had left. He told me if he had come, it would have gone far worse for me."

"I can well believe that. Why did you leave?"

Elise grimaced. "The reason was sound."

"Do you mean to extract a little revenge now?"

Elise looked at Sophie. "Things aren't always as simple as they seem."

Sophie nodded once. "And often not as complicated as we think. What stops you from leaving again?"

"He would only come for me again."

"But of course," Sophie agreed. "There is nowhere you could hide from *him*. I do see your point."

Elise looked sharply at her. Merriment danced in Sophie's eyes, and Elise realized she referred to Marcus and not Price, as her imagination had jumped to think. She was hallucinating—either that or drunk.

"Just how rich is my husband-to-be?" The countess's eyes widened, and Elise cried, "Good Lord, that didn't come right at all." She groaned and collapsed against the divan back.

"I imagine you wonder what sort of reception

you'll receive once you leave Brahan Seer?"

Elise's heart jumped, but the reaction was stalled by the honesty that shone in the countess' eyes. "I swear, Sophie, as foolish as it sounds, I had no idea he was a duke. Here at Brahan Seer... I knew him as Cameron's son and leader of the MacGregor clan. I knew they weren't destitute, but a duke!" She laid a hand on Sophie's hand. "I am no duchess."

"And I was no countess," Sophie replied.

"What?"

"I was only Lady Ashlund. Of course, my family has money." Sophie's eyes danced. "All Ashlunds have money. But, then, so does Justin."

"Ashlund," Elise repeated. "They are MacGregors?"

"Oh, no. Ryan MacGregor married Helena Ashlund about one hundred and fifty years ago. Helena was an only child, therefore, the dukedom fell to Ryan when Helena's father Coll Ashlund died." Sophie shook her head and a shadow passed over her face. "That was a terrible time. The MacGregor name had been outlawed."

"The clearances?" Elise asked.

"Oh, no. Those atrocities are much more recent," she said. "There was a great deal of political strife"—Sophie laughed—"when hasn't there been political strife in Scotland? In any case, the crown seized MacGregor land, and the MacGregors fought back. It is said in our family that, if not for Helena marrying Ryan, his brand of the MacGregors, Marcus's line, wouldn't be here today."

"Ashlund money," Elise murmured.

"You have it," Sophie said.

Indeed, Elise thought. *Now what am I to do with it?*

Chapter Fifteen

Much later that evening, Marcus pushed past the cluster of men outside the library doorway watching Elise and Sophie, each with a glass in hand as they sat on the floor in front of the fire giggling like school girls. He stopped and looked from the women to the decanter on the floor beside them. On the sideboard, other decanters sat in disarray. Some had been left uncovered—one actually lay empty on its side. Marcus turned his attention back to the women. He could scarce believe his eyes. They were drunk.

The women looked up as he strode toward them. "I suppose 'tis my fault for not looking for you here first." He stopped before them.

Elise and Sophie looked at one another and shrugged.

"I told you to inform someone of your whereabouts."

"Told me?" Elise's brows rose sluggishly. "I seem to remember you as-as-" Her gaze cut to Sophie. "A difficult word—asking me," she got out in a quick breath, then looked at him again. "But, then, I'm not surprised you remember it differently."

Laughter emanated from the men.

"And in case you hadn't noticed," she went on between hiccups, "I haven't left the confines of the castle." Despite the slight slur in her words, they were said with emphasis.

Another ripple of low laughter came from the men and Marcus shot them a quelling look. Cameron coughed and Kiernan raised a brow while the others' mouths twitched with amusement. Marcus turned his attention to Sophie.

"I see you are introducing my future wife to the niceties of polite society."

Sophie looked at Elise, who said, "I do believe he is blaming you." Leaning into Sophie, Elise added in a loud whisper, "Just like a man, wouldn't you say?"

The gales of laughter that swept the room increased when Elise gripped the seat of the chair with one hand, while clutching her glass with the other, and began scrambling to her feet. Marcus reached to assist her. She batted his hand away and rose onto unsteady feet. She swayed, grabbed the back of the chair, and leveled her gaze on him.

"Now see here, Marcus MacGregor, we'll have none of your lectures tonight." She pushed at his chest with the hand that held the glass. "Lady Whycham and I are enjoying ourselves and we don't need you or anyone else telling us what we should do. Isn't that right, Sophie?"

"Right," agreed Sophie. "We don't need you or anyone else."

"If you will excuse us." Elise reached down and grasped Sophie's hand. She pulled, nearly falling onto Sophie before finally helping her to her feet. Sophie smoothed her skirts as Elise faced Marcus. "Lady Whycham and I are going to see to the preparations for the banquet."

Shoving her glass into his hand, she headed for the door, Sophie on her heels. A picture of the two women falling down the stairs and breaking their lovely necks flashed in his mind, and Marcus sat the glass on his desk and started after them. The men parted for the ladies, stepping back an extra pace when he charged past. He grabbed the women as they reached the stairs, pushing Sophie toward his son and scooping Elise into his arms.

"Put me down!" she sputtered, but he ignored her, hurrying down the stairs and into the great hall. When he reached the table, he dropped her into a chair.

"He's peeved," Elise commented to Sophie, who had been set in the chair beside hers.

"Serves him right," she replied.

Marcus stifled an oath and ordered a kettle of tea. When the strong brew began to clear their senses, he watched with satisfaction as they rubbed their temples.

"Brute," Elise muttered, casting a dark glance in his direction. She rose and headed for the stairs, adding loud enough for all to hear, "I wager Sophie agrees with me."

"Damnation, Elise," Sophie paused in rising, "must you shout?" She, too, started for the steps.

Elise paused at the stairs and glanced over her shoulder. Marcus met her gaze, but she only shook her head and turned to go up the stairs.

"You're to be married in two days," Sophie said, taking the first step behind her. "Perhaps you should give serious thought to your decision, Elise."

Marcus jumped from his seat at the table. By God, he would strangle her. He strode across the room. Halting at the bottom of the stairs, he called up to them, "Sophie, you would do well to keep your thoughts to yourself." His voice echoed up the narrow staircase and both women halted, covering their ears.

"Of all the nerve," Sophie complained as they started up again. "Marcus, I never knew you to be so perverse. Mayhap you should reconsider, Elise. I wonder if any of us know him at all."

Marcus took the stairs two at a time and, in a flash, reached Sophie's side. "You will retire to your chambers *now*, Cousin," he growled.

Grasping her elbow, he hurried her up the stairs ahead of him until they reached Elise. Marcus grabbed her elbow with his other hand and forced them up the remaining steps ahead of him. He escorted them down the corridor until they reached Elise's chambers. He shoved Sophie in the direction of her room, opened

Elise's door, and thrust her inside.

"Don't leave this room the remainder of the evening. I will have dinner sent up."

Elise mumbled something unintelligible as he clicked the door shut behind him.

When Marcus reentered the hall a moment later, the low laugher of the men cut short. Those sitting at the table seemed absorbed in the odd task of examining the tabletop. Marcus looked closer as he neared them and discerned the collective struggle to keep from bursting into laughter.

"Out with it!" he boomed. "I couldn't live with the guilt of someone bursting a blood vessel."

No one made a peep, and he threw his hands into the air and headed for the sanctuary of his library. When he was halfway up the stairs, the hall filled with laughter. Marcus paused, torn between cursing the men and joining them, then shook his head and hurried up the stairs.

At the light tap on his library door, Marcus ceased speaking to Harris. The door opened and Sophie peered inside.

"Oh," she said, "forgive me. I didn't know you were busy."

She started to back away and Harris said, "We can finish later, Marcus. I have enough here to begin work." He lifted his notebook to indicate his notes.

"No," Sophie began, but Marcus waved her in. Harris rose, bowed to Sophie, then left them alone. She seated herself in the chair Harris had occupied, and said, "You seem to have accomplished a great deal this morning." She motioned to the open ledger on his desk.

"I rise early," he replied.

"It is a beautiful morning."

Marcus gave her an appraising look. "I would think after yesterday evening that this morning would not be so pleasant for you."

Sophie smiled. "I have a strong constitution, as

you well know." She settled back against the cushion and regarded him. "Do not say you are truly angry with me."

"Shocked. As Justin would be, I wager."

"My God!" she exclaimed. "Mayhap Elise was right."

"Right about what?" he asked sharply.

"She commented on the puritanical characteristic of the MacGregors."

Marcus tossed aside the quill he'd been holding and lounged in his chair. "I assume this is in reference to me?"

"You were the original topic of conversation. But never mind that. I like Elise."

"Aye?"

"Yes. She told me the harrowing story of how she came to be here. I am curious, though, what it is she is omitting."

"What do you mean?"

Sophie's expression softened. "It is plain you care for her."

"Sophie—"

"Don't become annoyed with me, Marcus. We have known one another too long for such foolishness. I am pleased you have found a woman to care for, and approve of the match."

Marcus raised a brow.

She gave him a dry look. "You comprehend what I mean. Now, tell me, what is she hiding?"

He took a deep breath. "I have yet to find out."

Sophie smoothed her dress. "She isn't given to talking about herself, even half in her cups. Which do you think is most likely: that she has committed a crime or has run away from her husband? Either one would allow for her gentle upbringing."

He prayed to God she hadn't run away from a husband. What would he do if that were the case?

"Those are not the only possibilities," Marcus said. "It may be her husband was in debt and she has no means to repay the creditors."

"Quite right," Sophie said. "I hadn't thought of that."

Thus far, his investigations had turned up no record of a ship sinking in Solway Firth, nor had any ship docked in the firth. There had, however, been a terrible storm the day before Shannon and Josh found Elise. The ship may have sunk as Elise said. The report of ships docking in Edinburgh and London gave no clues as to what ship she might have sailed on. The report on ships leaving Boston harbor had yet to reach him.

Marcus focused on his cousin. "I will have no meddling in this affair, Sophie."

She wrinkled her nose in distaste. "Of course not."

"I am serious," he added.

"Marcus, I don't interfere in the affairs of others."

He gave her a reproachful look.

She screwed one side of her mouth into a wry smile. "Not really, I don't, and you cannot deny that I have never interfered in your life."

"True."

"But that doesn't mean I can't see what is happening. What measures have you taken to discover the truth?"

"That is nothing you need concern yourself with."

Sophie sighed. "I feared you would say that. Marcus. I like the girl. Still, I would ask that you inform me if any… problems arise."

"I will keep your request in mind," he said, and wished her a good day.

Her wedding day brought with it all the promise of a hailstorm in June. Wind blew in clouds so dark, it looked as though God's wrath would rain down upon them. Elise sent up a prayer of thanks for Sophie's experienced hands. She held her breath while Sophie deftly fastened the buttons that went from the neckline of the yellow silk gown to the small of her back.

"There." Sophie gave a final tug to smooth out the

dress. Elise turned as Sophie reached for the matching lace veil. "Look at this beautiful work."

"Yes," Elise agreed. "Winnie is a master needlewoman."

Sophie smiled and positioned the veil's band atop Elise's hair. The lace fell to her waistline. A lace overskirt continued the illusion of fog amid petals to the floor. Sophie stepped back. Elise watched her soon-to-be-cousin, touched by the genuine pleasure on her face.

"Lovely." Sophie's expression sharpened. "Well, Cousin, you've done it now."

Elise glanced at the clock on her mantel. "I still have half an hour."

"A full thirty minutes in which to explain to Marcus why you changed your mind."

Elise jerked her gaze onto the countess.

"Come now, you know your anxiety is only due to the gravity of the vows you will take." A gleam appeared in Sophie's eyes. "Unless you fear you cannot keep your vows."

"You MacGregors," Elise began, then amended, "Ashlunds," at the look on Sophie's face. "Born troublemakers."

"A long line of troublemakers." Her mouth assumed an impish grin. "Perhaps you are nervous about the wedding night? I have not once seen Marcus making his way to your room."

"Good Lord! Is nothing sacred?"

"No," she said, then picked up the bouquet that lay on the bed.

Elise looked again at the clock, then back at Sophie. "I still have twenty-five minutes. Sophie," she began, but Sophie cut her off.

"I will await you in the drawing room."

Elise smiled her thanks. As Sophie closed the door behind her, Elise seated herself on the couch. Twenty-five minutes from now, the key that bound her soul to Amelia and Steven would lay at the bottom of the sea with them. She had considered using her position once she married to quietly bring about Price's fall, but had recalled Marcus's words *"The thirst for revenge will eat a man alive."* The same was true of a woman.

She was trading Steven and Amelia's rest for Marcus's safety. May they forgive her.

Chapter Sixteen

At sight of Marcus dressed in a new kilt, a crisp, white lawn shirt meticulously tucked into his waistband and buttoned to the neck, and a bonnet cocked to one side, Elise faltered the last few steps from where he stood at the altar. In minutes, this man would be her husband. Her gaze met his and she saw there an intensity that demanded she leap into his arms from across the final precipice that separated them. Her knees weakened. Marcus held out his hand. She flushed and dropped her gaze.

He grasped her hand in a firm grip, turning with her to face Father Whyte. The priest spoke the Latin vows slowly, then patiently waited until she repeated them as he had coached. Marcus repeated his vows and, before Elise realized it, he slipped a large emerald onto her finger. The ring was a size too large, but her heart skipped a beat at the weight of the jewel and the cool of the metal encircling her finger. Father Whyte gave the final blessing and a shout went up when Marcus took her in his arms. Her attention jerked from the emerald to him as he finalized the ritual with their first kiss as husband and wife.

Hand on her back, Marcus guided her around to face the guests who stood cheering. He urged her down the aisle and out the chapel doors. The crowd waiting outside shouted in exultation, and those following joined in more shouts. Waves, squeals, and cries of good wishes followed them to the castle. Marcus opened the postern door and Elise stepped inside.

With a sweep of her gaze, Elise took in the gold and purple swags adorning the walls, the velvet surfaces softening the light cast by sconces burning from holders erected while she slept last night. On the far side of the room, hung on each end of the wall, were two intricately woven tapestries depicting Highland men in battle. The table was laden with food, and serving girls dodged guests who had arrived too late to find space near the chapel. Another cheer went up and several women hurried forward, grasped Elise's arms, and whisked her across the room to a place near the hearth. She was instantly surrounded. Sophie stood among their ranks and she gave Elise a knowing look. Elise turned to see Marcus reach the opposite side of the room, a glass of whiskey already in hand, his friends clapping him on the back.

The men spoke loudly and, despite the din, Elise caught bits and pieces of their bawdy suggestions for the wedding night. Her female companions giggled, all but Sophie, whose mouth twitched, and Elise realized they, too, had heard the advice given her husband. Her cheeks warmed and she wished very much for the quiet of her bedchambers. *Her bedchambers.* Goose pimples prickled her arms. *Their* bedchambers. She would occupy the lady's chambers, but she wouldn't sleep there. The look in Marcus's eyes when the priest had pronounced them man and wife had dispelled any doubts about their wedding night. Sophie was right; she'd done it now.

Serving girls emerged from the kitchen, trays piled high with lamb, beef, chicken, delicately stuffed quail and wild pheasant. Salmon, perch, flounder and whitefish followed, all caught from the fresh waters of Loch Katrine and Lock Lommund. On the way to the castle, Elise had glimpsed the wagons loaded with meats, cheeses, fruits and vegetables that would be carted to the village so that all who had crossed MacGregor land for the   wedding could partake in the festivities.

She had overheard Marcus give instructions for fine liquors to be included in the bounty. Elise glanced his way. He stood among the warriors and peasants as though among equals. Who, but the wealthy—those who need not worry for tomorrow's bread—stood so casually? *And what of those who toil for the bread to feed those they love?* something deep inside her whispered.

Her heart pricked. Idiot that she was, not until two days ago had she found the presence of mind to go to Marcus's library and research the Highland clan system. Knowledge is power, her father had said. She had forgotten that precept. Had she followed her head instead of her heart, the moment her traitorous heart had stirred at the sight of Marcus MacGregor she would have made it her business to know his business. A chill stole through her and settled in her gut. What good had that done her with Robert? His family was counted among the elite of Boston, yet he had been a murderer. Elise focused abruptly on the man and woman who stepped before her.

The woman offered a bundle wrapped in simple cloth. "For ye, m'lady," she said in a thick accent.

Elise reflexively reached for the parcel. "Thank you."

She untied the twine that bound the bundle. The knot loosed easily and the cloth fell away to reveal a finely stitched linen blanket. Elise slipped a finger beneath the material's folds and, grasping it between her fingers, ran them along the edge.

"It's beautiful," she breathed, and opened the blanket to its full four feet. She placed the cloth covering on the hearth's mantel, then pressed the linen to her cheek. None finer had she found, even in the expensive boutiques of Boston. "How soft." She looked questioningly at the woman.

The woman blushed. "We grow the flax. I harvest the reeds, then make the linen."

Elise stared. She knew the arduous task of creating linen. As a young child, she had watched her great grandmother, a woman of seventy-two years, draw bundles of flax (straws pulled, not cut, her great grandmother stressed, for cutting made the stems useless) across boards filled with spikes set far enough apart to allow the flax stalks through but not the seed heads. That was but the beginning of the long process that led to the creation of the yarn used in the weaving.

Elise looked at the woman. "I've never seen finer work."

The woman blushed deeper and glanced from her husband back to Elise. "'Tis a blanket for the bairn."

"Bairn?"

The woman smiled. "The one sure to come next spring."

Emotion shot through Elise. The memory of Amelia as a newborn, wrapped in swaddling cloth, flashed before her only to be replaced by Amelia's lifeless body wrapped in a white burial shroud.

Another child?

She jerked her gaze onto Marcus. As though aware of her alarm, he looked in her direction. His attention focused on the blanket she still pressed against her cheek. His eyes softened and she knew he realized the blanket's significance. Elise dropped the blanket from her cheek and looked back at the man and woman.

"Thank you," she said in a hoarse voice.

The man looked at his wife, his pride in Elise's reaction taken as proof they had pleased the lord's bride. He gave a small bow and ushered his wife away. Elise turned and came face to face with Sophie.

"Shall I take that?" Sophie placed a hand on the blanket.

"Oh, Sophie," she cried in a small voice, "what have I done?"

"One never quite forgets the pain of losing a child," Sophie said.

The bagpipes struck up, followed immediately by the fiddle, then the remaining instruments blended into one for Elise. She watched as Sophie lifted the blanket and examined the intricate pattern.

"Society would pay a great price for such work," she commented. "And to think you found it here in the Highlands." Sophie looked up from the blanket. "Interesting what one finds in the most unlikely places."

Hours later, the revelry showed no signs of abating, so Elise retired. Sophie saw to her undressing, then the donning of the nightgown she had given Elise as a wedding gift. The gown made of pale-green silk brushed her ankles. She hadn't worn a night dress so fine since leaving Boston. Sophie slipped the sleeves of the matching robe over her arms. Elise examined the small satin rosettes encircling each sleeve hem.

"Lovely," she murmured.

Sophie stepped back and surveyed her. "*You're* lovely, and Marcus is sure to agree."

Elise grimaced, although inwardly she trembled. The heated look in his eyes when she'd turned before going up the stairs made her stomach do somersaults every time she remembered their passion. Why in heaven this should be so, she couldn't fathom. Tonight would not be the first time they'd made love. How much closer to *love* might tonight bring her?

Sophie assisted her into the large, four-poster bed and pulled the covers up to her chin. She kissed Elise's forehead then left. When the door clicked shut, Elise turned onto her side, facing the low-burning fire. Sophie had said the men would keep Marcus occupied well into the night. It seemed every time she had glanced in his direction, his glass was being filled. Father and son were following his example. She expected the lot of them to pass out on the stone floor of the great hall.

A glint from the corner dresser drew her attention. A gold chain, another gift from Marcus, sat beside a garnet-crowned heart brooch. A gift from Cameron. The brooch had belonged to Marcus's mother. Moisture had glistened in Cameron's eyes when he pinned it on her dress. Tears stung her eyes. What would Marcus's mother have thought of her son marrying a murderess? Elise slipped an arm beneath her pillow and hugged it close as she drifted off to dreams of ships tossed about by high winds, a child lost in the darkness, and a man who called from a place she couldn't distinguish.

"Quiet, lads." Marcus slapped Declan's shoulder. He rode atop the shoulders of Declan and Kiernan. "Ye are sure to wake the dead."

Declan pretended to misstep, jostling him. Marcus grasped Declan's shoulder.

"Don't make me fetch my sword and deal with you," Marcus laughed.

The procession of men stopped before the new lady's bedchambers. Declan kicked open the door. It hit the wall with a resounding bang and Elise bolted upright with a small cry. She blinked against the soft light of the candle illuminating her nightstand. At the sight of disheveled brown locks cascading down her shoulders and over the creamy rise of her breasts, Marcus's groin tightened. She looked from him to Declan. When her gaze came to Kiernan, her eyes widened and she snatched the sheet up to her chin.

Probably best, Marcus realized. Kiernan was no threat, but a band of drunken Highlanders barred the only exit. He bit back a laugh when her attention shifted to the top of his head where, earlier, had sat the now-missing bonnet. Her gaze traveled downward, her eyes narrowing when they reached the missing shirt buttons—a shirt open to his navel and only half tucked into a kilt, which looked as though it might come unpleated with a brisk sneeze.

Her gaze lifted to his face. "Is there something you want, milord?"

Guffaws followed, along with several straightforward answers to her query. Marcus noted her chagrin in the form of pink cheeks. He patted

Kiernan's and Declan's shoulders. They lowered him to the floor while Declan added his compliments upon Marcus's wisdom if he heeded their advice. The request they be allowed to remain followed as Elise's attention settled on Declan. Marcus glanced at Declan, who winked at her, and Marcus knew Declan was extracting a bit of revenge for the cuff with the frying pan.

"We have brought your new lord to you, lass," Declan said, his deep voice resonating above the general commotion. "He's a wee bit worn, but you need not worry. He'll have no trouble wielding his sword for you tonight."

The men fairly shook with raucous laughter. Elise gave a ladylike sniff, but Declan gave no evidence of noticing the cool look she sent his way.

She gave Marcus an appraising glance, then addressed Declan. "He looks worse for the wear. I suggest you put him in his own chambers. I have no need of a husband who is useless."

The men succumbed to more uproarious laughter. All, that is, except Marcus. He stepped forward and, heedless of her sudden cry and valiant attempt to keep the sheet wrapped around herself, pulled her to him.

"I assure you, sweet, I am quite fit for tonight's activities."

Whoops of approval went up as he kissed her quick and hard. With a jerk of his head, he cleared the room, never breaking eye contact with his wife. Finally, when everyone had gone and the last of the suggestions and general advice had faded from the room, Marcus released her. He stepped back and appraised her. She kneeled half naked on the bed, hair tousled as he remembered it on those occasions she had allowed him into her bed.

He wondered if she thought he wouldn't come to her, then noticed the sleeves of the filmy pale robe and night shift she wore. A gift from Sophie, no doubt. Did the wearing of the gift indicate his new wife anticipated his coming? She had uttered not a word about the discovery of his title, but she had married him. Was *that* enough? Had she forgiven him?

Marcus hadn't pressed her, fearing he would further tip the scales in his disfavor. She had gone about the business of the wedding as any bride might— any bride who considered marriage a business, that is. She had surprised him, unexpectedly joining him and his men yesterday when they went to the village. She had, when he'd made the mistake of addressing her familiarly, looked as though she would bolt for the castle. The look on her face then, he realized, wasn't so dissimilar from the look she wore now.

"Have you come to fear me so?" he asked. When she made no reply, he added, "You married me, Elise, knowing who I am."

She tilted her head as though to read his thoughts. His body pulsed. A wary look entered her eyes and he could have sworn she *had* read his mind.

"I have spent many nights in your bed," he said, adding in a husky voice, "Though, not nearly enough. Tonight and every night hereafter, you will be in *my* bed."

He waited for no response—needed no response— other than the reaction he would get when her body responded to his—and scooped her into his arms. She gave a surprised cry.

So, she was no mind reader, after all.

Marcus strode through the connecting closet into his room. He stopped before the massive bed. Her gaze shifted to the bed, then moved across her new surroundings. Her attention lingered on the fire burning in the hearth, then flicked upward to the sword which hung over the mantel.

Elise abruptly looked at him, seeming to have forgotten she lay in his arms. He kissed her. She wriggled as if to slip through the miniscule space between his arms and chest. Marcus flicked his tongue into her mouth, mimicking the motion he would soon replicate inside her body. She stilled, and he wondered if she was envisioning the same action.

At last, he broke the   kiss. He scrutinized her

face until her gaze fell to his chest. Slowly, he lowered her feet to the carpeted floor. He pushed the robe and night rail from her shoulders. His gaze followed the slither of their descent until they struck the floor.

Marcus tipped her head up until she faced him and whispered, "Touch me."

Elise didn't move, didn't blink, and he held his breath.

She shifted, only minutely at first, then lifted a hand to finger the topmost button still intact on his shirt. She reached with the other hand and unbuttoned the button, then the next, then the last. Her gaze remained focused on his chest. Marcus stifled heavy breaths when she slipped her hands inside his shirt and slid them up and over his shoulders. He dropped his arms to his sides, allowing the shirt to fall to the floor.

Her hands glided down his chest. Ripples of pleasure radiated through him. He hardened more with each inch she descended. She stopped with her fingers clasped around his belt. She slipped the leather from its loop. The clasp clinked in the silence of the room as she unfastened it. The plaid loosened and dropped into a pile at his feet. She didn't move, and he realized her gaze was fixed on the jutting, hard length of him. He didn't move—wasn't about to move. She could stare at him all night and, knowing her eyes were on him, he could maintain his arousal until she tired of the sight. Her gaze did move, though, back to his chest where she placed her palms.

"You're so hard," she said, as though marveling at something she hadn't the slightest notion could have been.

Marcus choked back a groan. He backed her against the bed and she fell onto the mattress. He scooted her farther up onto the bed, then rose over her, holding his body inches above her. He gently kissed her forehead, then the tip of her nose, her eyelids, cheeks, mouth. Here he lingered, rocking his hips against her in light motions as he drew the kiss out. Elise ran her hands along his back, hesitating at the curve of his buttocks.

"Aye, love," he whispered, placing small kisses at the corner of her mouth, then along her neck. "Touch me as you like."

He rocked again and, this time, her hands continued around and over the curve of his buttocks. Marcus groaned as he took a nipple between his lips. He gently parted her legs with a knee, then eased into her. He moved slowly, drawing out her pleasure. He suckled one breast, then the other until, at last, her fingers tightened on the tensed muscles of his buttocks. He quickened his movements. An instant later, she cried out softly and lifted her hips to meet his movements. Another instant, and he emptied into her. He waited until the throb of his body ceased, then hugged her close and slid to her side.

Elise relaxed against the carriage's cushion. She closed her eyes, allowing the motion of the carriage to lull her. The journey from Brahan Seer to the lowlands had been easier than expected. The stop at the Green Lady Inn earlier that morning had divided a tedious eight-hour ride into two, more comfortable, four-hour portions. Now, less than two hours from Ashlund, they would first stop at Sophie's estate.

She opened her eyes and looked out the window at Marcus, who rode alongside the carriage. He sat, as always, easy in the saddle. There had been little time to think of him today. Sophie had kept her distracted with plans for Ashlund and the visits they would make to the *modiste*, as well as a number of other merchants, who were sure to provide what Sophie said she needed to fulfill her role as the new Marchioness of Ashlund.

A tremor ran through her. She shifted her attention to him. Without Sophie's monologue filling her head with visions of jewels and bolts of rich fabrics, and without Mary's enthusiastic contributions as to which dresses and jewelry Elise should wear to the parties, she couldn't deny she was, completely and fully,

231

Elise MacGregor, Marchioness of Ashlund.

Her body warmed. There had been no denying that fact last night when Marcus had bedded her for the first time as his wife. She slid her gaze down his body to the muscled calf visible between kilt and boot. The memory of his thighs between her legs last night, then again this morning, dried her throat. She swallowed. Her throat moistened, but her heart beat faster as if in rhythm with his thrusts when he brought her to climax. How many nights such as that lay ahead of her? Was it possible they could live in peace? Could she could make him happy?

"He is a fine male specimen," Sophie said.

Elise jerked her gaze to Sophie, who regarded her from her seat in the far corner. Mary gave a titter of laughter, and Elise scowled. "You must make some people very nervous, Sophie."

"I do, indeed," the countess replied without hesitation. "I am pleased Marcus agreed to stop at Whycham House. You need a rest and I so want you to meet Justin."

"I'm glad as well," Elise said.

The carriage rounded a bend in the road and a rider became visible in the distance. Marcus kicked his horse and galloped to meet the rider. An instant later, Kiernan's horse passed the carriage at a gallop as he, too, sped to intercept the rider.

"What's happened?" Sophie demanded.

"A rider," Elise replied, without taking her eyes off Marcus.

Sophie moved from her side of the coach to sit beside her. Sophie leaned close and they watched as the man stopped and Marcus pulled his stallion to a halt beside him. Kiernan joined them a moment later. They spoke, then Marcus and the man whirled their horses in the direction the man had come and Kiernan spurred his horse back toward the carriage. The carriage halted as Kiernan arrived.

"What is it?" Elise demanded.

"A fire at Ashlund."

Both women gasped.

"It's the stables," Kiernan called. "The horses are safe, but there's been a casualty. My father and Jeremy are riding ahead. I will see you to Whycham House, then follow."

"We are nearly to Whycham House," Sophie said. "You needn't accompany us the rest of the way."

Kiernan shook his head. "Father instructed me to see you safely there." He shouted at the driver to move on.

The coach lurched into motion. Kiernan urged his horse to precede the coach and, twenty minutes later, they arrived at Whycham House. Kiernan waited only until the coach passed through the gates, then whirled his horse before Elise could ask any questions. She emerged from the carriage, her gaze following the boy as he disappeared from sight down the road.

"Don't worry." Sophie rested a hand on Elise's arm. "They know how to deal with such matters."

"But we don't know a thing about what has happened."

"Come along, Mary," Sophie instructed the maid as she hooked her arm through Elise's and started up the walkway of the imposing mansion. "Trust them to deal with the fire." Sophie led Elise across the threshold and into the foyer.

Elise tossed her riding vest onto the bed and crossed to the chair nearest the window as Mary closed the bedchamber door behind them when Sophie left.

"Now, there must be some water here somewhere," Mary said, as she glanced around the room. "There it is." She hurried across the room to the dresser.

Elise seated herself in the chair and bent to unlace her boots. "Freshen yourself first," she said. "I'll rest a few minutes then see to myself."

"I canna' do that," Mary exclaimed. She poured water from the pitcher into the bowl it sat in. "The laird would be displeased."

"The *laird* isn't here to care," Elise replied. She wondered if Marcus had reached Ashlund yet. The estate lay another hour and a half away by carriage. A fast horse could have gotten him there in half the time.

"Aye," the girl replied with a deep sigh. "It must be difficult for you considering the danger." Mary took a step back and surveyed the dresser drawers. She opened the top right drawer. "Oh, fine," she said, and pulled out a washcloth.

"By the time they arrive to Ashlund, the fire may be out," Elise said.

"Mayhap," Mary said. She dipped the cloth in the water and wrung it out. "Just pray the main house doesna' catch fire in the process."

Elise straightened from her boot. "What do you mean?"

"I'm going to Ashlund," Elise announced an hour later as she entered the drawing room.

Sophie looked up from the tea she was pouring. "Marcus said you were to stay here." She set the teapot down.

"He did not." Elise stopped in front of her. "Kiernan simply escorted us here so he could hurry to Ashlund."

"You know he intended for you to remain here."

"He probably thought I would be more comfortable here and that I might not want to arrive at Ashlund under such circumstances. Had we discussed the matter, I would have explained none of those things mattered."

Had Marcus told her the grove that separated the stables from the house had burned once before, nearly taking the house with it, he wouldn't have been able to keep her away. Winnie's story of how her uncle had burned while asleep in his house came back to Elise with the same horrifying realism it had when Mary described how the grove burned thirty years ago.

"Why the concern?" Elise said when the furrows

in Sophie's forehead deepened. "Daylight will last another two hours. I can reach Ashlund long before dark. I will take the driver, along with the men Marcus assigned to accompany us." Sophie still looked doubtful and Elise added, "Along with two of your men, they can help with the fire."

"Three of our men," she said. "Keep them as long as Marcus needs them. Perhaps I should send more? Oh dear, I should have thought of that earlier. I wish Justin were here. He would deal with this far better than I." She looked at Elise, adding in a hopeful voice, "He should be returning any moment."

"We have all the time in the world to get to know one another," Elise said. "Now, let's have the carriage readied."

Marcus slowed his stallion as he neared the stables at Whycham House. The boy Samuel emerged from the stables and Marcus came to a halt beside him. Marcus dismounted and tossed the reins to him.

"See to him, Samuel," he said, and started for the house.

He hurried along the footpath. Despite exhaustion last night, he had missed Elise. He entered without knocking and went directly to the drawing room where, as expected, Sophie sat on the couch facing the window overlooking the gardens. Elise, however, wasn't present.

Sophie looked up. Her brow furrowed. "What is amiss?"

"The only thing amiss," he replied, "is that my wife isn't here. Is she still abed? It is nearly—"

Sophie's eyes widened and she gave a soft gasp.

Marcus felt an instant of confusion, then his heart leapt into a furious rhythm. "What is it? Where is she?"

Sophie stood, the needlework in her lap falling to the floor. "She left yesterday, a short time after we arrived."

"What?" Marcus's head spun. "I instructed her to

wait until I came for her." He broke from the cold hand of fear and strode to Sophie. She looked up at him, panic on her face. He grasped her shoulders. "Why did Justin allow her to leave?"

"He wasn't here. Elise was concerned about you."

"And you let her go?" Marcus shook her hard enough to loosen several hairpins. Two curls struck her shoulder.

"It was still light," Sophie said, her voice so shaky Marcus realized she was close to tears. "I travel between Whycham House and Ashlund often. Marcus!" Tears streamed down her cheeks. "You know it is true. I have never feared traveling on that road, even at night."

Marcus released her, his hands working and reworking into fists.

"She took three of our men," Sophie went on. "I told her to keep them as long as needed at Ashlund. It was early. I had no reason to—"

"No reason to think!" he roared, and stepped closer. She didn't retreat. "She is not to travel alone," he shouted. "There have been threats—"

"Threats?" Sophie's gaze hardened. "Threats you say? I ask you, then, why we weren't told? Should Justin not have been informed? Should not some provisions have been made? My God, Marcus, why have you kept silent?"

He struggled to answer, but the words—his mind—nothing worked.

"What are these threats?" Sophie asked in a voice so reasonable, so firm, Marcus snapped from his indecision.

"There's no time for explanations." Sophie opened her mouth to speak, but he said, "First, we find her."

Chapter Seventeen

Marcus followed Elise's carriage tracks from Whycham House onto the road leading to Ashlund. Where a heavier-trafficked crossroad joined the Ashlund road, a myriad of tracks, all muddied by the night's rain, obscured hers. Marcus ordered Justin to return to Whycham House and check all farms and cottages near the road, while he continued onward and did the same. Two hours passed before he heard the pounding of hooves over the sound of his own mount's gallop. He glanced over his shoulder and saw Justin approaching. Sophie rode alongside and Kiernan followed with a dozen more men behind. Marcus slowed his stallion as they neared. He observed the haggard look on Sophie's face when they came alongside.

They had discovered no news.

"There are four farms between the point you left us and Whycham House," Justin said. "I did not wish to diverge too far off the road until we could better ascertain where she might have gotten lost."

Marcus's head jerked to the side and he glared at Justin. "Lost?"

"You have found nothing?" Justin went on.

Marcus looked forward again. "Nay."

"We are but midway between Ashlund and Whycham House," Justin said. "There is much territory yet to cover."

Two farmhouses down, they encountered a peasant who remembered Elise's entourage.

"When?" Marcus demanded.

"Yesterday," the man replied. "I was returning from MacLellan's down the road. Later afternoon, four-thirty or five, I would say."

"All was well with her?"

"As far as I could see."

"How many were in the party?" Marcus asked.

"I didn't see inside the carriage. Let me see, there was the driver, wheeler," he paused, then added, "there were three or four men riding alongside. Can't say for sure."

"Sounds as if the men are accounted for," Justin said.

"Come," Marcus directed the man, "you will show us exactly where you saw my wife."

They rode a mile south on the road, when the farmer stopped them. "Here."

Marcus dismounted and examined the tracks. "Bloody hell," he cursed. "It looks as though all of Edinburgh has traversed this road." He tried following his line of sight along one set of carriage tracks, only to lose them in the tangled web of another in the moist ground.

"Lord Phillip passed this way," the man said.

Marcus cut his gaze to the man. "Lord Phillip. When?"

"I passed him about two miles north of his estate," the man replied.

"Then you saw Lady Ashlund here?"

"Aye."

Marcus looked at Justin. "Phillip's estate borders mine."

Justin nodded. "Perhaps they passed one another."

An hour later, Marcus departed Lord Phillip's estate knowing nothing more than that the earl had set out to visit a friend to the north before heading south for Edinburgh. Marcus cursed the earl's timing, his absence, and his person.

Marcus glanced at the sky as he mounted his horse. The day had turned to dusk. He had ridden since morning and his mount flagged. He rode to Ashlund and exchanged his horse for a fresh one. He reached the outskirts of Ashlund property and encountered the search party.

"Exchange your horses for fresh ones at Ashlund," Marcus instructed. "I'll speak to the tenants of the two farms to the south."

"Father," Kiernan said in unison with Justin's, "Marcus."

"I left instructions for horses to be readied for you," Marcus said. "You will overtake me soon enough."

Dusk gave way to night as they extended the search into the countryside to the west. To the east, a high cliff butted the shoreline of an inlet from the bay. Now, they rode fifteen miles south of Ashlund, stopping at every village and home on the road to Edinburgh. The next village lay five miles farther south. Marcus urged his horse into a harder trot and the company following did the same. Sophie rode between Marcus and Justin with Kiernan behind them.

"Marcus," Sophie called above the clatter of hooves.

He looked at her. An overcast sky hid the moon, but four of the twelve men who accompanied them carried torches and he easily made out her strained expression.

Sophie shook her head. "Why didn't Elise——" She broke off with a stifled choke.

Marcus looked straight ahead. "I alone bear the blame. Don't cause yourself any further grief over the matter."

"No further grief?"

Her words hit him like barbs and Marcus snapped his attention onto her.

Her eyes blazed. "You can be an arrogant bastard,

Cousin. Whether or not I share blame, I will grieve as I please."

She yanked her horse's reins and Marcus pulled to the right in order to avoid her horse. She circled to the rear of the company and brought her stallion alongside Justin's.

A moment of silence passed before Justin said, "Seven men traveled in the company, all trained men of war. Not easy prey."

"Yet they are gone," Marcus said.

"True," Justin agreed, "but there will be news of them somewhere. A company of brigands large enough to take such a large party could not go unnoticed."

"Then let us find that news," Marcus said, and spurred his mount into a full gallop.

The morning sun had only begun to spread across the grey sky when Marcus brought his horse to a halt in front of Ashlund. Justin, Kiernan, and the messenger, carrying news of a priest who said he had knowledge of Elise's entourage, followed Marcus as he jumped to the ground and ran for the porch, then took the stairs two at a time. Pushing past the oak door, they strode down the corridor to the drawing room. Marcus threw open the door to find Sophie sitting on the couch. Beside her sat the priest, Father Fynn.

The priest stood and Marcus hurried forward. "Father," he said, "what news do you have?"

The priest hesitated.

"Tell me," Marcus demanded. "You have news of my wife."

"Forgive me, Lord Ashlund," Father Fynn began, "Yesterday, we found a woman's body washed ashore near Braemer."

Marcus's head reeled. He looked at Sophie, who had yet to rise. He turned back to the priest. "You can't be sure. We found no sign of foul play."

"Lord Ashlund, I wasn't aware you had married, and this woman was a stranger to us. Therefore, we began a search of our own. We traveled upstream and—" he broke off.

"What? What did you find that could possibly confirm your suspicions?"

"A carriage."

Marcus stared. "A carriage means nothing."

"I know the crest. All living in this area know it." Father Fynn pointed at the two-sworded crest hanging over the hearth. "The carriage bore your crest. It lies on the shore near Glenurcom."

Forty-five minutes later, Marcus stood with Justin and Kiernan at the edge of a wooded cliff overlooking Glenurcom. He looked down at a carriage, the front half of which was submerged in water. The horses' bodies were tangled in the mass of leather and iron, which had once been harness and axle. Marcus watched small waves lap at the bloated mass of flesh. He stared again at the broken carriage, then closed his eyes. Even from a hundred-foot distance, there was no mistaking the Ashlund crest.

He turned away.

Justin followed. "You say you found another woman's body in the carriage?" he addressed the priest, who had remained astride his mount.

Father Fynn nodded. "Young. By her dress, I assumed a servant."

"Mary," Marcus mumbled.

"And you found the bodies of how many men?" Justin asked.

"Four."

"How many men had you left with her, Marcus?"

He laughed bitterly. "Not enough."

"How many?" Justin repeated.

Marcus looked up, startled from his stupor by the earl's sharp tone. "Four. The driver, two wheelers and one guard. Kiernan rode with them. They were but twenty minutes from Whycham House—" he ceased speaking when Kiernan's mouth tightened. "'Tis not your fault, Kiernan. You saw them to Whycham House as I instructed."

"Three men are missing," Justin went on in a business-like manner. "Where are they?"

Marcus looked at him. He heard the words, but the meaning escaped him. "What?"

"Three men remain unaccounted for."

"You know full well where they are," Marcus said in a savage voice. "They ran from my wrath. And well they should. But they can't hide from me forever. When I catch them—"

"Don't be a fool," Justin cut in, his voice still calm. "There isn't a man in your personal entourage who would run rather than die. As for the three men from my household, I've trusted them with Sophie's life many times."

Justin began looking about the rocky terrain of the forest. He strode ten feet, then came to a halt. He studied the ground for a moment before saying, "The carriage came through here." With a sweep of his hands, he indicated a wide area between the trees. "I see only this bit of carriage tracks here," he squatted and ran a finger over two inches of ground, "and," he scuttled forward, "this here." He ran his fingers over another four inches of ground.

Marcus looked at the ground, but the imagined picture of Elise's terror-stricken face as the carriage careened through the forest toward the cliff's edge blurred his vision. He watched numbly as Justin rose, walked another twenty feet in the direction of the road, then stopped again.

He dropped to a squat and examined the ground. "Here is a hoof print." He lightly touched a mossy spot between embedded stones. "This stony ground challenges my limited skills as tracker."

Father Fynn dismounted and joined Justin in studying the ground. He glanced toward the road, then rose, strode several paces, and studied the ground. "Two rode here." The priest pointed to the ground a foot away.

Justin rose and walked another ten feet past the priest. He surveyed the ground, then the cliff. He looked at Marcus. "Why didn't the women jump?"

Marcus's stomach lurched.

Justin frowned. "The guards would have instructed them to jump long before they reached the cliff. The men wouldn't have willingly gone over with the carriage." Justin turned and walked toward the road until he disappeared among the trees. A moment later, his faint call sounded from beyond the trees.

Marcus didn't move.

"Father," Kiernan said.

Marcus looked at him and Keirnan gave him an inquiring look. Marcus started toward Justin's voice. He broke from the trees to find Justin examining the road. Father Fynn followed, his horse's reins in hand. Kiernan trailed with the remaining horses.

Justin didn't look up at their approach, only said, "Marcus, you are a far better tracker than I. Have a look."

Marcus moved forward as though in a dream and squatted next to Justin.

"This road is nearly as rocky as the shore," Justin said. "However, there is no mistaking these tracks."

Marcus looked at the inch long depression crushing the moss which grew between the rocks.

"And," Justin went on, "these." He pointed to another small rut to his right.

Marcus looked at the track. He frowned and looked up at Justin. "A second carriage"

The earl nodded. "Have you any idea if this could be Elise's carriage?"

Marcus looked from one carriage track to the other, then back at Justin. "Nay."

"They are two separate tracks, then?"

"Aye. They are spaced too far apart to be the same carriage." He surveyed the ground. "This road isn't used a great deal." The road branched off the main road to Edinburgh. He looked at Father Fynn. "This is the road you took from Braemer?"

"Aye," the priest answered.

"We found no sign of the carriage leaving the main road," Marcus said.

"True," Justin agreed. "But the rain the night before obliterated most tracks."

Marcus rose and stepped slowly toward the trees, all the while scanning the ground. When he saw the partial indentation of a hoof print, he looked up and stared at the trees through which Elise's carriage had raced.

"Kiernan," he called without looking back, "bring me my horse."

"Wait here," Marcus told Justin and Kiernan when they followed him down the chapel hallway. They had remained close—too close—on the ride to the church, and Marcus had no stomach for it when he faced what lie ahead.

They obeyed, and he continued to the door that separated him from the body of the woman Father Fynn insisted was his wife. Marcus reached for the door, his hand shaking so badly he gripped the doorknob with force enough to turn his knuckles white. He pushed the door open, stepped through, then shoved it shut behind him.

In the time it took to slide his gaze from the floor to her body, the memory of Elise turning to face him the day he'd happened upon her in the meadow flashed before him. Burned into his mind was the proud expression that revealed the indomitable spirit that would not be tamed.

The memory shattered at sight of the body lying on the small bed in the corner of the room. He reeled. Father Fynn warned that her skull had been damaged beyond recognition, but nothing had prepared Marcus for this. His belly roiled. He fell to his knees, his stomach finally giving up what little he had been coerced into eating the past two days. He wretched until he thought his liver would follow, then slumped forward.

A sudden pounding on the door jarred him. "Father!" Kiernan called from the other side of the door.

Amidst the pounding came Justin's calmer, "Marcus."

"Stay out!" Marcus shouted.

He leaned forward, his palms finding purchase on the floor amidst the vomit. The pounding ceased. Marcus slowed his ragged breathing, but no amount of effort controlled the shaking of his body. He forced his head up, steadying his gaze on Elise's skirts, torn and mud-caked. He recognized the light yellow damask. His gaze moved of its own volition to her hands, folded across her chest in an attitude of rest. Without thought, his gaze yanked farther up her body and he stared at the unrecognizable face.

Marcus jerked to consciousness as though roused from a slumber of years. Daylight had faded the sky to a purple haze. He rode between Justin and Kiernan. He searched his memory but found no recollection of how he had come to be there. He looked left, past Kiernan, and studied the forested land. There was something— something he couldn't quite grasp. He looked ahead at the road, damp from the day's shower. The recollection hit him like a bolt of lightning. He couldn't mistake the place. Marcus yanked on his horse's reins, wheeling the beast past Kiernan.

"Father!"

Marcus ignored his son and galloped through the trees toward the spot where Elise's carriage had run off the cliff. Hoof beats followed, but he cared nothing for his companions. He broke from the trees into the clearing at the cliff's edge and brought his horse to a halt ten feet from the cliff. Marcus leapt from its back and strode to the very edge of the cliff.

"Father!" Kiernan's shout preceded his burst into the clearing.

Marcus whirled. "Her wedding band."

"What?" Kiernan said, breathless as he jumped from his horse and hurried to his side.

Marcus looked past him to Justin, who was dismounting. "I didn't see her wedding ring. Did the priest give it to you?"

"No," Justin replied.

Marcus tightened his jaw as he pushed past Kiernan. "What have they done with her wedding band?"

Justin strode to his side. "The highwaymen would have taken everything."

Marcus shook his head. "Nay. The ring was a size too large. She feared losing it and packed it away for the trip."

The earl shook his head. "Surely the highwaymen would have searched the baggage."

"The emerald is three karats. It will not be easily hid. I can find it *and* Elise's murderers within the week."

For the second time that day, Marcus rode through the streets of Braemer. Elise's body was already on its way to Brahan Seer. Justin had made the arrangements. Marcus's gut twisted. He would retrieve her wedding band, find the guards who had deserted her, then return to Brahan Seer… and to her. He could offer no recompense for her death, but neither would he find peace for the remainder of his days. He stopped in front of the modest church.

"Wait here," he ordered Kiernan and Justin, then dismounted and went inside.

Father Fynn walked down the aisle toward the door. He halted when Marcus entered the sanctuary. They stared at one another for a moment, then the priest said, "You're here about the jewelry?"

Marcus felt another vicious twist to his insides. "Aye."

Father Fynn nodded. "Come with me." He turned

and started toward the altar.

Marcus followed him to the back of the church. He hesitated when the priest paused before the altar to make the sign of the cross. Left led to the room where Elise had lain. Father Fynn turned right, but Marcus's knees weakened nonetheless. They continued down a short corridor and entered a modest bedchamber. Father Fynn stopped before a desk in the far corner and opened a drawer. He retrieved a folded paper, then faced Marcus.

"I wanted no mistakes. When I saw the quality cut of Lady Ashlund's clothes, I assumed she had met with highwaymen. Therefore, the fact she wore no jewelry did no' surprise me. I thought no more of it until Sara MacPhee, one of my parishioners, arrived early this morning. According to her, her son discovered your wife. I didn't know that when I spoke to you earlier because it was James MacAlphie who alerted me to the presence of Lady's Ashlund's body in the loch." Father Fynn paused. "You must understand, the jewels represent a lifetime of wealth to these people." Marcus made no response and Fynn went on. "The long and short of the matter is that Sara's son took the jewelry."

Marcus clenched his hands into fists.

"The boy is gone. You could find him, of course, and would be well within your rights to extract payment. A man of your position could sentence the boy to a lifetime of imprisonment."

Marcus envisioned the boy hanging alongside the three men who had been entrusted with Elise's life.

Father Fynn unfolded the paper. "Sara saw the jewelry. She described a thin, gold bracelet and a brooch—"

"I am well aware of my wife's jewelry," Marcus snapped.

He strode to Father Fynn and snatched the paper from his hands.

"Of course." Father Fynn hesitated. "Lord Ashlund, I pressed Sara for information concerning the brooch. It was the most   valuable of the items, so I had hoped—"

"Most valuable?" Marcus demanded coldly. "My wife's wedding ring was far more valuable. The emerald is three karats. The gold, twenty-four karat. The ring has been in my family for generations. It is priceless."

Father Fynn looked startled. "Emerald? What emerald?"

"She packed the ring in her valise *with* the chain and brooch."

The priest pointed to the paper Marcus held. "I swear, Lord Ashlund, there was no emerald ring. Wait, there is this." He opened a drawer and withdrew a folded sheet of paper. He unfolded the document and handed it to Marcus.

He lifted the paper and recognized the pawnbroker's ticket for Elise's wedding band.

Thick gold wedding band his mind repeated the words on the document. Elise had kept the pawn ticket. Why?

Marcus riveted his gaze to Father Fynn. "Where is this Sara MacPhee?"

Fear crossed the priest's face.

"I will not harm her."

Father Fynn hesitated, then said, "I cannot stop you."

"No," Marcus said, his voice hard. "No one can."

In the predawn hours the next morning, the door to Marcus's study opened and Justin and Kiernan entered. The time of reckoning had arrived.

"Justin," Marcus said, without shifting his attention from the instructions he was preparing for Harris, "go home."

"Father," Kiernan said, forcing Marcus's attention to the chair Justin was settling into and his son standing beside it.

Marcus met Kiernan's gaze and he saw the pain on his face, but only broke the connection saying, "You will return to school."

"I will stay."

"Staying will not stop me." He looked at Justin. "Nor yours."

"*I will not leave*," Kiernan asserted.

Marcus swung his attention onto his son. "You *will* return to school. Refuse, and I will have you bound and taken back to Brahan Seer, where you will remain until I return."

"If you return," Kiernan shot back.

"You are old enough to understand—"

"Old enough to understand a fool's errand when I see one."

"The boy deserves an explanation," Justin said.

Marcus stared at his son, then looked at Justin. This was the first the two of them had demanded an explanation for his actions of the previous evening. He understood that he might appear insane. When he'd left the church in search of Sara MacPhee, he hadn't commanded them to leave, but neither had he explained the hurried ride to her home, nor the search of the immediate area when her cottage was found empty.

No words were spoken on the return trip home and Justin and Kiernan didn't accost him when he closeted himself in his study the length of the night. They knew nothing of what he'd read in the preliminary report entitled "Elisabeth Kingston" that had sat on his desk until last night. *Kingston.* At last, he knew her name. Marcus closed his eyes. *Why did you not tell me, Elise?* Too late, he knew her identity and why she was in the Scottish Highlands.

The daughter of a wealthy shipping baron, Elise had lost her father at age fifteen. She was now thirty—older than he'd thought. She married Robert Kingston—not Riley, as she had called him—seven years ago. Amelia Kingston had been born a year after the marriage. Amelia died aboard the ship that bore her name. Robert, too, had died. Only, he hadn't drowned in the wreckage of the ship but had been brought down by a bullet administered by his wife. Marcus's wife, the

Marchioness of Ashlund, was wanted for murder. What pushed a woman to murder her husband?

Marcus's man of affairs had attempted to find the *Amelia's* captain to answer that question, but ship and captain were on an extended voyage to Australia and wouldn't return for six more months. He'd located only one crewmember who had been aboard the *Amelia* on that voyage. The crewmember told of a nasty storm that had raged the night Elise had been lost at sea. Robert appeared on deck during the storm. He had a pistol, but before he could use it, Elise shot him. He returned fire as he fell. Steven was hit, but not mortally wounded. Elise had told him Steven went down with the ship. She must have believed Steven dead by her husband's bullet.

A massive wave struck the ship and swept Elise overboard. Everyone in America thought her dead, which didn't explain the notice advertised by her stepfather, Price Ardsley, that named her murderer. The investigator included in his report the rumor that Price Ardsley was unhappy with the twenty-five percent interest in Landen Shipping, which had fallen to Elise on her twenty-fifth birthday. If not for the twenty-six percent her brother controlled in Landen Shipping, her interest would be of small consequence to Price Ardsley.

The *Amelia* never docked in London, but did arrive back in Boston three weeks later. Two months ago, another ship owned by Landen Shipping arrived in the southern dock at Rotherhithe, Scotland. Price Ardsley had been aboard the ship.

Marcus picked up the envelope that contained the report on Elise and tossed it to Justin. He caught it and they made eye contact.

"You have one hour." Marcus looked at Kiernan. "Then I leave for Glasgow."

Marcus paused on the boardwalk outside the shabby pawnbroker's shop and scanned the dock.

Despite the early hour, hackneys passed in both directions on the street beside him and Justin, and sailors strode along the walkways, while others loaded and unloaded supplies and goods. A woman, likely one of the notoriously dishonest public house landlords the riverside teemed with or one of the brothel madams, hurried across the road. This was the neighborhood Elise had been in when Daniel found her. Marcus shuddered at what could have happened to her, then remembered what *had* happened to her less than half an hour from Ashlund.

"Are you all right?" Justin asked.

Marcus nodded, then entered the shop. A small man stood behind the counter in the rear of the room, his back to them as he examined an item Marcus assumed belonged to the man who stood on the other side of the counter. The man behind the counter turned. His gaze fell first on Marcus, then flicked to Justin and returned to Marcus. His eyes widened. Marcus glanced at the gold pocket watch the man clutched before the hand disappeared behind his back. Marcus strode toward the man with Justin following. The customer turned. He didn't step aside as they stopped beside him, only scrutinized Justin, who stood closest.

"Do we know one another?" Justin asked with a lift of his brow.

The man gave a rough laugh. "Nay, canna' say I've had the pleasure."

Justin turned to the man behind the counter. "Are you the proprietor, sir?"

The man shifted uneasily. "I dinna' know as I'd say the proprietor."

"What are ye talking about, Jack?" the customer cut in. "You owned this shop your whole life. Got it from your dad."

"Bart," Jack growled, "mind your business." Jack scurried toward the far end of the counter. He flipped a section of the counter up, passed through, and hurried toward Bart. Jack pressed the watch into his hand. "Be on your way," he growled, and shoved Bart

251

toward the door.

"Now, see here," Bart began, but halted when his gaze met Marcus's. He looked from Marcus to Justin. "Bloody gentry. Think they own the world." He continued grumbling as he shuffled toward the door.

The hustle and bustle of passing hackneys and men's shouts filled the room as he opened the door, then cut off abruptly when the door banged shut.

Jack hurried back behind his counter. He stopped across from Marcus and Justin. "Now, what can I do for you gentleman?"

From inside his jacket pocket, Marcus produced the pawn ticket for Elise's wedding band and placed it on the counter. "I am here about this ring."

The shop owner picked up the paper and began reading it. "Ahh, yes, I knew her husband would come for this one day. Yes, I did," he added as he scurried toward a curtained doorway in a corner behind the counter. "A fine piece of jewelry, this one. No' something a man is likely to be pleased about his wife selling." Jack paused, hand on the curtain and looked over his shoulder. "Your wife" He looked from Justin to Marcus. "Er, your wife, m'lord?"

Marcus nodded.

"I can see you have the situation well in hand." Jack disappeared behind the curtain.

A moment later, Jack burst through the curtain, a fragment of folded velvet in hand. He laid the fabric on the counter before Marcus and unwrapped it. Marcus stared at the gold band glistening against the black fabric.

"I—" he began.

"Well, there you are," Justin interrupted. "Just as you knew it would be." Justin looked at him. "That'll teach you something of a woman's wrath."

Marcus stared blankly at him.

Justin turned to Jack. "You know how women are."

"Oh, indeed, m'lord. Indeed, I do."

Justin produced a roll of banknotes from his

pocket. "How much did you pay her?"

Jack picked up the paper. "Here it is." He pointed a bony finger at the figure scrawled in the bottom corner of the paper. "Five sovereign."

Justin counted out ten pound notes. "I trust this will account for your efforts."

Jack's eyes glittered. "Aye, m'lord. Indeed, it will, indeed, it will."

He snatched up the notes as though expecting Justin to change his mind and stuffed them into his pocket. He rewrapped the ring, then produced a small wooden box from beneath the counter and placed the ring inside. He looked at Marcus and extended the box toward him.

"There you go, m'lord. As good as new."

Marcus took the box.

"Good day to you," Justin said, and looked at Marcus. "Come along, my good fellow. You'd best get back and deal with this matter straight away."

Jack snickered, but Marcus paid no heed as he followed the earl out the door. Justin took a few steps on the walkway, then stopped, looking toward the east.

"What is it?" Marcus demanded, following his line of sight along the busy dock.

Justin looked in the opposite direction. "We left Kiernan hours ago. I expected him before this."

"He is on his way to London as I instructed."

Justin grunted. "You don't know your son as well as you might think."

"What matters is that he knows me. I will make good on my threat to have him bound and taken back to Brahan Seer."

"It doesn't matter if you threatened to dismember the boy, he will appear sooner or later. You should hope for sooner; that will allow you to keep him under your watchful eye."

Marcus didn't reply. Instead, he opened the box containing the ring and removed it from the velvet wrapping. His heartbeat raced. The ring had been given to Elise by another man,   but it belonged to *her*—

was once a part of her. He closed his fingers into a fist around the ring. The cold metal warmed within his grasp. If he held the only remaining part of her, he could once again hold her.

"There is much in her past," Marcus said to himself.

"You're thinking of Price Ardsley," Justin said.

Marcus looked up sharply. "He's here. Or was."

"There is something going on with him."

"Imagine if she one day demanded the twenty-five per cent interest in Landen Shipping."

"By God, Marcus," Justin exclaimed. "You're as rich as the devil himself and still landed yourself an heiress."

Marcus started.

"Bloody hell," Justin muttered. "Deem me the fool I am. The words were out of my mouth before my brain could catch up."

Marcus gave a tired smile. "An uncommon state of mind for you."

Justin sighed, then gave him a long look. "You are going to America, then?"

"You won't dissuade me."

Justin nodded. "It is only right her brother know what this Price Ardsley is made of."

"I owe her that much," Marcus replied. His mouth tightened. "By now the body is buried. Aye," he said when his cousin opened his mouth to comment. "I should have been there."

"I can't blame you for being unable to bear seeing her lain in the ground."

Marcus gave a harsh laugh. "She will still be in the grave when I return."

Justin gazed at the ships in the harbor. "We had better see the harbormaster."

Marcus looked at him. "We? Nay, Justin. You aren't coming."

The earl started forward. "I would say his office is where we entered the docks."

Marcus hurried forward. Within arm's reach, he

grasped Justin's shoulder and forced Justin to face him. "I didn't ask you to come."

His expression remained impassive. "Of course not."

"I will not have you risking your life."

"Will you have me bound and sent back to Whycham House?"

"By God," Marcus burst out, "if that's what it takes."

Mild amusement crossed Justin's face. "You know me even less than your son."

"Sophie will not allow this."

"I already sent Sophie word I would be accompanying you to America."

Marcus gaped.

"I'm not a complete fool," Justin said.

"She won't be pleased."

"She won't be pleased we left her behind." Justin began walking.

"Justin!" Marcus strode after him.

The following morning, Marcus leaned against the railing of the *Sallinger*, absently fingering the wedding band in his trouser pocket. He stared across the harbor at the docks. The shouts of drivers in passing hackneys, dock workers, and merchants buying and selling wares faded into the background, replaced by a quiet whoosh as the brigantine skimmed through the water. Hearing footsteps behind him, he looked over his shoulder to see Justin approach.

"The captain has been kind enough to extend an invitation for breakfast," Justin said.

Marcus nodded. He glanced past the masts at the sun. Eleven years had passed since he'd last been outside Great Britain, fourteen since crossing the Atlantic. He squinted against the sunlight. A month from now, he would be seeing this same sun from Boston Harbor.

Only, it wouldn't be with Elise.

Chapter Eighteen

Marcus rolled onto Elise. The darkness prevented discerning even the outline of her face, but he heard her sigh. His chest pressed upon her breasts and she shifted, teasing him with a slight arch of her body. His heart beat fiercely, his body hard with an arousal that circumvented the disorientation clouding his mind. He yanked on her shift until he could spread her legs with a knee. He grasped her shoulders and, levering himself into position, thrust into her. With the first stroke, pleasure radiated through his body. Marcus pinned her against the mattress, each stroke increasing the deafening roar of blood through his veins.

Elise gasped. He lowered his full weight upon her, then rolled onto his back, keeping their bodies joined. Grasping the back of her knees, he slid them forward so that she straddled him. He gripped her waist and lifted her up until only the tip of his shaft remained inside her, then brought her down, up, down—she gripped his arms and he felt her weight shift as she threw her head back. He lifted her, slamming her onto him, faster, then faster, gripping her slim waist in a clasp that frightened him. Pleasure shot through him. He slammed her down harder. Arching to meet her—Marcus jerked awake, grasping the wet sheet covering his hips as he groaned. He continued to pump upwards for several strokes before slumping back onto the mattress.

His chest rose and fell in heavy gasps for several

moments before his senses cleared enough to recognize the cabin that had held him captive for twenty-eight nights. Shafts of muted light streamed through the small glass skylights. His gut wrenched. Another dream. He closed his eyes. In his mind, he saw the flutter of Elise's eyelids when he brought her to her release. His shaft twitched. A muted shout overhead brought the sudden realization that the ship no longer rocked as it had while slicing through the Atlantic. Marcus yanked the sheet aside and jumped from bed. He strode the three paces to the door and stuck his head into the hallway.

"Lad," he called to a boy at the far end of the corridor, "where are we?"

The boy turned. "We're in Boston, sir. We've docked."

"Can you get me a messenger? I need a note delivered immediately."

"Aye, sir," the boy said. "I'll go if you like."

"Good lad," he said. "I'll have it ready in ten minutes."

At five-fifty in the afternoon three days later, the door to the private dining room in the Boston Harbor Hotel opened and Marcus looked up from the glass of wine he had been staring at.

"A message for you, sir," the waiter said, and laid an envelope beside him on the table.

Marcus saw the return address from Colonel Shay. He tore open the letter and read.

My Dear Marcus,

I have only now received word concerning Steven Landen. The boy is a lieutenant in the US Army and functions as a tracker for them. As of three months ago, Lieutenant Landen was stationed with the 23rd Cavalry Division on the Tyger River in South Carolina. The

Army is slow in updating its records; the boy may have been sent elsewhere in the meantime. I hope this information will suffice to connect you with him.

Another bit of news I know will interest you. My wife is acquainted with Mrs Charles Hampton, of the Burlington Hamptons. (No, I do not expect you to know them, but you may take my word that they are among the Boston elite.) Mrs Hampton remembers the calamity which struck the Amelia *on that fateful trip to England. Apparently, the story was widely discussed amongst Mrs Hampton's class, a class, as you know, far above my own station.*

My wife related to me the tale as told to her by Mrs Hampton as follows: When the Amelia *docked and her captain advised Price Ardsley of Elise Kingston's fate, he was grief-stricken. Your wife's brother, the young Lieutenant Landen, was seriously injured and went into forced convalescence for nearly three months. Even before his release from the hospital, he demanded a search be mounted for his sister. The demand was flatly refused, most notably by Ardsley, though the directors of Landen Shipping did agree. They believed that had Mrs Kingston survived, she would have returned to Boston.*

None of this surprises you, as I well know. There is, however, one piece of information I believe will. Steven Landen contends that the night Elise was lost at sea, he came upon Robert Kingston strangling her. Steven thwarted the murder attempt, and he and Elise escaped up to the deck.

Marcus stared, his gaze fixed on the words *he came upon Robert Kingston strangling her.* Elise's husband had tried to kill her. His chest tightened. This explained why she shot him. Marcus closed his eyes. *Elise, why didn't you tell me?* He forced back the pain, opened his eyes, and refocused on the letter.

> *While they were on deck, Robert appeared. Elise shot her husband. Robert pulled a pistol from his pocket after she drew on him, and returned fire. Steven took the bullet he says was meant for his sister. When Steven regained consciousness, the captain informed him Elise had fallen overboard and that Steven had tried rescuing her by cutting down the longboat. Steven has no memory of this.*
>
> *Ardsley proposed that Robert Kingston wanted to eliminate Elise in order to claim her shares in Landen Shipping. Ardsley preached this philosophy with a depth of gravity that Mrs Hampton described as '"most admirable."'*
>
> *I wish I could be of more service. Travel safely to South Carolina. I look forward to learning of your success when you return.*
>
> *Sincerely,*
>
> *Colonel Martin Shay*

"South Carolina," Marcus said in a low voice, but his mind still staggered with the picture of Robert Kingston strangling his wife—*my wife*, Marcus's mind shot back. Memory of her broken body after the carriage crash filled his mind.

The clock that hung on the wall near the door gonged. He jerked his gaze onto the clock, dispelling the bloody vision. Six o'clock. Justin would arrive any minute. Even as he folded the letter with expert precision and set it beside him on the table, the door opened and Justin entered. A waiter followed close behind. The waiter pulled Justin's chair out as he seated himself across from Marcus.

Justin lifted the wine bottle sitting on the table and poured the remainder of the wine into his glass. He handed the bottle to the waiter. "Another bottle, if you please, and…" He paused, then focused on Marcus. "No dinner yet?"

Marcus gave a slight shake of his head.

Justin turned to the waiter. "Have you any pigeon pie?"

The waiter looked horrified. "This is not a port tavern, sir."

Justin raised a brow. "Can you name a port tavern that serves pigeon pie? Never mind. You do have filet mignon?"

The waiter straightened. "Of course."

"Be kind enough to bring two then, along with whatever you Americans consider appropriate accompaniments." Justin reached for his wine, clearly dismissing him.

The waiter looked as though he would like to bludgeon Justin with the wine bottle but turned stiffly and left the room.

Marcus leaned back in his chair. "You have a knack for condescension."

"Never say you think the fellow was right?"

"Not right," Marcus replied. "Simply not worth the time."

Justin snorted. "Had I not done it, you would have." Marcus started to reply, but stopped short at the gleam that appeared in Justin's eye. "Marcus, prepare yourself… she is alive."

Marcus's hand jerked, upsetting his glass. Wine spread across the linen tablecloth. Justin started, nearly tipping over his own glass.

"Bloody hell," Marcus cursed, and set the glass upright. He ignored the stain. "What are you talking about?"

"Three months ago, Ardsley announced that Elise had returned to America."

"Three months ago? But that was before we wed."

"Listen," Justin cut in, "there's a very interesting stipulation in her father's will. If Elise dies, a body must be presented as evidence, or five years must pass before Ardsley can take possession of her stock."

"How does that prove she's alive?"

"Ardsley claims to have her in a convalescent home."

Shock ricocheted through Marcus. "An insane asylum?"

"Yes."

His mind reeled. Elise, alive? And in an asylum. "'Tis not possible," he said in a hoarse voice.

"No?" Justin held his gaze. "For the past six months, Ardsley has been attempting to get Landen Shipping's board of directors to agree to a large loan he wants in order to expand the shipping company to include west coast trade. Many of the board members plan on retiring in the next few years and don't relish the idea of putting their life savings at risk. They have a date set three weeks from tomorrow to settle the matter."

"Ardsley needs Elise's twenty-five percent interest to control the vote," Marcus said in a near whisper.

"Fifty-one percent," Justin rejoined.

"What?"

"A year after Elise married, Steven Landen signed his interest in the company over to her."

"My God."

Justin's brows lifted. "It's rather late in the game for Ardsley to present Elise's *body*, don't you think?"

"An insane asylum," Marcus murmured. "If it is true…"

'*No Campbells, or anyone else, can harm you,*' he had told her. '*I can protect you.*' Wed only two days and he had utterly failed her.

"Marcus." Justin's sharp voice cut into the picture of Elise huddled in a tiny filthy cell, hands clamped over her ears to drown out the screams of the other inmates.

"I saw her body," Marcus said. "If that wasn't Elise, then who—"

Justin's mouth thinned. "That is a mystery to be solved—but not one we cannot solve from here. Agreed?"

Marcus stared. "Aye."

"What have you learned of Steven?" Justin asked.

Marcus's mind registered the letter lying on the table. He picked it up and handed it toward Justin.

The earl unfolded the paper and began reading. A moment later, he murmured, "Shay. Wait. *Shay.* This cannot be the fellow whose son you saved while on campaign in America?"

Marcus nodded.

Justin frowned. "What prompted you to contact him?"

"Landen Shipping informed me Steven Landen was serving in the Army."

Justin laughed. "Good of them to be so obliging."

"Colonel Shay located the boy."

"Boy?"

"He is twenty-five."

"I expected someone older than Elise."

"I thought the same," Marcus said.

"Something more you need to know," Justin said. "If Elise doesn't return from the dead, her shares go to the next living *blood* relative."

"Steven Landen would control Landen Shipping," Marcus said.

"Steven Landen *does* control Landen Shipping. Elise's stock isn't his—not until the allotted five years passes—but he controls her vote until then."

Marcus frowned. "Then why hasn't Ardsley simply killed him?"

"Because Steven's will bequeaths his shares and controlling interest to a distant cousin who lives in New York."

"My God," Marcus murmured. "Steven Landen is of no consequence—"

"If Price Ardsley has Elise," Justin finished for

262

him.

"Why the bloody hell is her brother not here?" Marcus burst out. "Where did you get this information?"

Justin grinned. "There is always a disgruntled employee to be found." The earl returned his attention to the letter. A moment later, he looked up, shock written on his face. "My God, she shot her husband? Surely, it can't be true?"

"I believe every word," Marcus said.

Justin glanced at the letter. "You knew nothing of this? Of course not," he added.

Marcus gave a hollow laugh. "I knew I wanted her. Nothing else mattered."

The earl nodded. "Love blinds a man."

As does passion, Marcus added silently, then said, "I meant to leave immediately to find Steven, but if it is possible Elise is here—" he broke off, still unable to grasp the possibility.

"You must find the boy. He's the key to getting to Ardsley. I never met his sister. If our story is to hold any weight, it must come from you."

"But Elise…"

A glint appeared in Justin's eye. "I will find her."

Marcus grasped his cousin's shoulder and squeezed, then released him. "I'll depart tomorrow. We—"

The door opened and the waiter appeared, a plate of food in each hand. He approached the table and began to set Marcus's plate before him but halted, his gaze falling on the wine-stained tablecloth.

He straightened. "I shall replace the linen." He turned to leave, plates still in hand.

"Nay," Marcus said. "Leave the plates. We will live with the spilt wine."

The waiter looked as if he'd been asked to strip naked and run through the streets of Boston.

Marcus rested his gaze on him. "Leave the plates, lad."

The man did as instructed. "If you need

anything—"

"We will call for you," Marcus cut in. "Until then, see that we aren't disturbed."

The waiter blinked, but gave a stiff bow and left.

Justin picked up his knife and fork. "I said you'd cut him to the quick."

"I'll be back well before Landen Shipping's next meeting," Marcus said. "Then I will cut Ardsley to the quick."

Marcus slowed his horse in the dense forest and scanned the ground. The tracks in the soft South Carolina ground were less than an hour old. He glanced up through the trees. At most, the afternoon sun would be in the sky another two hours. At a sudden commotion in the trees ahead, Marcus jerked his hand to the musket in his saddle holster, but relaxed when a flock of bobwhite quail took flight. The leather fringes on the sleeves of the buckskin he wore swayed violently, then came to a rest as he focused again on the tracks and urged his horse forward.

Only a moment later he caught sight of two horses picking their way through the trees about seventy-five feet ahead. He looked closer. One of the horses was riderless. He'd been following the tracks of *two* men, where—the distinct sound of a rifle being cocked answered the incomplete thought.

"Take the musket from its holster and toss it," a male voice said from above him. Marcus hesitated and a strong "Mister" settled the matter.

He slid the Brown Bess musket from its holster and tossed it to the ground. "I'm not here to cause trouble."

The sound of the rifle's hammer being uncocked from above was followed by the light drop of the man from the trees onto the ground behind Marcus.

"You tracked me some distance before I realized you were on my trail," the voice said. "Not bad for an Englishman."

Marcus slowly turned his horse and found himself facing a young man dressed like himself, except the other's clothes bore testament of the wearer's time in the saddle. This was Steven Landen. Those deep brown eyes—and the challenge they held—were all too familiar.

"Scottish Highlands," Marcus said.

"Well, Highlander, what are you doing in South Carolina tracking me?"

Marcus glanced at the Baker rifle the boy held loosely at his side—not so loose he couldn't yank it into position before Marcus was upon him. *Arrogant pup.* But perhaps it was an arrogance born out of experience. The British-made Baker rifle was known for its precision aim, a very good reason for a US Army tracker to carry the weapon.

Steven's gaze shifted past him and Marcus glanced over his shoulder to see the rider he'd spotted a moment ago standing a few feet away. He saw now what he hadn't discerned before. The buckskin-dressed man was Indian.

Marcus faced Steven. "How did you discover I was on your trail?"

"I'm the best tracker this side of the Mississippi," Steven said with unabashed candor. "White tracker, that is."

"You are Steven Landen, then?"

The boy gave no indication Marcus had hit the mark, only continued to study him.

"We need to talk. Privately," Marcus added.

"Anything you have to say can be said in front of Joseph."

"'Tis about your sister."

Steven's nonchalant demeanor vanished. "My sister is dead."

"Nay. She was lost off the coast of Solway Firth, Scotland."

Steven's jaw tightened. He looked at the Indian. "Joseph."

Marcus didn't hear   the man leave but knew

he had when Steven swung his gaze back to him.

"You have any idea how many people have *information* concerning my sister?" Steven's expression turned speculative. "None of them ever tracked me through the wilderness. You must feel damn confident about your information. You have five minutes. I should warn you, however, if I don't find your story amusing, I'll kill you."

A melancholy warmth rippled through Marcus. "That sounds like something your sister would say."

Steven's gaze turned icy. "If you want to delay dying, don't bother with the amusing anecdotes."

"I will begin with this." Marcus reached into the front pocket of his buckskin jacket.

Steven pointed his rifle at Marcus. "Easy."

Marcus paused, then slowly produced his and Elise's wedding certificate from the pocket. He dismounted, then strode to Steven and extended the certificate to him.

Steven rested his rifle against the tree he'd been hiding in. "Don't think we're alone," he said as he unfolded the document, "I saved Joseph's life once. He can't return to his Chickasaw tribe until he returns the favor, so he's hoping like hell someone will try to kill me."

Steven scanned the document. A moment later, he looked at Marcus and gave a short laugh. "You got the name wrong. Elise is not a Merriwether."

"Nay," Marcus said, "she's a MacGregor."

Half an hour later, Marcus laid Elise's death certificate on the ground between him and Steven. The boy stared at the document. The fire they had built flickered off his pale face in the waning daylight. He lifted his gaze to Marcus.

"No death certificate was issued for Elise." He stared at Marcus for a long moment before saying, "I have no way of knowing if a word of what you say is true."

"Perhaps you do." Marcus retrieved the gold band from his front pocket. He laid the ring on the death certificate.

Steven looked at the ring, his brow furrowing in thought, then he picked it up and held it up to the firelight. Marcus watched him read the words etched inside the band—*For all eternity*—words he'd read a thousand times over the last month.

Steven set the ring back on the document and looked at him. "Why tell me any of this?" He nodded toward the death certificate. "She's dead."

Marcus took a deep breath. "Mayhap not." He produced the next piece of evidence: the notice of reward for Elise's body that had appeared in the *Sunday Times*.

By the time Marcus finished with the more bizarre half of his tale, Steven's expression had hardened. "I knew Price was a fortune hunter, but this goes beyond anything I suspected. Twenty-six percent of Landen Shipping remained held in trust for me until I reached twenty-one. When the shares became mine, Price wasn't pleased, but he still held controlling interest. Elise married Robert when she was twenty-one, four years before she would come into possession of her inheritance. Not that it mattered; Robert controlled the purse."

"The woman you describe is different than the one I knew. Elise—" Marcus laughed, "She has done things many men would grow fainthearted over."

Steven picked up the stick he'd laid beside him earlier and poked the fire. "She never wanted for courage. That night on the *Amelia*, she surprised even me." Steven looked at him with sudden surprise. "Damn! Her journal."

Marcus tensed. "What?"

Steven plunged the stick into the ground. "Amelia's doctor instructed Elise to keep a journal in order to chronicle her illness. After she died, Elise began doing research. Actually, she began the research

267

before Amelia died but, by then, it was too late."

"Too late?"

"Amelia was diagnosed with everything from heart trouble to nervous disorders. No one could offer a cure. You won't believe this, I wouldn't have believed it either had I not caught Robert trying to kill her, but Elise suspected Robert of poisoning Amelia."

Marcus went cold. "Bloody hell."

"I learned of her suspicions from the journal. By then, Robert was gone." He gave Marcus a frank look. "Despite how I felt about Robert, if I hadn't walked in when he was strangling Elise that night, I would have attributed her suspicions to… well…"

Marcus clenched his fist. "If the bastard were alive, I would kill him myself."

Steven gave a cold laugh. "I would have done it long ago."

"Aye," he said. "I wager you would have."

Steven laid the stick back on the ground beside him. "Price being in Scotland and that bounty don't prove Elise didn't die in the carriage accident."

Marcus held his gaze. "Three months ago, Ardsley told the Landen Shipping board of directors that Elise was here in America."

Steven went white.

"Are you all right, lad?"

"When Elise married, I gave her my shares in Landen Shipping."

Marcus gave a slow nod. "The stakes are even higher. Ardsley has begun negotiations for a large loan to Landen Shipping. He wants to expand the shipping routes."

Steven started. "What?"

"He began negotiations six months ago."

"How can he hope to make the vote without me?" Steven's lip curled up in a derisive twist. "Of course."

"Aye," Marcus said. "He would not need you if he has Elise."

Chapter Nineteen

Marcus strode into the Single Penny tavern with Steven behind him. Marcus glanced back at his young companion. They'd spent seven days on the road and the boy looked none the worse for wear. No one would suspect he wasn't a regular in the establishment. The deception went beyond the rough clothes he wore. The metamorphosis from upper-class gentleman to the rough, bawdy character ready to yank his knife from its sheath and open the gullet of any man who looked in his direction was complete. Steven certainly wasn't the typical wealthy American.

The boy's gaze rested for an instant on a table in the far corner of the room, then moved on. Marcus glanced in the same direction and realized he had seen Justin sitting with another man. Even in the shadows of the dimly lit room, Marcus understood what had snagged Steven's attention. Despite the rough clothes Justin wore, the way his manicured fingers curled around the beer mug he drank from gave away the fact he wasn't a typical river rat.

Steven looked at Marcus. Marcus gave a small jerk of his head and Steven followed as he strode to the table. Justin set the mug of ale on the table and looked up at their approach. Marcus slid into the seat to his right. Steven circled the table and took the seat to Justin's left.

"Marcus," Justin's cultured English accent

remained evident despite the hoarse quality he injected into his voice.

"Justin," Marcus greeted in a thick, Scottish brogue.

"Meet William Sheldon of the Boston police department," Justin said.

"Shhh," Sheldon hissed, ducking his head down.

"Mr Sheldon," Justin said, "tell my friend what you told me."

Mr Sheldon looked about. He sat back suddenly and Marcus would have urged him on, but a tavern maid approached the table, two ales in hand.

"Good evening, gentlemen," she said, setting an ale before Marcus, then going around William to place the other in front of Steven. She straightened, saying, "You have a choice of jackrabbit stew or roast pig."

"Jackrabbit stew, my girl, all around," Steven spoke up.

Marcus hid his surprise at hearing the guttural accent Steven employed and nodded to the girl in assent when she looked at him. She started for the bar at the back of the room and Marcus focused on William.

"Lad," he said in low tones, "proceed with your tale, if ye please."

William cast a nervous glance about the room, then leaned forward. "Your friend here," he nodded toward Justin, "promised the remainder of the fee."

"Aye," Marcus said. "Whatever he agreed to, you'll get."

"If you don't mind, sir," William said, "I'll have my payment now."

Justin pulled forth a small pouch and set it on the table. William reached for it, but Marcus laid a hand on his when it covered the pouch. "The money stays where it is until I've heard what you have to say."

William nodded, and Marcus withdrew his hand. William released the pouch and placed his elbows on the table. "There's a place up north, a hundred and fifty miles or so, Bainbridge Hospital. A month ago, a man incarcerated his wife there because she believes she was Cleopatra in a past life."

"And what makes ye think this woman is the one we are looking for?" Marcus asked.

"The description your friend here gave. The woman is dark haired, late twenties and slim of build. The man is much older and seems to fit your description. He's rich, sure enough."

William sat back and Marcus saw the tavern maid approach again, tray in hand with four bowls of stew on it.

She set a bowl before each of them and looked at the men. "Anything else?"

"That'll be all," Steven said, and hunched over his bowl. He began clinking the spoon loudly against the side of the bowl.

The woman turned as he took a hearty mouthful. William gulped a spoonful of stew. He chewed, his gaze following her until she was out of hearing range. He took one more bite of food as two men passed, headed for a nearby table.

William pushed the bowl forward. "As I was saying, the man is rich. He's left strict orders that no one is to visit his wife and she is to be kept under heavy sedation."

Marcus's hand balled into a fist and, before realizing it, he started to push to his feet.

Justin grasped his shoulder and shoved him back into his seat. "Easy there, my fellow," he said, his voice all amusement. "You would think it was your own wife there instead of—well"—Justin flashed a grin—"you know how it is, Mr Sheldon, when a woman cuckolds a man."

William nodded. "Indeed, I do."

"Seems the lady was burning both ends of the candle," Justin said. "It's my guess her husband is teaching the wench a lesson far beyond that you could serve up, my boy." He gave Marcus a hearty clap on the shoulder.

Marcus slumped back into his chair. "She

didna' cuckold me," he muttered in a sullen a voice, and looked at William. "'Tis no' enough to be sure she's the one."

"She is the most likely one."

Marcus exchanged a glance with Justin. "What do you mean 'the most likely one?'"

"There's another woman, but she doesn't seem a good fit. A raving lunatic. Has nightmares about a child who was poisoned—"

Marcus started. Justin straightened and Steven dropped his spoon into his nearly empty bowl. William looked from one man to the other.

"Where is this woman?" Marcus demanded.

"Twenty miles outside of Boston in Danvers Sanitarium."

"Danvers?" Steven repeated in a loud voice.

Marcus shot him a warning look.

Steven lowered his voice. "That's an asylum for the criminally insane."

Marcus felt the blood rush to his head.

"What are her circumstances?" Justin cut in.

"Her father brought her," William replied. "She suffers from delusions that her child has returned from the dead." William shivered. "Most of the men working there fear her. There's nothing like the fear of the devil to put the fear of God into a man."

Or the fear of a courageous woman, Marcus silently added.

Marcus stepped from the tavern onto the dimly lit street between Justin and Steven.

Once out of sight of the tavern, Marcus looked at Justin. "I am the spurned lover?"

Justin grinned. "You weren't anything until I thought you would do poor William in."

"Who is this William?"

Justin gave a deprecating laugh. "A Boston law-enforcement officer."

Marcus addressed Steven, "What do you know of Boston law enforcement?"

"I don't know William, but many Boston police officers are in a position to know information like what he told us."

Marcus nodded. "Where does Landen Shipping hold its board meetings?"

"The Brill Building, downtown Boston," Steven answered.

Justin said, "Ardsley will have to transport her from the sanitarium to the meeting,"

"Aye." Marcus replied. "Only, we will meet him long before he reaches Boston."

The sun peeked over the horizon. Not a single traveler had appeared on the road leading to Danvers Sanitarium while they lay hidden under the cover of darkness. Marcus tapped Justin on the shoulder and signaled that he would return momentarily. He slipped from the trees overlooking the road east of them, crept through tall grass, brambles, and bush up a hill. The wildly growing foliage ended abruptly. Across a vast manicured lawn, the view of the sprawling, ivy-covered, brick building—his first in the light of day—chilled him to the bone.

The pointed towers and peaked gables had lost the haunting look their silhouettes projected in the twilight hours and became, instead, the bared teeth of *The Witches' Castle.* A shudder ran through him. What sort of twisted mind had built a sanitarium on the spot where John Hathorne, the most fanatical judge of the Salem witch trials, once lived?

Marcus's heart hardened at sight of the iron-barred windows. He brought his gaze down to the stone steps of the front entrance. Marked on both sides by wrought iron railing, they lead up to a circular, covered porch. Columns supported the porch roof on either side. He looked again at the windows, studying one, then another, of what seemed an endless array of cells.

Which of those tiny rooms held Elise prisoner? So

close. Marcus envisioned forcing his way past the attendants who fed off the brutality they inflicted upon the helpless inmates. The image, however, was violently replaced by the realization that those men would hold him until Price arrived. Then any power embodied in the information he held would become worthless—and Elise would be lost forever. He closed his eyes in an effort to banish the thought but saw, instead, her frail form, lying on a thin pallet, hands crossed over her breasts in readiness for the coffin. He shook off the vision, then turned from the menacing asylum. He crept down the slope and returned to Justin and Steven.

Marcus scanned the empty road before whispering, "What has gone wrong?"

"Mayhap Ardsley took her out before we arrived?" Justin asked.

Steven shook his head. "No. You heard what our scout said when we arrived yesterday evening. Price hasn't been to the sanitarium."

Marcus started to speak, but Steven cut him off. "The surrounding area is being watched. Had anyone ridden cross-country, we would have been alerted."

"A single man could have slipped past your men," Marcus said. "Does Ardsley ride?"

"Quite well," Steven replied. "But he couldn't have approached the hospital without being spotted. As you have seen, Danvers is surrounded by open country."

"He would need a carriage for Elise," Justin said.

"Aye," Marcus agreed, "but if he didn't plan on bringing her to the meeting today, he would have come by horseback."

"If he doesn't need her at the meeting, he may not have come at all," Justin added.

"He has no hope of swinging the vote without her," Steven said. "He must bring her. Why keep her alive if he isn't going to present her?"

That was a question Marcus couldn't consider.

Another day of living with the knowledge that Elise was locked in hell had worn Marcus beyond thin. The Single Penny's tavern door swung open and he snapped his attention onto the newcomer, his brother-in-law. His heart rate accelerated. The grim expression on the lad's face didn't bode well. Steven assessed the room in the same manner he had the day they'd met William Shelby, then pressed through the cluster of men milling near the door and shuffled across the room.

He slid into the seat opposite Marcus and without preamble whispered, "I'm a complete fool."

"What has happened?" Marcus demanded.

"We were so occupied with Danvers—so sure Elise was there—"

"Are you saying she is not?"

Steven shook his head. "No. Only that our knowing she is there created a distraction." He gave a harsh laugh. "If I didn't know any better, I would swear Price planned it." His mouth dipped into a deep scowl. "It occurred to me last night that I should question Price's servants."

"Wouldn't Ardsley stop you?" Marcus asked.

"If he knew, yes. There is little love lost between Price and his servants. The housekeeper, in particular, despises him." Steven halted and looked past Marcus. He realized the barmaid must be approaching with ale in hand. An instant later, she appeared at his right and set an ale before Steven.

"Any of that jackrabbit stew left?" Steven asked.

"Always got jackrabbit stew," she replied.

"Two," Steven said, and she left. He drank from his mug, then said, "Mrs Hartley is a jewel of a housekeeper and Price knows it. Every day, after lunch, she goes to the market. This afternoon, I met her there." Steven paused. "I've always wondered why she stays with Price. A woman with her skills could easily find another post. She doesn't live in terror of him as the other servants do.

"This is the only concession I have ever

known him to make in his household. That, too, puzzled me. Price isn't a man to tolerate being questioned. Today, I discovered why she stays. Mrs Hartley has a son. He is now thirty years of age. About fifteen years ago, he killed a man in a brothel brawl. The dead man was a well-respected businessman. All these years, Price has been holding this over her head."

"Why tell you this after all this time?"

Steven gave a low grunt. "Two reasons, I suspect. One, she likes Elise. The second, once I told her Price was holding Elise captive she must have realized that there was a great chance I would deal with him legally. That would free her from Price's hold."

"Bloody hell," Marcus burst out. "You didn't inform her of my presence?"

Steven glanced around the tavern and Marcus cursed his temper.

The younger man leaned closer. "Of course not. But the woman's no fool. She knew I was up to something. Nothing goes on in any household the servants don't know, sometimes even before other family members, and with good reason; they're smarter than the devil himself. Our stew is coming." Steven slumped back in his chair.

Marcus did the same as the barmaid set a bowl of stew before him, then Steven. She turned and headed back to the bar. Steven placed his elbows on the table and took another drink of ale before stirring the stew.

"Mrs Hartley knew that Price told the board Elise was here in America," he said, and took a bite of stew. "He's in the habit of having late meetings in his home with board members. Last night, a woman was brought in. She was dressed in black. Heavily veiled and heavily sedated. Price carried her to one of the guestrooms on the second floor. He wouldn't allow anyone into the room when he took her up. Half an hour later, he called for Mrs Hartley. Imagine her shock at seeing Elise in the bed, looking as if she had all but stepped into the grave."

Marcus's heart missed a beat. "How did he get her

past us—we left Danvers too soon."

"Don't lose yourself just yet, MacGregor. I thought the same, but there was something wrong with Mrs Hartley's story."

"What do you mean?"

"She said a single candle burned on a table in the corner of the room. The covers were tucked tightly around the woman's shoulders. Despite the dim lighting, Mrs Hartley observed the emaciated neck and hollow cheeks of the woman—and her hair—you know how thick Elise's hair is."

"Aye." Marcus remembered well the silky feel of the thick tresses between his fingers.

"Mrs Hartley said her hair was so thin that her scalp was visible in places."

"'Tis but two months since Arsdley abducted her. How is it possible—"

"It isn't," Steven cut in. "The resemblance must have been strong for Mrs Hartley to believe the woman was Elise, but Mrs Hartley said the woman was barely recognizable as the Elise she had seen just a year ago. Elise lost weight due to the stress of Amelia's illness, but she was, overall, very healthy."

Marcus nodded. "The housekeeper thought Elise had been wasting away an entire year."

"Right." Steven took another spoonful of stew. "Consider," he said between chewing, "it's not yet two months since Elise disappeared. Had Price starved her to the point of shedding that much weight, her heart would probably have given out."

"The woman is not Elise." Marcus leaned back in his chair. "Why an impersonator? Why not simply incapacitate Elise?"

"I can only guess," Steven said, "but—"

"But," Marcus interrupted, "he will not risk her leaving the asylum."

Steven nodded. "Price is… canny." His expression turned pained. "Had I been more aware—"

"Nay," Marcus cut him off. "The man is clever and he can't have done this alone."

277

Suddenly, Langley's words came back to Marcus. *"Ye have a spy, MacGregor."* Price Ardsley had help. The truth hit like a landslide. *The Campbells.* Marcus recalled the day they attacked the women at the loch and the look on the Campbell warrior's face when Elise called out that Nell had been taken. The man recognized the American accent. They had come for Elise—for the second time. Marcus suddenly understood why they hadn't accosted her when they kidnapped her: the ten thousand pound bounty. But how had they known—more importantly, who at Brahan Seer had aided them?

"MacGregor."

Marcus shook from his thoughts at hearing Steven's voice.

"What is it?" Steven asked.

"Ardsley may not be as omnipotent as he appears."

"What do you mean?"

"I believe some old enemies of mine were in league with him," Marcus said. "Elise had a bad habit of leaving Brahan Seer without an escort."

Steven paused in taking another drink of ale. "Brahan Seer?"

"Our home in the Highlands. She used to go alone outside the castle."

Steven grimaced. "I can believe she would be so foolish. Even as a girl, she drove Father to distraction, coming and going without permission."

"You are saying this is a fault of hers?"

The younger man barked a rough laugh. "MacGregor, if you're only now coming to this conclusion, I have no sympathy for you."

Marcus smiled faintly. "The woman can be a pain in the arse. She is mine, nonetheless."

"These enemies," Steven prodded.

"Aye. They kidnapped Elise once, tried a second time."

Steven regarded him for a long moment, then shook his head and took another bite of stew.

Marcus liked the lad. "The board meeting," he said. "The vote is to be held at Ardsley's home

278

tonight?"

"No, tomorrow. But the board members are to meet at Price's home tonight. I wager Price is going to let them see Elise in her sick bed then, when he presents the paper tomorrow—a paper signed by my sister—it will be a *fait accompli*."

"What time this evening?"

"Eight o'clock."

Marcus glanced at the clock hanging on the wall behind the bar. Four fifty-five. "We have three hours."

Steven raised a brow. "If we show up and claim the impostor..."

"Aye," Marcus said. "If he wants my wife's fifty-one percent of Landen Shipping, he will have no choice but to return Elise to me."

"We should have stormed the damned hospital," Steven muttered darkly.

Marcus tensed, remembering all too well the strength of will it had taken to keep from hiring fifty men and raiding Danvers. Strength of will. Nay. Justin had been the voice of reason. They weren't in Scotland, Justin had reminded him. Here, Marcus was naught but a British subject on foreign soil. He had always thought of himself as a man of logic and not given to rash action. But, until now, he hadn't realized how much he relied upon his position as the Marquess of Ashlund— even more—the son of the Duke of Ashlund.

Ah, Ryan, my ancestor, how far our paths have diverged.

For the first time in his life, Marcus understood the true nature of Ryan MacGregor. All these years, Marcus thought he understood him—thought it was Ryan who demanded recompense for the wrongs done to the MacGregors over the centuries. But, in truth, how could Marcus, a man of wealth and position, understand a man who possessed nothing? A man who fought with the only weapon he had: his mind. Marcus laughed inwardly. How many years had he fought his enemies with the sword—the very thing Ryan had fought against?

Marcus turned his attention to his brother-in-law. "We are far from finished with Price Ardsley. We shall deal with him in a way that brings about his demise because of his own actions."

Steven's gaze intensified. "All I ask is that I be allowed to witness his end."

"Aye, lad," Marcus replied in a quiet voice. "You will be one among many."

Marcus watched, concealed by the evening shadows among the trees, as the seventh carriage that night passed through the iron gates of Price Ardsley's mansion. The crunch of gravel beneath the carriage wheels grew fainter until the high and low seesaw pitch of cricket music again filled the quiet. Marcus's horse shifted beneath him and he gave the animal a soothing stroke. Steven's horse nickered softly, nuzzling his companion's nose, and Steven patted his shoulder.

Marcus looked at him. "What time is it?"

Steven pulled a pocket watch from the breast pocket of his suit. "Nearly eight," he whispered, and slipped the watch back into its place.

Marcus returned his attention to the mansion. "Is that the last of them?"

"Unless Brentley rode with one of the other board members, no."

"You are sure your vice-chairman will attend?"

Steven grunted. "Price would be glad not to have Brentley attend. Brentley is a thorn in his side. But Brentley has been chairman since the inception of the company and the other members would not attend a meeting of such importance without him."

Steven peered down the road and they lapsed into silence. The cricket symphony abruptly halted and, an instant later, the faint clop of hooves and turning of carriage wheels sounded on the public road up ahead. Marcus squinted until the outline of a coach took shape in the darkness.

"Brentley," Steven said.

The carriage passed through the gates and the darkness, once again, closed in around it. The nightlife sprang back to life. Still, Marcus waited several long moments, acutely aware of his companion's impatience before saying, "Now, Brother," and urged his horse from the cover of trees.

They slowed their horses through the gates and onto the gravel of the private lane. The cool air of fall brushed across Marcus's face, then snaked its way between his collar and neck in chilled fingers. The road wound through the grounds until, at last, a faint glow lit a beacon through the thick trees to the left. The road made a sudden left turn and the mansion came into view, two gas lights blazing on each side of the doors. No servant waited to greet them. All expected guests had arrived. Both men dismounted at the base of the stairs and hurried to the door. Steven entered with Marcus close behind. A butler appeared from a door at the end of the hallway carrying a tray laden with decanter and glasses.

"Sir!" he cried, rattling the tray.

"Simons," Steven replied, and started up the grand black walnut stairway to his right.

"Sir," Simons called again as Marcus followed Steven up the staircase.

"I'll see myself to the second floor," Steven called over his shoulder.

The tray was set down with a clatter and was followed by the light tread of feet on the stairs behind them.

"Simons is persistent," Steven said in a low voice, taking the stairs two at a time.

The staircase followed the wall straight up to the second floor. The landing turned sharply left at the top. Marcus strode down the corridor alongside Steven, who stopped at the fifth door on the left.

"Sir," Simons called from the landing.

Steven reached for the doorknob and Marcus saw his hand shake.

"Lad," he said, gently.

"Sir!" Simons cried, his voice nearly hysterical. "You know how Mr Ardsley does not like strangers upstairs." Simons had nearly reached them.

Steven looked at Marcus, gave a single nod, then said as he pushed open the door, "He's no stranger, Simons; he is my brother-in-law."

The words "brother-in-law" rang in the silence of the bedchambers.

Simons hit the doorframe with an audible slap. "Mr Ardsley, sir," he said between heavy breaths, "I tried stopping them."

Marcus locked gazes with the powerfully-built golden-haired man who stood nearest the bed. He looked to be about ten years older than himself. He outweighed Marcus by twenty pounds, but his fit frame testified that he wasn't a man given to excessive drinking or any such habits that would quicken the infirmities of age. Cold blue eyes stared back at Marcus. Here, at last, he understood what Elise so feared.

"I am—" Simons began, but Price Ardsley said in a quiet voice, "Go along, Simons. We're fine." Price shifted his gaze to Steven. "Steven, I wasn't expecting you."

"I am sure," Steven remarked.

Ardsley focused on Marcus, and said, "Sir?"

His tone was quizzical, but Marcus understood the flicker of expression that had said, *Lord Ashlund, you are a surprise.*

"Pardon me, Gentlemen," Marcus said, and brushed past the men who stood in stunned silence. He felt Price's eyes settle on him as he sat on the bed beside the woman Price claimed was Elise. Marcus took her cold, limp hand in his and lifted it to his lips. "Elise," he said in a choked whisper, then gently lay her hand upon her breast. Sliding his arms beneath her, he lifted her, bed covers and all, from the bed.

A chorus of protests sounded as Marcus turned toward the men gathered in the room.

Chapter Twenty

Elise felt herself lifted into a sitting position. Next came the familiar cold rim of the metal cup against her lips. *Do not drink*, she warned herself silently. *The thirst doesn't matter.* Her mouth felt like sandpaper, parched from lack of water, but the laudanum-laced water held a greater fear than death. She allowed her head to loll to one side. A meaty hand cupped her cheek and forced her into a more upright position. Liquid dribbled past her lips and into her mouth. She kept mouth and throat muscles lax and, despite the cold of the liquid as it trickled down her neck, none made its way down her throat.

"She can barely sit up," a coarse female voice said. "Why does she need more?"

"'Tis the doctor's orders," came the all-too-familiar Irish brogue of Ramsey.

"Bah!" the woman said. "If you want to waste your time forcing it down her throat, do so. I have better things to do."

The cup left Elise's mouth and the hand released her face. Again, she allowed her head to loll to one side.

"You're right," Ramsey said.

Her head was laid back on the pallet.

"They will dose her this evening. She's not likely to come out of this stupor before then."

The woman laughed. "She's not likely to come out of that stupor *ever*."

"How is the bleeding?" Ramsey asked.

Elise tensed inwardly, calling forth every ounce of strength not to react openly to what she knew was forthcoming. She felt her skirts lifted, then cool air washed her legs as the woman drew back the fabric. Elise bit back tears when her legs were spread, though only slightly this time.

Soon, she told herself, *soon. If I can convince them for just one more day that I don't need the laudanum, I will find a way out of this madhouse.*

There came a prod to the rags between her legs, and the woman said, "Not so bad."

"Let the night shift deal with it," Ramsey muttered. "The things they ask us to do."

The skirts were yanked back over her legs and she lay motionless, counting the ten steps her jailers took to the door, then the creak of the door as it opened and the echo of the clank being pulled shut. She waited a long moment.

Was he still there?

How many times had the Irishman stared in at her through the small, barred window on the door? Twenty—thirty times? She had lost count. There came the soft but distinct scrape she had come to know. She willed her body not to tremble. Ramsey had, again, waited for the woman to go, then opened the shutter on the window to stare at her from the other side.

Minutes passed—more, she thought, than he had taken before. It wouldn't matter if she screamed. In this place, everyone screamed. The opening swished closed. Elise began to tremble so badly she feared her teeth would chatter. Most rooms were built to keep the sound in, but her room seemed to amplify sound. She imagined her persecutors listening for the slightest sound so they might pounce upon her, pronounce her *stupor* a lie, and administer more laudanum.

Tears rolled from the corners of her eyes. She had lost her child—Marcus's child—less than two months in the womb. Even in her laudanum-induced state, she had known the moment the blood began to flow. How many days ago that had been, she couldn't say. There had been no pain, the laudanum had ensured that, but she had known. The degradation that followed paled in comparison to the despair.

Laudanum had been the instrument that had taken the child's life, but Price was the babe's murderer as certainly as if he had squeezed the life from the infant with his own hands. Robert had taken her child and her brother. Now Price had taken her second child. Between them, they had stripped her of all she held dear. *Not all,* her mind reminded her. There was still Marcus. More tears flowed.

Dear God, let him accept my death. Do not bring him to America.

Marcus locked gazes with Price Ardsley. "My wife and I are leaving." He started toward the door.

The men, transfixed by the strange happenings, parted as he brushed past them. All but one—standing closest to the door—who stepped in front of him.

"Pardon me, sir," he said in a low, firm voice, "if you would explain."

"Brentley," Steven said, and stepped up beside Marcus. "Please clear the doorway."

"Steven," Price said. "Explain yourself."

Steven opened his mouth, but Marcus spoke. "I am Marcus MacGregor, the Marquess of Ashlund, and this"—he nodded to the woman in his arms—"is my wife, the Marchioness of Ashlund."

An instant of stunned silence passed, then the man standing closest said, "I assume you have proof of this claim?"

"My brother-in-law has the wedding certificate." Marcus motioned with a nod of his head in Steven's direction.

Steven retrieved the certificate from the front pocket of his great coat and handed it to Brentley. The older man took the paper while reaching into his pocket and pulling out a pair of spectacles. He wrapped the wires of the spectacles around his ears, then read the certificate.

"The ceremony was officiated by a Father Whyte of Badachro, Scotland," he said.

"I know nothing of that person or place," one of the other men said.

Brentley looked at Marcus. "Forgive me, sir, but you will understand this"—he indicated the wedding certificate with a small shake—"isn't enough."

"Steven," Marcus said, "take the ring from my breast pocket."

Steven pulled back Marcus's coat and reached inside the pocket. He retrieved the ring Robert had given Elise and handed it to Brentley. "The inscription," Steven said. "Read it.

Brentley took a step closer to the door, holding the ring out so that the light from the hallway glinted off it. He squinted, reading aloud, "For all eternity." He looked questioningly at Steven.

"That is the ring Robert gave Elise on their wedding day."

From the corner of his eye, Marcus saw Price's mouth thin.

Another of the board members cleared his throat. "What sort of proof is that?"

Brentley looked from his companion back to Steven. "You are sure?"

"Absolutely," Steven replied.

Brentley whipped his glasses off and faced Price. "What do you make of this, Price?"

Price stepped up to them and extended his hand. "May I see the ring?"

Brentley placed it on Price's open palm. Ardsley stepped into the doorway and examined the ring. An instant later, he turned his gaze onto Marcus. "It looks very much like the ring Robert gave Elise." He handed the ring to Steven.

"It could be a forgery," Brentley said.

"Possibly," Price agreed, then said to Marcus, "Have you other proof of your claims?"

"The night Elise was washed overboard, her husband tried to strangle her. She was forced—"

"That is common knowledge," Price interrupted.

Satisfaction surged through Marcus. So this was to be the line Price would not have him cross. "True," he agreed, "but there are details which wouldn't have been common knowledge."

Price inclined his head. "Gentlemen," he looked around the room, "in the interest of privacy, perhaps it would be best if we reconvened in my study."

The men gave a general nod of agreement. Price grasped the servant's bell hanging near the door and tugged. A moment later, Simons appeared in the doorway.

"Simons, show my guests to the study."

"Indeed, sir," Simons replied. "If you would, gentlemen." He bowed.

"I cannot leave Elise," Marcus said.

The men hesitated, and Price said, "Gentlemen, if you will allow me, I will reassure Lord Ashlund that Elise will be well tended in his absence. Go with Simons. We'll be along directly."

The men filed out of the room until only Steven, Marcus, and Price remained.

Price closed the door, then faced Marcus. "What do you want?"

"My wife," Marcus said, and turned to carry the woman impersonating Elise back to the bed. He gently lay her on the mattress, straightened the covers about her neck, then faced Price.

"And the stocks?" Price asked.

"Yours, once you deliver her to me."

"They are mine now."

"All assets will be frozen for a minimum of three months," Steven interjected. "That is the time it will take to confirm the Marquess's claim. And"—he added with a slight smile—"that could easily turn into six months. The board will wish to be extremely thorough in this matter. In the end, they will be mine."

"It's a shame Robert's aim wasn't

better," Price commented.

"Be that as it may," Steven replied evenly.

"You have until tomorrow evening to deliver Elise to the *Josephine*," Marcus said. "The ship is docked in Boston Harbor and awaits our arrival before departing for England."

"I have a signed affidavit giving me Elise's stocks," Price said.

"I care nothing for your money," Marcus said. "Return her to me, and I will not contest the documents."

Price looked at Steven.

"My sister's life is worth the shares I gave her."

Price returned his attention to Marcus. "You will dine with me tomorrow evening."

"An early supper. I have a friend aboard the *Josephine*. He *knows* Elise and will send me word once she arrives."

"And what about this puppy?" Price motioned to Steven.

Marcus looked at Steven.

"I, too, will be waiting at the *Josephine*." His expression hardened. "I wish to see my sister before she returns to Scotland."

Price looked at Marcus. "You will sail on the *Josephine*?"

"Aye."

"And you"—he turned again to Steven—"will remain here to deal with me." Steven didn't reply, and Price said, "Let us adjourn to the library and explain how poor Elise was so out of her head she forgot her husband in Scotland. You can assure them you have no interest in her fortune."

"This woman leaves with us tonight," Marcus said.

For the second time that evening, Price showed a flicker of emotion. "A woman in her condition shouldn't to be moved."

Marcus shook his head. "I will not arrive tomorrow evening to find my sick wife dead."

"It's unlikely she will die. The only real thing

wrong with her is malnutrition. That and the laudanum."

"Is malnutrition the only thing wrong with Elise?"

"Elise is quite well."

"Alive and well?" Marcus pressed, maintaining a firm grip on his fury.

"Very much alive."

"Then let us speak with your guests. Steven will remain here."

"Of course," Price said, and opened the door for Marcus.

At nine o'clock that night, Marcus settled the woman impersonating his wife into the carriage, then assisted the maid, who would tend to her on the short ride to the *Josephine*, into the carriage. He strode to his horse and took the reins from Steven. They mounted, then urged their horses after the carriage. They remained silent until long after leaving the estate.

"He has no intention of allowing you to return to the *Josephine* tomorrow evening," Steven said in a low voice.

"Aye," Marcus replied, and lapsed back into silence.

Elise started awake, her eyesight finding and fixing on the sliver of light that jabbed beneath her door into the darkness of her cell. The stench of sweat, urine, and blood met her nostrils. Hers, she realized with a clarity she hadn't experienced in weeks. Memories washed over her in a tidal wave.

Scotland. The carriage careening down the road. Shots fired. *Price.* Price was in Scotland! No—he had been in Scotland—he—they—were now in America. He had brought her back to Boston. He waylaid her coach. She squeezed her eyes shut. Six—seven men murdered in cold blood. And Mary—the memory of the girl's pleas for mercy as Price forced her into the carriage left Elise as cold now as they had then. Mary was the informer Marcus sought.

Marcus. Elise sobbed. He believed her dead. She ceased crying. She was dead. She had signed her death warrant when she signed over her shares in Landen Shipping. But the death of the unborn child he had used to coerce her now stirred something within her.

The child is dead! she mentally screamed. *Price has no more hold over you.*

He wanted her dead. Yet, his affirmation, when she demanded to know if he knew Robert had been poisoning Amelia, had shaken her in a way she hadn't thought possible. He had looked out through those expressionless eyes and answered "Of course" in that cool voice her mother had so loved.

The stirring flared into anger, and with anger came the realization her mind was free. No one had come the previous night to administer another dose of laudanum. She hesitated. Was this the next day? Perhaps two, three, or five days had passed. She couldn't know. But she could think, could find out. Was she strong enough to leave this place? Her heart skipped a beat. Was she strong enough to even rise from this putrid pallet?

Elise took a deep breath, then pushed up to a sitting position. Her pulse raced. The movement had been effortless. Could she—she shoved to her feet. She tripped, one foot having landed on the floor, the other on the pallet, and she stumbled sideways, slamming into the wall. She slid to the floor, head swimming.

"Too fast," she told herself between the gasps for breath she prayed was fear and not lasting effects of the laudanum.

Her pulse slowed and she, at last, rose. Her head remained clear, despite the lurch of her stomach with the first step. She halted, waited a moment, then, eyes fixed on the light, she edged forward until her fingers touched the cold steel of the door.

Marcus closed the door to Miss Lisa Poteck's cabin aboard the *Josephine*, then followed the narrow corridor to the captain's quarters. With a perfunctory knock, he entered. Captain Garret sat at a large table, studying navigation maps that covered the large oak surface. He looked up as Marcus approached.

"How is Miss Poteck?" he asked in a refined English accent.

Marcus seated himself opposite him. "She will be fit enough for the meeting. All is in readiness?"

"It is, Lord Ashlund."

A loud knock sounded at the door and Steven entered.

Marcus came to his feet when he recognized the man behind Steven as one of those hired to watch Danvers Hospital.

"Ardsley has gone to Danvers," Steven said.

"When?"

The man answered, "I rode the moment he arrived. Less than two hours ago."

Adrenaline coursed through Marcus.

Steven was already consulting his pocket watch. "It is twenty-five past one." He stuffed the watch back into its pocket. "Price did just as you said he would."

"Aye, lad. He had no choice." Marcus turned to the messenger. "Wait for me on deck."

The man nodded, then left.

Marcus waited for the door to shut, then faced Steven. "The board members are ready?"

"They're waiting at a nearby tavern." He shook his head in obvious disbelief. "I thought you were wrong. Had I gone to Danvers as I wanted…"

His brother-in-law had no notion of the will it had taken Marcus to remain idle on the *Josephine*. He, too, wanted nothing more than to catch Price Ardsley on the road to Danvers, but he couldn't chance Elise being hurt in the gunfight. Justin would follow her. If worse came to worst, he would attack and take Elise from Price.

"Ardsley had to be sure you and I were aboard the *Josephine*," Marcus said. "You can be sure he knows of our continued presence here." Marcus faced the captain. "Captain Garret, please have your doctor prepare Miss Poteck."

"As you say," Garret replied crisply.

Marcus started for the door, Steven on his heels. Once in the corridor, Steven closed the door and called out to Marcus. He halted.

"Did you inform your cousin of your plan not to sail back to Scotland with Elise?"

"Instructions await him on the ship they are to sail on," Marcus replied.

"He will not be pleased. As for Elise—"

"Elise will be well looked after. Justin knows what he's about."

"And if you don't make your ship?"

"I will."

Elise's hand shook as she pressed a palm against the iron door. She pushed gently. The door swung open. A cry of surprise rose in her throat before she could stifle the sound. Why was her door unlocked? They believed she was still in a stupor!

She stepped as far as the doorway and peeked into the hall. The long corridor was empty. She stepped from the room and stopped two paces into the hallway. A single light lit the hallway near where she stood. Doors lined both sides of the corridor. She looked left, then right. Both directions turned into what seemed yet another hallway. Which way was out? Out—out to where? Where was she going? Marcus. No. She would not endanger him.

Blood roared through her veins; her head pounded. Panic rose. Which way? Choose a way, any way! She started forward. Her courage grew with each infinitesimal step forward. Near the end of the hallway, the tip of a banister extended out to where the hallway turned left. *Stairs.*

A scream shattered the silence. Elise bit back a shout and hugged the wall. Another cry, fainter this time but close, rent the air again. She peered in the direction she had been moving. A door stood three feet from her. She edged toward the room. The door stood slightly ajar and she peered inside.

"No!" a woman wailed in a low voice. "Please, Ramsey, not tonight, not tonight." Her voice trailed off repeating the plea.

Elise jammed her eyes shut. *Ramsey*, the monster who had been watching her.

"No," the woman cried again.

Elise entered the room. "Shhh," she said.

The huddled form in the far corner jerked upright. "Who's there?" the woman said. "Sara? You're not Sara."

"No," Elise soothed. She stopped near the woman and knelt.

The woman shrank back. "Ramsey sent you. He wants to know if my monthly flux has passed. Tell him no! It will never pass. Tell him—"

"No," Elise whispered. "Ramsey did not send me."

"Liar," the woman hissed. She jabbed a finger at Elise and Elise scrambled to her feet. The woman began weeping. "Never," she repeated. "My flux will never pass. I won't spread my legs for him again." She fell into a fit of loud wails.

Elise backed up. The poor soul was mad. Tears streamed down Elise's face. Ramsey. She couldn't remember his face—Price had drugged her before bringing her to the sanitarium—but she could imagine all too easily what he was like. How many other women had he abused? She turned and fled the room.

Ignoring the feel of the stiff, filthy fabric, she ran toward the stairs. Her stomach roiled. Still she ran. A noise sounded behind her. She jerked her head around to glance over her shoulder but saw nothing. Another inmate of the many rooms? She faced forward again, slamming into what, at first, felt like a stone wall. She recognized the fingers of steel that gripped her shoulders even before she looked up into the face of Ramscy.

Chapter Twenty-One

"Release me!" Elise shouted.

She thrashed wildly and Ramsey's grip on her shoulders turned painful.

"Well, now," he said, his Irish brogue sharpened with raucous laughter, "what have we here?"

"Let me go!" She struggled harder, despite the pain of his beefy fingers digging still deeper into her skin. "My husband—" she began, but he cut her off with more foul laughter.

"Your husband committed you, my bonnie girl. So don't bother threatening revenge."

"Price Ardsley is *not* my husband."

"Don't know the man's name. Don't care. He put you here and plainly doesn't plan on you ever seeing the light of day." Ramsey yanked her to him and, with one hand, stroked her hair. "That leaves you and I to sport, eh?"

Elise raised a foot and stomped on the top of his boot. He yelped and leapt back. She whirled and lunged forward.

"Bloody fool wench!"

He seized her from behind and flung her against the wall. Ramsey crashed into her back, knocking the breath from her. He snaked a hand around her waist. Elise wedged her hands between herself and the wall and clawed at his fingers.

"Damn—" he hissed, pulling his hand free.

He grabbed her arms and yanked them back. Her

arms felt as though they would tear from their sockets as he crushed her to the wall.

"You're a plucky one," he wheezed in her ear. "Most wenches here are too daft to even know their names. Takes all the fun out of the play."

He pinned her arms between their bodies with one hand, then rammed the fingers of his free hand into her hair. Elise jerked her head aside, but he mashed her cheek against the wall.

"You haven't had a bath since coming here, but Sara kept you cleaned up where it counts." He thrust his hips against her.

Elise's stomach churned, more at the knowledge of the shared intimacy when Sara had tended to her than the feel of his erection digging into the cleft of her buttocks.

"Not a pretty sight," he went on. "Until she cleaned you up, that is. Then," he roughly ground himself against her, "I knew you and I would be spending time together. I was waiting for the right time." He laughed again. "You decided you wanted me now, eh?"

She shoved hard against the wall in an attempt to thrust his body away from hers, but he slammed back all the more brutally, groaning when their bodies jammed together. His fingers tightened in her hair and she cried out in pain.

"Aye, my girl," he rasped. "Scream. In this place, no one will care, and I like it."

He released her hair and forced his hand into the small of her back where his belt had been digging into her flesh. His belt jingled and, for the first time, Elise felt loathing and fear vie in earnest with outrage. Her body trembled and her knees weakened. She twisted, but he yanked back on her arms, and she felt her arms begin to separate from their sockets.

His belt and trousers hit the floor with the buckle landing with a dull clank. He grabbed her skirts and yanked them up. Elise kicked backwards with the heel of her foot, hitting the   hard bone of his shin. He grunted, but only spread his legs and thrust his hips into her.

"I will not be another of your victims!" she shouted.

She grit her teeth and jerked her head backwards. The back of her head struck Ramsey's hard skull. He shrieked, yanking hard on her arms as he fell back a pace. Pain reverberated through her head. Elise bit her lip to halt the pain as he unexpectedly leapt back from her. Iron fingers seized her arm and she barely registered the difference in this and Ramsey's hold as she was spun her around.

Elise gasped.

Price Ardsley stared down at her.

Two hours after the messenger arrived informing Marcus that Price had arrived at Danvers, a messenger arrived at the *Josephine* directing Marcus to come immediately to Price Ardsley's home. Half an hour later, Marcus was shown into his private study. A fire crackled in the hearth and Price sat behind the mahogany desk he had occupied when they had explained Elise's situation to Landen Shipping's board of directors. A tumbler of whiskey sat before Price. How would this man explain Elise's situation when the board members appeared here later this morning?

"Please," Price motioned to the chair in front of the desk, "have a seat."

Marcus sat.

"Would you like a drink?" Price asked, straightening.

"Nay."

Price leaned back. "Word will arrive any moment that Elise has been safely deposited aboard the *Josephine*."

"You had until this evening. Why bring her so early?"

"I thought her speedy return would please you."

"Her not being abducted would have pleased me."

"Rest assured she is safe. So long as she—you

both—remain in Scotland. You've said nothing about the boy." Price sipped his drink.

"He is no threat to you."

"He won't take lightly that I kept his sister prisoner."

"I have convinced him to accompany us to Scotland," Marcus gave the planned answer.

Price seemed to contemplate this. "The longer the stay, the better."

"Aye," Marcus agreed.

The sound of boots on carpeted floor were heard, and Price said, "That would be our young friend now."

As if on cue, the door opened and Steven entered. "Elise is safely on the *Josephine*."

"She is well?" Marcus asked with as much calm as he could exert.

Steven turned his glare to Price. "She has a dislocated shoulder and looks as if she hasn't bathed since her abduction."

Marcus jerked his gaze back to Price and barely managed to check the compulsion to lunge across the desk.

"Your brother-in-law will now take a message to the captain that he is to set sail before the hour is up," Price said.

"I will not leave," Steven shot back.

"Aye, you will." Marcus prayed the boy wouldn't pull the pistol he'd noticed stuffed into his waistband. "You have pen and paper?"

Price produced paper from a desk drawer and laid it before Marcus as he scooted the quill, sitting at his left, up alongside the paper. Marcus wrote the note instructing the *Josephine* to set sail immediately, then folded the missive and extended it toward Steven.

"Anyone can deliver this," Steven protested.

Marcus shook his head. "You take it, lad, and be on the ship when she sails." This Marcus had *not* discussed with Steven, for the boy would not have agreed. Chances were, he wouldn't obey now.

Steven looked from Marcus to Price, then snatched the note from Marcus's grasp. He settled his gaze on Price. "We aren't finished."

Price nodded with a sigh and Steven faced Marcus. "You shouldn't have come here."

"Take care of Elise," Marcus said.

"That I will," he said, and left.

Marcus focused on Price. "My father, the Duke of Ashlund, will be waiting for the *Josephine* when she arrives. If anything happens to Elise or Steven, if any attempts are made to harm either of them, someone will set sail from Scotland before I step onto Scottish soil."

"I have no intention of harming Elise."

Aye, neither will you harm her brother, Marcus silently added. "How long am I to wait here?" Marcus asked.

"Until word arrives that the *Josephine* is well out of Boston Harbor. I estimate two hours."

"A guard stands outside this door?"

Price gave a single nod.

"I would have preferred to wait at one of the harbor taverns," Marcus said, not feeling the slightest twinge of guilt at the lie. He had planned all along to be here when the men of Landen Shipping arrived on Ardsley's door about the same time the *Josephine* left Boston Harbor.

"Shall I have refreshments served?" Price asked.

"Nay," Marcus replied. "I dine only with friends."

Nearly two hours of silence later, there came a quick knock on the library door. Price looked toward the door as it opened and Simons entered.

"Sir," the butler said out of breath, "Mister Brentley and the other gentlemen from Landen Shipping are downstairs. They are demanding to see you—" A pounding of footsteps in the hallway intruded into Simon's speech. "There they are, sir. I feared they would not wait."

Brentley appeared in the doorway. The rest of Landen Shipping's board of directors piled up behind him. Brentley stepped inside the room and looked at

Marcus, who rose.

"We have just come from the *Josephine*," Brentley said.

"The *Josephine*?" Price asked evenly.

"Yes," Brentley replied, and the room broke out into a babble of voices. "Gentlemen," he shouted. "Gentlemen, please!"

Another figure appeared behind the men. The din quieted as Steven pushed past them and halted beside Marcus.

"You should have sailed on the *Josephine*," Marcus said.

"As should you have," Steven replied.

"Price," Brentley said, "we have just spoken with Miss Poteck and Elise."

"Miss Poteck?" Price said as if he had never heard the name in his life.

"Don't," Brentley cut in, his quiet voice harsh. He produced two folded pieces of paper from his front coat pocket. He unfolded them and held up one. "This is a signed affidavit from Miss Poteck, explaining in detail how you paid her to impersonate Elise Kingston." Price frowned, but Brentley went on. "This," he lifted the other document, "is Elise's statement." He continued in a half strangled voice, "She swears you kidnapped her in Scotland and brought her to Boston against her will, then incarcerated her in Danvers Hospital." Marcus's heart raced as if hearing this for the first time. Brentley lowered the papers. "If I had been given this information without the benefit of witnesses, I would put a bullet between your eyes."

A murmur circulated through the men. Surprise flickered across Price's impassive face. Marcus had the sudden urge to slip the knife from his boot and throw it at him. However, the mental image of Price's fine white shirt darkening with his blood dissipated when Brentley said, "As it is, I will have to satisfy myself with the punishment allowed by the law. As you may know, Judge Quinley and I are well acquainted. I will see to it he takes a personal interest in this case. I have always known you were a scoundrel, but this"—Brentley faltered—"this goes beyond anything I could have imagined."

He shook his head, his blue eyes clouded with disbelief. "The things Elise claims in this document..." He paused and held Price's gaze. "It's a wonder the girl survived." He looked at Marcus. "You have my deepest sympathies, Lord Ashlund."

Marcus's gut twisted. What more was wrong with Elise than Steven had admitted? What had Brentley seen that the younger man hadn't? Marcus gave a single nod and, once again, everyone began talking. He glanced at Ardsley. Price met his gaze with the same unruffled expression he always wore. A chill passed through Marcus. He turned and left the room.

A moment later, Marcus and Steven stepped from the mansion out onto the front steps. Marcus looked from the boy who stood at the bottom of the stairs holding his and Steven's horses across the trees surrounding the mansion to the sky that hinted at dawn. He and Steven strode down the steps, mounted their horses and urged them into a walk. They rode in silence until passing from the gates.

"Elise is safely sailed on the *Surrey*?" Marcus asked.

"Justin smuggled her off the *Josephine*. An easy feat with the *Surrey* docked only two slips down. I watched the ship sail. No one suspected a thing, including Brentley and the others."

Marcus allowed the first breath of relief since Elise had gone missing. Autumn was just beginning. The journey would be an easy one. "Steven," he said in a quiet voice, "is she truly well?"

"As I said, her shoulder is dislocated and she hasn't bathed since leaving Scotland."

"Otherwise?"

Steven hesitated, then said, "In a way, she's the Elise I knew; in a way, she isn't." He paused. "She has passed through fire since I last saw her, but losing

Amelia changed her, and there is her marriage to you."

"We were wed but a night when Price took her."

Steven blew out a breath. "You didn't mention that."

Marcus looked at him. "She is my wife. It doesn't matter whether for a day or a year."

"I suppose not." Another moment of silence passed and Steven said, "She had no idea you were coming for her."

Marcus jerked his gaze onto Steven.

"I believe she had hoped you wouldn't come."

"Bloody hell," Marcus burst out. "Why?"

"It's easy to see she lied to you."

"She didn't tell me about Ardsley."

"Neither did she tell you she shot Robert."

"Nay," Marcus replied.

"She saved my life. You think she knew about the bounty on her head?"

"How could—" Marcus stopped, remembering the night at Michael's when she laid the onion before Michael *after* removing his copy of the *Sunday Times*— the copy Erin had brought.

Everyone in Brahan Seer knew how Michael loved reading the newspaper. Anyone passing through Edinburgh brought a copy at least as far as the *Glaistig Uain*. From there, the copy, eventually, made its way to Michael. Elise lived at Brahan Seer for four months before Marcus returned. All that time she had been going to the cottage and searching the paper for news. By God, on his return from London the last time, he had brought a copy of the paper. It still sat on his desk.

"Why not simply ask to have the paper brought to Brahan Seer?" Marcus whispered.

"What?" Steven asked.

"I thought I had never met a woman more stubborn."

"And something has altered your assessment?"

Marcus smiled, but the smile faded as quickly as it appeared. He looked past the trees that lined the road up to the sky. The ship he was to sail on awaited him. Three more weeks would pass before he got his answers. His gut tightened another notch. He had enough answers to last a lifetime. Elise hadn't wanted him to come for her. Did he need more?

"She asked about you," Steven said.

"What?" Marcus looked at him, startled.

"We had no time for discussion." Steven gave a mirthless laugh. "Seems that's how it has been with us for some time. Had I taken more time—never mind. We had a devil of a time convincing her to get on the ship this morning. She didn't want to leave without you."

Relief mingled with frustration. "By God," Marcus muttered.

Steven laughed in earnest this time. "Surely, you expected no less."

"I expect her to have some common sense."

"What is common sense, Ashlund? Well, never mind. She's made a mess of things and knows it—"

A shot rang out.

A bullet whizzed past Marcus's ear. His horse lunged forward. Marcus yanked on the reins, following Steven, who already galloped for the cover of trees. Another shot resounded and Marcus saw wood splinter in the tree he sped past. He pulled his horse up alongside the place Steven had leapt from his horse.

"*Price*," Steven hissed.

He yanked the pistol from his waistband and crept toward the edge of the trees. Marcus jumped from his horse and started after him. Steven halted just before the trees gave way to the road, then darted from the cover of the forest.

"Steven!" Marcus shouted, and raced after him.

Marcus's heart hammered against his chest. He dove into the trees across the road and came to a skidding halt at seeing Steven, pistol raised and aimed at Kiernan.

"Son-of-a-bitch!" Steven yelled, and squeezed back on the trigger.

Chapter Twenty-Two

Marcus paused on the deck of the *Dauntless*, one foot on the gangplank, and scanned the Edinburgh dock. It was not quite noon, yet storm clouds filled the sky, casting dark shadows reminiscent of nightfall. The docks teemed with activity. Bales of dry goods and crates of supplies lay stacked on the boardwalk. Sailors and dock workers hurried to load them onto ships before the rains fell. Marcus spotted Erin near a crowd of sailors.

Erin caught his gaze, and Marcus nodded, then started forward. He avoided a man carrying a bag of provisions on his shoulder and stepped onto the dock. For the thousandth time, Marcus swore an oath to go to the grave before setting foot on another ship bound for America. He had been forced to make too many hard choices these last three months—more than enough to last a lifetime. Elise might never forgive some of the choices.

He stopped before Erin, who was looking past him. "What is it?" Marcus demanded.

"I don't see Kiernan."

Marcus's throat tightened. "Kiernan—"

"Father!"

He turned at hearing his son call.

The boy was hurrying down the gangplank. He dodged his way through the people and passing hackneys before reaching Marcus.

"Kiernan," Erin said with obvious relief. "Your

grandfather sends word you are to come immediately—"

"Kiernan will be going straight to London," Marcus said. "I will deal with my father." Marcus looked pointedly at Kiernan.

"Yes, Father. Directly to London."

"Do not return to Brahan Seer until I send for you."

"That's rather unreason—"

"You have no say in the matter," Marcus cut him off.

Kiernan sighed. "As you say, Father."

"If I hear you have left London before I give permission to do so, I'll come for you myself."

"So you have said," Kiernan replied.

"Then you comprehend the situation."

"I do."

Marcus gave him a curt nod. "I assume you can make your way from here?"

"Of course."

The sailors who stood nearby suddenly let up a cheer and several among their ranks jostled Marcus and Kiernan. Marcus motioned Kiernan and Erin to follow. He strode several paces from them, then stopped and faced the two young men.

"It's early yet," he said to Kiernan, "you can cover at least a third of the journey if you start immediately." Marcus looked at Erin. "You brought three horses?"

"Aye. They are at the Bliney tavern."

"Good. Kiernan, you may have lunch before leaving. Erin and I will begin straightaway for Brahan Seer." Marcus started in the direction of the tavern but stopped when Erin said, "Laird." He turned. Neither of the young men had moved. "What is it?"

"Lady Ashlund is not at Brahan Seer."

"Not at—where the bloody hell is she?"

"Ashlund."

Marcus frowned. "Is something amiss at Brahan Seer?"

"Nay," Erin quickly assured him. "She simply

refused to go there."

"Has my father seen her?"

"He is at Ashlund."

Erin reached into his pocket and produced a note. Marcus recognized the paper his father used on the rare occasions he wrote missives. He took the letter, tore open the seal, and read.

Marcus,

Elise is safely in Ashlund. When she refused to come to Brahan Seer, I left for Ashlund. She gave me your letter. I read it, then read it to her, but only after she confessed to me what she says is her entire story. It seems she knew nothing of your travels in America. I believe the danger you faced genuinely upset her. That is only right.

I thought it better not to force her to return to Brahan Seer, so we await you in Ashlund. Bring my grandson with you.

Cameron

Ashlund lay a three-hour hard ride away. He would see Elise before the evening meal.

Three hours later, Marcus and Erin rode into the stables at Ashlund. The stables were empty when they arrived, so Marcus left Erin to attend his horse and hurried to the mansion. His butler met him.

"Welcome home, Lord Ashlund," Nelson cried.

"Nelson." Marcus smiled. "Where will I find my father?"

"He is in the library, I believe."

"And my wife?"

Nelson looked thoughtful. "She planned to go to the solarium."

Marcus didn't move.

"Was there something else, Lord Ashlund?" Nelson asked.

"Nay," Marcus replied, and strode down the hall

toward the solarium.

Marcus jerked open the solarium door with unexpected violence. He paused, startled at the intensity of feeling, then, regaining his composure, stepped inside and closed the door softly behind him. He had a clear view of the aisle ahead of him and Elise wasn't in sight. He started forward, scanning the foliage and flowers that separated the aisle he walked down from the other aisle. Suddenly, he caught sight of her through the *calanthe rosea*. She stood gazing out the window, her back to him. The small lavender orchids snaked up their fragile vines, framing her body between their branches.

He halted. The lush hair that hung loosely about her shoulders didn't hide the thinness of those shoulders and arms. He detected a difference in her stance. Gone was the lofty air. In its place was a stronger sense of being in the here and now. Steven was right; she was the same yet wasn't.

Marcus continued forward. When he reached the end of the aisle, Elise turned as if she heard his approach. The faint smile on her face snapped into a gasp as their gazes met. She gave a cry and collapsed onto the stone bench beside her. Her hand flew to cover her heart and her wide eyes remained fixed on him. He halted a few feet from her. He discerned dark smudges beneath her eyes—eyes that weren't the clear brown he remembered. They wore a haunted look, one that perhaps mirrored his own. No joy shone in her expression. That, too, he knew, mirrored his own. Still, she was beautiful. Damn her—damn her beauty.

During the month-long trip to America he had remembered every lovely line of her face, the soft timbre of her voice and sweet gestures that had enchanted him so. Upon arriving in Boston, his thoughts had been consumed with finding her and bringing her safely home. Those months had distanced him from the goddess she had become in his mind and she had become the woman who stood before him now—more flesh and blood than angel.

As if reading his mind, she said, "I told you that you couldn't know."

"I could have, had you told me."

Elise dropped her gaze. "So easy to say now. I couldn't be sure—there was no time—"

"How much time would have been enough, Elise?"

She looked at him and he saw the tears pooling in her eyes.

The sadness in her expression deepened. "You're right." She turned so that her profile was barely visible to him and he realized she fought tears. "I cannot believe you're here," she said in a whisper. "Cannot believe I am here. You should have left me there. Were you hurt?"

"Look at me and see for yourself." Her head jerked up and he locked her gaze. "Do I look well?"

"I—"

"Do I resemble a man who has lived the past three months in wedded bliss?"

"I know I endangered you," she replied.

"And Kiernan."

She blanched. "Yes, Kiernan—and the others. I didn't intend on returning. I wouldn't have done that to you."

"Wouldn't have done *that* to me?" he thundered. "Instead, you would have left me in misery the remainder of my days?"

"If I am here, you are in misery; if I am gone, you are in misery."

"Misery of your making."

Elise shot to her feet. "I am aware of my mistakes. I've had plenty of time to recount them."

"Aye," he replied. "And did you recount the biggest mistake of all?"

Her eyes blazed with a bravado he believed bordered on hysteria. "Which biggest mistake would that be, Marcus MacGregor?"

"Leaving me before I had the chance to really love you—and be loved by you."

She faltered as if she would crumple back onto

the stone bench.

His hands worked into fists at his sides. "We are finished with lies. God knows, I'm as guilty as you. I knew you feared something. I have been a fool." He stared at her astonished face. "I won't make you a prisoner, but I must know you will use good sense in the future. Do you understand that, as my wife, you cannot go about like a peasant's wife?"

"I used good sense when I left Whycham House," she retorted.

"Aye?" He clenched his fists tighter. "You can say that when you knew Ardsley had a bounty on your head? You didn't tell me, the one man who could have—would have—protected you. You married me but didn't trust me. I told you I would not fail you."

Elise burst into tears and covered her face with her hands.

"Surely, you expected no less?" he pressed.

This, Marcus suddenly realized, was to be his revenge. She would have to live the rest of her life with him loving her, no matter her faults. Mayhap she would love him in return, despite his faults. Love him, aye. Forgive what had happened in Boston… what had happened to Steven? Perhaps not.

She reseated herself. Marcus sat beside her. He placed a hand on her shoulder. She stiffened, but he recognized the reaction as fear not loathing.

"I must know what happened," he said. *Then we shall see what you think of my sins.*

He waited. Her sobs at last subsided into a deep sigh. She faced him but avoided his gaze. "I left Whycahm Hall. Mary told me—" Her gaze abruptly jerked to meet his. "Oh, Marcus," she cried in a voice so full of sadness it startled him, "Mary—" She choked.

"Aye," he said quickly. "I know."

"No! Mary was the spy. She was giving the Campbells information."

"What?" Blood pounded through his veins, the rushing sound in his head making it hard to think.

"Yes," Elise went on hurriedly. "She argued with

Price. I heard enough to understand she had been passing information to the Campbells. That's why they were on MacGregor land. I didn't believe you when you said their presence had something to do with me. I am at fault, and I don't deserve to be here, but I swear, I wouldn't have left Whycham house if not for her urging."

"What happened?" Marcus demanded.

"After Sophie showed us to the guest chambers in Whycham House, Mary told me about Ashlund and how the stables were too close to the main house. I remembered Winnie telling me of her uncle who died of terrible burns, and Mary was so vivid in her descriptions of Ashlund—"

"Mary had never been to Ashlund," Marcus cut in savagely.

The anguish in Elise's eyes nearly did him in. "How could I know?"

Aye, how could she know? "I was wrong not to understand how little of us you understood," he murmured.

"You can't blame yourself, that is—"

Marcus leapt to his feet. "You are ignorant of a great many things here, Elise. Don't make the same mistake you made before."

She blinked and he knew he'd hurt her, but he wouldn't allow her ignorance to go unchecked this time. "Mary has received her just rewards. Forget her. What happened next?"

"About forty-five minutes after we left Whycham House, we were accosted by highwaymen—or I thought they were highwaymen." Elise shuddered with such obvious fear Marcus clenched his hands at his sides to keep from slamming a fist through the solarium's glass wall. "I thought they were simple highwaymen so threw my wedding band out the window of the carriage." She looked at Marcus. "I am sorry. Sophie told me the emerald was in your family for centuries, but I meant to give you a clue."

So, Sara McPhee hadn't taken the ring.

"You did right," he said.

Gratitude flickered across her features, then she went on. "When we reached the point where they were gaining on us, more men appeared from within the trees and intercepted us." Tears streamed down her cheeks. "Your men fought valiantly. Price shot Richard and Taylor."

Two of the men he had planned on hunting down and killing. "They were good men."

"Price pulled me from the carriage. He left Mary inside. The men…" Elise faltered. "Three—no—four of them, they were beaten half senseless, then the carriage was run off the cliff."

Marcus's mind raced. The woman who he thought was Elise must have been put in the carriage after it crashed into the water. What poor soul had Ardsley snatched from her life to take Elise's place?

"The other man," Elise rushed on, "I don't remember his name." She turned an anguished look on him. "I should remember his name."

"What happened to him?"

"I don't know. Price forced laudanum down my throat. I awoke aboard a ship. He made threats. I didn't fear his threats against me, but…"

"He threatened me?" Marcus asked quietly.

"Yes. But…" she halted and he saw the agony on her face.

"Kiernan?" he pressed.

"Not him…" Her gaze dropped again and she said in a whisper, "Your other child."

"My other—" Marcus fell back a pace, feeling as though he had collided headlong with a horse racing toward him at breakneck speed. "What are you saying?"

Elise was shaking. "I-I couldn't be sure so early on. I had missed my monthly flux by only a week. When Price told me he knew, I was so startled that he instantly knew."

Marcus grasped Elise by the shoulders. "You are with child?"

310

She slumped in his grasp and began crying so hard that Marcus was shaken to the core.

"Elise," he insisted with more gentleness.

"The laudanum." She forced back the tears. "They fed me laudanum every day—every hour, it seemed." She appeared to deflate even more. "I lost the child."

Hot rage flashed in a thick lightning bolt of red across his vision. He had sat across from Ardsley, stared into his eyes, and all along the bastard had known he was responsible for the loss of the child—*my child*. Yet the man had returned his stare and smiled.

"If I faced Ardsley now—" Marcus cut off the statement at seeing the sudden terror on Elise's face, but her expression said she understood all too well the unfinished words. *Nothing could stop me from killing him*—nothing *will stop me from killing him*. The oath never to set foot on American soil again rang in his head—a vow he would break.

"This is why I didn't tell you the truth before our marriage." Tears streamed down her cheeks. "I am sorry. I realized too late you would st-stop at nothing to—"

Marcus crushed her to him. Her body melted against his and he prayed the action was the first in the weakening of the wall between them.

Marcus shifted his gaze from the flames in the hearth of his London study to the Earl of Loudoun. The shocked expression on the earl's face when Marcus had laid the edict signed by King George on the desk was far better revenge than any Marcus could have devised.

"You drag me here for this rubbish?" Loudoun demanded.

"By King George's command," Marcus replied evenly.

"Ridiculous," he muttered.

"Would you have preferred I continue to take matters into my own hands?"

The look on Loudoun's face said he would have

preferred just that.

"You do not seem to comprehend," Marcus said. "I tire of the fight. It will end one way or another. I can raze every keep between Brahan Seer and Castle Kalchurn. You cannot doubt I have the power."

"You have the power," Loudoun snarled.

"Yet you crave the war—a war you would most assuredly lose."

"We have not yet lost," Loudoun snapped.

"You have not won."

"The Campbells are a force to be reckoned with."

"How many more of your men must die to prove that?"

The earl's mouth tightened.

"You need not love a single MacGregor for us to live in peace, Loudoun."

"We cannot live in peace."

"King George disagrees." Marcus motioned to the document. "You may keep this copy. Copies have been sent to every Campbell leader of consequence."

Loudoun placed the tips of his fingers on the paper, then slowly slid it inch by inch into his hand until it formed a ball. He abruptly threw the paper at Marcus. Marcus didn't flinch when the paper rebounded from his chest and landed on the floor.

"A law purchased with Ashlund gold," Loudoun sneered.

Marcus held his gaze. It mattered not if Loudoun knew that half the Ashlund fortune had been the final bargaining price that induced King George to sign the law condemning both Campbell *and* MacGregor to death for murdering any man—or woman—from the opposing clan. A sense of weary finality washed over Marcus. Ashlund gold had bought MacGregor freedom, but it was the wisdom of one MacGregor so long ago that had illuminated this better path.

"Bought with MacGregor blood," Marcus murmured, then louder, "and Campbell blood."

The earl rose in one graceful motion. "Forgive me, Lord Ashlund, but I find it likely King George will countermand this foolishness with the next turn of wind. He will find fault with you *and* your clan soon enough."

Marcus gave a short laugh. "I wager King George would be just as pleased to find fault with you as he would with me."

Loudoun's face reddened. He whirled and headed for the door.

"Loudoun," Marcus called.

The earl halted and faced him.

"I will make sure King George enforces this edict."

Loudoun's lip curled upward. "Even if it takes *every last* crown in the Ashlund vault."

"Even if it takes every last crown."

Loudoun turned and left the room.

Only a moment passed before the library door opened again. Marcus turned from staring at the hearth and smiled as Elise's head appeared around the edge of the door.

"I saw the earl leave," she said. "How did the meeting go?"

"As to be expected."

"Your son is waiting to speak with you."

Marcus raised a brow. "Why not come himself?"

She laughed, opening the door another inch but didn't enter. "He tells me you forbade him so many things when he last saw you he fears forgetting one of your rules."

"He has done as I instructed and we're in London, after all. He has free reign here." Marcus grimaced. "Nay, 'tis best you not repeat that." He regarded her. "Do you intend on standing in the doorway the entire day?"

Elise blushed and opened the door fully. She wore a simple gown of soft turquoise muslin. This was the most festive dress she had worn since returning from Boston. Perhaps she was truly beginning to forgive herself—and him. The softness in her eyes gave him hope.

She remained in the doorway. "I'll send Kiernan to you."

"Will you return later?" Marcus asked as she started to turn.

She looked at him. Her expression displayed some of the shy reticence he had seen during those first months at Brahan Seer

"Perhaps," she replied with the hint of a smile, and turned to close the door.

Marcus's gaze fell upon the mail he had received just before Loudoun arrived. A letter from Boston lay at the bottom of the mix.

"Elise," he called.

She paused and looked over her shoulder.

"Have Kiernan meet me in the stables in fifteen minutes. I have something to attend to and I planned a ride before lunch. He can accompany me."

She nodded and left him alone.

Marcus seated himself at his desk and fished the Boston letter from the pile. He tore open the envelope and removed a letter, two folded newspaper clippings, and a sealed envelope addressed to Elise. He laid the two letters aside and unfolded one of the newspaper clippings. The title read:

November 10, 1826

The Wellington *leaves Boston harbor carrying twenty-five American convicts headed for Australia.*

Marcus scanned the report, which listed the twenty-five men, their crimes, and sentences.

He picked up the second clipping and unfolded it. The report read:

November 10, 1826

BOSTON SHIPPING MOGUL MISSING

Boston shipping mogul Price Ardsley, recently charged by the board of directors of Landen Shipping with fraud, has been

missing since November 9. Landen Shipping contends that Ardsley fled the country to avoid prosecution.

The night Price Ardsley disappeared, Mister Jacob O'Riley reported witnessing two men outside Ardsley's estate accost a lone rider. A hood was thrown over the victim's head, then he was tied and thrown into the back of a carriage driven by his two assailants.

William Sheldon of the Boston Police Department interviewed Mister O'Riley but determined the event O'Riley witnessed is not connected with the disappearance of Price Ardsley.

Anyone having information about Mister Ardsley's whereabouts is directed to report to Captain Sheldon immediately.

Marcus reread the first clipping. *Price Ardsley in Australia.* Heated satisfaction shot through him. So, he would not have to return to America after all. He refolded the two clippings, slipped them back in their envelope, then opened the letter and began reading.

Ashlund,

Six weeks have passed, and I am fully recovered from the knife wound you inflicted. Had the doctors not insisted on the long convalescence, I would have caught the next ship bound for Scotland and run a dagger through your leg for good measure.

I imagine you've read the newspaper clippings I sent. Strange things are afoot. I can't say what lies ahead. Though I feel certain Price Ardsley won't be in a position to pay anyone to kill another man—or two men, as the case may be—again in the near future.

See that Elise gets the letter addressed to her.
Take care of her.

Steven

Marcus refolded the letter and placed it in the envelope with the clippings. He took the letter addressed to Elise and went to her chambers. He sighed upon finding her room empty. Perhaps when he returned she would be here and... He left the letter on her dresser, then headed for the stables.

Marcus heard the approach of footsteps even as Elise called out his name. He exchanged a glance with Kiernan before turning from the stall where his son was saddling the stallion he had chosen to ride. As she hurried down the stable aisle toward them, Marcus's heart began to hammer out the heavy beat he had been experiencing more and more of late when in her presence. He noticed a letter—Steven's letter—tightly clutched in her hand.

Elise had nearly reached them when she lifted the letter. "This came today?"

"Aye," Marcus replied.

"Steven says he is fully recovered and out of the hospital." She stopped beside Marcus. Her expression clouded over. "Marcus, please, don't lie. How bad was the wound? Is it possible he truly is out of danger?"

"I told you the truth, love," he said. *Except for the fact Steven had turned at just the wrong moment and the knife Marcus had thrown pierced the breastbone above the heart instead of his arm, as intended.* Marcus shuddered inwardly as he always did when remembering how close he came to killing his wife's brother—and how close the brother came to killing his own son.

"The wound wasn't life threatening." *Or so the doctors said two days later, when Steven began to show signs of recovering from the loss of blood.* Marcus would have arrived back in Scotland a week earlier had he not tarried in Boston to assure himself the boy would recover.

Kiernan stuck his head out the stall. Elise jumped, bumping into the small table against the wall. The brush and trimming scissors lying on the table skittered across its surface. She quickly righted the table before they fell to the floor and looked at Kiernan. He flushed and Marcus knew his son was remembering his part in nearly getting killed, *and* nearly getting Steven killed. Marcus had also feared Elise wouldn't forgive Kiernan's part in her brother's brush with death. But she had, or so her warmth toward the boy seemed to indicate.

Would her warmth eventually extend to him? Would she forgive him? He wouldn't forget the sight of her pale face when he told her how Kiernan had saved him and Steven from Price's assassins, and how Steven had mistaken Kiernan for those assassins. When Marcus gave her the short letter Steven had written for her, she noted the shaky hand the letter had been written in and wouldn't be completely consoled—until today.

She blushed in response to Kiernan's embarrassment, and Marcus's body pulsed. He suddenly wished his son far away. Perhaps, if he and Elise were alone, she might allow him to make love to her. Marcus turned to Kiernan.

"Mayhap you should go on without me." He looked at Elise. "Will you walk with me?"

She looked as though he had asked her to puzzle out the secret of the universe, and Marcus repressed a laugh. He extended his hand. She slipped her hand into his. He glimpsed a figure entering the door at the far end of the stables as they turned to leave.

"Silas," he called after the new stable hand, "see to Alexis. I won't be taking him out as planned." Marcus turned back to Elise and urged her toward the door at the far end of the stables. "Did Steven have much to say?" he asked.

"He will return to duty in the Army." She hesitated. "He mentioned Price is missing."

"He cannot harm us, Elise."

Her gaze swung to his face. Her brow furrowed, then she nodded. They exited the door and took a few steps down the path before she exclaimed, "The letter!" and broke free of his hold on her hand. "I must have dropped it."

"Elise," he called, but she had already

disappeared back into the stables. Bloody hell, at this rate it would be another six weeks before he got his wife back to the house, much less into his bed. He strode back inside the stables.

His heart jumped into his throat. In the instant before he broke into a run toward Elise, he took in the sight of Kiernan riding through the stable doors, Silas stepping from the stall next to the door, knife poised for throwing, and Elise grabbing the trimming scissors from the table. She hurled them toward Silas as she had thrown the *sgian dubh* that day at Brahan Seer.

The scissors hit their intended victim with deadly accuracy between the shoulder blades. Blood darkened the dirty shirt he wore. Silas faltered and turned, eyes wide with surprise. His expression contorted into rage. He roared and lunged toward her. Kiernan whirled his mount around to face the sudden commotion. His gaze met Marcus's, then Kiernan shouted and dug his heels into his horse's ribs. The beast's nostrils flared as he dipped his head and charged. Marcus forced his legs to pump harder. Silas would still reach Elise before either of them did.

She pivoted and grabbed the hoof pick hanging on the wall. The hair on Marcus's neck rose when Silas clutched at her. She swung the hoof pick. Kiernan reached them as she slashed Silas's arm. The horse slammed into Silas and he was knocked forward and into Elise. He grabbed her, but Marcus leapt between them, shoving her behind him. The table crashed onto its side and Elise cried out. Marcus seized Silas's collar and pounded his fist into the man's jaw.

"Father," Kiernan shouted as he leapt from his horse.

Marcus swung Silas around and sent him flying through the door of the stall. Silas banged into the wall and crumbled to the ground. Marcus whirled to face Elise. His breath came in quick, deep gasps—much like hers. She met his gaze, eyes blazing. He looked at Silas. The scissors had fallen from his back onto the straw-laden ground beside him. Marcus looked back at Elise.

"You never told me where you learned to throw a knife like that!" he shouted.

She blinked as if yanked from a dream. "Steven—" her voice caught, but Marcus realized it was the last vestiges of fear—and rage. "Steven learned as a young boy. I-I always feared he would hurt himself, so I attended his practices."

Elise yanked her skirt above her ankles and strode to the stall opening. She stared at Silas, her hands clenched on the fistful of skirt she held. She pivoted as Marcus stepped up behind her and collided with him. He grasped her shoulders.

She grabbed his arms as though to steady herself. "Will we ever be free of him?"

In her eyes, Marcus saw the fear he had felt when he saw Silas poised to murder his son. Marcus glanced around and spotted the bucket of water he was looking for several stalls down. He fetched it, then pushed past Elise and Kiernan and threw the water on the unconscious man. Silas awoke with a sputter. Marcus seized him by his collar and yanked him to his feet.

"Who sent you?" Marcus shouted.

Silas cowed.

"Tell me or I'll kill you here and now."

"That woman." Silas cringed.

"Woman?" Marcus gave him a hard shake.

Silas went silent.

"Kiernan! Give me your pistol."

"No," Silas cried.

Marcus lifted his fist for another blow.

"Ross!" Silas shouted. "Lady Ross."

Chapter Twenty-Three

Elise stilled at the sound of Marcus's bedchamber door opening. She rose and stole through the closet which separated their two rooms, then knocked lightly on his door, and entered. He looked up from where he stood near the nightstand on the far side of the bed. Her heart lurched. She had suspected he kept a mistress, but seeing him now, hair tousled, cravat missing, the top button of his shirt undone, there was no mistaking the fact he had just risen from another woman's bed. The mental picture of Marcus kissing the rise of her breasts, then taking her nipple into her mouth filled her vision.

"Elise?"

She snapped back to the present. "I—" Her gaze caught on his hands—hands that had once touched her, had once—the urge to cry sprang up. No, she wouldn't cry. She had made her bed. She would live with the consequences.

"I wondered how things went with Lady Ross's trial," she said. "Is it over?"

Marcus reached around his back and pulled out the revolver stuffed into his waistband.

Where had the revolver lain when he made love to his mistress?

"It is over," he replied. "She claims to know nothing of a plot to kill Kiernan." Marcus glanced at her. "I suspect she wanted you dead. Though she denies that as well. I don't know how, but it is clear she was in league with Ardsley. Margaret had no reason to kill

320

Kiernan."

Elise started to ask how he could be so sure when he said, "She won't face prison." He gave a mirthless laugh. "England is not about to put one of her noblewomen in prison, even if she is Scottish. She is to go to America." Marcus's expression abruptly darkened. "Do you intend on standing in doorways the remainder of our marriage?"

She blinked.

"Or is it that you simply find it too abhorrent to be in a room with me?"

"I… no. I only thought—"

"Thought what?" he demanded.

"I didn't want to intrude. It is late—"

"So it is." Marcus began unbuttoning his shirt.

"Good Lord," she muttered. "It's not as if you have invited me into your bed—chambers." She added "chambers" in a rush, seeing his fingers halt on the third button and the sudden gleam in his eyes.

His eyes narrowed. "Am I to understand it is I who have stayed out of *your* bed?"

"You say that as if you're surprised," she snapped.

"By God," he thundered. "I will settle this now." He started around the bed.

Elise rolled her eyes. "You have no energy to *settle* anything."

He stopped short. "What the blazes does that mean?"

"It means, I have made my bed and I'll lie in it." *Alone.*

Marcus charged across the room. Elise backed up. He grabbed her and tossed her on *his* bed before she could blink. His lips crashed down on hers in a bruising kiss. Shock ripped through her. Energy pooled in the pit of her stomach, then between her legs. His hand covered a breast. Elise arched into him. She wanted him, but could she live with the fact he had another woman? He yanked up her night rail and reached between her legs. *Yes.* She could live with anything if

321

she had him. His fingers probed. Marcus abruptly pulled away from her.

He touched her cheek. "Steven is well," he said. "There is no need to cry."

"Cry?" She lifted a finger to her cheek, but even as she did, she realized she was crying.

"Unless…" Marcus said.

Elise looked at him.

"You can't forgive me for Steven. I am sorry. I understood the consequences. I could not change—"

"Forgive *you*," she interrupted. "You have done nothing to forgive. It's my fault, even your taking a mistress. I can't blame you for wanting—"

"A what?" He looked startled.

"What?" she repeated.

His brows puckered in a fierce frown. "We have been in Ashlund two weeks and already you have me consorting with other women?"

"There's no better explanation for the late nights, your state of dishevelment."

"My state of dishevelment?" His gaze swept across her body. "You seem to have forgotten what my *state of dishevelment* is like when I make love to a woman." He kissed her mouth, her cheek, her ear. "When I make love to you," he whispered.

Elise drew a sharp breath as he rocked against her. She wrapped her arms around his neck.

"There is no more Margaret," he whispered. "No more Ardsley, and"—Marcus slid a hand beneath her and lifted her hips to meet each thrust of his hips—"there is no mistress."

He pulled his arm from around her, then reached between them and unfastened his trousers. His erection sprang free of its constraints and Marcus drove himself into her.

"There is only you," he said, and began the rhythm that bound them together as one.

From the Author

I hope you enjoyed Marcus and Elise's journey of discovery and love in My Highland Love. Feel free to drop me a line and let me know what you thought of the book. Next in the Highland Lords Series will be *My Highland Lord*, which continues the saga with Marcus' son Kiernan MacGregor. The boy grew up good.

For your reading pleasure, I have included a bonus chapter of my Scottish Historical *Lord Keeper*.

Tarah

LORD KEEPER
Scottish Highlands 1508

CHAPTER ONE

Iain might have been standing on the edge of a dream when the abbey door opened and she stepped out into the morning light. Though separated by a small earthly measure of holy ground, he sensed her mind to be as far from him as heaven was from hell. His heart stilled with the sudden blaze of auburn hair against the Highland sun and he determined to learn what color eyes matched such fire.

With a nod in response to Father Brennan's statement that the Menzies clan was rumored to be raiding land to the north, Iain slid a hand along his horse's neck. The beast nickered and shifted beneath him. An answering whinny followed from one of his men's horses behind him. Careful not to give away his intention, Iain slid his gaze across the heather covered hills in the background, and covertly monitored the woman's progress as she strolled along the grounds, a book in hand. Another moment and she would be off Montrose Abbey.

She slowed.

Annoyance flared. Curse the archaic law that kept her safe on holy ground. What if he ignored the civilized directives instilled by his education, and simply took her? He dropped his attention to the intricately carved leather wristband that covered his arm from wrist to elbow. A deep scratch spanned the leather, a reminder of the battle that almost took his arm, had taken the lives of many good men, a battle fought in the name of justice.

Iain looked up in response to Father Brennan's report that four Menzies clansmen had passed the abbey yesterday afternoon. He was in no mood to encounter marauding Menzies on his return home, particularly considering his change in plans. He breathed deep of the Scots pine scent carried on the keening wind. The law forbade him taking the woman while on holy ground, but sanctioned the kidnapping once she entered the outside world. No law would be broken, no war begun when he claimed her.

Ticking off the seconds in his mind, he gauged her progress away from the grassy expanse that marked the distance needed to intercept her race back to the monastery. Any resistance would be hampered by the heavy skirts of her expensive brocade dress. She took the last fateful step. Iain flashed Father Brennan a grin as he grasped the hook on his claymore's scabbard and unhooked latch from hook. Sword and scabbard dropped to the ground. The priest's eyes registered surprise, then understanding. He whirled as Iain dug his heels into the horse's belly and broke ranks with his men.

"Run!" the priest shouted.

She looked up from her book. In seconds, Iain drew close enough to discern the expression of a doe catching first sight of the bowman. His heart surged. Mayhap the wide-eyed stare wasn't fear, but fascination? Understanding lit her features and Iain laughed at his folly. The doe realized the bowman meant to have her, after all.

She dropped the book and yanked up her skirts to run. Iain veered right and leaned from the saddle as she darted left. He seized her waist. She gave a muffled 'oof' and kicked when he dragged her against the side of the galloping beast, her legs tangled in her skirts. The horse snorted, his gait faltering with the uneven burden; he steadied and Iain hauled her across his thighs.

His groin pulsed with the weight of her derriere across his lap. He laughed to himself. If she understood the pleasure her struggles afforded him, she would cease. His horse snorted and Iain threw a leg over the lass' shins, hugging them close to the belly of the beast. She grunted with the effort of trying to slide from the saddle, then stiffened with his firm grip on her thigh.

"Iain," Father Brennan said in a loud voice.

Iain forced his attention from the disheveled mass of velvet hair that cascaded down slim shoulders and looked to where the priest had retreated onto holy ground. Father Brennan motioned him forward. Iain smiled and gave a shake of his head. The hand at Father Brennan's side fisted.

Good. The priest understood no MacPherson would set foot on holy ground today.

The woman's muscles tightened in another attempt to throw off his leg, and Iain gave the flesh a warning squeeze without breaking eye contact with Father Brennan. The priest ran the back of a forefinger in a slow line along each side of his mustache. Iain understood his shrewd look, but the curiosity in his eyes was a surprise. He strode toward them, and the warriors who had ridden in with Iain drew up alongside as the priest neared.

"It doesna' seem she is taken with your charm, Iain," Father Brennan said.

"Charm?" his captive snapped. "What madness is this?"

"Patience, lass. It is a simple mistake." The priest looked pointedly at Iain.

"Aye," she blurted, "and this barbarian would do well to release me before he discovers just how grave a mistake."

Iain glanced at his companions when someone unsuccessfully stifled mirth.

Father Brennan clicked his tongue with impatience. "Iain, you cannot take her."

Iain responded with a raise of his brows.

"Aye, then," Father Brennan muttered, "you can take her, but 'tis not fair play. I had not informed her of this tradition. A tradition long dead," he added with asperity.

"I believe it was you who said ignorance of the law is no excuse," Iain reminded him with a low laugh.

Father Brennan hesitated. "You must know she is English. Are you sure you want her?"

The lady gasped. Iain started to demanded explanation for the slur, but forestalled at something unknown in the priest's demeanor and replied in an unruffled tone, "If I did not want her, I would not have taken her."

Relief flickered in Father Brennan's eyes, but his voice remained insistent. "This is wrong. She did not know it was unsafe to step from holy ground."

"Unsafe?" Iain echoed.

Father Brennan's expression darkened. "You heard what I said, Iain MacPherson, unsafe."

"Is she entering the convent?" Father Brennan's frown deepened, and Iain added, "It is, no doubt, a grievous sin to lie about such matters."

"By the saints. Nay, you scoundrel, she has no such intentions."

"Why is she here?"

"Sweet Jesu," the lady cursed. "What concern is that of yours?"

Iain shifted his gaze to her. Fury ruled her gaze, but it was the challenge in the lift of her chin that gripped his heart. "Where is your husband, lass?"

Silence hung thick in the air and every nerve stood ready for the answer he dreaded, hadn't considered, until this moment.

"In a grave in England," she answered at last.

That was unexpected and Iain wasn't sure whether to praise God she was free, or feel compassion she had lost a loved one. Guilt surfaced with the realization that he gladly chose the former. He wheeled his horse around.

"Nay!" She kicked the stallion's belly.

The beast reared. Iain yanked back on the reins, but she kicked again. The stallion reared a second time. Iain seized the pommel, but felt their bodies slipping from the saddle. He rolled, hugging her close so that she landed on top of him as they crashed to the moist ground. She shoved away from him. He held tight, laughing in spite of the dull pain in his shoulder when she growled. She jabbed an elbow into his ribs. Pain lanced through his gut. His grip faltered and she broke free. The closest of the warriors shot after her and was upon her in a few short strides and grabbed her.

Iain leapt to his feet and lunged after her. "Release her!"

The man dropped her. She jumped up, tripped on her skirts, and barely scrambled up again as Iain brought her down like a wild animal.

He flipped her over and straddled her. "I should have let you break my fall."

She grabbed his shoulders and dug nails into the hard muscle. Iain seized her wrists and shoved them above her head. He slid his body along hers until he covered her length and his face was an inch from her mouth. She continued to struggle.

His groin thickened. "At least you might have been knocked senseless long enough for me to get you to my bed and shackle you there."

She stilled, eyes wide. Regret stabbed at him. He had enjoyed the thrust of her slim hips against him.

The lower edge of Father Brennan's scapula came into view beside them. "Let her up, Iain."

Iain shook his head. "Nay. I am enjoying this more than anything else this morning."

A round of approving grunts and laughter went up from his men. As an afterthought, Iain lowered his mouth on hers. She stiffened, but the scent of rose water mingling with the heather crushed beneath her assailed his senses and he breathed in the arousing scents. Shifting, he found the curves of her body held the expected promise. He couldn't help a glance in the direction of the forest where privacy lay but a moment away.

"MacPherson," the priest growled.

Iain jerked his gaze back onto her. Fear tinged her expression. A twinge of guilt gave way to the desire to kiss away the small tremor on her lower lip.

"Iain."

"Aye." He rose, pulling her to her feet.

She bolted, but he yanked her to his side.

"Please." She worked to pry his hands from her arm as he led her in the direction of his horse.

The desperation in her voice halted Iain's march.

Father Brennan gave her a fatherly pat on the arm. "All will be well, lass."

She scowled. "What an absurd statement."

Iain laughed and received a kick to the shin for the offense.

"I am to blame, child." Father Brennan sighed. "I did not warn you to remain on holy ground when we had visitors."

Iain angled his head in acknowledgement, then faced her. His brief inspection earlier suggested her long skirts hid feminine curves and shapely legs. Yet, her carriage had intrigued him above all. A woman of intellect and gentle breeding, she would suit him well. To his surprise, she had spared but a cursory glance in his direction before turning back to her book.

He touched the spot where cheekbone met eyes. "As blue as the waters of Loch Ericht."

Startled understanding appeared in the blue depths and satisfaction rippled through Iain. Luck was with him today, luck and his captain's suggestion that he visit Montrose Abbey to investigate rumors of trouble with the Menzies.

Her eyes narrowed. She shoved his hand away and faced Father Brennan. "You are saying that because I took one step too many in the wrong diretion this . . .

this man can take me and I have nothing to say about it?"

"Well, 'twas more than one," Father Brennan corrected.

She gave an unladylike snort.

"Lass," Iain cut in. "I am Iain MacPherson, leader of my clan. I will provide you a fine home and swear by God to keep you safe."

Her severe expression turned with deliberation on him. "King are you—"

"Clan chief," he corrected. "A difference King James is sure to appreciate."

She raised a scornful brow. "That gives you the right to take me prisoner?"

"Nay, my lass." Iain yanked her to his chest. "The fact I am a man gives me that right."

Determined fury darkened her eyes. He tangled a hand in the soft tresses behind her neck and pulled her mouth to his. She shoved at his chest. Iain tasted her with slow consideration, not forcing the tightly clamped lips apart, despite the compelling desire to thrust his tongue inside. The length of him hardened to near pain and his heart pounded at breakneck speed, but he ended the kiss. She twisted in an effort to free herself, yet Iain didn't miss the tremble in her body.

"Nathan, fetch my horse."

The young warrior broke from the band and, a moment later, brought the horse up alongside, with Iain's sword strapped to its side.

"Hold fast the reins."

Nathan complied and Iain lifted her. She braced her hands against the horse's ribs, but he hoisted her into the saddle.

"You will keep her?" Father Brennan crossed his arms over his chest.

"Aye." Iain kept an arm around her waist as she tried to slide down the opposite side.

The priest nodded. "Since you take advantage of her stepping from holy ground, you will abide by the law and wait until she consents."

"She will wed me of her own free will," Iain stepped into the saddle and encircled her waist as he took the reins that were handed to him.

"That is not what I mean and you know it."

"I do not force women," Iain replied.

"Perhaps because no woman has ever refused you before?"

Iain locked gazes with the priest. "Beware that your good intentions do not take you too far, Father. You know I have never taken an unwilling woman."

"Liar," the lady interjected.

Iain leaned her back in his arm and stared into her eyes. "You do not know me, lass. Why say such a thing?"

"I am unwilling, yet you force me to go with you."

For an instant her logic confused him and memory of another woman made captive by a man who claimed love flitted through his mind. "Aye," Iain agreed, through tight lips. "But you will choose to marry me." He gave a quiet order to one of his men and pulled on the reins, once again wheeling his horse away from the abbey. "Come to us in ten days, Father," Iain threw back before they were out of earshot.

"He will only come to bring me back," she said through clenched teeth. "I will never marry you."

NOW AVAILABLE AT YOUR FAVORITE DISTRIBUTOR

Author Bio

Award-winning, published author Tarah Scott cut her teeth on authors such as Georgette Heyer, Zane Grey, and Amanda Quick. Her favorite book is *A Tale of Two Cities*, with *Gone With the Wind* as a close second. She writes classical romance, suspense, horror and mainstream.

Born in New Mexico, Tarah grew up in the Southwest. Fifteen years ago, she relocated to Westchester County, New York, where she and her daughter reside in a lakeside community. Don't be fooled by what sounds like a quiet life. The city that never sleeps is only an hour away, and this Texas girl and her New York bred daughter wouldn't have it any other way.

Also by Tarah Scott:

Lord Keeper
A Knight of Passion
The Pendulum: Legacy of the Celtic Brooch

Labyrinth
An Improper Wife
Double Bang!
Born Into Fire

My Highland Lord
Highland Lords series

As T. C. Archer

Chain Reaction
Full Throttle
Sasha's Calling
Trouble at the Hotel Baba Ghanoush
For His Eyes Only
Sin Incarnate

Award Winning Titles:

Lord Keeper

Golden Rose Best Historical of 2011
First place in the 2004 RWA CoLoNY Happy Endings
contest.
Third place in the Greater Seattle Chapter RWA's 2003
Emerald City

Made in the USA
Lexington, KY
09 March 2014